THE HOUSE OF TONGUES

ALSO BY JAMES DASHNER

The Maze Runner Books

The Maze Runner

The Scorch Trials

The Death Cure

The Kill Order

The Fever Code

Crank Palace

The Maze Cutter Books

The Maze Cutter

The Godhead Complex

The 13th Reality Books

The Journal of Curious Letters

The Hunt for Dark Infinity

The Blade of Shattered Hope

The Void of Mist and Thunder

The Mortality Doctrine Books

The Eye of Minds

The Rule of Thoughts

The Game of Lives

JAMES DASHNER

THE HOUSE OF TONGUES

AKASHIC
MEDIA ENTERPRISES

All rights reserved. Published in the United States by Akashic Media Enterprises, also doing business as AME Projects. Visit us on the web at AkashicMediaEnterprises.com. Printed in the UK by CPUK Print Publishing. Interior formatting by Hannah Linder Designs.

Publisher's Cataloging-in-Publication Data
(Provided by Cassidy Cataloguing Services, Inc.)

Names: Dashner, James, 1972- author.
Title: The house of tongues / James Dashner.
Description: Second edition. | [Red Bank, New Jersey] : Akashic Media Enterprises, [2022]
Identifiers: ISBN: 979-8-9859552-7-9 (hardback) | 979-8-9884215-1-1 (paperback) | 979-8-9859552-9-3 (ebook)
Subjects: LCSH: Serial murderers--Fiction. | Kidnapping--Fiction. | Murder--Fiction. | Blessing and cursing--Fiction. | South Carolina--Fiction. | LCGFT: Horror fiction. | BISAC: FICTION / Horror. | FICTION / Southern. | FICTION / Occult & Supernatural.
Classification: LCC: PS3604.A83 H68 2022 | DDC: 813/.6--dc23

Second Edition

PRAISE FOR JAMES DASHNER

A #1 *New York Times* Bestselling Author
A *USA Today* Bestseller
Author of *Kirkus Reviews* Best Teen Book of the Year
An ALA-YASLA Best Fiction for Young Adults Author

"Wonderful action writing—**fast-paced**... but smart and well observed."—*Newsday*

"[A] **nail-biting** must-read."—*Seventeen*

"Breathless, **cinematic action.**"—*Publishers Weekly*

"**Heart pounding** to the very last moment."—*Kirkus Reviews*

"**Exclamation-worthy.**"—*Romantic Times*

"**Take a deep breath before you start** any James Dashner book." —*Deseret News*

EPIGRAPH

I wake to sleep, and take my waking slow. I learn by going
where I have to go.

—Theodore Roethke

The mouth of the just bringeth forth wisdom;
But the perverted tongue shall be cut out.

—Proverbs 10:31

PROLOGUE

I am an old man.

At least, that's what my kids tell me. If I'm honest with myself, and with you—something I've promised within my heart to do in the telling of this tale—it's not just what my kids *say*, it's what they truly think. They actually think I'm old. That I'm one double-cheeseburger away from the heart attack that'll send old pops to his watery, muddy grave. Well, kids are stupid. I'm not old. I'm 44. People fly in airplanes older than that—at least let me turn 50 before we stir the coroner from the couch in his cold, stale office. Maybe even 70 or 80. (I have no interest in seeing 90, though, so let's not push it.)

But. *But.*

Do I *feel* old? That's another question, entirely.

I do. I feel as old as the pecan trees destroyed by Hurricane Hugo, torn from the beautiful earth of my parents' grass-spotted yard, a feat I would've thought impossible unless I'd seen it myself. I felt an incredible melancholy looking upon those clusters of roots, their long, white fingers clodded with mud, ripped from their warm home beneath. Never to return, destined to burn with the rest of the tree in some field no longer rich enough to yield crops. I could dwell on that, and perhaps it'd be appropriate, but I must move on in the telling.

Yes, the telling. There's always a story to be told in this neck of the woods.

And the following is mine.

There'll be no trickery in what I'm about to share, no deceit. So let me say this from the start: there are many who think I'm a murderer. Worse than a murderer. A monster. A monster so monstrous that never before has a world seen such a monstrous monster. A bit melodramatic, to be sure, but it's how I perceive these perceptions. You can imagine, can't you? Knowing that such things are said about you? How that would make you feel?

What can I do, but tell you the truth? It's the only thing that's warranted.

Fair warning, this is a dark tale. Things will be said that you won't believe—your heart will deceive you into thinking such darkness can't exist in the world. I wouldn't blame you. Hell, if I hadn't lived the things I'm about to share, if I had not seen them with my own two eyes, I'd scarce believe them myself, not unlike the uprooted tree and its forlorn roots. There's not a moment goes by that I wish my story weren't true, that it were some incantation of a dream beset upon me by a sorcerer, to relive day by day, night by night in the cellar of my mind.

But alas, it's the truth, the whole truth, and nothing but the truth, as the lawyers are wont to say. It gives me peace that I begin the tale with such honesty, displaying before you that which hurts me most. That so many people think me a monster. All I can counter with is this: in my heart of hearts (as Dickens was wont to say) I know that I am indeed *not* a murderer, much less a monster.

And so, let the telling begin. It must be presented in two parts, neither one more important than the other. For I was once a child, when the horrors began, and when the horrors returned, the child had become a parent. I will leave nothing out; this, I promise.

And you, unseen stranger, will be my final judge.

CHAPTER ONE

Sumter, South Carolina
December 17, 1979
7 Years Old

I could smell Christmas in the air.

A cold breeze swirled the dust, making it dance in the cement gutters of Main Street, and I could almost touch the excitement that filled it. As the same wind pierced my skin, sending shivers all the way to my bones, it felt no different than the trembling anticipation I'd experienced just a few minutes before, perched atop the lap of Santa Claus himself. (If Santa Claus also worked part-time at the Brogdon Auto Shop and smelled faintly of gin.)

I had asked for one thing and one thing only, figuring my odds improved with every elimination of non-essential requests. The sole object of my desire was the new Tonka Truck that had just been released: a full-on bulldozer that came with its very own dump truck. I, of course, fully understood this actually constituted *two* Tonka Trucks, but I hoped that old Santa would count it as one since they were of a pair. That, too tired to give a hoot about the distinction.

"Tonka, huh?" the grizzled voice had cheerfully grumbled back at me as his plump leg bounced beneath my rump. "That's a mighty fine gift for a young'un your age. You think them dang old elves up yonder in the North Pole can whip that up?" He smiled, his teeth a mighty yellow, especially glimpsed through the fake white beard.

"Yes, sir, I do," I had replied, trying to show all the confidence one can muster in such an anxious event.

"Well, then," Santa said, "I reckon we'll just have to wait and see. Best be gettin' on, now, and be a good boy for your mama and daddy down at the farm. Those are some good folk if I ever seen any in my life. Tell 'em old Jeffrey says howdy do."

I had laughed then, finding it hilarious that Old Man Brogdon didn't even bother pretending he was actually *The Man*, himself. But all kids know very well that Santa has plenty of helpers, scattered all over the world. It didn't bother me in the least or test my steely faith. My joy was uncapped, unfettered, then. If only I could've frozen the universe, time itself, halted my inevitable growth. An insect preserved in amber.

A few minutes later, standing on the sidewalk beneath the sign for the Rexall Drugstore, I rubbed my hands together, then hugged myself, trying to conjure some warmth out of the thin, cold air. My daddy was scheduled to arrive at any moment; he'd gone to market to sell a few bales of dried tobacco they'd saved from the autumn harvest. Normally, I begged to go with him, listen to the auctioneers talk faster than an album with the RPM speed set too high. But I couldn't very well pass up a chance to speak to Santa, now could I? (Well, Santa's helper, anyway.)

A vehicle turned onto Main Street up ahead, and I almost stepped forward until I saw that it wasn't my daddy's truck, despite being black, dusty, beat all to hell, and huge. It wasn't a truck at all, in fact. It was a hearse—those big, scary things that transported smaller, scarier things—with WHITTACKER MORTUARY stamped on its side doors. Not that you could actually read the words after a decade or two of wear and tear. Just a few letters of the logo had survived, along with a depiction of an old church's steeple sticking through the letter "O" in MORTUARY. But, legible or not, there was only one place in town that collected dead people, and only one man that drove the battered old hearse.

Its engine burped and spat toxic fumes as it rumbled down the two-way lane, the windows so dusty that I couldn't see the tiny man I knew sat behind the wheel: Pee Wee Gaskins, jack-of-all- trades when it came to the recently-departed. Whatever Whit Whittacker needed, Pee Wee provided—picking up the deceased, cleaning the deceased, embalming the deceased, dressing the deceased, burying the deceased. People around town said old Pee Wee Gaskins could dig a grave faster than Parson Fincher could say a burial prayer. I wasn't so sure about that, but figured it'd be a tight race, anyhow.

The hearse lurched to a stop, not 20 feet from where I stood. As its engine growled and burped, finally shutting off to a series of clicks and hisses, I imagined a great dragon settling in for sleep after a long day of hunting sheep and princesses. I'm not ashamed in the least to admit a chill crept up my spine in that moment, something beyond normal for such a wintry day. The door popped open, and for a split second I was absolutely certain that a demon would step out, its red skin glistening, its mouth open and full of sharp teeth, its eyes yellow and slitted. My shoulders actually sagged in relief when little Pee Wee Gaskins hopped through the door and landed on both feet, as if he'd just stepped out of a big rig. My daddy always had this to say about Pee Wee's wanting stature: the man could get lost in a field of wheat standing on his tippy toes, and no one in town knew how on Earth he handled all those dead bodies.

"How you doin' there, pipsqueak?" Pee Wee called over when

he saw me huddled beneath the Rexall sign. The man was skin and bones and barely five feet tall, his head half-bald, with what was left of his hair wispy and scraggly, some of it almost reaching his shoulders. He kept his face clean-shaven, as if to show off the pockmark scars he'd gained from his youthful acne. Like a badge of honor. The man did have kind eyes for the most part, his one saving grace, but they seemed as out of place as if they'd been situated on his elbows, one each.

"Just fine, sir," I answered back, still shivering from the unnatural chill Pee Wee had brought along with the hearse. I craned my neck to see around the heap of a vehicle, hoping my daddy's truck would magically appear.

"Your mama in the store or somethin'? Don't seem too bright standin' out here—you gonna catch the death of a cold, boy."

I could've been forgiven for thinking there'd been a glint in the man's eyes when he said that. Maybe business was slow this week, and old Pee Wee needed some work to cut the boredom.

"Just waiting on my daddy is all," I replied. Then quickly added, "Should be here any second now. Any second." I shot another look down the street.

"Any second, huh? Well ain't that just the best daddy I ever heard of." He spit on the sidewalk. "Ya'll be good, now. I got me some shoppin' to do."

Pee Wee nodded, then walked to the back of the hearse. He twisted the lever of the handle until it clicked, then lifted the great door open. The hinges squealed an unhappy tune and I grimaced, sure he'd awakened whatever dead fella might be lying in the back. Pee Wee reached deep into the hearse and pulled something out, then slammed the door closed. The thump of it echoed down Main Street, chased by the bitter wind.

With no surprise at all, I saw that Pee Wee was holding his faithful shovel, the splintery wooden handle gripped in both hands. It was well known around town that the man liked carrying around his grandpa's shovel, almost like a security blanket, often using it as a makeshift walking stick. They were a good five miles from the cemetery, but that never stopped Pee Wee Gaskins from hefting that shovel around. I swear on the graves of my ancestors that I'd once seen him holding it across his lap in church.

Pee Wee lifted the shovel onto his shoulder, the scoop-end hanging over his back. The metal had rusted, the edges jagged and caked with dirt clods that just might've dated back to the last century. Some even said that very shovel had been used to bury soldiers from the Civil War. (Hopefully dead ones.)

My daddy's truck finally—*finally*—turned a corner up the road apiece and headed in our direction. This gave me a sudden and inexplicable surge of courage, and I asked the question that would prove to haunt me for the rest of my life. I'd think about it long into the nights, even decades after the authorities had excavated the bodies sunk deep within Puddin' Swamp—some of them with heads still attached, some without.

"Hey, Pee Wee," I blurted as the man passed within five feet of where I stood, making his merry way down the street toward some unknown "shopping" destination.

"Yeah, boy?" he replied, pausing for a second, gripping the shovel with both hands as the tool lay across the back of his shoulders.

"Why you always carrying that thing around?" I asked. "Even when you ain't got no work to do?"

Old Pee Wee Gaskins nodded a few times, as if pondering the perfect response. When he finally answered, he let out a grin that registered close to a nine-point-six on the creepy scale.

"Well, son," the man said. "You never know when you might find a body needs buryin'. You just never know."

And then he walked off, that old shovel bouncing with every step.

CHAPTER TWO

Lynchburg, South Carolina
March 1989
16 Years Old

Time passed as time does, a flowing river, my life nothing but a leaf upon the waters—I always knew the general direction laid out before me, but never quite where I'd end up. In the short span of my 16 years on Earth, life on the farm had changed drastically. Whereas my older siblings had spent their tender childhoods picking tobacco and drying tobacco and bundling tobacco, their arms perpetually covered in black, sticky tar—a nemesis that never quite washed off, no matter how chemically creative one might get—my world was a different thing entirely.

In the twilight of my first decade, our dad up and decided he was too old to be a farmer and rented out the vast acreage he called his own, content to watch other poor saps do the hard work. This, of course, meant less money. But if ever there was a man who didn't need much to get by, it was my daddy. Poor mama, though...

But I need to stop.

I'm doing this all wrong.

This isn't the right way to lay out my path.

Yes, the story of my teenage years needs to be and will be told, for a story without a proper beginning is pretty worthless by the time the end comes around. But how can I make any of this matter—how can I press upon you the significance of these occurrences without presenting the key characters to whom these horrors would someday visit? *They* are what matter.

They are the only things in this *world* that matter, and my diabolical tale is an empty husk until they have been presented unto you.

I'm talking, of course, about my children.

CHAPTER THREE

I-20 Freeway
July 2017
44 Years Old

I

"Dad! Wesley elbowed me again!"

My hands on the wheel, the freeway stretched out before me like a great stone river, I watched the painted lines of the road dying one by one as they disappeared beneath my car. With the low whine of the tires like a song of alien sea creatures stuck on one note, I closed my eyes for a brief second. I took in a deep breath, and then I let it out. Opened my eyes. Saw that the road hadn't changed and we weren't much closer to Grandma's. In fact, we had four hours left to go, at best.

"Dad!"

I breathed in again, felt the cool air go straight from the A/C vent into my lungs, then reluctantly come back out, almost like the burning mist of a drug. I did keep my eyes open this time.

"*What*, Mason?"

His little voice, so sweet at times that it hurt my heart—panged it with love—now sounded like the very screech of Satan's angels. "Wesley keeps touching my leg! And he's only doing it to bug me!"

There are people in the world—perhaps even you, reading my tale—that think it's a baseless cliché, the whole he-or-she-is-touching-me bit. If nothing else from my narrative you take away as fact, this one is as solid as gravity: if you have a child, and they are sitting in proximity of another child, as sure as the Earth spins and the moon shines white, the one child will touch the other child, whereupon the aggrieved child will make it plain to any adult within earshot that he or she has been offended greatly by said contact. I believe I mentioned earlier that kids are stupid?

"Wesley," I said over my shoulder, trying to keep my own annoyance at bay, "please stop touching your little brother." I looked at him in the mirror—16, blond hair hanging a bit in his eyes, which showed a profound wisdom belonging to a 60-year-old man. He smiled a grin at me, one that said so many things. That he'd just been teasing Mason, that he was sorry, that he was bored, that he loved me. Everything good in the world shone in that smile.

"Yes, father," he responded, the sarcasm as heavy as the car in which we drove. "I'll obey your reasonable command if you ask Mason to kindly stop burping after each chip he eats. It's making me nauseous."

"I'd like to insert a comment, here." This came from Hazel, who had the misfortune of sitting on the other side of the belch-happy Mason.

"Please do," I said, genuinely interested. Hazel had a knack for talking like a professor despite being 10 years old, and I always looked forward to the next thing that might pop out of her mouth. My eyes found her in the mirror now—you might be worried that I wasn't paying much attention to the road and could kill my children in a violent wreck at any moment, but I assure you that wasn't the case—and smiled at her beauty. Dark skin, her head adorned with black, tightly curled hair. Face of an angel, to give you a cliché worth complaining about. (And yes, she's adopted, to get that out of the way. All of my kids are, after Wesley. There's one, sitting in the far back, sound asleep, that I haven't even mentioned yet. His name is Logan, just like the Wolverine.)

Hazel, after a little bit of pontificating, her index finger actually pressed against her lips for a moment, finally gave us her thoughtful answer.

"Mason's burps *do* stink. I think he has a gastrointestinal problem. We need to have him diagnosed by a proper physician." Two things that Hazel loved: Use of the word "proper" and calling a doctor a physician. Ten years old, remember.

"I concur with the well-spoken madam from Atlanta," Wesley added. "Mason doth stinketh in a most profound way. Perhaps even from both ends if I'm not completely mistaken." He only spoke like this to mock Hazel, but he did it so lovingly and agreeably that it swelled my heart. "Let us hope the physician chooses not to remove his innards."

Understandably, Mason chose to cry at this morbid statement, bursting into a bellow that hurt my ears. He's seven years old, so we can forgive him. Logan, who we mustn't forget in the back, is four, still strapped to a car seat though he thinks it ridiculous to imprison such a big boy. As you may have guessed, my wife and I were able to have one child by natural means, Wesley, before going through several years of no luck (despite our very best efforts, I might add). And if there was ever anything my sweet wife and I wanted in life, it was a big family, just like the ones from which we hailed. So we went the adoption route, picking up kids from all over the world—Africa, China, Detroit. In that order.

My wife wasn't in the car during all this burping and

complaining and pontificating, and I'm sad to say that the reason is a very melancholy one. She died two full years before the road trip of which you read. She'd been on a business trip to far-off Singapore and perished in a very suspicious way, but that's a tale for another time. I'd tell you more, but it's the kind of love that sounds way too good to be true. Maybe some day. But I miss her as much, and as painfully, as you can imagine.

"I tell you guys what," I said after Hazel's proposal that we get a medicinal authority involved (with Wesley's concurrence). Mason had gloriously quieted to a sniffle. "Let's make a deal. Mason, you can only burp once—when you're finished with your entire bag of chips. Hazel, I promise I'll ask the doc—the *physi-cian*—about Mason's gastrointestinal issues at his next checkup. Wesley, if you'll stop touching Mason I'll let you drive after our next pit stop. Do we have a deal?"

My eyes met theirs in the mirror, one at a time—again, I assure you my senses perceived the road just fine while doing this necessary exercise—and watched each of them nod. Of the three, Wesley seemed most satisfied.

Approximately seven seconds later, Logan—don't forget, four years old, in the back, unwillingly strapped to a car seat—woke up and announced with an extraordinary if inexplicably happy voice that he'd peed his pants.

I breathed in; I breathed out.

And watched the road.

2

Two gas stations, one change of clothes, a jaunt through the drive-through of a non-brand hamburger dive, at least a dozen pointless if not sometimes entertaining arguments, and one deeply philosophical discussion with Wesley on mixing religion and race in the analysis of bigotry later, we arrived at Grandma's house. I'm not sure why Grandpa got the shaft so universally, but the home in which I grew up was always referred to as the abode of Grandma's and Grandma's alone. I first knew my parents as Daddy and Mama, which slowly transformed into Dad and Mom by the time I was a teenager. So many names for such simple, kind people.

They lived smack dab in the middle of nowhere, along a dusty, narrow lane—literally called Narrow Paved Road—that stretched like the world's longest and straightest arrow across the farmlands of Lynchburg, South Carolina. Being the middle of summer, the black pavement of the infinite road shimmered with heat, the air above the lane practically boiling as we cut through it. Crops went past in their beautiful rows—the lines of white dirt flashing like an odd sort of strobe light as we sped by. I never tired of looking upon those beautiful crops when we came back home—the broad leaves of tobacco, the billowy white balls of cotton filled with their prickly seeds, the humble, rather ordinary-looking soybean plants. I cracked the window to sniff the welcoming smells of earth and greenery and manure, all mixing together to grace my senses with an assurance that I had returned to the land of my birth.

Houses were far and few between, but soon the porch and brick chimney and white siding of my parents' century-old structure slid into view, up on the right, and every one of us quieted for a moment of awe. My kids revered this place—and the people who lived within—as much as I did. We weren't your normal family, saving up every dollar to go to wild, magical places like Disney World and New York City. When we had time off, when summer hit, when Christmas rolled around, we did what each and every one of us wanted to do—visit Grandma and Grandpa. Visit my gazillion cousins and aunts and uncles. Eat lots of food and tell stories of the old days on the farm.

This very place, I thought as I pulled onto the gravel driveway that wrapped around the front yard, *was the place we all wanted to be.* At least this is what I told myself. Maybe my kids wanted to go see Mickey Mouse and only spared my feelings. Or maybe I was at fault for not showing them more of the world. Either way, in my memories a shadow hung over the home that day. A shadow that failed to darken my joy. Even thoughts of Grandpa Fincher's ghost in the old house's attic—an apparition I'd heard with my own two ears, I swear beneath God, angels, and witnesses—couldn't penetrate my elation. The ghost probably —*probably*—wasn't real, but we sure loved pretending that it was so.

I put such things out of mind when my mom and dad appeared on the cement porch, letting the creaky screen door flop shut behind them. My dad, all grey hair and whiskers, waved his bony, wrinkly hand, the skin so weathered by the sun you could've made a fine baseball glove out of it. My mom smiled her beaming smile, too busy wiping her hands on an apron to wave,. Stereotype or not, the only thing the woman loved to do more than cooking was cooking for company. And no one has ever tasted anything finer than the morsels blessed enough to come out of her oven or off her stove.

"Howdy-do, pardner," my dad said as I opened my door, the same thing that always came out of his mouth at this point. Whether he said it ironically or not, I never quite figured out. "Glad you made it safe and sound, just in the nick of time. Storm a-brewing yonder south, blowing up this way."

My dad, a man who'd rather check the weather report than breathe air.

"Hey, son." My mom had me in her arms before I could fully stand, pulling me tight, kissing both my cheeks. And then the kids were out of the car and bedlam broke loose.

"Grandma!"

"Grandpa!"

"Mason!"

"Hazel!"

"Grandma Grandpa!"

"Wesley!"

"Grandpa!"

"Grandma!"

"Where's my little Wolverine?"

"Someone get me out of this stupid car seat!"

There were hugs, someone fell down, my dad pulled a muscle in his back, and I think I saw a tear or two wiped away in embarrassment, but I can't remember who it was amongst the blur of movement. The reunion was all joy and bluster, the excitement of the next several weeks filling the air almost like the snowy thrill of Christmas. We were back at Grandma's, dammit, and all was right in the world.

"Let's get our bags, kids," I said, shooing with my hands in no particular direction.

I looked at my dad in that moment, and saw something that made me pause. A wave of sadness, perhaps. It was gone as soon as it came, but I felt a little crack in my tray of welcome. He'd always been a bit mysterious, sometimes gloomy.

The trunk was opened, bags were lifted, somebody pinched somebody, somebody screamed.

"How was the drive?" Mom asked.

"Not too bad," I said, already forgetting the forgettable parts of our sojourn. "Mason might need some Tums, though." All four of my kids snickered at that, Mason especially.

"What've you been up to, Wesley?" Mom asked my oldest child. Everyone exaggeratedly grunted with strain as we carried our bags up the porch steps.

"Not much, Grandma." He shrugged, a move perfected by prehistoric teenagers, an art never lost since. "I kinda miss my friends since school got out, just been looking forward to coming back here, I guess. Can't wait to hang out with the cousins. And for you to stuff me with food until I explode." He always spoke with an... *adultness* that never failed to amaze me.

I could see the same feeling in my mom's eyes as she responded. "Just wait until you try my new casserole. It's got something in it that'll make your toes curl up."

"Is that a good thing?" Wesley asked. "I kinda like my toes straight."

Grandma laughed hard at that one, a little in disproportion to the quality of the joke.

And so, we had arrived.

With a sigh that spoke a million words, I followed everyone else into the house.

3

Dinner was everything that my mom had promised. I didn't know if anyone's toes had curled inside their shoes—mine, in fact, had not—but it was one of the finest meals I'd ever been blessed to partake. I'm not sure if Grandma liked having leftovers in the fridge or if she thought we'd all turned into elephants, but heaps of food still remained on the table long after we sat back, hands on stomachs, with slightly distressed looks on our faces. I'd thought myself full at least 20 minutes before I'd stopped eating.

But before that, at some point during all that exercise of transporting meats and vegetables and baked goods from dishes and trays to plates and utensils to our mouths and finally down our throats, Hazel paused with a loaded fork frozen in midair and spoke in a clear, loud voice.

"Would you mind telling us a story about the old days, Grandpa?" she said, her words and tone as likely to have come from any woman I've ever known as from a 10-year-old child. "A proper story, please."

"Yeah," Wesley pitched in. "Tell us about the dead pig in the bathtub."

I smiled through a mouthful of food, knowing exactly what he was referring to. It's not nearly so morbid as it sounds.

"You mean the fall barbecue?" Dad asked, always willing to spin a tale for his grandkids. He put down his own fork and leaned back, a wistful look peeking through his whiskers and wrinkled brow. The shadowed countenance from earlier seemed to have disappeared. "Good times, those were. We had more people packed in this yard and house than ants in an anthill. We'd go out to the pig sty and grab the biggest fella we could find, string the poor thing up, pull out a honking big serrated knife—"

My mom leaned over at this point and tapped my dad on the arm. "Maybe leave out the most gruesome details, sweetie."

"NO!"

I'd never heard my kids speak so clearly and in such perfect unison before.

"Definitely tell us the gruesome parts," Wesley said, throwing an *I'm-sorry* glance at his grandma. "Blood, guts, intestines, everything."

"Yeah!" Mason echoed.

"Bloody guts!" Logan yelled.

Dad looked pleased as punch, a phrase he taught me. "Well, let's just say we took care of business—and I was always quick about it. I loved those swine, and never woulda harmed a one if we didn't need to feed our children. And that day we were feeding a god—uh, er, a galdern army of relations. But yes, anywho, there was a mess of blood and guts, and not one inch of my body clean by the time we had that poor beast ready to cook."

"What does a bathtub have to do with this?" Hazel asked, her face as innocent as the day we picked her up.

"It was an old iron washtub used by your grandma's papa," Dad said. He meant Grandpa Fincher, whose ghost had taken up residence in the attic—no one really disputed this. "Kept it in the shed out back by the safe. That thing was perfect for cutting up a pig—even comes with its own drain. We did all of this on the porch, mind you." He shifted in his seat, pointed at the back door which led to the killing ground of which he spoke. "Yes, sir. Right out there. Oh my babies, I hope you never have to hear the squeal of a slaughtered hog."

"All right, then," Mom announced. "I think that's quite enough of the washtub story. More pork casserole anyone?"

Several dazed faces shook their heads in unison, along with a few silent-but-mouthed *No, thank you*'s. I shrugged my shoulders and obligingly accepted another shovel-full. Eventually, everyone gave in and loaded up, but soon enough we came to that moment mentioned previously, sitting back in our chairs, hands on stomachs, in disbelief that we'd ever felt hungry, even once, in our entire lives.

"Grandma," Wesley said, "you need your own TV show. That shit was good."

His sentence had fully come out before he realized quite what he'd done. He looked at me, and I looked back at him. He looked at Grandma, then Grandpa, and they looked back. Hazel had a mouth so open it looked downright unnatural, like the mouth of a bear's cave. A spoonful of gravy-soaked mashed potatoes was halfway to Mason's own mouth, but it splashed back onto his plate. Logan was oblivious, either taking something out or putting something into his nose.

Mom laughed a short bark of a thing she tried to cover up. Dad tried not to grin as he shook his head. Wesley blushed.

"Sorry," he muttered. "I was gonna say crap but that just didn't seem to give your food justice."

We all sat a moment, pondering this profoundly confusing statement.

Dad shook his head again, grunted a sound that was somehow amiable, and stood up to clear the dishes. We all knew he had no intention of doing it alone so we immediately began to help. A flurry of clinks and clanks filled the warm room.

I leaned into Wesley as we carried some plates to the kitchen. "In front of my parents? Really?" I thought it the only rebuke I could give without seeming like a grumpy old curmudgeon.

"Come on, Dad," he responded. "Grandpa's a farmer—you really think he's never used that word before? When the... whatever, cows bit him?"

"Cows? When they bit him?"

"I don't know. Or when the tractor ran over a chicken or something?"

I let out a very exaggerated sigh. "Fail."

Wesley gave our plates a good scrape over the sink then slid them into the dishwasher. "Guess I should've played that farm game on my phone more often."

"Double fail," I replied.

"Maybe I should quit school and become a farmer."

"Okay, stop talking."

Just then the doorbell rang. Everyone looked up at once, as if we were expecting God himself to have dropped by for a visit.

"That must be Aunt Evelyn," my mom pronounced.

Because we loved my sister almost as much as we loved Mom's cooking, at least one chair toppled over as we raced for the front door.

4

It wasn't Aunt Evelyn.

The spring door creaked its crooked squeal as my dad pushed it open. I was standing right behind his shoulder, looking through the glass and mesh at a man I'd never seen before. He stepped aside to reveal himself better as the door clicked into its propped position. He was a nervous stretch of a thing, all sinew and darkly tanned skin, his eyes cast down to the ground as if he'd come to confess his awful sins.

"Can I help ya?" Dad asked.

The stranger fidgeted, playing the tips of his fingers like a musical instrument. Still he did not raise his eyes. I guessed he was in his mid-30s, maybe pushing 40. Hard to tell with the bushy beard that marooned itself on his face and neck. His dirty-blond hair had been severely combed to the side, greased with something of industrial caliber. His entire head shone like polished bronze.

"Sir?" Dad intoned firmly, making it clear that this man's presence better be explained quickly or there was going to be trouble.

With that, the stranger finally looked up. He had the darkest eyes I'd ever seen, the surrounding whites moistened with recent tears, his skin puffy from crying.

"I'm—I'm sorry," he mumbled. "I don't mean nobody no harm. No, sir."

"Then what in God's name are you doing here on my front porch?" Dad asked, his voice matching the unease that hung in the air like mildewed drapes. "Do I need to call the authorities?" He nudged me with his hand, as if he wanted me to do that exact thing, or at least pull out my phone to make a show of it. I did, held it up for display.

"No, sir, please!" the stranger pleaded. "I ain't here to harm nobody—I the one been harmed!" He spoke with such earnestness that the tendons of his neck bulged and jiggled under his beard. "Please, I just need... to take care of somethin'. I ain't got no gun or nothin'—you can check."

At this point my dad turned to me, a look on his face that I would better understand a few days hence. It was a look of compassion, almost pleading, but it also rang heavily with falseness, as if he he'd been hired to do a commercial, a piss-poor actor to boot.

"Now look, Dad," I started to say, but something he did—a slight tremble of his lips, a furrowing of his brow, his eyes seeming to think on their own, lost in words too profound to speak aloud—stopped me. Confused me, really. With a hearty sigh, I turned my attention to our visitor. "What's wrong, man? Do we need to call an ambulance? The police? Are you in some kind of trouble?"

The stranger shook his head in the negative so voraciously I would've only been a little surprised if the thing had tumbled off into the bushes. "No, no, I'm finer than frog hair, I swear it. I just come here to say a few words is all. I heard you was in town and figured I'd make my way over here before sun sets a-yonder."

His eyes focused on me so suddenly, and so absolutely, that I took a step backward. They cleared as he looked at me, any sense of the rambling, sad, stumbling persona gone.

"Me?" I asked, feeling rather stupid, as if our positions in the odd situation had just switched. "Do I know you?"

"You . . . You knew my papa."

I find it impossible to describe the change that came over his face when he said this, and, as I recognized the resemblance that I saw there, the even greater transformation that came over me. All color drained from his pallor, as I'm sure it did from mine, seeming to magically mutate into storm clouds above us, making the world suddenly and blackly dark.

I know that my mouth opened in that moment, that I intended to speak, but I can't recall if any words actually came out.

"Now don't go judging me," the stranger said, an almost visible wall of defense shimmering before him. "I ain't nothin' like my daddy and I ain't got nothin' in my blood that'll ever make me so. Sins of the father and all that—ain't nothin' but a bunch of horse shit."

The man on the porch, standing before me, facing the home where my own grandmother had birthed my mother, was Dicky Gaskins. You've heard me mention his father in this telling, and a chance meeting I had with him as a little innocent, fresh off the joy of meeting a fake Santa Clause. That was but our first encounter, and the last to ever be pleasant.

"You're Pee Wee Gaskins' boy, huh?"Dad said in a breathless whisper. Again, something rang untrue in his tone. I had the feeling he knew very well who the guy was but for some reason didn't want *me* to know that.

Dicky nodded, trying his very best to put on a look of humility—all bowed head and sunk shoulders, hands clasped before him sanctimoniously. "Yes, sir, I am. And I've spent every last day of my wretched life trying to apologize for it. I ain't my daddy."

I don't think I'd moved a muscle in these long, eternally tormenting moments. A better storyteller than I would've set things up properly, so that you could know the hellish dread that had settled upon me. But there is a method in my madness (said the Bard) and I ask your patience as my story unfolds. Suffice it to say that I would've felt no more fright and dismay if Satan and all his devils had stepped upon my parent's lawn.

"Get the hell out of here," I said, fighting my instinct to rain blows upon this kin of my plague. "Don't say another word and get off my dad's property." If blood were said to boil in anger, mine was downright cooking like a stew. I felt the heated flush in the skin of my face.

"You're gonna hear what I come to say," Dicky Gaskins insisted.

I yelled something at him then, something laced with every word my mom taught me to never say. Then a compulsion took over, as if I'd been emotionally hijacked, and I barreled forward, grabbing Dicky by the shirt, pushing him ahead of me. Finding strength I didn't know I had, I lifted him clear off his feet and slammed his back onto the concrete floor of the porch, heard the air rush from his body. No matter his ancestry, the look of genuine terror that came over him triggered a spate of unwanted guilt deep inside me. All the same, I reached back my hand, balled into the mightiest fist I'd ever wielded, and readied to punch him in his vulnerable, weak, Pee Wee Gaskins-like face.

"Dad?"

It was a soft voice, angelic. Coming from my right. Holding my fist in its position, hovering somewhere between Dicky and the heavens, I looked over. All four of my kids stood there, watching my fit of rage. They must've gone out back to come round the side yard. Hazel had spoken, but the harrowing tone of her simple word had conveyed properly the feelings of them all. Even Wesley, who I often thought of as someone older and wiser than I, stared with a childlike confusion. Although I might've expected it more of Mason, Logan whimpered, tears streaming down his cheeks.

I snapped out of my trance. Stumbling, I lifted myself off of Dicky and scooted backwards until my shoulders hit the front wall of the house. Dad still stood at the open screen door, motionless and silent.

"I'm sorry," I whispered, although I'm certain no one heard it, least of all my children, to whom I was really speaking.

"It's no problem," Dicky said, misunderstanding, rising to his feet as he dusted himself off. "Now let's get down to—"

"Just go!" I yelled, now angrier at what he'd made me do in front of my kids than anything else. "Just leave and never come back!" My eyes weren't focused on him, however. They rested squarely on Wesley, who studied me like the wisest owl from every children's fantasy tale.

I didn't know what to say. I didn't know what to do. I wasn't so worried about Wesley—all of them—seeing my temper tantrum as I was about being forced to explain the *reason* behind it. In Dicky's face I saw his dad, and in his dad I saw everything bad that had ever happened to me.

I was standing now, breathing as if I'd done a hundred sit-ups. My kids needed to hear words from me, needed to understand my reaction. I'd thought to spare them these horrors, but no other choice lay before me. I opened my mouth to speak, with no idea what might come out.

"Guys, listen . . ."

But that's as far as I got. Dicky made a gagging, retching sound, a sharp exhale of noise that echoed across the lawn. I looked at him, bewildered—reflecting back, I'm ashamed to say I didn't feel the least bit of concern, only a morbid curiosity. It had been a strange sound, one of those unnatural sounds that, when coming from a human body, makes one immediately understand that something has gone terribly wrong, that death is knocking and only a doctor can keep it outside the door.

Dicky spasmed on the ground, both hands clasped around his own neck. Eyes bulging, face puffy and red—shading toward purple, tendons sharp as piano strings beneath his skin, the man writhed in agony on the edge of the porch. He finally toppled off of it, falling the three feet that had once seemed a dozen to me. A blooming azalea bush squashed under his weight. All the while, those awful noises coming from his throat filled the air.

"Dammit, do something!" my dad shouted, at everyone and no one.

The kids, huddled close for protection, a little pack of wolves, had come around the front of the porch, keeping their distance but unable to *not* watch. The fear in their eyes was something I'd hoped would never assail them, and it was only the first of my many failures that summer.

"David!" Dad was finally leaving his perch at the screen door, heading for the spot where Dicky had fallen. I'd needed to hear my name to snap me out of my trance, but I moved quickly, and got to the writhing, suffering man first. I jumped down into the azaleas, feeling the prick of their branches, knelt, felt more pricks, and assessed the situation.

Our visitor was in bad shape. His entire face resembled an awful bruise, the skin so puffy it might've popped if stuck by a pin. It was a wonder his eyes stayed inside his head they bulged so much from their sockets. No physician needed for this diagnosis—the man was choking and about two licks from dying right there in the bushes. But unless I'd missed Dicky clandestinely pull a Slim-Jim out of his pocket and start munching away, I couldn't imagine *what* had lodged in his gullet to make him suffer so.

"Dad, call a doctor!" My hands hovered in the air, fingers outstretched, not a single one amongst the ten with a clue of what to do, Dicky twisting, gagging, squirming below them. The purple marshmallow of his face looked ready to burst, if his eyes didn't do it first. He was on his back, staring toward the sky as if he expected angels to come take his soul away.

"Dicky," I said, trying to hide the terror in my voice. "Be still a second. I need to . . ." I didn't know what I needed. What *he* needed. I reached down and touched his hands, still clasped around his neck, then his chest, then the area around his mouth, which was open wide—he'd gone quiet, which meant it had gotten worse. "Dicky! I'm gonna try the Heimlich maneuver!" As if announcing my intention would make me any more capable of doing it.

Digging into the azaleas with my knees for support, I grabbed Dicky's shoulder and heaved him onto his side, then onto his stomach. I straddled his back, then wrapped my arms around his body, clasping my hands at his stomach, the branches beneath him scraping my skin. More than aware that I wasn't strong enough to pick Dicky up, I squeezed him tight and did my best to lift him.

"Get up!" I grunted. "Dicky, get up!" I pumped my arms in and out, digging my two-handed fist into his abdomen each time, while simultaneously trying to get my feet under me to stand. If only it had been a safety drill, my kids would've had a good laugh at how ridiculous I must've looked. "Dicky, get your ass *up*, man!"

Somewhere in the midst of all that struggling and silent retching and dying, Dicky's brain still had its synapses sparking, because he heard me and was able to do the little he could to get us both in a standing position. Once we were upright, I was able to do the famous Heimlich maneuver more properly. I know because I've seen a million movies.

But it wasn't working.

I heaved my fists into his stomach, pulling with all the force I knew, lifting his entire body with the effort. He came down and I did it again. We repeated this hapless dance at least a dozen times to no effect. Dicky was obviously weakening now that his air pipe had been completely blocked. The man was fading, dying, right in my arms.

A heavy force slammed into my side, a bony shoulder that shocked me when I saw it belonged to my son, Wesley. He'd hit me hard enough to loosen my grip on Dicky, and the man fell to the ground once again, this time missing the bushes; he flopped onto the grass, his eyes no longer bulging.

"It's his tongue, Dad," Wesley said. I'm not sure, in my entire life, I'd ever heard a more confusing string of four words put together. At least in the heat of the moment, it made not the least bit of sense to me.

"Huh?" I asked dumbly, but Wesley hadn't waited on a response. He'd dropped to the ground, kneeling so that his knees touched one purple, puffy cheek of Dicky. Then I watched in amazement as my son squeezed the man's cheeks—squeezed hard—with one hand while using the other to force Dicky's mouth open. It resisted at first, but then popped open as easily as a soap bubble bursting. Wesley reached into the gaping maw of the mouth with the hand that had been pinching Dicky's face. The hand went deeper and deeper, Wesley's bottom lip bit between his own teeth as he looked sideways at the ground with an intense expression of concentration. I'll swear to the day I die that his arm disappeared all the way to the elbow.

"Got it!" Wesley yelled. He pulled his hand out of Dicky's mouth and collapsed backwards into the azalea bushes. As for Dicky, he was now heaving in breaths, one after the other, sucking and blowing air like a human bellows. Then came the coughing and choked gasps and all the other unpleasant sounds you'd expect from a man who'd almost died swallowing his own tongue.

I was close enough to the edge of the porch to sit down in a daze. Everything around me had become surreal. My other kids were all crying now. Dad was nowhere in sight. The air seemed too still to be natural, as if the substance of the universe had locked into place.

The bizarre string of occurrences once again flashed before my mind. The son of a serial killer shows up at our door, the son of the man who'd done more harm to me than all the other villains of my life—great and small—combined. This son of a killer said he came to see *me*. He then choked on his own tongue, for no apparent reason. And my son, who'd never showed us the slightest hint that he knew the first thing about saving a person in such dire straits, had done just that.

But as strange as it all was, I must tell you that what lay beneath the surface—what had truly transpired in those terrifying moments—was a thing so dark that I can't bear to describe it just yet.

We must now go back to where it all began.

CHAPTER FOUR

**Lynchburg, South Carolina
March 1989**

I

All the horrors of my life can be traced back to one day—the day that Andrea Llerenas and I went for a walk in the woods.

It started when Andrea uttered the words that destroyed my heart. The words that almost literally hurt my ears as the vibration of her sound waves passed through those waxy canals. Words that slashed and burned and ruined what I had thought was the most perfect young woman to ever walk the earth.

"Led Zeppelin is no better than all those other hair-bands you listen to."

We were walking along the old abandoned train tracks, their long rails still straight if not a little rusted and worse for wear. Every good thing that comes with the end of winter and the onset of spring was in full view around us. Oak trees and birches and maples dressed themselves with green leaves, taking some of the glory back from the pines that had stood their ground through the cold months. The undergrowth of the forest was alive again, the bushes and vines and weeds filling in those lonely, wintry gaps, making the whole place seem crowded and happy. There were even flowers peeking out, some reds and blues, but mostly yellows at this early stage. It all smelled fresh and vibrant, somehow made all the stronger by the constant hum of insects, a buzzy roar that becomes its own kind of silence.

We were surrounded by beauty and I walked with the greatest friend I'd ever known, as happy a moment as I can remember, until she said those words and dampened the mood.

"Wait a second," I said, stopping to stand on one of the rotted wooden railroad ties. "I think my hearing just hit the skids." I stuck a pinkie in my ear and gave it a wiggle as if digging for worms. "You can't possibly have just said what I think you just said. Even though you said it. I'm pretty sure you said it but you couldn't . . ." I gave up trying to be funny.

"Mmm hmm," Andrea replied, "that didn't make much sense, but okay. Poison, Skid Row, Guns 'N Roses, Led Zeppelin— they're all the same. And by same I definitely mean crappy."

Still perched atop the rotten wood, my feet sinking as if it were clay, I rubbed my temples with both hands. "All right, first of all, that's wrong on at least two levels. For one thing, every single one of those bands is awesome. *But*, Led Zeppelin is nothing like them. Totally different. Totally another level. I mean, they're all awesome, but . . . Zeppelin is awesomer."

"Do they all have long hair?" she asked.

"Yeah, but—"

"Do they all wear ridiculous clothes?"

"Yeah, but—"

"Do they all have that excruciating guitar solo in the middle that no one wants to listen to?"

"They're *not* the same. All awesome, one is awesomer. End of discussion."

"So eloquently spoken I don't know how I can possibly argue any further." She folded her arms and exaggerated a sigh of defeat. "Except to say that they all suck."

"Yeah, not nearly as good as Madonna and Tiffany."

"Take that back. Take that back right now."

But even as she said the words, a laugh was rising from her chest and she pulled me into a hug, wrapping her arms around my neck. A few kisses might've followed.

How to describe the pure pleasure of those three things—her laugh, her hug, her kiss. I'm not one to embrace the cheese when it comes to matters of love, but she embodied happiness for me, a beacon of pure joy amongst the darkness and fog that so often accompanies the teenage years. If she hadn't been in my life over the next couple of months, I'm absolutely certain I wouldn't have survived.

She stepped back, sadly dropping her arms away. "Can we *please* go find the path now?"

"If you insist." I took a moment to admire her—the brown hair, the brown skin, the sharp curve of her cheeks. But it was the eyes—so dark and so full of intelligence, a window to her brilliant mind—that were always my favorite. *She* was my favorite.

"Why are you staring?" she asked.

"Just trying to look into your soul. Trying to see if you could possibly be so damaged that you think Led Zeppelin and Poison are the *same*."

"That's it. No more lame band talk."

She turned and ran, and I gave chase.

2

Like most things in life, there were pros and cons to living in the farm country of South Carolina. I won't go into the cons right now—of which there were plenty (again, like most things in life) —but the pros were pretty magnificent. No 12-lane highways, no smog, no gangs, no traffic; in other words, things that *big-city folk* had to deal with. Was there some naivety in all this? Of course. Looking back, I was a ridiculous person in so many ways. But we were content.

The greatest pro of all was the sheer . . . *expanse* of the environment in which we lived. Vast stretches of fields, forests, and swamps—nothing around those parts ever seemed to quite come to an end. Andrea and I loved to explore, and I swear we could've done it for 10 hours a day for 10 years and still have had wonders galore left to discover. Hidden rocks beneath the surface of the swamp, stepping stones to a little island that no one else knew about. Family cemeteries in the middle of nowhere, their creepy grave markers covered in grime and kudzu. Creeks full of crawdads, waiting to be captured and set free again, leaving a pinch or two just to remind everyone who's boss. Trees to be climbed, lakes to be swam, rivers to be waded, fruit trees to be ransacked. All of it, there for the taking, there to be relished.

But the woods were my favorite. The endless variety of trees, some thick of trunk and as old as the first settlers, some thin and straight and reaching the sky, all of them with their own scents and bountiful leaves and needles. The kudzu, that creeping vine that grows faster than babies and covers anything in its path— I've seen entire houses lost under its heavy green skin. The undergrowth, the squirrels, the deer, the intermittent meadows filled with wildflowers, that buzzy roar of the insects already mentioned. It was a haven for me, and if my family and society hadn't generally frowned upon such a thing, I would've gladly lived like Mowgli amongst the wolves. Except that we didn't have any wolves.

"How do we lose this spot every single time?" Andrea asked.

She and I, hand in hand, had walked up and down the same

stretch of railroad for 10 minutes, searching for the beginning of a path that had become our latest favorite. But at the rate things grew around there, you could lose a cousin in the weeds, much more a narrow trail.

"There it is!" I yelled in triumph, pointing to a barely noticeable gap between two heavy bushes. It's hard to see the head of an unofficial trail in such a place of constant growth, but you know it once your eyes have truly settled on it. The foot-trodden earth, a broken branch or two, the slender passage between plants that seem to have recoiled from recent human touch.

"Finally!" Andrea responded with a huff.

We entered the forest with the usual sense of awe, stepping through those welcome-bushes into a world of green and wood and shadows. Sunlight streamed through the canopy of leaves far above us, dappling the ground with a constant shift of golden color. We followed the winding path, beaten down by the feet of those before us, who seemed to have missed the notion of a straight line being the quickest way from Point A to Point B. But it was no matter to us. The more crooked the path, the longer we'd be in there.

After a few minutes of craning our necks this way and that, Andrea broke the silence (the drone of insects not counting as actual noise).

"You up for climbing something today?"

"Only if I get a reward when we get to the top."

"Fair enough." She pointed at a giant oak, the kind that had branches thicker than most men, a couple of them bending down to kiss the ground before rising back up again. Easiest thing in the world to climb. "Your reward will be to quiz me on our Biology test. Look at that moss."

I did. The willowy stuff hung from the limbs of the oak in a thousand places, grey-green. Most people compared it to an old man's beard, but to me it looked like the tree was simply melting with age, sad, forlorn. Weeping, maybe.

"Wanna race to the top?"

She always beat me so I had no intention of accepting her offer.

"How about we just sit on that limb over there and talk?" I weakly suggested. "I'm kinda tired today."

"Okay," she replied, sounding much more disappointed than I'd expected. "But then we're racing to the top."

I'm not sure how long we sat on the wide, low branch on that spring afternoon. A chill had risen with the shade, and Andrea snuggled in my arms for a good long while without us even saying a word. There was a history with us, something grown ups might have the weakness to roll their eyes at, but was nonetheless profound to both of us. As is the case with my future lost wife, this history is a tale for another time, but it's enough to say that she saved me, and I saved her. And, mind you, that was long *before* the horrors of this particular tale began.

Andrea yawned and leaned harder into me, stretching to clasp my left hand, and squeezed five fingers amongst her ten. Her head lay upon my shoulder as she spoke.

"Where do you think he is now?" She'd asked me this question more often than I can count, but she said it without the least tremble in her body or quiver in her voice. Time had healed some wounds, the axiom true. And maybe, just a little, I'd had something to do with that.

"Far from here," I replied, truly believing it. "You and your mom are safe. That bastard would have to be a complete idiot to ever step foot in this state again. And we know he's not an idiot."

She answered with a simple, mind-ticking "huh."

"The guy's too narcissistic to come back here," I added. "It was never about power or jealousy or some . . . sick . . . sickness to hurt people. Everything he did was about himself, trying to put *himself* higher on some God-forsaken mountain he'd envisioned for life. And getting arrested and thrown in jail is not something he'd ever risk. It'd hurt *Mister* Llerenas too much for his liking."

Andrea broke into a terrible British accent, perhaps a new tactic to hide her pain. "You don't think he'd fancy jail, do you?"

"No, my lady. He'd find it quite . . . extraordinarily insufferable." The only thing worse than Andrea's British accent was mine. She didn't have much of the southern twang, if any, but I did, and mixing those two sounds was a bad idea.

"I think you're right," she said, growing serious. "Too much time has passed for him to have any *real* anger left. Right? The kind that would make him wanna come back and do something stupid like . . . I don't know, hurt us or whatever. There's nothing to gain—no money, no house. He'd only be ruining the fact that he practically got away with it."

"Exactly." I turned my head to kiss her on the forehead.

"So, really, I don't get scared anymore. I asked about him just because . . . well, I'm curious, I guess? He's out there somewhere, my own loser dad. Alive, sleeping, waking, going about his day. It's impossible not to think about."

I kissed her on the forehead again. This display seemed like something a grown man would to do his one true love, and I'm sure I'd never felt more like a grown man in my life.

"Maybe it'd be kinda fun to imagine what he's doing," I suggested, the thought just bursting out. I was actually a little taken aback at how brilliant it sounded. "Make fun of it."

She pulled back from me, sitting straight on the limb, her feet clasped at the ankles and swinging. "That's actually the most perfect idea I've ever heard! That's how we'll deal with this from now on. Kinda like *Where's Waldo* but much more dark and twisted and . . . and therapeutic." Her face beamed with a smile and I felt like the world's greatest psychologist.

"Okay, who should go first?" I asked.

"Definitely you. You're the one who came up with it."

That, I did, I almost wanted to say. (Whether I actually felt so cocky about such a simple thing or if I'm just looking back on it a little wistfully, I'm not sure.)

"Okay, here goes," I said, rubbing my hands together, something we all know makes our brains work more efficiently. "We'll call it *What would I be doing if I were Antony Llerenas.* So—"

"What? No. A little unwieldy don't ya think? Let's just call it *Where's Antony?* It's not like we're going to get sued for copyright infringement out here in the woods."

I nodded, sufficiently humbled. "Okay, here goes again." Once more with the rubbing-hands bit. "*Where's Antony?* Right now, he's . . . He's coming out of a CATscan, and his doctor is slowly shaking his head back and forth, looking all worried and shit. Your dad—"

Andrea cut me off. "No. Don't call him that, ever. Just Antony."

"Got it. So, Antony, CATscan, worried doctor, etc. You caught up?"

"Yes, I'm caught up, David."

"So, your . . . *Antony* asks him, 'What's wrong? What's wrong? Oh, please tell me, Doctor Spitz.'"

"Doctor *Spitz?*"

I shrugged. "First thing that popped in my head."

"That's weird."

"Are you going to let me finish my *first* turn, or not?"

She made a revolving loop gesture with her hand as if to say, *Get on with it.*

"*Anyway,*" I said, "Doctor Spitz comes up to old SOB Antony, puts a hand on his shoulder, and gives him a compassionate frown. 'I'm sorry to report,' he says—the doctor, not Antony—'that it's just as we suspected. You have an ass for a brain. Not sure how it got in there, but tomorrow we'll do a colonoscopy to see if they somehow got switched at birth.'"

At some point in all this, Andrea had started to giggle, and by the time I finished I was barely able to talk for having joined with her.

"That was good," she finally said, wiping a tear from her eye. "I don't know what the hell I was expecting, but that got me. Good start."

"Why, thank you." I bowed my head ever so royally. "Your turn, now. Then we can climb the tree."

"Yeah," she agreed, "but speaking of asses, mine hurts. Let's hit the trail and walk awhile and I'll take a swipe at our new game when I'm ready."

"Deal."

3

And so it was that we hiked our way ever deeper into the darkening woods. The trees grew bigger and huddled closer, their web of leaves thickening like a rising tide of green sea. The sun stretched its fiery arms for the horizon. Shadows slanted sharply now, making a forest of dark poles on the ground taller than the trunks towering above us. The air took on a gloom, somehow still golden but deeper, more sorrowful, as if mourning the beautiful day's inevitable end. Andrea and I walked, hand in hand, enjoying the sights and sounds and each other on equal terms.

"Come up with anything yet?" I asked her after a particularly long stretch of silence between us.

"Yeah." She stepped over a root the size of an alligator then ducked under a low-hanging branch; I followed suit, glad to have a brave trailblazer before me. "But it's not really funny. Just . . . stupid."

"I bet it's great. Hit me, honey."

She stepped past another hanging limb, this time pushing it out of the way and letting it fly back and smack me. "Don't ever call me honey again. I don't care if we get married, procreate, survive cancer together, stay faithful until we're 99 years old then die hand-in-hand while parachuting, don't ever call me honey."

I'd only been kidding, because I already knew this. "Sorry... Genius?"

"Much better. Honey is what old fat people call their . . ."

I sensed she was touching on something way deeper than I could guess—probably related to the very subject of our game—and I waited to see if she wanted to talk about it. She didn't.

She stopped and turned to me. "Okay, I'm ready. Don't laugh."

"But what if it's funny?"

"*Then* you better laugh. But it's not funny so don't."

"Those are some very confusing instructions."

"Are you ready or not?"

I jerked forward and gave her a quick kiss. "Ready, Freddy."

"Don't—"

"I know. Don't ever say that again. Now, *Where's Antony?*"

She nodded then took a deep breath. "He's at a bar. A woman comes up to him, asks if the seat next to him is empty. He says yes. She sits down. He orders her a drink, a . . . Martini. She sips it. She sighs, like she's, ya know, satisfied, or relieved. Then this lady turns to my—to Antony, and says, 'Did you have both of those eyeballs when you hurt your mom and left your family with nothing?' Of course, he'll look at her in confusion because that's a crazy question, right?"

"Right," I repeated, absolutely captivated.

"So she repeats it, word for word. He nods, already thinking that he needs to get the hell out of there. But before he can move, she pulls out a knife and *stabs* him in his right eye"—she made a quick jab with her fisted hand—"the blade slipping in and out just enough to make the whole thing burst. As he screams, falling off of his stool, writhing on the floor, she calmly gets up and walks away, saying over her shoulder, 'You only deserve one, now.'"

Andrea stopped, not looking at me, but looking at the dried pine straw to the side of the trail. I'm sure my jaw had dropped in the proverbial expression of shock.

"Wow," I said, "that was . . . dark."

"I'm glad you didn't laugh."

"How could I? More likely to laugh at little slaughtered babies." I'd meant it light heartedly, but it was the wrong thing to say. She turned from me and started down the path. I quickly caught up to her. "I'm sorry, I'm sorry." I grabbed her arm and pulled her around to face me. "Seriously, I'm sorry. That was a perfect story. That's the point. It lets us vent about him in a weird way. Sometimes it'll be funny, to make fun of the bastard— sometimes it'll be dark, like what you just said. Can we keep doing it? Every once in a while? I think it'll be a good thing."

She smiled, although it was one of those bittersweet sad ones. "Me, too. That actually felt *really* good."

"And it made me love your mind even more."

We hugged, then we walked.

4

Five minutes hadn't passed when we realized we had to turn around or we'd be stuck out there when full darkness came. Twilight had truly taken over the world, now, casting the forest in a shadowy murk. We headed back the way we had come, feeling more than a little sad that the adventure for the day must come to an end. They always did.

"My dearest young David," Andrea said as we walked along the trail. Trees loomed above us like old rocket ships, retired in a hanger. The insects buzzed even louder, excited for the nocturnal orgy of activity to come. "We never climbed the tree or talked about the Biology test. You were supposed to quiz me."

"Oh. Yeah. Well that's no fun."

"Come on, just until we get back. I can't bomb this like I did the last one. Gotta keep my four-point-oh, ya know."

"Bombed?" I repeated. "I believe you got an 87%."

"Right."

I waited for more, but nothing came. "Right. Well, okay. Let's see . . . Something something mitochondria and osmosis. Tell me all about it."

"*David.*"

"Fine. What are the three . . ."

I stopped because Andrea had stopped, almost in mid-step. It was the first sign that something was wrong—the way she'd . . . halted, abruptly, instead of slowing. Her body also stiffened, as rigid as the trees around us. She held up a hand behind her, one finger pointed at me, lightly touching my chest.

Interpreting it as a signal to be quiet, I very softly whispered, "What's wrong?"

Andrea took a careful step closer, finally turning her face so that I could see it. My heart froze a little when I saw the odd look she gave me. It wasn't fear, exactly. More like... abhorrence, her face screwed up in questioning disgust, like she'd seen something awful that had no explanation.

Worried to speak again, I frowned my own question back at her, holding my hands up in a *what's going on* shrug. She leaned in until her lips brushed my left ear.

"There's a man up there. Just off the trail. Doing something . . . weird." She pulled back enough to make eye contact, then poked her head in the direction she meant. My eyes followed, searching until I found the stranger. And then, as if spotting it awakened my eardrums, I also faintly heard the sounds. Small cries of suffering.

The man, slight of build, had his back to us, stooped over as he worked at something on the ground before him. He was almost all shadow, but his movements were jerky and evident, oddly off-kilter, as if his joints and bones were metallic machinery in need of oil. His right arm lurched up every second or two, then dove back down. It was worrisomely bizarre. The things I heard only made it worse—squelching, his grunts of effort, that soft moaning, like someone in pain. Maybe not digging. Maybe stabbing.

"Is he killing a damn deer?" I whispered, desperately hoping it was so.

It was Andrea's turn to shrug back at me. "What do we do?" She mouthed the words, and I saw my sudden terror mirrored in her expression. The man did his deeds off the path a ways, but close enough to it that we'd never sneak by without him noticing. And if we left the trail, we'd make plenty of noise to arouse him from his dark duties, whatever they might be. We could go back, but that would only take us deeper into the forest, and make certain we were out there when full dark came.

I shook my head at Andrea, although my mind ran through several possibilities, everything from climbing a tree to rushing the guy and tackling him. Nothing that popped in my head seemed worthy of pursuing, however.

Andrea slowly crouched to the ground, pulling me with her until I had no choice but to sit on my butt or I'd topple over. She leaned in to whisper. "Let's just stay here and hope he doesn't notice us. He obviously didn't come from this direction, so when he leaves he'll probably go toward the tracks. We'll follow when he's good and gone."

With a nod, I tried to relax. A futile effort. For all the world it looked like we had a crazy person about 30 yards from us. I peeked around Andrea's shoulder and examined him as best I could. With the growing darkness, if anything the stranger worked harder, slashing, poking, ripping at something near his feet. Even if the thing at which he enthusiastically maneuvered was a deer or a squirrel or any other wildlife, the fella had serious problems. His every jerky motion screamed imbalance. I felt a spike of panic that took a monumental effort to repress.

Andrea seemed to sense it. "It'll be okay," she said. "Let's just make a run for it. Down the path, right past him. He looks older, kinda skinny. We'll either outrun him or outfight him."

Although her bravery thrilled me, it also made me wish I'd never met her. I didn't want to die that day.

"Are you serious?" I said too loudly.

On instinct, we both whipped our heads to look at the stranger, but he hadn't heard me. That, or he didn't see us as a concern. Even as we watched, he dropped to his knees and leaned forward, his whole body now moving with effort as he appeared to saw at something. Every part of him trembled as his arms, working together, went forward and backward, forward and backward, like one side of a two-person lumberjack crew.

"What in the *hell*," I murmured, mostly to myself.

The insects were so loud, I couldn't tell if the small, pitiful moans had stopped altogether or just been drowned out. It had become too much. We needed to move, just like Andrea said, or I'd go insane and start screaming.

"Okay," I whispered. "Let's run for it."

"You sure?" she replied.

"I trust you." I didn't like putting the burden of our survival on her shoulders—hadn't meant to—but she seemed to take it in stride. I'd never seen her so resolute.

"We'll fly right past him, go tell the police. Or if he comes after us, we can take him together. There's one of him, two of us."

I nodded as firmly as I could muster. "You say when."

She grabbed my hand, putting weight on her knee for leverage to get me back into a crouching position. We then rose together, our eyes glued to the sicko in the woods. He was still earnestly sawing away, and I didn't hear a thing from that direction except insects and a scraping sound that became horrible things in my imagination. Whether human or beast, the object of his efforts was now surely dead.

"Hurry, before he's done," Andrea said. "Now."

Still holding my hand, she leapt forward on the path, not letting go until she was sure I'd followed right on her heels. Our feet thumped against the narrow, worn trail of leaves and dirt as our shoulders knocked away the branches and bushes leaning in our way. The sounds of it didn't seem very loud to my ears, but as we approached the man—still on his knees, leaning forward—he stopped what he was doing and snapped his head around to look at us. Even in the dusky light, shade upon shadow, his eyes shone white and fierce, widened to a degree I'd never seen before in another human being.

I stifled a yelp within my chest, fought the urge to turn back, run *away*, not towards him. But Andrea was ahead of me, obviously with no intention of slowing down. I doubled down my efforts, pursued her with a newly found will to survive. We'd cut the distance between us and the stranger by half, and then by a half again. Very soon we'd be past him and have a clear advantage to make it out of the woods first. He jumped to his feet, turned his whole body around, stepped forward. We were now even with him, us on the path, him about 20 feet to the side. I couldn't tear my eyes away, knowing that I *knew* this man, and the realization filled me with a consuming shudder of horror. Still moving as fast as possible, a second later I was actually looking *behind* me as I ran.

My foot hit a root, jutting from the ground like a swollen vein. I stumbled into Andrea and she was able to keep me upright. It only slowed us a bit, and helped break me from the trance of staring at our hideous companion. But even though the man had taken a few more steps toward us, he showed no signs of actually making chase. As I could no longer both watch him *and* flee, and despite the unknown danger of having my entire back to him, we ran on.

"Andrea," I said between heavy breaths. "Do you know who that was?"

"No."

I couldn't find enough air to tell her yet, not while we sprinted through the forest. We wrapped around the big oak tree we'd considered climbing, its many branches jutting out and bending toward the ground like a magnificent octopus. Although we had a good jaunt remaining before we reached the train tracks, it still gave me peace knowing that we'd put that behemoth between us and *him*.

Him.

My chest ached from the sudden burst of expended energy, with no let up. The cooling air hurt my lungs and I couldn't bring in breaths as deeply as I needed or wanted. I must've sounded like a vacuum cleaner in desperate need of maintenance. Maybe she was drowned out by my own embarrassing, gasping heaves, but I swear Andrea was like an Olympic marathoner ahead of me, light on her feet, breathing evenly, not a bead of sweat on her skin. As for me, my armpits had already soaked themselves and I had the thought—I swear to God I did—that I hoped I'd worn deodorant that day.

The fear drained slightly—only slightly—as we put space between ourselves and whatever horrible spectacle we'd witnessed far behind us. There'd never been any sounds or signs of pursuit, which both shocked and pleased me to no end. Maybe he was too exhausted, or too old, to bother chasing two youngsters he had no chance of catching.

Him.

Had it really been him?

As we flew through the trees, and as I saw the familiar shapes in the shadows that signified the train tracks were close, I remembered a cold winter day a decade ago, when I'd seen a man carrying a shovel perched upon his shoulder, off to do some shopping, two things that didn't much fit together. I'd seen that same man today, rapturous in his unnatural enterprise, or my eyes had gone kaput.

5

When we burst out of the woods, the sky a light purple against the dark shadows of the trees, I couldn't take it anymore. My heart told me so—the thing felt fit to explode and end every-thing right then and there. Doubling over, hands on knees, I sucked at the air around me, trying to inhale every last molecule of oxygen remaining in Lynchburg, the other citizens be damned.

"Are . . . you okay?" Andrea asked; with one hand on my back, she'd leaned over to catch a glimpse of my face. I was too embar-rassed to let her see it, bending over even more. At least she was breathing heavily, human after all.

A few seconds more and I felt like I'd at least staved off death. Straightening, hands on hips—our nifty gym teacher had taught us that was the best way to open up your lungs—I nodded to her that I was fine. But then I realized my back was to the woods from which we'd just fled, and I swore I could feel Gask-ins' peepers on me. I spun around to examine the dark shadows between the trees, half expecting to see a pair of glowing eyes.

"We better keep moving," I said, having the sudden and awful thought of maybe *why* he hadn't chased us—because he knew a shortcut, was planning to cut us off somewhere down the tracks. This made my entire body shudder, once, literally from head to toe. I grabbed Andrea by the hand and pulled her after me until we were on the actual tracks, then headed for town. But she stopped me.

"Who was it?"

I looked at her, looked at the woods—so dark I could only see the outermost trees now—then back at her. "Pee Wee Gaskins."

Her expression went through several lightning-quick phases of confusion. She thought I was kidding, but then knew I'd never make a joke at such a stupid time.

"The guy who works at the mortuary?" she asked.

"That'd be him."

"You're sure?"

"No doubt."

"I was too busy trying to see what was on the ground . . ." She glanced at the woods. "Pee Wee? Really?"

"Yes. Really. And who knows where he is now. We need to get the hell out of here and tell the police. *Man* that was weird." With a little distance and time having passed, my brain couldn't accept that Gaskins had been hurting an actual person—it'd just been a fancy of the dark woods, haunted fairy tales, my imagination leaping to the worst case scenario. But I also knew that whatever he'd been doing was about a nine-point-five on the creepy scale. What Andrea said next ratcheted it up to a full ten and reversed any placating line of thoughts I might've had.

She placed her hands on both sides of my face to make sure I was looking directly into her eyes. Somehow they still shone despite the darkness that had fallen. Then she spoke.

"I saw a *head*, David."

CHAPTER FIVE

Lynchburg, South Carolina
April 1989

I

S eeing a mangled, bloody head lying amongst the leaves at
the end of town gravedigger is the stuff of nightmares, and
those happened aplenty for both Andrea and myself over the
years. And there was far more source material waiting in the
wings that long-ago summer. We kept in touch after high school,
Christmas cards and occasional visits, slowly letting go of the
special connection we'd had, beautiful and bright but ultimately
severed by the horrors we'd go on to witness.

All of it came back to me when Dicky Gaskins visited almost
30 years later.

After my son Wesley's heroic efforts to save the poor man
from his own tongue, it'd taken a while to settle the children
down. They each reacted in their own unique way. Logan, the
youngest, looked like a carving robbed from the Louvre statue
garden—stock still, mouth slightly open, face drained of his

usual brown color, eyes fixed on some indeterminate point in the distance. Mason, seven years old, the crier in the family, earned his reputation stronger than ever, bawling without the usual drama. It was as genuine and heartbreaking as a cry can get. Hazel, our ever-wise 10-year-old, did her best to fight the tears, but they came in a steady flow. She stood straight, however, arms folded, daring anyone to accuse her of cowardice.

And then there was Wesley, the hero himself. The only word to describe him was stunned, like a rabbit in an old-fashioned snare. He barely spoke a word for the rest of the night, and no matter how many times I asked him where in the world he'd learned to save a man choking on his own tongue, he simply shrugged and said that he didn't know. That it had been instinct.

Paramedics came. The police came. The few farmland neighbors came, their noses nosier than ever. And then they all left.

"You think he'll come back?" Hazel asked from the floor next to the couch on which I lay.

Several hours had passed and everyone was down for the night. As Dickens might've said if you'd asked him, even in the best of times or the worst of times, a person's gotta sleep. In typical fashion when we visited Grandma, we'd all huddled in the main living room, no one daring to go off on their own to one of the dark, dusty, mysterious bedrooms once occupied by my siblings and me. This had nothing to do with the events of that evening—it was a time-honored tradition, birthed long ago because we were all semi-scared of the supposed ghost in the attic. It's also why we had a couple of box fans blowing at full blast, no one in the mood to hear old Grandpa Fincher's footsteps creaking above our heads. (We also loved the sound of the fans, a humming lull that could put a cranked-up crackhead to sleep.)

I reached down and softly caressed Hazel's head, though I could hardly see her in the nighttime gloom.

"Don't worry, sweetie," I replied. "Old Dicky's never hurt a fly in his life." This wasn't true, not at all, but my mind had done a pretty good job of blocking the worst memories of my child-hood. That would change soon. "He's just one of those men who had a tough life and didn't quite know how to deal with it. Ya know?" Memories or no memories, I still half-wished my son hadn't succeeded in saving the bastard.

"What was so bad about his life?" Hazel asked.

Another pair of eyes shone in the darkness—Mason, lifting himself onto an elbow and leaning in to listen. Logan was zonked, but a glance at Wesley showed that he was awake, too. He liked to sleep in my dad's recliner, which was roughly the size of New Hampshire, magically nestled next to the smallest stone fireplace you've ever seen. At the moment, the recliner wasn't even reclined. *What're you thinking about over there*, I wondered. Because he probably couldn't hear me over the box fans and their hurricane-force winds, I gave him a nod in case he could see me.

"Dad?"

I turned my attention back to Hazel. "Oh, sorry. What'd you ask me again?"

"Why was that man's life so hard?" Even in the dark, I knew the sweet expression on her face as surely as I knew how many toes I had on each foot.

"His dad..." I hesitated. I always prided myself on not keeping things from the kids, but the haunting tale of Pee Wee Gaskins went too far. "His dad was a bad man, a horrible father. The absolute worst. You guys are lucky to have the best papa of all time, right?" It had been a terrible attempt to break the ice, steer the conversation in a different direction, but it didn't work at all.

Mason asked the next question. "What did his daddy do?"

I looked at the gloomy spot where my son lay propped up. Had I actually said anything that should've made a seven-year-old ask such a specific question? The phrasing usually referenced jail time, and seemed mature beyond his years.

Unable to lie, I simply said, "He hurt some people. Well, killed them, actually. But this was 30 years ago—you guys have nothing to worry about." A ridiculous statement to little kids in a dark house on a scary night with a purported ghost tramping around in the attic. I sensed the fear in both of them.

"Come here." I swung my legs onto the floor and patted the couch on both sides of me. They scrambled up as quickly as if I'd declared a hot lava game in-session. Wrapping my arms around their shoulders, I squeezed them both. "Look, it's been a crazy day. Let's not talk about any of that stuff, okay? Let's talk about... I don't know. Bunnies. Let's talk about bunnies."

"Did Dicky's dad ever kill any bunnies?" Mason asked.

Lord save me, I thought. The man probably had. He'd probably killed them and skinned them as a boy, hung their bodies up to rot, ate their entrails, did voodoo or black magic with their blood. I didn't share this pessimistic likelihood with the kids.

"No. I'm sure he loved bunnies like everyone else." I'm glad they couldn't see me wince at such an absurd response. "Seriously. Something else. Any cool new games on your phones? Something that's charging my credit card against my wishes?"

"Dad?"

"Oh, good. Hazel has something. What, sweetie?"

"Can you tell us about the ghost again?" When I sighed she hurriedly added, "I know it's just a silly story, but it's fun to hear about Great-Grandpa Fincher."

The honest truth is that it *wasn't* just a silly story to me, at least not completely. I wanted it to be true. I'd heard those creaks and groans on the attic floorboards way too many times. Although it never ceased to creep me out, gave me the chills like Hades himself had risen from the underworld to give me a back tickle, I'd accepted it in a funny way. Grandpa Fincher just didn't want to leave the house in which he'd been born, and the man would never harm a soul, especially one related to him. He was my mother's father, after all. Let the old man stay up there with no bother—no need to call one of those ghost-hunting TV shows.

"Guys, come on," I finally said, deciding not to talk about the ghost. "Think happy thoughts. Disneyland. Ice cream. Leprechauns. Naked dancing leprechauns."

Hazel giggled and Mason yawned.

We settled into silence as they snuggled deeper into my arms. The best feeling in the world.

I remember two things before finally falling asleep: Laying them back onto their blankets, and, at some indeterminate, hazy point later, hearing the metallic clunk and chunk of my dad's enormous chair finally reclining.

2

Later that night, to my great surprise, I woke up in the woods.

I'm not sure exactly what awakened me. Being outside in South Carolina, in the middle of summer, lying on the ground in a forest, provides one with countless possibilities. The deafening roar of insects. A scuttling mouse or squirrel. The snap of a twig, stepped on by a deer. The sting of a house-sized mosquito. Anything could've jolted me from my inexplicable slumber. The question is why in the hell was I out there in the first place?

My eyes fluttered open and consciousness swarmed in, snapping me instantly awake. I felt the leaves and sticks beneath my face, heard the drone of insects, felt the humid nighttime air. And, as stupid as it seems, I heard no box fans blowing. Pushing off the ground with both hands, I jumped up and looked around. The moon was just bright enough to silhouette the countless branches above and paint the ground beneath with lines of shadow barely darker than the forest floor itself.

I was in the middle of the damned woods, and a spark of panic ignited my heart.

Dazed, I staggered a bit, instinctually brushing the debris off my shirt. I must've turned a full circle a dozen times, trying to make sense of how I'd ended up outside. An overpowering sense that I was being watched also gave me the chills.

"Hello?" I said in a hushed whisper, feeling as foolish as I ever had. Not really wanting anyone to know about this odd turn of events, I decided not to call out again.

Finally, my mind and vision adjusting, I was able to make out my surroundings. I hadn't gone very far—the outline of my parents' house was visible through the trees, the yard no more than 50 feet away. Breaking into a light jog, I headed in that direction, hoping I could sneak back in without being noticed. As I passed the thinning trees at the edge of the forest, I tried to remember if at any point in my life I had sleepwalked before. Something tickled the edge of my memory, wiggling its way through the fog of things long forgotten. I *had* sleepwalked, I knew it. But the details were lost in the mist.

The vast back yard was empty and dark, the massive pecan trees jutting from the ground like black mushroom clouds. There was an eerie silence, as if the insects had taken a 15-minute work break. Something chilled my skin, again, gave me goosebumps. It was probably just a light breeze brushing the sweat on my arms, but I was thoroughly creeped out. Maybe Grandpa Fincher had decided to leave the dusty domain of the attic and take a stroll on his old stomping grounds. I full-on sprinted for the back porch, damned sure there was a presence hanging right behind my shoulders the entire time. My chest gave a shudder as I ran.

I bounded up the steps and tried the door. Locked. Dammit. Must've gone out the front. Turning around, half-expecting to see the ghostly image of an old man cackling—and far too relieved that I didn't—I made my way back down the steps and then booked it around the house. Snuggling once again under those blankets on the couch had never sounded so good. I fully planned to pull them over my head and fool the boogeyman, convince him that I'd disappeared. This thought actually made me laugh out loud, surprising the insects just as much as me— their buzz returned to the air with an airplane-like roar. Spooked as I was, exhilaration filled my insides, and I have to admit I felt like a kid again as I took the front porch steps in one single bound, just like Superman.

The main door was locked, too.

I stepped back and stared blankly as the screen door shut automatically.

What was going on here? Surely I hadn't sleepwalked to such a coherent degree that I'd made sure to lock things up when I exited the house. Surely not. Pondering my options, I slowly wandered the cement porch. Did I dare try a window? With my luck, Dad would think Dicky was back and pull out his shotgun, fire a warning shot. And with his aim, that warning shot might fill my chest with lead. Maybe I could curl up in one of the porch chairs and sleep the rest of the night off, claim that I'd come out super early to watch the sunrise. Already, I could imagine Hazel's response: *Yeah, right, Dad. Without your coffee? And with the door locked? Make up something better, next time.*

Oh man, I thought. I had to knock. I had to knock and tell my kids the embarrassing truth that I'd sleepwalked. Slept-walked. I didn't even know how to say the damn thing.

Something rattled.

The sound was at first deceiving, deflected by the porch roof which had always possessed magical powers for doing such a thing. I looked behind me, saw nothing but shadows. Then the metallic rattling rang out again, and I realized it was the door-knob. Rushing forward, I swung the screen door wide, almost ripping the thing off its hinges, and waited for the main one to open. But the handle just shook and clanked without turning.

That tingling sensation of irrational terror once again chilled my skin, made my entire body shudder. Grandpa Fincher was trying to get out, I just knew it. Then I heard the faintest voice coming from the other side of the door.

"Daddy? I'm scared."

It was Logan. I'm ashamed at the relief I felt—not only that it wasn't a ghost (ridiculous, yes, until you're in the dark in the middle of the night and hear a rattling straight out of *A Christmas Carol*), but also that the culprit was my youngest child. Maybe I could get away with this after all—he'd probably forget by morning, or even if he didn't, his four-year-old tattle-tale rant could be brushed off as a dream.

I crouched down so that my head was level with the knob, which had just been given another shake. "Logan? Can you hear me?" I spoke barely above a whisper.

"Daddy?"

"Yeah, it's me. I accidentally locked myself out. Do you know how to unlock the door?"

"I'm scared." Even through the barrier of wood, his voice was as pathetic as a child in a bad TV commercial. I wanted to squeeze him in a hug.

"I know, buddy. Me, too." I winced, no idea why I'd said that. "See the little... smaller thingy on the doorknob? Right in the middle. You need to turn that. Grip it with two fingers and turn it. The little flat thingy. See it?"

He didn't respond, and he certainly didn't do what I had just so eloquently described.

I stood up and sighed, arching the stiffness out of my back, wincing at the pain in my knee joints. I felt as old as those pecan trees. "Logan?"

The doorbell rattled again, then it twisted and the door popped open. I opened my mouth to say something condescending like, "Good boy," but stopped when I saw my three youngest children standing in a little group, staring up at me.

"Oh," I said, chagrined. "Looks like you're all up. Well, this is embarrassing."

Only Hazel got the subtle humor in my statement and stepped forward to take my hand. "What in the world are you doing outside, Daddy? A man your age should be getting a full night's sleep whenever possible."

I'd never been so happy to hear that wise-beyond-her-years-smart-ass voice. Pulling her and then the other two into a family hug, I squeezed tightly. "Mm. I love you guys. So much. Come on, let's get back to sleep."

"You didn't answer my question," Hazel persisted. Did she always have to be so smart?

"I just went for a walk, couldn't sleep," I replied. "Must've locked the door on instinct before I pulled it shut. No biggie— thanks for saving me. Come on." I gently ushered them into the house and closed the door, this time locking it very much on purpose. "It's a miracle we didn't wake up Wes..."

I trailed off because my eyes finally fell upon the gargantuan chair of my dad, empty, no sign of Wesley anywhere else in the room. His phone lay atop the side table. At any other time, in any other circumstance, I wouldn't have blinked at this. He'd obviously gone to the bathroom. Gotten a snack. Something.

But not tonight. Tonight was weird as hell and seeing that empty chair struck another spark of panic within my chest.

"Where's your brother?" I asked.

Hazel had just plopped down onto her pallet of blankets and lazily looked over at the chair.

"Huh," she said.

I'll never forget it. I'll never forget the ominous sound inflected in that simple word as it passed through her lips. She knew. Of all the things in my life that I may doubt, this is not one. Hazel knew something bad had happened, as surely as I felt it in my heart.

I sprinted through the family room and into the middle

hallway that led to the kitchen. The bathroom door was open and no light shone from within. I stepped inside and flicked the switch. No one was there. Fulfilling that most cliché act of thoroughness, I swept the shower curtain aside to make sure he hadn't decided to take a completely insane middle-of-the-night bath. Empty.

The spark of panic ignited into a small flame, a pilot light burning steadily atop my heart.

There was only one other bathroom in the old house, and I got there as fast as one possibly could. It, too, was empty. I then marched through every last inch of the home, urging my rational side to come up with an explanation of why there was no sign of my son anywhere. My parents' room came last, and concern for their sleeping habits didn't enter my mind at all. I opened the door without knocking and stepped inside; the light from the hallway revealed the two of them in bed, no one else around. My dad was on *top* of the blankets, just adding to the weird night. I marched over to the closet and peeked inside. I've often thought since, in odd, quiet moments, what would I have thought if I'd found Wesley huddling inside his grandma's closet, for no apparent reason, in the deepest part of night? Perhaps relief would've overwhelmed the complete strangeness of such action.

But he wasn't there; he wasn't anywhere.

"What about the attic?"

Hazel's voice startled me so much I cried out.

"Oh, sweetie," I somehow managed to say, touching her shoulder as we left my parents' room. They stirred in their bed but didn't speak, and I wasn't ready to bring them into the developing situation.

We went back to the front family room, where—as far as I knew—the only access point to the attic was cut into the ceiling, a small square with a simple flat board lying atop it. Never, not once during my entire childhood or adult life, had I so much as peeked inside that scary, mysterious place. But without hesitating, I pulled over the chair from the small desk by the front door and placed it under the attic entrance. Stepping on it, I held out my arms to catch my true balance. Then I reached up and pushed aside the board. A wispy cloud of dust fluttered down upon my face.

Coughing, I wiped my eyes. Then I did what would have surely seemed comical at any other time but now probably terrified my children, who could sense my growing fear. I jumped as high as I could, just enough for my head to pop through the square opening and catch a quick glimpse of the attic space. I did it again four or five times so that I could scan every angle. Though very dark, I saw the outlines of boxes and piles of random items long forgotten by the occupants of the house. No silhouettes of lurking humans or pacing ghosts.

All the while, the flames of panic hopped and burned inside me.

Outside. He'd obviously gone outside, although it wasn't like him and I couldn't fathom a reason.

"Stay here," I said curtly to my other three kids. Looking back, I should've offered them a word of comfort or encouragement. But my mind wasn't working properly, not at all. Something white and hot seemed to occupy my head, almost literally obscuring my vision.

I opened the front door and ran outside, saw the first, faintest hints of dawn lightening the sky to the east. And then I did everything I could to magically make my son appear, looking everywhere, not caring what his explanation would be when I found him in a weird place, hiding from his family and the world at large. Searching, searching, every last inch of the yard, the old barn, the shacks and sheds, behind every last tree. By the time I started on the forest lining the back of the property, my parents had been awakened, either by my kids or by the noise of my increasingly frantic actions, accompanied now by a constant shouting of Wesley's name. They joined in.

But I can tell you that nothing came of it.

The panic, now an inferno, raged inside my chest, making every breath a struggle.

My son was missing. My son was gone. If he'd left voluntarily, he would've taken his phone.

Finally, barely able to speak, I called the police.

CHAPTER SIX

Lynchburg, South Carolina
April 1989

I

It's a tired image, I'll admit, but a perpetual storm cloud hung over my life in the days after seeing Pee Wee Gaskins in the woods, a severed head at his feet. The same cloud hung over Andrea's life as well. It didn't matter how brightly the sun shone down, my vision was tinged with a shadow that refused to quit, a pressing outline of blackness that tainted my bearing. Andrea could hardly talk about it, which was just fine with me. We made some silent pact to pretend it never happened, that we never saw what we saw. It was a flippant attitude, but on a deep level within us, I believe it was literally happening. Blocking our memories subconsciously.

Of course we'd gone to the police, told them everything. I could see the condescending glint of humor in the officer's eyes —the man probably thought we'd stumbled upon a hit or two of acid and had ourselves a good ole time in the forest that day.

Visions aplenty to go with some hot teen sex on top of an old termite-infested log, to be sure. But all it took was a trip out to those woods, where we showed them the blood and the gristle, where we all smelled the scent of decaying human. Pee Wee was nowhere to be found, of course, nor any trace of his victim larger than a chunk of barbecue. The cop we'd reported to looked as pale as a woman struggling in childbirth.

My mom and dad hated the whole affair—hated that I'd seen such horrors, hated that the police hounded us for hours and days until we'd told our story a thousand times. Andrea's mom was worse, so distraught that she targeted the blame on me for an irrational few hours, forbidding her daughter to ever speak to me again. That vanished by the evening of the next day, the three of us hugging and sobbing in the Llerenas's foyer, each apologizing for things that needed no apologies. There's no preparation for such things, and all is forgiven as soon as it happens.

Three weeks had passed. Every cop in the state was looking for Pee Wee Gaskins and no one had found him yet. No details on the investigation had been released—other than the victim; a man named George Holloway I had never met; others were missing—but I had to assume they'd found some nasty surprises at Pee Wee's home. Who knew where the tawny little man could be hiding, but there were plenty of spots when 95% of your county consisted of woods and farms and swamps. For some reason I kept imagining him holed up in a hollow cypress tree, its bone-white roots stretched out like tentacles into a flat morass of black, murky waters, even the gators fearing the evil that emanated from this man.

My one bright spot—a flicker of light against the dark pall— was meeting Andrea for a cup of coffee after school at the Rexall Drug soda counter. The caffeine boosted our spirits, made us talk about movies and books and music videos, anything creative and not of this world. We sat together on a Thursday afternoon, a spring rain shower spattering drops against the panes of glass in the huge windows looking out on Main Street. It's possible that I failed to notice the hollows under Andrea's eyes at first, or maybe she hid them well. But the rain comforted me, externalizing the storm within, and on that day I felt genuinely better, even before old Betty Joyner brought us our cups of black delight.

"There ya go, my little darlins," the saintly woman said as she placed two steaming cups onto the counter. I know I'd yet to see my 17th birthday, so it wasn't saying much, but I swear Miss Betty had been 80 years old the day I was born, and was 80 years old still. She hadn't changed in the slightest since my first memory of her. "On the house, today, after all you've been through."

"You've said that every day for three weeks," Andrea responded with a gracious smile. "I think it's high time we actually paid for something."

Miss Betty waved a hand as if swatting a fly. "Oh, fiddlesticks. It costs Henry about two pennies for what's in your cups. That old buzzard ain't got the slightest clue I've been slippin' you some free Joe for weeks." She winked with conspiratorial glee, as if she'd been passing us cocaine and armed contraband instead. "Just don't go asking for my banana bread on the lam. That stuff ain't free." With a whooping laugh, she walked away, her aged body showing no signs of weariness.

I lifted my cup toward Andrea, and she did the same, clicking our hot drinks in a silent toast.

"That's the best old lady that ever lived," I said. "I wish she was my grandma."

"Me, too." Andrea took a careful sip—you never got lukewarm at the Rexall. "I hope she lives to be a hundred."

"A hundred? She's gotta be pushing that now."

"Don't be an ass. She just celebrated her 70th birthday last

November. I guess you weren't invited to the party like the *rest of the entire town*."

My memory had been officially jogged. "Oh, yeah. I remember, actually. Pretty sure we skipped it to go to the Clemson game." I sipped my coffee, relished the burn on the back of my throat, the heady taste of the brew. "Huh. Seventy. I could've sworn she was 97. If not 98."

Andrea snickered at that, making me feel good. "What're you up to this weekend?"

"Oh, crap." I put my cup on the counter. "The Fox Pen. The annual Thomas Edgar Fox Pen. Thanks for reminding me."

Andrea laughed again, slapping her knee to make sure I knew she found this especially hilarious. "How can you contain your excitement? An entire night holed up with a bunch of drunk old men, hounds baying and howling all around you? Can I please come? Please, please, please?" I could've sliced her sarcasm with a dull knife.

"Stop. It's not that bad."

The truth was, I had a great time every year at the Fox Pen once my dad dragged me out there and I picked a bunk in the drafty cabin where everyone had misguided intentions of sleeping. I was usually the only one who even pretended to try. But listening to those men talk, hearing the stories and jokes that popped out of their mouths once they'd been loosened up with beer, was a highlight of my year. I could write a book and make a million dollars, but the town would never recover from all the scandals.

"Do they let *women* come to this ridiculous ritual?" Andrea asked.

I shrugged. "I've never heard otherwise. Wanna come?"

"Thanks but no thanks. I can smell the body odor and beer breath just thinking about it. I'll save my feminist statement for something more civilized."

"You're very wise," I replied. "At least Alejandro will be there

—I can hang out with him." He was a friend from school. I spontaneously leaned over and kissed her on the cheek. We had a strange relationship, no doubt, tainted with an underlying darkness. Who knows where things might've led if one Pee Wee Gaskins hadn't wedged his way into our lives that dreadful year.

After a few sips of coffee in a slightly awkward but not uncomfortable moment of silence, Andrea spoke first, bringing us back to reality.

"I dreamed about him last night."

At first I thought she meant her dad, but then common sense pointed at Gaskins. Thankfully I stopped myself before asking because I would've seemed like a total douchebag. "Oh. Man. So... Have you before? What happened in it?"

The coffee-induced brightness in her eyes had faded. "It was bad. Really bad." She paused, and I hate to admit it now, but my curiosity burned like a torch. So I didn't interrupt.

"And no," she continued, "I've never dreamed about him before. But last night made up for it. I woke up in my bed—like, in my dream, not for real—and the house was dead silent. Like, unnaturally silent, almost as if someone had stuffed cotton balls in my ears. I got out of bed—again, *inside* the dream—and went out of my room, down the hall. Couldn't hear a thing, and it was hard to move, like wading through water, with a current against you. Really dark, air pressing in... I can still feel it. I've never had such a realistic dream I don't think."

"Did this dream have a really bad ending?" I asked, pretty mesmerized by her storytelling—we might as well have been sitting around a campfire.

"Worst ending possible." She looked at me with melodramatic eyes and I almost laughed, thinking now that she was just pulling my leg. I narrowed my eyes instead, trying to hint at my suspicion. "I'll spare you the details. But let's just say when I finally made it to my mom's room, Pee Wee was in there, leaning over a blood-soaked bed, sawing away at her neck. He finally cut through some vital bone or tendon when I walked in because the head snapped off and rolled away, eventually bouncing off the floor with a wet thud."

I swallowed. "Are you serious?" I asked, now completely mortified.

Something in Andrea's face changed. She gave a weak laugh. "Nah, just messing around. Trying to make light of it. Dumb idea. Sorry."

We didn't say a whole lot after that, even as the rain slowed to a sprinkle outside, then stopped altogether. It was right about the time the sun popped out, turning the streets into rivers of sparkling, liquid crystal, that I decided she'd been telling the truth about the dream after all. In the end, she wanted to protect me, as if I might take her dream and transform it into a premonition.

My mood thoroughly ruined, and feeling selfish because of it, I brooded until Andrea said she had to get home for dinner. This time she kissed *me* on the cheek, then practically ran out the door, its jingling bell far too cheerful for the occasion.

I raised my hand at Miss Betty. "Could I have another cup? This time I'm paying for it."

2

It's hard to believe that the very next night started out as fun as any I've ever had, despite the things weighing on my mind.

The annual Thomas Edgar Fox Pen is a wonder of the world that follows the old mantra that you have to experience it to believe it. I always dreaded the over-nighter a little bit because I'm the type of guy who likes his own bed and wants to take a shower in the morning to clean off the oily night-stinks. But you see, the namesake of this fine country event is a relative of mine, and we were obligated to attend. Not obliged, just obligated, as my dad liked to say. Although I know he enjoyed shooting the shit with all those old fellas as much as anyone.

Almost secondary to the shooting-the-shit part, and definitely secondary to the drinking-the-beer part, was the actual event itself, where dogs chased foxes inside a huge fenced-off area of woods on the Whittacker property. It was probably a hundred acres or so, and the purpose was to train the dogs, I guess. Get their sniffers and barkers in top shape after a long winter of no hunting. Honestly, I don't have a clue if there was a purpose. More likely the old men wanted an excuse to get out of the house once the weather turned.

Either way, my night usually consisted of four parts, and that night was no different.

First came supper, a meal that made the whole ordeal worth every last second of longing for home. These men knew how to barbecue every beast of the field, and some of the air, in ways that a person's tongue could never forget. Smoky, sweet, and spicy are words that come to mind when I think back on it. And then there were all the fixins, as they were called—fried potatoes, corn bread, green beans, lima beans, baked beans... there may have been a slight obsession with legumes. It's a happy feeling being so stuffed with food, but that's not to say there wasn't some discomfort as well. And the poor little bathroom at the cabin had a hell of a time keeping up with things afterward.

Next came the activity portion of the festivities, which meant different things to different people. For me, it consisted of a white-knuckled ride on the back of a four-wheeler while an absolutely insane kid named Rusty Johnson drove like a drunk motocross reject. My old friend, Alejandro, usually ended up on there with me, and we always had a running bet on who'd die first. He was a quiet kid, kept to himself, mostly, but we'd known each other since birth and that counted as friendship in these parts. So far neither one of us had won the bet.

It's a wonder we didn't kill any dogs or humans that night

in particular, as Rusty seemed hell-bent on catching every piece of the action as the canines chased the foxes. My senses could hardly handle the overload of input—the smells of pine and manure and churned mud, the feel of the wind on my face, the incessant barking and baying of the dogs, the rev of the engine as we chased them, Alejandro's startled giggles on every bounce, the trees and brush eerily lit up by our headlight, the world telescoped down into what lay before us as we jumped and jostled along. And, every once in a while, even bat-shit crazy Rusty would stop and admire the stars above us, switching off the light so they could shine down their brightest.

Of all the moments so engrained in my memory, the star-gazing is what touches me most, still to this day. And on that night, with thoughts of Pee Wee Gaskins and Andrea's maybe/maybe-not dream fresh on my mind, it actually helped to know that I was only a tiny speck of dust in a gigantic, infinite universe. It made me feel safe, tucked away in a forgotten corner, an abandoned mote that no force of evil would ever bother looking for.

But the night was young, and the night was long.

3

Parts three and four of these Fox Pen adventures were always simple enough—sitting around a hefty bonfire, listening to the old men talk, and then finding a bunk bed in the vast cabin built by some forgotten Fincher relative a half-century ago. After eating all that food, and after two hours cruising on a death-mobile, my fingers aching from their clutch of the grill on the back of the four-wheeler, and after who-knows-how-long sitting next to a warm fire, even the most resilient person gets dog-tired. Call me a wimp, but I swear I was always the first one—

maybe the *only* one for all I knew—who toddled off to bed in the middle of those chilly nights.

It was probably 11:00 or so when I hurried to find a good position near the fire, dragging a lawn chair to a spot not too far from several men who'd already settled in, including my dad. Each man sat with one leg crossed over the other, their arms draped across their armrests, beer cans hanging from their dangling fingers, seemingly by magic. Orange light from the roaring fire flickered on their faces, creating and destroying tiny shadows that lasted only milliseconds. But the glow in their eyes was steady as they stared into the flames, as if that's where they discovered the agenda for the evening's topics of conversation.

The closest thing to a beer they'd let me drink was of the root variety, and I had a special disdain for root beer. So I had a sip of my cold Mountain Dew, fresh from the cooler, its sweet nectar icy on my throat, and leaned in to hear the good ole boys shoot the shit.

"Ya'll remember the Dixon boys?" a man named Kentucky—I swear to Heaven above his name was Kentucky—asked. He was a large fella, worked at the dairy, had the ugliest beard I'd ever seen. Looked like Spanish moss, which doesn't go too well with a human face. "Grew up down Shiloh way, by the brick church?"

Alejandro was sitting across the fire from me, and he caught my attention, raised both of his thumbs and made a goofy expression of glee. He loved all the stories as much as I did.

"*Remember?*" my dad replied. "How you expect us to forget those two knuckleheads? It's a wonder the school's still standin' after they came through."

"Thank God their daddy got laid off," a man named Mr. Fullerton griped. He was a lawyer in town, as tall as he was smart. "I think they moved down to Charleston, chasing a port job. Good riddance. You think the boys were bad, well... let's just say the fruit didn't fall far from that rotten tree."

"That bastard was a sumbitch amongst sumbitches." This

came from an ancient man known only by the name of Gramps. I think he was so old that no one remembered his name.

"Sure was," Mr. Fullerton the lawyer agreed, "and coming from Gramps, that's saying a lot."

This brought a few chuckles, even from the old man himself. I laughed a little harder than I should have, and Gramps gave me a side-eye that made me shrink back in my chair for a minute or two.

"Why'd you bring those two kids up, anyway?" my dad asked Kentucky.

"Say what you want about their good-for-nothin' daddy," the man answered behind his scraggly beard, "but those boys told us a story one night that made me laugh till my cheeks hurt. They were helping over at the dairy and set up like vaudeville comedians at lunchtime, had the whole cafeteria lending their ears. By golly it was the funniest thing I've ever heard in my life."

"Well, spill it, then," a man named Jimmy One-Sack urged. I never discovered why people called the guy One-Sack, and I'm not sure I wanted to. But he was nice, younger than most of the other men, worked behind the counter at the hardware store in town. "We ain't got all night."

"Yeah, we do," my dad replied, and this brought another round of chuckles. Except for Gramps, who just shifted in his seat and scratched his nether regions.

"Alright, then," Kentucky said, sitting up straighter. He rubbed his hands together in anticipation. "Not sure if those boys are twins or not, but might as well be. Poor bastards got their looks from their daddy's side of the family, and he ain't much of a looker if you know what I mean. Got a nose like a squashed school bus, and that's his best attraction. Anyway. Both them boys tell a story about the day they figured they'd try flying off the watchtower with a damned bed sheet for a parachute."

"What?" several men asked at the same time.

"Done heard this story," grumbled old man Gramps, who

proceeded to spit a wad of something dark directly on the ground at his feet. It was powerful enough to splash onto a kid's shirt sitting nearby.

Kentucky continued on as if no one had interrupted him. "Now I ain't got a clue what those kids' names were—we just always called them the Dixon boys, like they were of a piece. I'll just call them Dumbledee and Dumbledumb. Anyhow, they got this fool notion in their heads they was gonna jump off the watchtower out by the Fullerton place, tied up to the end of a bed sheet, planning to drop down to the corn field like paratroopers in World War Deuce. Well, at the last second before they climbed those rickety stairs of the tower, Dumbledee makes the suggestion of a lifetime."

"What was that?" my dad asked.

"Henry."

A moment of silence passed, the question obvious.

"Henry was their damned dog, you bunch of slowpokes. They decided to test the parachute idea on the poor little pup."

"Who the hell names a dog *Henry?*" Gramps barked. "At least call the sumbitch Hank for Pete's sake."

"*Anyway,*" Kentucky said, his feigned annoyance fooling nobody. He was enjoying every second of this. "Dumbledumb agrees with Dumbledee that this is a fine idea, just to be safe, ya know. I mean, the odds of disaster were slim to none and Slim just left town, as they say, but *just in case*, you see, they decided to have a try with old Henry. So there they climb, tromping up those rattling stairs, around and around they go, till they finally reach the top. Then the Dixon boys proceed to tie two ends or four ends or I don't know what of that sheet around the dog's body then rightly threw him off into the wind."

"You have *got* to be shittin' me." I didn't notice who said this, too mesmerized by the story.

"I ain't no judge to tell ya how true it is," Kentucky responded. "Just shut the hell up and let me finish, would ya?"

He took a deep breath, and I could tell he was prepping for the big ending. But when he started talking again he could barely keep the snickers at bay. "Well, needless to say that old bed sheet made a piss-poor parachute, that's for sure. The Dixon boys told me it looked like nothing but a shoe string"—here the man had to pause to gain his composure, his whole body shaking with laughter—"nothin' but a shoe string as that dog plummeted to its death amongst the corn stalks below. Just a dog with a string trailing it like a kite. Later, when their mama asked 'em if Henry was dead, they said 'Sho 'nuff, Mama, it's *graveyard* dead.'"

I looked around me and the men were laughing along with Kentucky; most of the boys looked somewhere between confused and horrified. Alejandro was loving every minute of it.

"To this day," Kentucky said, "when you come across those boys, they'll say the same thing if you ask them about it. 'If it weren't for old Henry the dog, there wouldn't be but *one* Dixon boy today!'" He laughed a bit, then said it again through his snorts, "There wouldn't be but *one* Dixon boy today!"

At this point, Kentucky completely lost it, and so did I. It wasn't so much the punchline as seeing just how hilarious the man thought it was. I'm sure the beer helped, but he practically fell off of his chair, and several others actually *did*, pounding the ground with their fists as they shook with laughter. It filled me with indescribable joy to see such gaiety among these men that I'd often thought cold and distant and rough-edged. Alejandro was outright giggling on his side of the fire. The whole affair went on for another five minutes at least, flared up again anytime someone repeated the infamous last line or, even better, "Sho'nuff, Mama, it's *graveyard* dead." Even my dad joined in. More guffaws, more dirt pounding, so on and so forth.

It was a good time, a time to remember.

Shockingly, it was another half hour before anyone brought up Pee Wee Gaskins. But bring him up they did.

4

The conversation started oddly enough. As you can imagine, the beer was flowing like the Nile by this point.

"Boy, you ever been wid a *girl?*"

It took me a moment to realize that I was the one who'd been addressed. Somebody kicked me and I looked up.

"Huh?"

"I asked if you'd ever been wid a girl." It was Kentucky. Good thing my dad had gone off to take a piss or he might've whopped the man a good one. That, or laugh, I honestly don't know.

"Shut your fool mouth, 'Tucky," someone named Branson said. He'd been quiet most of the night so far. "Cain't you see that boy ain't but 13 years old?"

"I'm actually 16," I said quickly, and rather defiantly I might add. If there's one thing for which a young person will rise to the occasion, it's to defend their age.

"I don't care if you're votin' come November," Branson responded. "You're way too young to be courtin' them ladies."

Alejandro barked a laugh, pointed at me mockingly.

"Courtin'?" Kentucky repeated. "Too young? Branson, I swear, you are perpetually stuck in the 50s and there ain't no help for you."

It was all said in good fun and Branson did nothing but flip the appropriate finger at his longtime friend.

"Ya'll know good and well what you *should* be asking young David."

I turned around and saw that the honorable Mr. Fullerton had returned from getting another beer. My heart started sinking before the name even sprung from his mouth.

"Pee Wee Gaskins." He said it like a death sentence, like a pronunciation of the Black Plague. "This fine young man has seen and heard more about it than any of us. And I think it's high time we quit acting like a bunch of pussies and talk about what's troubling this county of ours."

My dad stepped up right then, and I've always wondered if it hadn't been orchestrated beforehand.

"Now just a minute, there, Jackson," he said. "My boy's been through enough."

Mr. Fullerton held up a hand. "Edgar, I've got all the respect a man can have in this world for you. And you're one of my oldest friends. But I think it needs to be talked about. Talked about before we find somebody else with a head missing. George wasn't the most handsome fella this side of the Appalachians, but I would've liked to see his face in that casket at the funeral."

"Well why didn't Sheriff Taylor or his deputies come tonight?" my dad asked feebly.

"Too busy with the investigation, is what they told me. That and a 'kiss my ass' is about all they'll say on the matter. Hence we need to talk to David, here. He's smart and he's tough and he can take it. Can't ya now, David?"

I nodded because I didn't know what else to do. Alejandro looked kinda guilty for poking fun just a minute earlier.

My dad folded his arms and looked into the fire for a few seconds, the reflective spark in his eyes a little too demonic for my taste. Then he sighed and came over to me, knelt down, and spoke quietly.

"Do you *wanna* talk about it, son? You don't have to, now. Say the word and I'll march you into the cabin, myself. But..." He paused and looked at the ground. "Sometimes it helps to get things off your chest, and frankly I think it might help these boneheads to hear some things straight from the horse's mouth." He squeezed my knee. "Sadly you're the horse in this here situation."

I smiled and he smiled, though his seemed a little forced.

"It's fine with me, Dad."

He gave a stiff, authoritative nod. "Alright, then." He stood up and faced Mr. Fullerton. "This boy's going to bed in 20 minutes. Until then, he's all yours, counselor."

This brought another round of low chuckles, but there wasn't a whole lot of spirit to them, the subject matter too grave.

Mr. Fullerton put his hand on my shoulder from behind. He had to stoop to do it—like I said, he's so tall his head brushes the clouds. "David, you're one of the good'uns, I swear to God Almighty. Why don't you stand up and just tell us whatever pops in your head about what happened. Start from the beginning and work your way through it. In a half hour you'll be snug as a bug in a rug—Tommy'll find you the best bunk in the house."

I wanted to say that sleep—unfurling a canvas for all kinds of dreams about Pee Wee—sounded like the worst idea of the night, but I refrained. Just nodded instead, and the nod Mr. Fullerton returned had so much confidence woven into it that I sprang from my chair bursting with something like pride, as foolish as that sounds. I felt like Alexander Hamilton himself, facing the original Congress. Addressing the crowd of old men and a scattered few younger ones, I began.

"Well, it was three weeks ago. My friend Andrea and I were hikin' in the woods—ya'll know where, down by those old, rusty abandoned tracks—and we came across Pee Wee."

"That sumbitch," Gramps muttered.

"Yes, sir, that's what he is. It was kinda dark so it was hard to make out much, but he was grunting and breathing heavy and obviously sawing away at something. There was blood, that's for sure. When he looked up at us, we ran, and luckily he didn't follow. But Andrea saw"—here my voice faltered just a titch and I hoped they didn't notice—"she saw a head, just lying there on the ground like a rock." One of the boys listening, a kid named Fenton, had eyes as wide as the moon.

I continued. "We went straight to the Sheriff's office and they called our parents, wouldn't let us talk till they got there. We told everyone there what I just told you guys. I mean, there wasn't a whole lot to tell. There was Pee Wee, blood, and some-body's head, cut clean off." I shrugged as if to say we'd stumbled across a dead possum in the road, though that was far from how I felt. Recalling that evening brought something sharp and weighty onto my chest.

"What happened next?" Mr. Fullerton asked.

"Sheriff Taylor asked if we'd mind too much going out with them to the scene of the crime. My dad and Andrea's mom came along. Pee Wee was long gone by the time we got there, and so was the body. And... the head. They shone the flashlights down" —I shuddered; the memory of those white lights on glistening red will forever haunt me—"and there was a bunch of blood and... little chunks, I guess. But nothing else." I wanted to vomit.

Mr. Fullerton was slowly nodding, stone-faced, his lawyerly instincts having kicked in. But most of the others were looking down, as if ashamed they'd made me recount this awful tale. No one said anything, so I felt like I needed to keep on talking.

"They let my dad take me, Andrea, and her mom back home, asked us to come back the next day for more questions. And we did. We were there for three or four hours, pretty much repeating the same junk over and over again. But... I mean, there just wasn't much. It was definitely Mr. Gaskins, and he'd defi-nitely lopped off Mr. George's head. That about sums it up." I no longer wanted to vomit, I just felt stupid at that point. Like I'd disappointed everyone by not having more information. "I swear I don't really know anything else."

"Two others have gone missing," Mr. Fullerton announced, though everyone already knew this. "Gloria Perez from the bakery and old Tink from the motel. Anyone seen hide or tail of those folks? Heard anything?"

Heads shook around the fire. No one.

Mr. Fullerton nodded like someone trying to accept a cancer diagnosis. "Looks to me like Pee Wee's killed at least three, then. Probably got their heads racked up like trophies."

"Okay," my dad said loudly, stepping up to me and taking my arm. "Time for anyone under 21 to go beddy-bye. Come on, now." He tried to hide it but I saw him shoot a dirty look at his looming lawyer friend. "Ain't no harm coming to folks in this Fox Pen, I can promise you that."

A few minutes later I was lying down in a top bunk, staring at the ceiling, blankets pulled up to my chin, only able to think of one thing. My mom *wasn't* in the Fox Pen. Sure, she had a shotgun, doors locked up, and was as tough as any person I'd ever met. But still.

In times like this, how could we have left her alone?

5

I'm not sure what woke me up later that night, deep in the witching hours. Alejandro had waddled in sometime after I had and was zonked out on the bunk beneath me; maybe he'd snorted in his sleep, something he was prone to do. Maybe there'd been an especially loud roar of laughter from the still-drinking adults outside. Dogs constantly barked everywhere, had almost become background music you didn't hear, but maybe one got extra close, yelped extra loud. Hell, maybe I'd grown a sixth sense.

All I know is that when my eyes fluttered open, there was a man in my room.

My entire body chilled, despite my heart thudding against my rib cage.

Nothing more than a shadow, a silhouette, the dark figure stood in the far corner, stock still, and if the wall behind him hadn't been painted white, I might never have noticed him. I hadn't moved much upon waking—nothing more than a shift to my side—and the darkness may very well have hid the fact that I was no longer slumbering. Whatever the case, the man didn't move. He stayed perfectly still, standing in place, like a demon sentry waiting for the devil himself to return. The outline of his shadow revealed no details, and I can honestly tell you that the sight of him scared me 10 times more than when I spotted a bloody Pee Wee Gaskins sawing a man's head off in the woods.

Squinting to hide the whites of my eyes, their lids almost completely closed, I calmed my breath even though it wanted no part of calmness. Heart and lungs churning like a powered-up engine, I breathed through my mouth and nose at the same time to alleviate the pressure, lessen the noise of rushing air. And with slitted eyes, I stared at our visitor.

It was definitely a man, and any chance it might be something so absurd as a statue or cardboard cutout had quickly been eliminated—the shadow moved, ever so slightly. The shadow breathed, ever so shallow. Just enough to remove any doubt. He wasn't tall, wasn't large—nothing like the monster my mind wanted to turn him into—he looked as normal as one can standing in a dark room for no apparent reason. Bald or close to it, a little stooped at the shoulders. He began to sway just a little, the line of his silhouette shifting to the left and then to the right, no more than an inch or two but steadily, left then right, left then right, left then right. I saw nothing of his face, but my every sense told me he was staring back at me. Waiting. Waiting for what?

The man took a step forward, the floorboard creaking beneath him.

It took every ounce of will hidden in my bones to prevent myself from screaming. He took another step then stopped, standing at attention once again, although four feet closer than he had been. I squeezed my eyes closed like a child, hoping this boogeyman would disappear when I opened them again. Winking hard with one and barely cracking the other, I saw that my foolish wish had not come true. My thoughts raced, my mind desperately trying to find an explanation for this visitor.

Any reasonable person would've already jumped to the logical conclusion of who stood in my room in a cabin in the middle of nowhere. But my mind was far from rational, still lost somewhere between the real world and the one of nightmares. It seemed far-fetched that somehow Pee Wee Gaskins had appeared at my bedside, one of two kids who'd witnessed his heinous murder. How could he have gotten past the dogs, the hunters, the old men outside? My dad had to have let him in. Surely this was someone he'd sent up to watch over me, worried about my well-being after all I'd been through. I tried to match the size and shape of the shadow with any one of my dad's friends...

The man took another step forward.

My heart no longer raced. I swear it stopped, dead in its tracks, for an interminable moment. No air would come in or out—I choked on a fear I'd not thought possible until that moment. The man was now only an arm's length away, facing me, his dark-hidden face about even with the top bunk. Level with my slitted eyes. I heard his own breaths now, shockingly even and calm, like the gentle breathing of a lion at rest, one paw draped over its slaughtered prey. And as I listened to the air whistle in and out of his lungs, two things became murderously apparent to me.

One, I finally accepted—knew without the slightest of doubts—that Pee Wee Gaskins was the man in my room. It was like my mind had tried to deny it, block it out as a possibility. But the image of his bloody self in the woods matched perfectly with the outline of the person standing right before my eyes.

Also, I couldn't possibly fool myself for one more second— Pee Wee knew full well that I was awake and staring back at him. Frozen by terror, literally unable to move, I surprised myself by speaking with a whimper of a voice.

"They know you're here."

If my words threw him off guard, he showed no sign of it.

The shadow didn't move, the breathing continued on as steady as ever.

"It's a trap," I added. "They're coming."

Looking back on those frightening moments, I'm touched by the bravery of my words, though at the time they seemed reckless. But they had no effect on Pee Wee. For at least a minute— each and every second drawing out like a wave that slowly washes into shore from the horizon—he neither moved nor spoke. An entire lifetime seemed to pass, my mind urging my body to get up and run. To kick him and flee, scream for help. I did nothing.

Finally, this horrid man, this demon made flesh, spoke to me.

"I'm gonna tell them it was you."

His words threw me. I didn't know what I'd been expecting —perhaps for him to say, "I've come to take you away, away, I've come to take you away." Or maybe an "I'll tear your soooooooul a-paht." But not this. Not, "I'm gonna tell them it was you."

Quietly, I replied, "What do you mean?"

Pee Wee came half a step closer, the floor creaking like a haunted house. He leaned forward. If he'd have sneezed I'd have felt its wetness, caught his disease.

"I'm going to tell them I came for you," he said in a fierce whisper, "and that you *begged* me to kill your friend instead."

I trembled from head to toe, an actual wave of movement traveling through my body. My ability to speak from just moments earlier vanished completely. Shuddering, I backed away, scooting all the way to where the bunk bed met the wall, and pulled the blanket to my chest as if that would protect me. I couldn't so much as whisper a plea for mercy.

"What's his name?" Pee Wee asked, voice so soft, motioning to Alejandro, who snored softly below me.

I only shook my head in response, chest hurting from the lack of breath.

"Tell me his name," Pee Wee said. "Tell me his name or I'll kill you both."

I shook my head again.

"*Now.*" Though still whispering, the command was as close to an animal growl as I'd ever heard from a human.

A perfect fear made me tell him.

"Alejandro."

"Alejandro," Pee Wee repeated, almost tasting the name with his lips. "Now, go." He took a step back and gave his head a swift jerk in the direction of the door.

Instead of obeying or responding directly, I whimpered, "Please don't hurt him."

He once again surprised me with his next words.

"You saw me in the woods. You and the girl. Don't tell me you didn't."

I shook my head then nodded, not sure which answer he wanted.

"Can't kill you, now, can I?" he said. "You already done told them everything. There's another reason, too, much more important. But they'll never find me, boy. They can't even see me. No one sees me unless I want them to. Keep sayin' what ya want, tell the po-lice what ya want. But no one's ever gonna forgive you for beggin' me to kill..." He pointed at the lower bunk. "For beggin' me to kill Alejandro, here. Now go on, boy. Make me say it again and my knife'll cut a pretty smile on your face. A *red* smile that ain't never gonna frown."

My vision had been adjusting to the darkness upon waking. That, or he'd stepped into a pool of bare light from the window. But I could see him better, now. Could see the pockmarks on his face, see the gleam of hate, of something *wrong*, in his eyes. I've told you how short he was, but in that moment he seemed taller than the ceiling, as impossible as that sounds. A giant monster that wanted to eat me, straight from the storybooks.

He pulled in a breath to speak again but I hurried and swung my legs over the edge of the top bunk. That quieted him. I turned over and slid on my stomach until my feet hit the floor. Having my back to him sent a fresh wave of terror across my skin, goosebumps rising. Then I faced him again. Not out of bravery. It was completely, utterly, an act of cowardice.

"That's it, boy," Pee Wee said. "Get out and don't come back for a half hour. Tell anyone and I'll kill your mama by sunrise."

I like to think I hesitated. That I showed the briefest moment of rebellion. But before Pee Wee could've possibly said or done anything, I turned and ran out of the room. Behind me, I heard a quick shuffling of feet, a muffled groan, a wet thunk of a noise that replays in my mind when it's dark and silent and I'm all alone, to this very day.

With a shame so deep I can barely type the words, I tell you that I didn't go back or talk to anyone at the camp until I knew Pee Wee had had enough time to kill Alejandro.

Enough time to cut off his head.

CHAPTER SEVEN

Sumter, South Carolina
July 2017

I

f I were a poet, I'd say that mine has been a life of darkness, storm clouds above and sharp rocks beneath. My hair is cold and soaking wet, my feet bloodied. (Speaking metaphorically, of course, though I've felt those things in a literal sense from time to time.) But I've never stopped walking, really. There's always been a spark of hope shining through those clouds and smoothing out those rocks, just enough to endure. When I was young, I had my parents and siblings and friends. And when I grew up, I had my kids and Andrea to lean on in the dark, dark days after my wife died.

Always, there was hope. Always, light on the horizon, no matter how dim.

Until my son disappeared in the middle of the night.

Since I'd made that frantic, high-pitched, insanity-laced call to the police, my world sank into an abyss of such black despair I hardly know how to describe it. There were a lot of phone calls, shared descriptions and stories to the press and the police, search parties of family and friends and complete strangers. A lot of tears. But all of that was done in a haze of such sadness and fear that I was barely aware of my surroundings.

Life was no longer linear, but a loop of terrifying anticipation. Like those interminable moments rattling up the first incline of a roller coaster, infinitely waiting for the raised horizon, the plunge into unknown depths. Yet we never reached the top, even as I simultaneously wanted to and didn't want to.

Each and every second stretched out to infinity, a constant dread of potential bad news hanging over our heads, making me wish my life could freeze before someone told me the thing that might shatter me once and for all. This, mixed with the urgency of finding him as soon as possible, created a confusing relationship with time that made me inconsolable and relentlessly restless. I had not slept—had barely so much as sat down.

We searched. That's what we did. My parents, Aunt Evelyn, Uncle Jeff, their kids, an army of locals. We searched.

Time lost all meaning. Things like the rising and the setting of the sun ceased to exist in my sphere of understanding, the darkness of my days no different from the lightless nights. There was no such thing as seconds, minutes, or hours. Only a swampy morass of *right now*, a universe that had ground to a halt, stuck in a quagmire of fear and anxiety. Not one thing from the past, present, or future mattered anymore, not until we found my son.

I didn't know what to do with my other kids. I couldn't lie to them, set up false hopes. Against my parents' urging, I just told them everything, kept them near, let them hear all my conversations, made them work tirelessly in the search parties. I think it kept both them and me on the barest side of sanity. I know for sure it stole a piece of their innocence that they'd never get back —even little Logan. But it seemed the only choice.

On the third day after Wesley had gone missing, I walked

through a cornfield over by the Frierson place, the stalks green as limericks and barely brushing my shoulders. The sun was pushing its way up the sky, the heat on my neck finally reminding me that the giant ball of fire even existed, 90 million miles away. I didn't care for it, wished that it would supernova or whatever the hell those celestial bodies do when they die and take us all with it in a blast of flame and glory. That had been one of my more cheerful thoughts of the morning.

Hazel was in the row next to me, craning her neck to look around each and every stalk that passed by, as if Wesley just might actually be hiding behind one. She did it with an earnestness that came close to breaking what was left of my heart. That girl loved her brother, missed him terribly, and I know that her young mind processed what had happened in a very different way from mine. I didn't understand it and refused to pretend that I did, but something told me that she fully expected Wesley to pop up and say, "Boo!" at any time. That she held onto a hope I could only wish for.

I wanted to say something to her, even opened my mouth. But every word to my kids had been a chore the last two days, a lifeless attempt at displaying what I didn't feel inside. Tears welling in my eyes, I quickly leaned through the stalks and patted her head, attempted an encouraging smile. It was all I could do. We kept walking. Shouts of "Wesley! Wesley! Wesley!" filled the air, had become our constant soundtrack. My own throat was hoarse from it, and nothing came out today.

"Daddy?" Hazel asked.

I looked over at her, comforted just a little by her voice, glad she spoke when I couldn't. "Yeah, sweetie?"

"Well," she replied, falling into her usual contemplative stare. "I was going to ask if you're okay but I know you're *not* okay, so it'd be dumb to ask."

"I'm trying, sweetheart. And I *will* be okay as long as I have you next to me." You may think I didn't quite mean it, but I did.

I needed that little girl like I needed blood in my veins. And after two days of hopelessness I was starting to realize that more than ever. I felt a surge of unbearable love and suddenly wept like a child.

"Daddy!" she exclaimed, and jumped over to my row and put out her arms for a hug. I dropped to my knees and pulled her in close, squeezed her so hard I just might've rearranged her ribs. But she didn't complain, only tried to match my strength. The sun was directly above us now, meaning our shadows had mostly disappeared, just for a moment.

"We're going to find him," she said, once again speaking well beyond her years. "We're going to find him and he'll be safe and sound. You'll see. He probably just got lost is all."

Unable to speak, I nodded through my tears and held on tight.

2

We didn't find anything in that cornfield, or in the woods that bordered it, or in the swamp that bordered the woods. Calls came in from the other search parties, some lead by Jeff and Evelyn, some lead by old friends, some lead by police deputies. But they all had the same thing to say.

Nothing.

Nothing.

No one could find my boy.

3

I have no recollection of time passing that third day. There was a morning, an afternoon, and an evening, but they could've switched order and I wouldn't have noticed or cared or thought it particularly unusual. Sometimes the sun was on one side of the sky and sometimes on the other. I do remember the point it shone straight from above. Other than that, it came as a complete shock when my mom stepped up to me and said, "It's time for supper."

We stood at the edge of a soybean field, having just finished scouring a copse of trees on the other side of the road. It had been a swampy, thickly vegetated spot of land, and I was filthy and soaked from sweat and swamp water.

"I guess it *is* almost dark," I muttered.

My mom nodded, seemingly encouraged that I had at least responded with words. Most of the day I'd just ignored everyone. "We're too far from home for me to make us a good meal. Let's head on over to the Compass and have a nice sit-down."

I was shaking my head before she'd finished talking. "Mom, there's no way I'm going over there. We gotta use this last bit of daylight to search..." I hesitated, having no idea what came next. I pointed in a random direction, toward a farm with a huge barn, one of those new fancy ones with actual paint, no holes in the roof. "Maybe he tripped and fell in someone's ditch. You know who owns that place over there?"

My mom leaned even closer and put a hand on my arm. "Son."

"Mom, you never know—"

She squeezed, hard. "*Son.*"

Caught by her tone, I looked into her eyes, and they were hard. Probably as hard as mine.

"We're going to have a nice meal," she said. "Your kids need it. I need it. You sure as shit need it."

My mom never swore, and I found myself on the edge of tears again. My chest hitched.

"Come here." She pulled me into a hug and I let it out again, just as I had with Hazel. I sobbed, letting the tears drop on her shoulder. Then she whispered in that loving Mom-voice I had always under-appreciated. "You've exhausted yourself, David. We all have. We've worked ourselves to the bone and others will keep doing it. You have three kids that need to see something normal, like us sitting down for dinner. Not to mention that we all need a good dose of food in our bellies. We can take an hour or so, okay? Let's go over to the Compass and do the seafood buffet. Jenny probably won't even let us pay for it. Come on, now."

"But Wesley," I said. "How can we just sit there and eat good food when he's out there somewhere? Hurt or..." I couldn't finish, and wouldn't have allowed myself even if I could. "How can we do that to him?"

"Because he'd want us to," she replied. "Because he loves us and he would want us to."

She pulled away and took my hand, smiled as best she could through her own tears. I know she felt the worry and pain as much as I did, and she was being strong when I couldn't. After wiping my eyes, I nodded.

"Okay. One hour. But then we gotta keep looking."

With a heavy sigh, she agreed to my terms.

4

It turned out to be true that Jenny wouldn't even hear of us paying for our meal. As soon as we walked in, the matronly, ageless woman hemmed and hawed over us, with hugs and sweet words aplenty. She settled us down at a big table in the back and insisted that everything was on the house tonight. Her Ed was out working with a search party even as we spoke, she said.

After going through the buffet, feeling a pang of guilt with every greasy, fried item I put on my plate—Wesley loved this place, and we went at least twice every time we came to visit Grandma—I sat down at the table with my parents and the kids.

I kept thinking about how I'd blanked out or sleepwalked and ended up in the woods the night Wesley disappeared. I'd yet to tell anyone, thinking it would only confuse things, even as I kept telling myself that the two events were completely unrelated. Lying to myself, although I honestly didn't know the truth. All I had was a faint feeling that something similar had happened to me in my youth.

"This is the best shrimp in the world," Hazel announced to the table, "and I don't even like shrimp." She popped a nice juicy one, slathered in cocktail sauce, into her mouth and chewed with relish.

"Then how do you know it's the best in the world?" Mason asked, seeming pretty genuine with his enquiry.

"What do you mean?"

"If you don't like shrimp, you probably don't eat it very much. So how do you know *this* shrimp is the best in the world?"

"Silly boy," Hazel responded with perfect confidence. "It's just an expression. It means I like it a lot."

"I think it's the best in the world," my mom contributed. "And I've been as far as Florida."

That one went right over Mason's head, but Hazel giggled even as she stuffed two shrimps at once into her mouth. Although it hurt, just a little, to see everyone act like nothing was wrong, I also knew that I'd hate the alternative. If my kids had been as big a mess as me, I'm not sure I could've handled it. And I knew my parents were trying on their behalf, although my dad couldn't hide his despair, looking as gaunt and miserable as I'd ever seen him. Which was exactly how I felt. But I did eat, and I tried to smile, and I did my very best not to cry again.

"What's a shrimp?" Logan asked. That kid wouldn't eat a single thing that hadn't been lopped off a chicken. Right then he had two halves of a fried chicken strip gripped in both hands, his fingers already greasy. Chewing with his mouth open.

"It's kinda like a fish," Mason responded.

"A fish?" Hazel repeated. "It's nothing like a fish."

"Now, now," my mom input. "They both live in the ocean. Give him a break."

Hazel was not to be thrown off track. "Well, Grandma, a Tiger and a snake both live in the jungle, but they're nothing alike."

My mom's mouth dropped open at this ingenious statement, and then let out a little laugh. "You got me there."

Hazel turned toward Mason. "A shrimp is a crustacean, meaning it's a shellfish..." She immediately trailed off, realizing she should've stopped at the word *crustacean*.

"Ha!" Mason shouted. "So it *is* a fish!"

Hazel shook her head adamantly. "No, they're completely different!"

"How is a shellfish not a fish?" Mason held his hand up, fingers pressed together, and made a swimming motion. "It says fish right in its name!"

I saw a light flash in Hazel's eyes as she came up with the perfect comeback. "Oh, I guess you're going to tell me that a seahorse is the same as a regular horse now? You can take rides on both of them around the farm?"

Surprised, I realized that I had leaned back in my chair, enjoying this banter more than I would've thought possible two minutes prior. I wouldn't go so far as to say I had a smile on my face, but I certainly wasn't frowning.

"What about a tiger shark?" I asked, just to keep it going. "Do those have stripes on 'em? I can't quite remember. And are they fish or cats?"

"I think those are actually in the whale family, so they'd be mammals," my mom responded, a statement so unexpected that I laughed, purely from instinct. Everyone looked at me as if I'd just started singing old jazz tunes.

"Sorry, Grandma," Hazel said after gazing at me with something like relief. "Tiger sharks are sharks and all sharks have gills and therefore it's a fish. Doesn't really seem like a normal fish but it's fish."

"Thank you, sweetie," Grandma responded, forking a shrimp into her mouth just to sum things up. "I wasn't completely sure."

My appetite had come back a little. I leaned forward, feeling slightly better, and scooped up some of my own food, shoveling it down now like a switch had been flipped inside me. The shrimp and cod and hush puppies and mashed potatoes all melded together into one salty taste, but it satisfied the hunger that had been unleashed. I ate voraciously, as if I tried hard enough to act normal then things would go back to that. Soon I'd stuffed myself silly.

"Eat much, Dad?" Mason asked, rolling his eyes in exaggerated fashion.

"Not lately," I mumbled.

My mom smiled. "It's good to see you eat, son. You need the energy."

I faked my own smile and speared another piece of shrimp. Just before it got to my mouth, my cell phone buzzed. Dropping the fork, I hurried to get the thing out of my pocket, something that seemed impossible for about three seconds, my hands getting snagged on the tablecloth, the napkin, the lining of my jeans pocket. Finally I was able to pull it out and take a look at the screen.

Sheriff Taylor. (Like father, like son, he'd become the sheriff just a few years after his dad had died of a heart attack.)

You can imagine the horror that seeped through my bones in the moment it took me to answer the call. He could've been calling for any number of reasons, but my mind jumped to all the worst conclusions. Dead, murdered, cut up, a litany of evil things.

"Hello." The word snapped out of my mouth.

"David, he's okay. We found him."

5

How to convey the range of emotions I experienced as I drove to the address Sheriff Taylor had provided. As soon as our phone conversation ended, I told my parents and my kids that he was okay, that he'd been found, that I needed to get over there right away. After giving the address to my dad—they could come over at their own pace; I planned to break all land speed records, myself—I sprinted to my van, got in, started it, practically shaved the tires bald peeling out of the restaurant parking lot.

And then the news hit me, even as I put my motor skills on automatic, hyped up to a 10 on the adrenaline scale. The news hit me hard and fast. My boy was alive. Even okay, by the sounds of it. Nothing else mattered. I could tell over the phone that there were some weird details, about to be discovered, some shock still to come. But he was alive and well. Maybe not *well*, per se, but okay. The Sheriff had *said* that he was okay. So he had to be.

A sob exploded out of my chest, hurt my throat on its way out. Tears streamed down my face. And then I laughed, a series of wet coughs that would've terrified anyone within earshot. More tears, more laughs. I was hysterical, and on some level I knew it. But who cared? A whole realm of dark possibilities had been eliminated with one phone call, death not even being the worst of them. The unbearable stoppage of time, the looming potential for horrific news, the heavy, heavy weight of the unknown—we'd all been saved from it at last.

Only a few more minutes and Wesley would be in my arms. I didn't care that he was about as big as me now—I planned to lift him from the ground and cradle him in my arms and rock him back and forth for at least three weeks straight. I thought maybe I'd even feed him from a bottle and burp him afterward, have him wear diapers so I could take care of his every need, just like when he'd been a baby. I laughed again, so violently that snot sprayed from my nose.

As I said, hysterical. I'd gone completely, temporarily insane.

The GPS mapping app on my phone lead me to a dirt road, barely visible now that night had fully come upon the world. I saw nothing more than a hole on the side of a forest, trees and branches forming a small gateway into darkness. A cave in the woods, into which a poorly maintained road of gravel looked fit to be swallowed. On any other given night, I would've shrunk from this entrance into the unknown wilderness, wondering what terrors awaited me in that abyss of blackness. But now I drove recklessly, the tires spinning dirt and rocks as I turned off the paved road and gunned the engine to bullet down the unpaved one.

My van bounced and jostled and made crunching sounds that I knew couldn't be good. The headlights bobbed up and down, revealing a thick canopy above and water-filled potholes beneath. The road was straight as a cornrow, but so far nothing revealed itself within the range of my lights. The surreal glow against the bordering trees and branches was a spooky sight. Still, I drove on, yearning for any sign of people, cop cars, Sheriff Taylor. Any sign of my boy.

Then I saw something.

An image flashed from the right side of the road, a man, erupting out of the woods and directly into the path of my car. Even as I slammed on the brakes, the man stopped and turned toward me, his face illuminated brightly by the headlights. A pale face, shining with moisture, eyes burning with some kind of emotion I'm not sure I understood. Something alien to this world. It made me shiver where I sat. And then I realized who it was, although he was barely recognizable, fear and sweat staining his features.

Dicky Gaskins.

He took a step toward me, a look of utter uncertainty now

filling his features, replacing the fear-inducing glare from before. But then he seemed to recover, realized that I could be nothing but bad news for him, and he turned and ran. He disappeared into the brush on the other side of the road from which he'd come. Not more than three seconds later, a fully dressed officer of the law appeared out of the woods, obviously chasing Dicky. With barely a glance in my direction, he pursued him further, entering the trees in the exact spot Dicky had. At least he was on the right track.

A generous portion of my elation had vanished, just like Dicky in the forest. They had found my son, somewhere up ahead, and yet the spawn of my lifetime haunt was on the lam, being chased by the police like an old bank robber in a 70s flick. Things were obviously not in order, and my heart shriveled a little, suddenly scared again for what might lay in my immediate future. I didn't know what to do but call Sheriff Taylor.

He answered on the second ring.

"David? Where are you? On your way I hope."

His tone put me a little at ease. He didn't sound overly worried or panicked.

"Yeah I'm on my way, on the dirt road somewhere. Dicky Gaskins just ran out in front of my car, chased by one of your deputies. What's going on?"

The Sheriff sighed, a sound so loud I might've heard it even if we hadn't been on the phone. "You must be close, then. Don't worry about that—we'll catch him. Just come and see your boy. He needs his daddy."

"Is he okay?"

"He's okay, David. I promise. Come on, down."

I ended the call without saying goodbye, even felt guilty about it for an absurd second. Then, recovering a little from the shock of what had just happened with Dicky, I pushed the gas pedal to the floor and continued my way down the long, bumpy road.

. . .

6

A few cop cars—their blue-and-reds spinning and flashing like psychedelic disco balls—lit the way for the last half mile or so, the pot holes now roughly the size of Lake Marion. I had to maneuver my way around the last two or three, my heart thumping so hard that I could feel its vibration through my arms, all the way down to the steering wheel, where my fingers gripped the rubber so tightly they shone white.

I saw Wesley before I saw anyone else, as if my eyes had some familial magic power that sensed him out. He had a blanket draped over his shoulders as he sat on the rear bumper of an ambulance, its doors wide open and spilling light. Thus my boy's face was in complete shadow. The scene reminded me of the end of every action movie ever to grace the silver screen, the hero or heroine only safe once they had that blanket and that ambulance.

I noticed no other details of the location or cared much, not until later. I stopped the car and I swear it took me a full minute to loosen my seat belt if it took a second. Stumbling out of the car, I felt half foolish and half giddy, but recovered myself and sprinted forward until I reached Wesley, then I pulled him into the fiercest hug one human has ever given another. Tears streamed from my face and I shook with joy and sadness both. Wesley returned the hug but barely, and didn't say a single word. What had Dicky Gaskins done to my eldest child? Oh, the horrors that sprung from that question.

"Are you okay?" I asked. Looking back, it seems the most unoriginal thing to say, without much feeling, but no other words came to me. I'll always wish I had just said, "I love you," instead. How could those words not have been my first proclamation, the only thing that mattered?

"No, I'm not," was his reply, as lifeless a voice as I'd ever heard.

"I'm so sorry." Empty words. I sat down next to him, my arms still wrapped around his shoulders, and pulled his head to my neck. He resisted a little, and his entire body trembled like a frightened puppy. At some point Sheriff Taylor had come to stand beside us, and he looked down at me with all the compassion in the world. He was a father. He knew.

I thought finding my boy would take away the pain, make everything better. But it was only increasing by the second. A different kind of pain, no doubt about it, but no less hurtful. My mind ran with all the damage that might've been done to him. I didn't know what to do, what to say, didn't want to upset him any further. So, for the moment, I just held onto him and finally looked around at this place that would terrorize my dreams for the rest of my life.

The dirt road had ended in a clearing, maybe an acre in size, bordered on all sides by a wall of trees, their branches seeming to dance in the flashing lights of the cop cars. In the middle of that clearing stood a large wooden shed, leaning to the right as if a strong wind blew from the west. It was a dilapidated thing, looking much like you'd expect here in the woods, a long throw from any kind of civilization. Built with scraps, built in stages, with never a care for aesthetics or longevity, the wood warped and splintered, not a lick of paint to be found. I saw two broken windows, the remaining shards looking sharp and deadly. There was one door, and it hung open and askew, the doorknob busted and lying on the ground.

"What is this place?" I asked the Sheriff, but then remembered Wesley and shook my head. This wasn't the time to talk about what had happened.

Sheriff Taylor seemed to agree, just giving me a nod and one of those smiles one gives at a time like this, really nothing more than pinched lips and cheeks pulled back a little.

The clearing around the shed looked as trashy and uncared for a place as I'd ever seen. Everything from milk bottles to beer bottles, every kind of paper product, even garbage bags that had been ripped open, their contents scattered—all of this was strewn about the entire area. I saw an old bike without its wheels, a couple of random car seats that had been ripped from their home, an abandoned fridge that hadn't been used in at least a decade. The dump was like the world gone ill, having caught a disease that could never be cured.

Man, I thought. *Does Dicky actually* live *here?* At first I had assumed it was just the remnant of a home that had once thrived and Dicky had come here to hide, but now I wasn't so sure. Nothing in sight necessarily pointed to the shack being currently lived-in, but it suddenly seemed the type of place where a Gaskins would take up residence.

I wish I could use the power of words to tell you how much my heart hurt in that moment. But I find none to do it justice. It was simply a bottomless, indescribable pain.

"David," Sheriff Taylor said gently.

I was staring at two old truck tires, one leaning against the other. I looked up at the Sheriff.

"We better get Wesley here to the hospital," he said, then quickly added, "Just for a routine checkup, now. Nothing tells us that he's been harmed in any way. But let's get him safe and sound and get him reunited with your sweet family. Sound like a plan?"

I nodded, unable to speak.

"Okay, then. Let me—"

A strangled cry from the woods cut him off and made me jump. Wesley tensed up, as rigid as stone beneath the blanket, and then he suddenly came to life, looking left and right, trying to find the source of the sound. His eyes blazed with fear.

"It's okay, it's okay," Sheriff Taylor said. "They caught Dicky, that's all. Everything's fine. Let me take care of this." He walked off, to our right.

In that direction, three figures were coming out of the forest. Two of them were deputies, dragging the third by his arms—Dicky Gaskins. The man kicked and flailed his body, screaming obscenities between his cries of anguish, so much noise that it blended together into nonsense.

Sheriff Taylor looked back at us and then to his deputies.

"For Pete's sake," he yelled, then lowered his voice. "Randy, why'd you bring him back up here?" Another worried glance over his shoulder at us.

"Sorry, boss," the man replied. "What else'd you want us to do?"

"Just get him in the damned car. Hurry!"

The deputies changed direction and dragged Dicky toward the closest vehicle, another cop already opening the back door. I felt such rage for Dicky that it's a wonder I didn't run to him and start beating him with both fists. Wesley and I were feeding off each other, both shaking, though I believe his was from the purest fear I could imagine. Mine was only anger.

"You did this!" Dicky yelled. To my horror, he'd gotten an arm free and was pointing directly at me. "Your whole family! You the one should be going to jail, you—" A hard smack from an officer cut him off.

Wesley let out a little cry next to me and burrowed his face into my shoulder. The officer smacked Dicky on the side of the head again and got both of his arms pinned behind him. Then they were shoving him into the back seat of the car. But he wasn't done talking. He wasn't done hurting my boy.

"It's your turn, now, Wesley!" Dicky screamed at him. And then he uttered it again, almost spoken softly, reverently, before the thump of the slammed door shut him up.

"It's your turn."

CHAPTER EIGHT

Lynchburg, South Carolina
April 1989

I

I t still hurts to think of what the younger version of myself went through in the days after Pee Wee Gaskins killed my friend, Alejandro. It's almost like a different person altogether lived out those dark days, an innocent who will always remain a child in my memories. I ache for him, feel guilt for him, shed tears for him in the deepest part of sleepless nights. No one should have to experience such a thing, myself or anyone else, in some odd way rendering it moot that it *was* me. As if it created some ethereal, otherworldly being that forever occupies residency in my head. That doesn't make a lick of sense, I know, but tragedy warps the mind.

Two mornings after the night in question, I sat on the bottom step of the farmhouse's back porch, staring dully at the fields, recently planted with soybean. The weather had forgotten all about spring and moved right into a sweltering, humid heat that made my shirt stick to my skin, beads of sweat trickling down my sternum to settle, cool and wet, in the folds of my skinny stomach as I hunched over. It was Monday, school in session, but my parents said I should take a day or two off, not bothering to give a reason. None was needed.

I felt completely awful, utterly alone, without hope of ever being consoled. I think I was smart enough to know that blame for Alejandro's death couldn't reasonably be assigned to me— that no rational person could possibly have expected me to turn into Captain America and fight off Pee Wee Gaskins amidst his threats.

I was a kid. He told me to run. I did.

But what ripped at me, what tore holes in my heart, was the fact that I hadn't told anyone, hadn't screamed for help the instant I stepped out of the cabin door. Men were everywhere— some sitting at the campfire, some cleaning up, some returning from another jaunt with the hounds. I was too terrified, too petrified. I understand the meaning of that word, *petrified*. There is a level of fear that hardens your mind, your insides, your every muscle and nerve, making it impossible to act, rationally or otherwise. I stumbled out of that cabin and into the woods, found a tree, collapsed against its trunk. And remained there, as frozen as the hard wood which I leaned against.

Time had passed, interminably slow. Until the scream came from within the cabin, followed by shouts, blurs of movement, cries of anguish. It didn't take long for my dad to find me, as distraught as I'd ever seen him, and he held me fiercely in his arms, right there in the mushy pine straw of the forest floor, until the cops finally showed up. I'd told him everything, then, about a half-hour too late.

The thump of a car door pulled me out of my memories. My head had slowly sank until it hung like a sack of laundry from my neck, but I looked up at the solid thunk of a sound, which had come from the front of the house. Despite the shining sun and the unusually oppressive heat of the mid-spring day, the world felt dark and cold for a moment. Because I knew who had come for a visit.

A woman named Wendy Toliver, crime reporter for the local newspaper, *The Item*.

She had questions about the murder of Alejandro Mondesi.

2

The distraction broke me from my gloomy stasis of reliving that night over and over in my head. I crouched right behind the corner of the house and leaned forward, just enough to see Ms. Toliver standing at the bottom of the porch steps. She was well-dressed, her wheat-colored hair pulled back into a ponytail. My dad had come out to greet her, and she was looking up at him, although I couldn't see him. I didn't want to risk being spotted.

"Thanks for agreeing to meet me," she said.

"No problem." My dad's voice had a hint of warning, as if saying it could become a problem very quickly if she weren't careful.

Ms. Toliver reached into her purse and pulled out a small tape recorder, then held it up for show. "Do you mind if I record our conversation?"

"Actually, I'm sorry, but I do mind. I think I'll be a hell of a lot more comfortable if that thing's not on."

The reporter didn't seem fazed at all by this response. "That's completely understandable." She made a scene of putting the device back into her purse, then pulled out a small notebook and pen instead. "May I at least take notes of our discussion?"

My dad said nothing, so I imagined that he'd given her a curt nod.

Ms. Toliver gave an unsubtle look at the front door. "Where would you like to talk?"

"Here's just fine."

I risked leaning forward just a little more, saw my dad take a seat on the top step, resting his elbows on his knees, somehow looking defiant. This left the reporter with no choice really but to remain standing. But then she surprised me—and certainly my dad—by plopping down on the step right below him and casually crossing her outstretched legs at the ankle.

"I assume you've heard about the note left on the boy's body?" Looking back, I know her question and actions were all maneuvered to catch my dad off-guard, but it had only one impact on me. Dizziness quivered in my head and I had to sit down.

"Of course I've heard about the damned message left on the body," my dad replied.

Toliver nodded and wrote something in her notebook, but I could hardly see her do it. I had stars flashing in my vision, nausea trembling in my gut. I knew nothing about a note, and I certainly didn't know they'd found a body. There'd only been blood on Alejandro's bed in that cabin. Lots of blood.

As if she'd realized her hard-boiled approach wasn't working, Toliver visibly softened, putting her materials down with a sigh. "I'm sorry," she said. "I guess... I guess I didn't think this would be as hard on you as... Well, since it wasn't your son that was killed."

I could almost feel my dad tense up, as if my spirit had momentarily jumped into his body.

"Are you *trying* to get thrown off my property?" he asked in a dangerously steady voice.

"No, sir. I'm... I'm sorry." She paused. "Can I say something personal to you? Something totally honest? You're a respected man in this town. More than that son of a biscuit mayor, that's for sure." Another awkward pause. "Uh, don't quote me on that."

My dad actually laughed at this, and I wondered if maybe this Wendy Toliver lady wasn't the smoothest act in town.

"What'd you wanna say?" he asked.

The reporter stood back up and faced him. I noticed that she'd left the notebook stranded on the porch step.

"Mr. Player, I'm torn up as heckfire over this story. Split right down the middle to be honest. Half of me is jumping up and down, excited over the chance to cover the story of a lifetime. The other half is scared, hating every second of this. I didn't wanna come here and make you uncomfortable. I don't wanna dig through everybody's crap and make things worse. And I'm scared that flippin' monster is gonna come after me because of what I'm reporting. But ever since I was a kid I wanted to be a journalist and here's my chance. I can't fudge this up. Can I?"

It was starting to hit me that Ms. Toliver had a bit of a pretend-swearing problem. Now sitting on my ass, legs crossed below me, I leaned forward and propped an elbow on my knee. I'd stopped caring if they noticed me at this point, my curiosity overwhelming my dizzy spell.

"Wendy, let's sit down," my dad offered. "That kind of honesty will get you far in these parts."

Ms. Toliver blushed and nodded humbly, but then she picked up her notebook on the way to the porch chairs to which my dad had gestured. Once they'd settled down like two old-timers about to have iced tea, I had to scoot forward a few inches to continue my spying ways.

Dad put one foot up on a knee and looked at Ms. Toliver very seriously. "Listen,

I know you've got a job to do. An important job. Hell, the more word gets out about this man and the things he's doing, the better. Right? People will be more aware, more on the lookout, protect themselves better. Blast his picture all over the front page, I say. I'll help you, okay? I will. But my son is 16 years old and he needs to be left *out*. Period. Do we understand each other? He's still a minor and I refuse to let you talk to him or say anything *about* him. That's my only chance at talking."

Ms. Toliver nodded, her head bobbing like it'd been attached to a loose spring. "Yes. I understand. Completely. We'll avoid the parts dealing with David. No problem."

It took me a second to realize just what my dad had unwittingly revealed. The first thing she'd asked about was a note attached to a body, and now he'd made it clear that the subject of one David Player—*me*—was off limits for her story. Unless all this terror had lowered my IQ, that meant the note might have had something to do with me, and *that* meant that Pee Wee had probably kept good on his word that night in the cabin, right before I ran out of the room. That he'd tell people I'd begged him to spare me, to kill Alejandro instead.

"Okay, then," Ms. Toliver began, her notebook and pen at the ready. "Can you just give me your version of the events that night? At the Fox Pen?"

"My *version*?" Dad asked. "What's that supposed to mean?"

Sheesh, Dad, I thought through the haze of all my worries. He seemed determined to make this woman's life miserable. Maybe he hoped she'd never come back for more information.

"I'm not implying anything," she responded without a hint of defensiveness. "Bad word choice, maybe. I'm just trying to get as many perspectives as I can on what happened leading up to the discovery that Alejandro Mondesi was missing. Until the blood was discovered. Do you mind just starting at your arrival to the camp and give me as many details as possible?"

"That sounds reasonable enough."

"Anything and everything will help."

My dad started talking, and even I was bored after 10 minutes. I'd lived it, after all. One thing did bother me slightly, though I later shrugged it off as paranoia—my dad seemed to be hiding something. It had just been a feeling, and I'd forgotten about it by day's end.

3

An hour after the interview, I was out in the heat, wandering the freshly planted fields, the sun sapping the strength from my thin body. I could've filled a milk bucket with all the sweat pouring down my skin, but I didn't care. It felt nice to suffer physically, taking some of the pressure off the mental anguish that had consumed my every minute. A lot was on my mind, a long list that kept running through my thoughts without ceasing. I could almost see the scroll-like paper unrolling before my eyes, each terrible item writ in calligraphy, the whole thing like Santa's naughty-or-nice list from a Christmas cartoon.

But one problem dominated the rest. Pee Wee Gaskins was still out there somewhere.

"David!"

I jumped at the word, then looked around, confused, as if I'd temporarily left the world and hadn't been ready to return. My mom was walking briskly toward me, offered a wave when we met eyes. It wasn't until later that I realized she must've been horrified at the thought of me out there by myself, a killer on the loose. A killer who seemed to have some kind of sick interest in her son. It was a wonder my mom was able to hide that fear from me, certainly aware that I was on the cusp of breaking from it myself.

"Hey there," she said when she got close, a little out of breath. "What're you doing out here?"

"Just taking a walk."

"Yeah? You do realize it's about 300 degrees out here?" She shaded her eyes and looked up toward the culprit.

"It's not so bad," I mumbled.

She leaned in and made a show of smelling my armpits, her face screwing up in mock disgust. "Well, next time you decide to sweat your problems away, wear deodorant."

"I did!" My instinctive reaction was about as childish and innocent as I can imagine, now, looking back.

Mom laughed. "Cool your jets, I was just kiddin' ya. I'm trying to be one of those hip moms. Why don't we go back to the house, drink some cold water? Your dad asked me to have a talk with you."

"About what?" It was probably one of the dumber questions I'd ever asked her.

"Really?" She folded her arms and raised her eyebrows. "You really think your dad didn't see you spying on him and Wendy?"

I smiled, my best defense.

"Come on."

Despite my being soaked with nasty sweat, she put her arm around me and squeezed, then we started walking back toward the house.

"I really did put on deodorant," I said.

"Yeah. I know. God bless ya for it."

4

I was on my second glass of ice water, sitting at the kitchen table, before Mom said anything. It was so cold and refreshing on my parched throat, I momentarily forgot that I could very well be in mortal danger. It was a reprieve, a short one, but it brought me a strange peace.

"You want to know about the note, don't you?" my mom finally asked.

Kids complain a lot—I sure as hell did—but deep down, maybe even subconsciously, they're always comforted by the fact that their parents are the smartest people in the world.

"Yeah," I said. "She said it was found on the body. So..."

Mom only nodded in response.

"They found his body?"

"Yes, they did." She sighed, then, and the weight of the world seemed to crash down on her all at once, her face melting with a heavy sadness. "Half-submerged in Pudding Swamp, near the old Fincher fishing hole. And..." She paused, and I'd never seen my mom so uncomfortable.

"What?"

Shaking her head, she replied, "I don't know what else to do but be honest with you, son. You're whip smart, were born an old man, and you can probably handle this stuff better than I can."

In all my life, I don't think I ever felt so proud of myself as I did in that moment. She continued.

"His head was off, though I imagine that doesn't surprise you all that much. I reckon he did it right there in that cabin based on all the blood they found, then carried the body out."

"Was the head with the body?" I asked, surreal words to come out of my mouth.

"Nope. It wasn't. I can't imagine what he's doing with... those." Her body shuddered, and I felt it, too. "Anyway, like you heard from Ms. Toliver, there was a note attached to the body. The paper was in a little sandwich baggie, protected from the swamp water. It..." She rubbed her face with both hands, seemingly so traumatized by the contents of this note that I was terrified to hear it for myself.

Nonetheless, I asked, "What did it say?"

She looked at me, her eyes red and rimmed with moisture. "You need to know that I don't believe a word of what Pee Wee wrote, and even if it *were* true I wouldn't blame you, son. You have to know that. You're just a kid for crying out loud, no matter how mature you may be. But I don't want you to hear about that note from anyone else but us."

"What did it say?" I repeated.

"That he had gone to the camp that night to kill you, that he wanted to get rid of the witnesses. You and Andrea, I guess. But then his heart was softened—he used those exact words—when you begged him to spare your life. He said that you begged him to kill Alejandro instead of you. And that's why he did it. That sick monster of a man actually tried to peg the blame of cutting off a teenager's head... I don't even know what else to say about it. Maybe I shouldn't have told you. How in the world are people supposed to know how to act when something like this happens?"

Feeling oddly like our roles had reversed, I reached out and pulled her into a hug. Her news hadn't shocked me at all—it was, after all, exactly what Pee Wee Gaskins had said he would do. But it did scare me that he actually went through with it.

"I didn't do that, Mom," I said. "I was a chicken, and I acted like a baby, and I ran away, and I didn't yell for help, but I never said anything about Alejandro. I swear I didn't, Mom! I swear!"

My voice had risen in pitch with every word and by the end they were exploding from my chest along with a sudden burst of sobs. Mom squeezed me as tightly as if she were wrangling a calf.

"I know, son. I know. My sweet boy, I never thought it was true, I didn't. And you can't feel shame for running out of that cabin, for being terrified. You hear me? Not one person on this planet would expect you to have acted any differently. Okay? Don't you ever think such a thing again. You did *not* act like a baby, you were not a chicken. That's total nonsense. Absolute bullshit."

When it came to swearing, my mom was lacking considerably, so her liberal straying of vocabulary showed me just how much everything had affected her. It meant a lot to me that she cared so much, that she loved me so much. I had no doubt, not even the slightest bit, that if Pee Wee Gaskins had stepped into our yard right then, my mom would've found the strength to murder him, strangle him with her own two hands.

Mom gently gripped me on both sides of my face. "Do you understand what I'm telling you? You have no blame in this.

None, zip, zero. It's beyond absurd to even consider it. Okay? Gaskins is a monster, pure and simple, and he's trying to get in your head. If he does, then he wins. Let's not let him. Let's not give that SOB one ounce of satisfaction."

I'd calmed down as she spoke, somehow feeling better. Maybe my brain was too young to truly grasp what it meant to have a serial killer interested in you.

"You also don't need to fret over that newspaper article. Your dad made it clear as noonday that Wendy didn't have our permission to write one word about you. Not a single one. And if she mentions that note on Alejandro's body we'll lawyer up and sue every last penny from *The Item*'s coffers. Got it?"

"Got it."

"Come here," she said. "I want you to see something."

She escorted me back outside and we walked to the front yard, stopping in the shade of a gigantic pecan tree. She gestured with her chin to a spot across the road from our house, where a police car was parked on the shoulder, its far side probably hanging precariously on the edge of Mr. Johnny's irrigation ditch.

"You know who's in there?" Mom asked.

I shook my head.

"Mark Fuller. He's a young deputy for Sheriff Taylor, and he's here for one reason and one reason only. To make sure nothing happens to you."

"Really?" I looked up at my mom with wide-eyed wonder. An actual blood-and-flesh cop, assigned to protect *me*? The idea sounded miraculous and magical.

"Yep. He's the one that told your dad you'd been eavesdropping on him and poor Wendy Toliver, and he's the one who told me you'd gone out into the fields all by yourself. You were in his sight the entire time. He's not gonna let Pee Wee Gaskins get within a country mile of you or anyone in this family, okay? You're safe. *We're* safe. There's nothing to worry about."

That last sentence was a bit much, but I understood the sentiment.

"Thanks, Mom." I didn't know what else to say, and I could only hope that she felt my gratitude. I suspect she did, because it was so strong that my eyes were wet.

"Enough of that iced-water business," she said. "Let's go get us a Mountain Dew."

We did just that, adding a couple of moon-pies for good measure.

5

The next morning, as the first traces of dawn made the shade pulled over my window glow like a yellow moon, I awoke to a consistent tapping. Like most noises, it first came to my aware-ness in a dream—I stood in a great banquet hall, inside a castle, worthy of King Arthur himself, and some low-level landowner was striking an iron knife against his wine glass to garner the attention of his liege—when I finally snapped awake, frightened in the ethereal light of early morning. Someone was knocking their knuckle against my window.

I scrambled out of bed and stumbled to the only source of light, slightly disoriented as I lifted the shade to peek out. There I saw Andrea, standing in my yard, peering back at me as if this were the most natural way in the world to greet a person.

"What's going on?" I asked, even though I knew she couldn't hear me—probably couldn't even *see* me very well.

But she responded anyway, holding a newspaper against the glass.

Oh no, I thought. This had to have something to do with Wendy Toliver and her story on Pee Wee Gaskins. I unlatched the window and with both arms heaved it up on squeaky tracks. You may think this is something we'd done often, clandestine meetings without my parents' knowledge, but this was a first. I kinda liked it. And despite everything, I remember having the immediate worry that I hadn't brushed my teeth yet and all future romantic possibilities with Andrea would come to a screeching halt.

Slightly embarrassed at the effort it took for me to get that damned window open, I let out an involuntary grunt as it lurched the last few inches. Before I could say anything, Andrea climbed up and toppled through the opening. I stepped back as she arranged herself into a sitting position on the floor and once again thrust the newspaper toward me.

"Prepare yourself," she said. "This is the worst article written in the history of articles. It's not good."

My heart had leapt to full-speed-ahead, and it had nothing to do with my morning exercise of lifting an 80-year old piece of warped glass and wood. The look on Andrea's face terrified me. She was trying to keep it cool, but I could see in her eyes that whatever had been printed on those thin, smudge-ready papers was bad, indeed.

"What does it say?" I asked in a thin voice.

"I think you just need to read it." She still held the paper in the air, gave it a little shake. "Just read it and get it over with. Then we can hug and make you feel better."

I reluctantly took the bearer of ill news from her hands, held it stretched out in front of me. I'd subconsciously avoided looking at the front page, but now I saw that Ms. Toliver's article on Pee Wee Gaskins was the lead story. My rapidly beating heart seemed to sink in my chest, its thumps now rattling my stomach.

With a sigh as heavy as my body, I sunk to the floor and sat facing Andrea. We exchanged a look that can only pass between best friends, one that said we'd get through this together, all the adults in the world be damned.

"Do you want me to read it to you?" she asked, as sincere a thing as she'd ever said to me.

"Nah, I got this."

The first part of the article summed up a bunch of things I already knew, all too well. Several people, brutally murdered, their bodies discovered submerged in various locations throughout the grand, delta-like reaches of Pudding Swamp. Several others were missing, presumed dead based on the bloody crime scenes left behind. Overwhelming evidence led police to believe that Pee Wee Gaskins, a quiet, reserved, enigmatic worker at Whittacker Mortuary was the man responsible (and yes, the cliché nature of his workplace has never been lost on me, but I can only tell the story in all its ironic truthfulness). Ms. Toliver provided lots of sensational, gruesome details, using words like "severed" and "gator-fed remnants" and "rotted." I swear to you she even threw in the word "chunky" in a way that made my skin crawl.

But then came the part that I knew was about to change my life significantly. I grew angrier with every single word that passed my vision:

One local resident has found himself inexorably and tragically connected to the crimes in question, having faced the accused killer on at least two separate occasions. Because he is a minor and parental permission had yet to be granted at press time, *The Item* has chosen not to include his name. For the purposes of this article, the minor will be referred to as John.

John was one of two minors first to witness Pee Wee Gaskins in the act of an alleged murder, a scene that took place in the wooded area located near the abandoned Shiloh Line of the South Carolina Railroad. Police found gristly evidence of the body of George Holloway, whose further remains were the first to be found in Pudding Swamp, as previously stated.

John allegedly had an additional encounter with Gaskins at

the popular Thomas Edgar Fox Pen gathering on Friday evening past. Having retired to bed in the onsite cabin before most of the others, John later told authorities that Gaskins appeared in his room, making threats, whereupon John fled the scene and hid in the forest. His bunkmate at the time had been Alejandro Mondesi, age 15. He was soon reported missing, with grim evidence at the scene suggesting he'd met a similar demise as earlier victims of Gaskins.

In the late afternoon of the next day, that assumption was proven correct when trawlers in the swamp discovered the body of Mondesi, his head having been brutally severed from his torso. *The Item* can now reveal that a handwritten note was also found with the deceased, attached to his clothes with a safety pin, the paper contained within a plastic bag to protect it from the elements. Though police refused to divulge the exact contents of the message, citing the ongoing investigation, unnamed sources have revealed, exclusively to this paper, certain details of what it presented.

The message was signed by Pee Wee Gaskins, and several people who know him have allegedly confirmed that the handwriting on the note matches his perfectly. Gaskins claims in the message that when he approached John in the cabin at the Fox Pen, John broke down in hysterics and pleaded for his life. Gaskins then told the boy that he had come to kill and he wasn't going anywhere until his bloodlust was satisfied, whereupon John allegedly begged Gaskins to murder Alejandro Mondesi instead. Gaskins ended the note saying that such cowardice should be considered more shameful than what he himself is doing, and suggested that the Mondesi family should seek their own vengeance upon John for what he had forced Gaskins to do.

The Item will continue to seek information from the authorities as well as from the parents of the minor involved. A representative speaking on behalf of the Mondesi family said that a full statement would be coming soon.

I tossed the paper to the side, heard its pages flair and flutter as it settled to the ground. Then I gave a long, hard look at Andrea, showing with my eyes what I couldn't find the words to say. It hurt. The article hurt. Caused physical pain in my chest. All the fear and worries and trauma seemed swept aside, replaced by a deep ache that pulsed.

"How could she write that crap?" Andrea asked. "Like calling you *John* is going to make one lick of difference. Every person in this town with one ounce of brain inside their heads is going to know it's you. What bullshit!"

She yelled that last word so loud that I immediately heard steps outside my bedroom. There was a knock and then the door opened. My mom poked her head in.

"Oh," she said, seeing Andrea sitting with me on the floor at 6:30 in the morning. Then her eyes flicked up to the open window. "I didn't know you had company, sweetie. Did Andrea come for breakfast?"

There were so many unspoken questions in her greeting that I had to admire my mom's skills. And I figured at this point honesty was the only policy.

"She came to show me *that*." I pointed at the discarded newspaper.

My mom's demeanor shrank, and I knew immediately that she had already seen the article. This made me feel at least twice as much pain, thinking what this would do to her. But it was, in a way, a relief that I didn't have to tell her everything.

She came over to me and knelt on the floor, our eyes now level. Hers showed an aching as deep as mine. Probably deeper.

"I'm so sorry," she said. "Sometimes a parent doesn't know how to protect her own children." At this she burst into tears and so did I, the world of my troubles eclipsing all else, its shadow dark and vast. On some peripheral level I might've understood that crying in front of Andrea should've been embarrassing, but she did what I still consider one of the coolest things I've ever had a friend do. She crawled over and joined my mom and me in a big group hug full of snivels and tears.

"I didn't do that," I said when I gained enough composure. My chin was pressed up against Andrea's shoulder. "I never said one thing to him about killing Alejandro."

Both of them pulled away from me and looked as if I'd just told them I had lost an eyeball.

"Of course you didn't," my mom said. "Oh, son, I told you yesterday we never thought for the slightest second that you did such a thing."

"Yeah," Andrea added. "Give me a break. No one's going to fall for that stupid note."

I nodded, wiping tears from my cheek, wondering if I should tell them about how I ran, about how I never called for help. But I couldn't do it. "What happens now? What do we do? Has Dad read this yet?"

My mom visibly slouched. "No, he hasn't. He went out to fix a leak in the west irrigation pump. Don't you worry, I'll be with him when he reads it and help soothe his... wrath. It won't help things if he goes and murders this Wendy Toliver hussy."

My mouth opened slightly; I couldn't believe my mom had just called another woman a hussy.

"As for what we're going to do," she continued, "we're going to keep you safe and wait for them to capture Pee Wee Gaskins, which they *will* do. Soon. I know it."

"Maybe I should go to school," I said. "I can't stand the thought of sitting around here all day thinking about that article and imagining what peopleare saying about it. I'd rather face it head on."

"I'll stick by his side," Andrea said quickly.

My mom put on her "let me think about that" face.

"No. At least not for a couple of days. But Andrea can stay for breakfast."

I made to protest but didn't make it very far.

"No, this is not up for negotiation."

I sighed. "Okay, maybe in a couple of days. Like you said."

Mom asked Andrea to help her in the kitchen, leaving me to get dressed. I still hadn't even brushed my teeth, and couldn't help but wonder what unpleasant odors had floated around our group hug as I spoke. That inexplicably brought a smile to my face as I turned on the shower and waited for the water to get hot. I was sad about not going to school, but more than that, I hated that I'd be home when my dad came home and saw the paper.

He was gonna piss fire when he read it.

CHAPTER NINE

Lynchburg, South Carolina
July 2017

I

After Wesley's dramatic rescue from Dicky Gaskin's shambled wreck of a home, my boy didn't say much when grilled by the authorities—one of whom was an FBI agent of all things, since this had been a kidnapping in every sense of the word. Either not much had happened or Wesley was too traumatized to talk about it. I hoped and prayed to every god I'd ever heard of that it was the former, not the latter. Even in a quiet moment back at home, just me and Wesley together, out in the shed on the pretense of his helping fix a leak in the roof, he'd stuck with his story. I'd held him by both shoulders and looked into his eyes with all the love and concentration I could muster, and asked him, directly, to tell me if Gaskins had hurt him in any way. I swore to not tell a soul unless he wanted me to.

"No, Dad. He didn't physically harm me."

"Okay. Okay. Good."

"Dad, what's in that safe?"

Under the workbench, an old metal safe sat like a forgotten tombstone. It had been there for many years, and all my own dad would ever say about it is that we'd be given the combination for its lock when he died. Not before. We were under no circumstances to ever open it before he died. I used to wonder all the time, but the mystery had worn off.

"I don't know, actually. Some secret of your grandpa's. Let's hope it's big stacks of hundred dollar bills."

"Yeah, let's hope."

I realized I'd just fallen for the old *what's over there* trick to stop talking about his ordeal. And that was okay. We threw an old football for a while then came back to the house.

He said nothing had happened. What could I do but believe him? They'd given him a full inspection at the hospital before he'd been released to come home, and everything had checked out. I remember the nurse had used that word, *inspection*, like we'd taken him in for an oil change. What the hell was wrong with "check-up" or "physical?"

All had settled for the moment. My family was safe. Together. Inside the house as I went for a walk to clear my head and think through these many things. The air was warm but had an electric tension to it, the golden light of twilight tinted by distant cloud-cover encroaching from the southeast. Remnants of a hurricane, of all things. It had been two days since Wesley's rescue, and he seemed his old self, alternating between the usual phases—grumpy, happy, silly, contemplative, annoying, hilarious, grumpy again—sometimes he went through the whole gamut before one inning of the Braves game passed on the TV. But there was nothing unusual about this. That was our Wesley, 95% perfect, and a trip to the bathroom and back usually helped you avoid the other five.

At the moment, they were all watching that idiotic talent show that came on at least 17 times a week and seemed to have a hard-on for ventriloquists. If it weren't for the Gaskins family, there would've been only two things in my life that I thought of as creepy: ventriloquists and clowns. I could do just fine without either of those monstrosities popping up on my TV screen. Thank you, no.

I walked along the edge of the woods on the backside of the property, the place wherein I'd awakened so surprisingly the night Wesley vanished. It seemed like a million years ago, as if there'd never been a time in my life where my son hadn't been abducted by a maniac. It was even harder to believe I'd lived so many years before those damn kids even *existed*. Seriously. My mind couldn't grasp it. How had I ever blinked awake in the morning and *not* longed for some kid to bounce on my bed before I could even get up to take a piss? How had I not missed them every minute of every day, even though they hadn't been born yet? Surely I wasn't the only nutcase dad in the world who thought such ridiculous things.

I caught a distant flash from the corner of my eye, followed several seconds later by a low rumble of thunder, rolling toward us like a living beast. It looked like the storm my dad had so proudly pronounced upon our arrival was finally here. The trusty weather people seemed confident our area would only get the scattered showers and intermittent gusts of wind that drifted off the main thrust of the hurricane, like lost sheep straying too far from the herd. It certainly wouldn't be like the Hugo of my childhood.

A small wooden bench nearby beckoned to my ass. Dad had built the thing decades ago, and I used to sneak out there while the dishes were being done to read my latest library book. The spot was hidden from direct view of the house by a giant oak tree, several of its branches having been lopped off recently because the thing had grown too large, like a spider too big for its web. I took a seat, folded my arms, breathed in a big chest full of air, then slowly let it out. I loved this time of year, especially with a storm coming in. The breeze was strong enough to defeat the heat and humidity, and the air just smelled... alive. Fresh. *Bouncy*. I don't even know what the hell that means but the word came to mind and it fits.

The wind picked up a beat, rattling the leaves of the oak tree and the countless branches and limbs of the woods behind me. The air seemed to darken so quickly that I could almost watch it, as if some great god in a celestial back room had slowly rotated a dim switch. Clouds covered the sky completely, now, and any golden trace of the burgeoning sunset had vanished. Though my heart still hurt from the tragic return of the Gaskins family to my sphere of life, I relished the feeling of being outside in such conditions. It brought pleasant memories of childhood, of the good years before my first encounters with that wretched family. Despite being the middle of summer, I was suddenly feeling like Halloween had come early, and could almost smell pumpkin pie baking, just a faint trace of it on the moving air. My breaths came easy and soft. I could've stretched out right there and taken a nap for the ages.

But then that would be a waste, wouldn't it? The rain would come soon enough, ending my chance to enjoy the weather out here where it happens, not locked away inside, watching from the porch or through the ancient windows—thought that had its own appeal. Good grief, I was in a sentimental mood. I decided to take a walk, venture out into the swampy parts that had so entertained me as a boy.

I stood up from the bench, stretched, took in another deep breath of that buzzy air. When I was young, defined trails lined these woods like veins, taking you to any one of a hundred places within a few square miles. Most of those had grown over with time, although my kids had kept at least a few of them looking clean. One of my favorites had been so worn with usage that I don't think even a century of growth could've hidden it. That's the one I took, entering the woods, zigzagging through it until I got back to where the swamp made things more treacherous.

Pudding Swamp was a complicated thing to define. It's not like a lake, even the most sinuous of lakes, with clear-cut borders, something you can draw on a map. In a geological sense, my entire town was *in* the damn swamp, even the sturdiest building we've got—the ugly hunk of stone and mortar we call the courthouse. I'm not sure what came over our forefathers when they stumbled over this vast land of cypress-studded murky water filled with snakes and gators and all kinds of spoiling things. Vegetation started rotting pretty much the day they burst from their seed in these parts. Half the animals did, too. The balls those settlers had, seeing all of that morass and thinking to themselves, "Bah, a few ditches and dams and we'll be right at home!"

Well, I reckon they were a lot smarter than I am. One thing you can say for a bunch of rotten stuff: it makes some damned good fertilizer. It was crop heaven. And so they started draining and diverting and damming things up, and pretty soon they could walk 10 feet without sinking into mud. Farms and villages and cities came next as the decades and centuries passed. The result? Well, it's not like they killed Pudding Swamp forever. It still exists, mostly incognito. It's here and there and everywhere, sometimes under you, sometimes in front of you, sometimes behind you. Manipulate a swamp all you want, but it'll always outlast its conqueror. Like entropy, the land is always moving toward chaos, no matter how much concrete and lumber you throw in the water.

I moved through the woods, thinking these things I'd thought a million times over the years. I came upon a little branch of the swamp, jutting out like a skinny arm that ended in a pointing finger, somehow accusatory and ominous. The water, black as if a skein of tar had been laid upon its surface, did not move even the slightest. No ripples, no flow, no lava-like popping bubbles. Water spiders danced across its surface, but their tiny feet couldn't disturb the eternal stillness of the swamp. As I always did, partly out of hope and partly out of dread, I searched for the eyes of a gator, often poking out of that dark flatness, a frightening and exhilarating sight. I saw nothing.

Walking along the edge of the swamp, stepping over the bone-white roots of cypress trees, I kept my eyes on the water, hoping to at least see a turtle or snake. I'm still a child in many ways, and catching sight of any creature of the wild is a part of that. What they say is true: those things are usually more scared of you than you are of them. But that doesn't mean you should go chasing them or poke their noses with a finger.

I kept walking, feeling more peace than I had in days. This was so different from when I was a kid, when Pee Wee Gaskins had been *out there*, free, haunting my every minute with his potential appearance. In the here and now, Dicky was in jail, locked away. I could be out here and not worry about my family back at the house, watching some seven-year-old girl swallow a flaming sword while her attention-hungry parents clapped and cried for the cameras. I knew my dad had his shotgun close at hand, just to be sure, and that made me feel even better.

The air was very dark now, heightened considerably by the thickening canopy of the woods. The blackness of the water also seemed to magically melt upward, making everything gloomy. But I couldn't turn back. Not yet. I kept moving along the trail. The ever-increasing wind wound its way through the many trees, stirring all but the water. Insects buzzed and chirped; small creatures scuttled through the undergrowth. Somehow, impossibly, the air smelled of cinnamon. The world was a fairy tale.

Up ahead, I saw a large bump in the water, near the makeshift shore of pine straw and roots. Such a thing wouldn't have garnered any special attention except that there was something too perfect about it, unnatural. A dark crescent curved at the top of the object, perfectly round. Three steps closer and I could plainly see that it was the heel of a boot, jutting through the black surface as if its owner had gone diving for crawdads and hit an unexpected sinkhole.

The boot wasn't moving, and I felt no alarm. To use an old classic, if I had a nickel for every time I'd found an abandoned piece of footwear somewhere in the vastness of Pudding Swamp over the years, I'd have at least 20 bucks. Some quick math would tell you that's 400 shoes, boots, flip-flops, sandals, high heels... you name it. Honest to goodness, that sounds about right. It was always just the one, never a pair, often making me snicker as I imagined all these poor saps waddling back to their homes with one bare foot. But it was almost as common as seeing a squirrel scoot up the side of a pine.

So I'm not sure what possessed me to grab a stick from the ground and poke at that forlorn boot. Instinct, curiosity, who knows? The fallen maple branch I chose was old and moist, and it bent like stiff rubber when I pressed its end against the heel of the boot. I pulled back and then shoved the stick forward again, harder. This time the boot moved, though only a little before it seemed as if my makeshift prod might break under the stress. My troubled mind jumped to the worst conclusion. And it only took a few more pokes to prove me right.

That boot was attached to a leg. That boot still had a foot inside.

2

I sat on the ground, staring at my discovery. Five minutes had passed. Maybe more. My right hand still gripped the slimy end of the broken branch I'd used, a wooden sword in case the owner of the submerged footwear decided to rise from the dead. Not that the stick would do much good against a rampaging cat, much less a zombie.

I don't know what caused my sudden catatonic state, but I absolutely couldn't move. There were plenty of solid options— run back to the house, call the police. I could grow a pair and pull the body out, make sure it wasn't someone I knew. But then Sheriff Taylor would tan my hide for messing with a crime scene.

I just sat there and stared, even as the woods grew darker and darker, full night almost upon us. A compression squeezed my chest as I wondered how it is that such awful things always seem to follow me, like smoke from a moving torch. It trailed and trailed until you stopped, and then it caught up with you, surrounded you. I had no idea what to do, as if my brain had said to hell with it, just sit there until a gator eats you.

It turned out someone made the decision for me.

A man was shouting my name.

3

I think my mind was too preoccupied the first few times my name wafted through the early evening air, and even when I took notice I couldn't quite tell the source. It seemed older, and I assumed it was my dad, until a sheriff's deputy came running up the trail—evident from the scant light shining off his badge. It had grown very dark.

"Mr. Player!" the man yelled as he stopped right in front of me. Even in the near-complete shadow of night I could tell it was the man who'd dragged Dicky Gaskins out of the woods when I'd been sitting with Wesley after his rescue. Randy, I believe his name was. "Mr. Player, your dad told me you were out here somewhere." He doubled over, heaving in breaths like a man with only one lung.

Every alarm system known to man had started clanging inside of me—my family. Something horrible had happened to my family, even though I'd only been away for an hour at most. Even though they were only a slight jog's distance from me.

"What's wrong?" I got out, breathlessly awaiting the bad news, preparing myself for the damage I knew was coming. But it didn't, at least not directly. At least not with immediacy.

"He escaped," the deputy said between sharp heaves of air, looking at me intently, obviously curious how I'd respond.

But my mind didn't compute at first. It tried to process the good news that my kids hadn't been mentioned. Or my parents. That a hole of despair hadn't opened up at my feet like a great chasm splintered into existence by an earthquake.

"Escaped?" I asked weakly.

"Dicky Gaskins. He escaped from his jail cell. The overnighter they had him holed up in."

The implications were vast, so vast I had no idea what to do. But before I could react or say anything, the deputy's eyes sank toward the ground and settled on the jutting boot heel, a lump of dark shadow on the water.

"What's that?" he asked. He had no way of knowing in the weak light—I was surprised he thought anything of it, that he didn't just think it a protruding root.

"It's a body," I replied, as numb as I could possibly be. "At least I think it is." The urge to get back to my family suddenly snapped to the forefront of all thoughts. "I have to get back to my kids. Are they okay? Do we know where Dicky went? What if he's going after my son again?" The questions rattled out faster than Randy could attempt to answer. I moved in the direction of home, but the deputy grabbed my arm.

"Sheriff Taylor is there right now, fully armed. He sent me to get you. But what the hell's this about a body?" He motioned toward the potential swampy grave at our feet.

Still stunned, I shrugged in frustration and lack of knowledge. "I don't know, man. That's a boot and it's attached to a leg. So I assume someone's dead, dumped right there to rot." It seemed an awfully cold response but I had bigger worries now than I had five minutes previously. With the sheriff's protection or not, my family needed me. *Wesley* needed me.

Deputy Randy nodded in the darkness, slowly but not stopping, his head bobbing in a sluggish rhythm, as if some somber tune played in his head that I couldn't hear. He still held onto my arm, though his grip had loosened. The wind rippled through the trees around us, shaking the leaves like a thousand rattles. The air smelled of dampness and tang—the rain couldn't be far away.

"What do we do?" Randy whispered. "How'd you find this? Who is it?"

I'd been waiting for that most obvious of questions, but I had no answer.

"You better call it in," I said. "I mean, we shouldn't touch it, right?" I asked because a morbid curiosity had taken over me—I wanted to know who lay dead at my feet, on my parent's property. I wanted to know how it had happened.

"Yeah, yeah, I need to call it in," the deputy responded, reaching for the radio mike attached to his shoulder. Without answering my second inquiry, he pushed a button, which was followed by the familiar squawk and hiss of police communications. It went silent when he started talking. "Dispatch, I've got a possible body in the swamp back behind the Players' residence on Narrow Paved Road. Looks like it's been here awhile, no suspects in sight."

As he spoke, I realized he'd trusted me beyond reproach—not only that there was, indeed, a dead body submerged in the water and not just the remainder of the boot, but also that I had nothing to do with the demise of said body. They exchanged a few more sentences while I thought about this, their conversation ending with the conclusion that a full team would be sent out right away, and then another squawk, hiss, and a click. Deputy Randy clipped the mike back onto its shoulder holster.

"Damn," he said, staring down at the water. "You better be right about this."

It had grown so dark, I could barely see a thing. "Do you have a flashlight?" I asked.

"Yah, I do." He pulled one from his bulky utility belt and clicked it into life. A bright beam shone down like a light saber, temporarily blinding me. Its round spread of illumination ran over the swampy black waters like a SWAT helicopter looking for bank robbers. The boot somehow looked even darker when the light shone upon it, and nothing else revealed itself other than fleet-footed spiders skipping along the murky surface.

"Hold this," the deputy commanded, handing me the flashlight. "I'm not gonna look like a complete ass when they get here." The accusation in his voice bothered me—I wasn't the trained professional, here. But I took the device anyway and pointed it at the boot.

Randy crouched down, then leaned forward onto his hands, letting his knees bump down into the soft undergrowth. He crawled to the very edge of the water then braced himself with his left hand while reaching out with his right. His fingers slipped into the water beyond the boot, searching, probing. He bit his bottom lip with concentration, now scooting to the right as he felt along what I presumed to be a bloated, decaying body, wrapped in soggy clothes as clingy as the wraps of a mummy.

He'd gone four or five feet, investigating meticulously by touch, when he stopped. On instinct I directed the light onto his face and his eyes squinted up in annoyance. But before they did I could tell his expression had taken on something strange.

"What?" I asked.

He looked up at me, then back down at the water, where his arm was submerged all the way to the elbow. Surprising me, he reached his other arm out and sunk it into the water next to his other one. Then, bracing his body, he yanked upward with all his strength, grunting as he did so. Pointing the light directly on that spot, I watched in horror as he lifted the shoulders and neck of a dead human out of the black wetness.

It had no head.

Whoever the person had been, and it looked to be a male, was wearing a T-shirt at the time of his demise, and his skin now looked puffy and white, small hairs skewed this way and that on his upper back and lower neck. The neck itself ended in a mangled mess of flesh and bone and sinew, roughly hewn and lacking any color. I'd expected it to be red and meaty-looking, but it was gray and dull purple, pockmarked with black as if the whole thing had been dipped in crude oil. Deputy Randy let out an agonized sigh, then let go of the shirt he'd gripped with both hands; the body splashed back into the water and quickly disappeared. Only a matter of seconds passed before the thick morass of a surface settled once again into flatness. Only the heel of the boot remained to reveal the poor man's final resting place.

The deputy seemed too shaken to speak, which is just about how I felt.

"It's the same," I whispered.

This snapped the deputy out of his petrified state. "Huh?" he asked rather goofily.

"It's the..." my words trailed off. What was this? What was happening? My mind leapt to ridiculous explanations. Maybe this body was one they'd failed to discover decades earlier, when they searched Pudding Swamp from one end to the other, probably a dozen times. But of course it wasn't. The thing would've decomposed long, long ago. This guy had been killed within the last few days, maybe even within the last 24 hours.

"It's the same," I whispered again after clearing my throat and making a stronger effort.

"Same as what?" the deputy asked, standing up from his crouched position. He looked over at me, his face barely visible because I'd inadvertently dropped the flashlight to the ground, where it had rolled to the very edge of the swamp and now pointed in the opposite direction. I had absolutely zero recollection of when it had fallen.

"It looks just like what he did. All those years ago." My voice sounded weak and sad to my ears, almost false, coming from miles away, conveyed by speakers on the fritz. I considered the possibility that I was slowly cracking up.

"You're talking about Pee Wee, aren't you?" the deputy asked me.

"Yes, sir," I said matter-of-factly, incongruent to the situation. I looked over at my new friend, peered into eyes hidden by shadow. "I'm talking about Pee Wee."

4

"I don't know if we can stay here, Dad."

We sat on the front porch, my dad sipping a beer while I stuck with ice-cold water. The rain had come, hard sprinkles making a rat-a-tat-tat on the tin that lined the shed out back. I could hear it from here. Above us, hitting the tiled roof, it was more of a soft series of thuds, like tiny drums helping ants march to a beat. The wind had picked up, seemed to add a few miles per hour on the hour, and I would've enjoyed it on any other night. But not this one.

"You can't leave." My dad said it with that tone of his, the one that said, *Save us both the trouble and don't argue. This is the law, boy.*

"Can't? We have to." My response was weak because I didn't want to leave. Not really. My oldest son had been through the trauma of his life, and a dead body had been found in the swamp not one mile from where we sat. A headless dead body. And yet every ounce of me said that leaving would be a mistake, even if anyone with a lick of sense might say otherwise.

"This storm is gonna get worse before it gets better," my dad said. "And you're the one that found that poor fella out in the woods. They're going to need you for their legal this and that. Plus, quite frankly, I'm scared as hell and I want my son here to make me feel better."

"The kids, dad. I can't keep them here if some maniac is running around killing people and lopping off their heads." *Just like Pee Wee Gaskins did three decades ago*, I didn't bother saying.

"Well," he said, "you'll do what you gotta do, David. I'm not gonna stop you."

I rolled my eyes, hoping as soon as I did that he hadn't noticed—the porch light had been turned off so there wasn't much chance that he had.

Feeling obligated to at least make a case, I laid out the facts. "There's a whole team of cops, coroners, forensic investigators, whatever out there in the woods. Excavating a dead body out of the swamp—someone who was killed in the same way Pee Wee did it back in the day. You want my kids to be in that kind of environment?"

"Excavate? Not sure that's the right word to use for something like that. Sounds more... archaeological, something they'd do with dinosaur bones. I think maybe you meant extricate or exhume, something like that."

I glanced over at him, sure that he was joking.

"Whatever, Dad. This is serious."

That was the wrong thing to say. He jerked as if I'd slapped him, then dragged his lawn chair over to sit right in front of me. Leaning forward, he spoke with his face no more than ten inches from mine.

"Serious? You don't think I'm taking this seriously? Did some earwig crawl up in your brain and take out the smart parts? I was here, you know, when Pee Wee was wreaking havoc and murder on this town. I was forced to watch my own son go through the absolute definition of living hell. Don't start preaching to me about taking things seriously."

"Then you should *want* us to go," I replied, ashamed at how defensive I felt. "You should want us to get as far away from here as possible."

He shook his head adamantly and sat back a little in his chair. "No. That's not the answer. Players don't run from their troubles. We face them and we conquer them. We did it then, and by God we're gonna do it now. It'll all be over soon."

"Easy to say, Pops, easy to say. Harder to do. But Dicky Gaskins escaped from jail and someone was murdered. Maybe others. I'm scared for my kids. I don't *want* them to go through what I went through."

"Well, let's give it some time." He sounded a little defeated. "Sheriff Taylor promised to have someone watch over us night and day. Please, son. Please don't leave yet. You have to trust me."

I didn't have the heart to point out that back when I was a kid, we'd had a deputy watching over us then, too. A lot of help that had been. But my dad's plea was so heartfelt, so sincere, that I couldn't argue one more second. I didn't want to leave, anyway, like I've said.

"Okay, Dad. We'll stay here and huddle together, keep each other safe, figure things out. I'm sure they'll catch Dicky soon enough, anyway."

"Glad we see eye to eye." He leaned forward and patted me on the knee.

"We still have two weeks left," I said when he sat back in his chair. "And if we're going to stay, then there's something I want to do. It's been over a year, but I have to try."

"What's that?" my dad asked, the curiosity in his voice ringing high and clear.

"I'm going to see Andrea."

CHAPTER TEN

Lynchburg, South Carolina
May 1989

I

Going back to school could've gone one of two ways. Mortifying, scary, terrible, awful. *Or...* warm and welcoming and safe and happy. At least this is what I told myself all through the night, waiting for morning to come. After the bombshell of a newspaper article, telling the world (or at least the greater area of Sumter, South Carolina) that I was a cowardly scaredy-cat that sobbed and begged a murderer to kill my friend instead of me, my parents had seemingly settled on keeping me home until I turned 80 years old.

But I couldn't stand the thought of that. That long day after Andrea had sneaked through my window, thinking about that article, imagining her and all of my other friends at school, wondering where Pee Wee Gaskins was hiding out, wondering what Alejandro's body must look like buried in a swamp somewhere, just about drove me crazy. So I pleaded with Mom and Dad to let me return, to let me brave the waters. I used every argument my strained little brain could conjure, flat-out making stuff up, telling them I'd learned it in my Psychology class at school. Words like *trauma management* and *absenteeism damage assessment* were bandied about, and I swear I even worked in a reference to Dr. Spock (the famed child psychiatrist, not the pointy-eared fella from Star Trek.) More than anything else, I knew that each and every day I missed would exponentially make it worse when I finally *did* go back. And I couldn't bear the thought of sitting around in that house again, my mind wandering the vast, scary world outside of it.

Eventually, I won the battle.

Still, I couldn't sleep the night before. My eyes stared at the shadowed ceiling as I speculated on just how well I'd be received come morning.

Andrea came by to walk with me, and it was a relief to see her come through the front door without so much as a knock. That's when you know you're a true friend. Breakfast was just about ready, my mom going the extra mile once she heard Andrea would be joining us again. Instead of grits and eggs, we had grits, eggs, sausage, biscuits, and gravy, and the glorious smells were wafting through the living room air from the kitchen when Andrea closed the front door behind her.

"Hey, guys," she said.

My dad was in his chair, pouring through the paper, probably to see if they'd had the gall to write additional nasty things about his son. He'd gone down to their offices on Main Street to give them a piece of his mind yesterday afternoon. I didn't know what he said, but I was happy I hadn't been in the same room, especially if Ms. Toliver had been around when he arrived.

He grunted a hello, not bothering to lower the edge of the newspaper, as I walked over to give her a hug.

"Hey there," I said, holding on a little longer than socially acceptable. Luckily my dad was too preoccupied to notice. "Thanks for coming out of your way *again*. I feel special."

She pulled back and snickered. "Keep dreaming." She walked over to my dad's boat-sized chair and tapped on the newspaper hiding his face. *Man*, I remember thinking, *she's got some balls.* (Figuratively speaking, of course.) "How're you doing, today, Mr. Player?"

He lowered his reading material and looked up at her with a surprisingly grumpy face.

"Good morning, Ms. Llerenas," he said wearily. "You came all the way over here to steal my son?"

She shrugged. "Gotta make sure he hits the books, you know. Get him ready for college. So he can get rich and buy you a new house in the city."

"You do know how to sweet talk, don't you?" He folded up his paper and placed it on the end table, then folded his arms. "I hate to say this right before ya'll head off to school, but they found another body. That sicko seems to be spreading them all over the damned county. I can't even believe I'm letting you leave this house."

The news had definitely soured things a little, but I wasn't about to let him change his mind.

"Officer Fuller will be right on my tail, right?" I asked. "He can watch over me at school just as easily as he can here. It's probably even safer there, with all those people around."

"Oh, don't worry. Mark's gonna be on you like flies on a cow patty. If he lets you out of his sight, I'll make sure Sheriff Taylor puts him on guard duty with the chain gang. I think they're cleaning the dump this month."

"Don't you worry," Andrea said. "I'll protect him, too. Old Pee Wee will have to get through me first if he wants to mess with your son."

I looked at her and blinked. This whole conversation was absurd.

My dad stood up and, shocking all of us, pulled Andrea into a genuine fatherly hug. "I'm sorry you're a part of this."

"It's okay," she whispered as he stepped back.

Tears glistened my dad's eyes and for a moment he struggled to say anything further. This was an uncommon sight in my house—something I'd seen about as often as I'd volunteered to clean out the septic tank—and it struck me hard. It struck me that everything that had happened was tougher on him than it was on me.

He finally got some words out. "It just means a lot that he has a friend like you."

"Thank you, Mr. Player. That's really sweet." I assumed she felt a bit mortified at the moment, and that was a pretty good response considering.

Feeling a little awkward myself, I went for the always-reliable culinary rescue.

"Mom's got all kinds of yummy food waiting for us," I said. "And we don't wanna be late."

Dad gave me a look of gratitude then made a beeline for the kitchen.

2

"He's killed four people. At least."

Andrea said this just as we passed Mr. Johnny's store, its namesake an old man who was far less sweet than the sodas and ice cream he sold out of his tiny establishment. The wispy-haired geezer wore a constant scowl, even as he thanked you for stopping by. I saw him through the stained window, staring our way as if one of us might be Pee Wee Gaskins in disguise.

"How many of them did you know?" I asked her.

"Well, I guess just Alejandro, really. I mean, my mom knew *of* all of them, had probably crossed paths a few times with two or three. But I didn't. Just... Just Alejandro."

Hearing his name hurt at the time, and still does today when I write it. No matter how many pep talks my parents and Andrea and the police gave me, and no matter what I told myself at the time and over the many years since, I knew I'd always bear some guilt for his gruesome death. But that morning I had to push it aside for my own sake.

"Let's just not talk about it," I said. "At least not for a little while."

"Happy to oblige, pardner," she replied with a fake twangy accent.

The morning was cool and bright, a stark contrast from the day before. A nice breeze blew over the recently planted fields, and I could already imagine the rows of corn and the barrel-sized tobacco plants and the seemingly snow-dotted crops of cotton. I wondered, as I squinted against the rising sun, looking out over the freshly turned dirt and barns and farmhouses, if all these terrors might come to an end by the time everything was grown and ready for the Harvest. Maybe they'd capture Gaskins by then, and his looming presence over my life would begin to fade into the mythical realms of childhood nightmares. They say kids tend to block out horrible things that happen to them. I could only hope I'd be so lucky.

"You okay over there?" Andrea asked. We'd just reached the corner of Kenwood and Kensington, where we needed to take a left, about a half-mile more to go. We headed that way.

"Yeah, I'm fine. Just enjoying the peace and quiet."

She snickered at that one, but didn't pursue it any further.

"Hey, I've got an idea," I said. I really did, and it was a good one. "Let's play *Where's Antony?*" As soon as I said it I worried it might remind her too much of that awful night in the woods, or conjure up her deadbeat dad when she didn't want to, but her eyes actually lit up.

"Absolutely yes," she replied. "It's about time we had another round of that. I'll go first."

"Alright, go for it."

"Hmmm." She tapped her mouth. "Let's see. Okay. Antony is on a bus. In... Sweden."

"Sweden? How'd he get to Sweden?"

She gave me her topmost look of annoyance. "Seriously?"

"Okay, then. Sweden."

"The bus is riding along, going up some mountains. Sweden has mountains, right?"

I shrugged. "It probably has mountains, yeah."

"Up and up it goes, winding all of these treacherous roads. Oh, and he's the only one on the bus. Except for the bus *driver*, of course."

"Of course."

She stopped walking—as did I—and she turned to me, her eyes focused on the ground in concentration. "Then it reaches the top... 50... *thousand* feet above sea level..."

"Mount Everest is only—"

She shushed me with an upraised hand. Very effective. "Okay, then. He's not in Sweden. He's on Mars, somehow transported to the future, and it's a self-driving bus, invented in... let's say 2030. And he's naked because you can't wear clothes on Mars."

Her story had grown absolutely absurd but I wisely said nothing this time.

"Then, suddenly, the bus is approaching a huge cliff. Like something in a Saturday-morning cartoon. Ya know, some of that roadrunner-coyote shit. Sheer drop off, everything is desert red, half-a-mile drop to certain death. There's even a sign that says, 'You're about to die.' But the bus doesn't slow down. In fact, it speeds *up*."

She paused for a breath then continued at a fast clip. "Antony realizes something's wrong. It took him awhile because he's an idiot, right? The bus is churning, shooting

Mars dust out behind the tires, going 532 miles per hour, now—"

That's really specific, I thought.

"—and Antony is panicked as hell. He stands up, naked as a jaybird, and yells to no one in particular that they need to slow the hell down and *turn*. Well, there's some kind of computer thingy that obeys his orders and the bus *does* turn. It veers sharply to the right and throws him against the window to the left. He smashes through it, the broken glass slicing him up, down, and sideways, gashes all over him, bleeding like a stuck pig. He lands on the Mars dirt and it's poisonous, seeps into his bloodstream, makes him feel all kinds of internal pain—"

I wanted desperately to ask her how he could even breathe at this point but she was speaking too fast for me to interrupt.

"—so he rolls to a stop, screaming in agony, wrenching in pain. Well, the bus kept turning right. Right, right, right, in a circle, because no one was inside to tell the thing what to do. Turning, turning, turning, and sure enough—BOOM!—it runs right over Antony. His head gets caught in the tire well and it's dragging him, now, even as it's squishing his brains out. Well, what happens next is obvious."

"Yeah. Obvious." I found myself enraptured and didn't know what happened next.

"The bus lost control and went off the side of the cliff, taking Antony with it. His head detached from the tire well and somehow he fell faster than the bus. Aerodynamics, something like that. He landed flat on his back, crushing his spine and every last organ. But he wasn't dead yet. No, sir. He looked up, full of every pain known to man, and his last conscious thought was seeing that bus come down and land right on top of him. Antony is finally dead."

She breathed in a satisfied sigh then looked at me. "Well?"

I gave her a couple of slow nods, my mouth bent in a

thinking man's frown. "Impressive. There's a plot hole or two, but definitely impressive."

"Smart ass. I'd like to see you do better."

Laughing, I said, "I might have to do mine after school. We're gonna be late."

"Oh! Yeah. Let's go."

We jogged the rest of the way.

3

I had thought that school would go one of two ways. Great or terrible. Thankfully, it was mostly the former. Turns out that when there's a serial killer loose and he plays mind games with one of your classmates, you take the side of the classmate. People were either overwhelmingly nice and supportive, or they just kinda looked the other way, obviously feeling too awkward to say anything. There were ample examples of both at lunchtime.

"Oh, David, it's so good to see you back at school." Mrs. Medlock said this to me as she pumped my hand—clenched firmly in both of hers—up and down, up and down. A nice lady with a giant poof of gray hair stacked on top of her head, she taught Trigonometry, and claimed I was the smartest student she'd ever taught. Unbeknownst to her, I once overheard her say the exact same thing to Holly Davis. "My family has been praying for you and yours, I can promise you that. Just let me know if you need any help, anything at all. Okay, sugar?"

"Yes, ma'am." Calling your student "sugar" was something that still happened back in the day. She'd barely let go of my hand when Mr. Kim came out of nowhere and whacked me on the shoulder, almost knocking me over.

"Hey there, David!" He was a thin, olive-skinned man, a third-generation Korean-American. Taught Social Studies.

"Don't worry about all that dadgum nonsense in the newspaper, boy. Not a single person in this-here school believes the hootey-patootey about you begging that pipsqueak lunatic to kill poor Alejandro." Mr. Kim was sort of a no-nonsense guy.

"Thanks, Mr. Kim," I said, my shoulder sore and my spine slightly misaligned.

It wasn't just the teachers, though there were several more of those—and the principal, Mrs. Moore, who's tight-lipped smile and quick, "Glad to have you here, son," was about all a kid could ask from the overly-stressed woman. Most of the students were nice, too. Being a small school, I knew every last one of them, many for over a decade, and had for the most part avoided making enemies through the years.

Missy Severinsen, a mousy little thing that had to watch for high winds in case she got blown to the next town, gave me a soft pat on the arm while looking up at me. "Hi, David. We've all been thinking about ya. Let me know if that Andrea girl dumps you." Missy always said things like that, so it made me feel right at home.

Blake Canton punched me on the arm, his knuckle as sharp as a knight's lance. It hurt like a son of a bitch. But that's how Blake showed affection so I couldn't complain, despite the three weeks it'd take for the bruise to go away.

Andy Benetendi, a skeevy kid who hadn't showered since the 70s, gave me a high five as I entered the cafeteria, something he'd never done before and never repeated. He and I had never talked much, and really never did after, but his small display on that day somehow warmed my heart a little.

Lots of other kids offered pleasantries, or at least gave me the cool-guy nod as we passed in the hallways and classrooms of the majestic Mayewood High School. Ronard Howell. John Hannon. Kerry McCallum. Craig Casalou. Brandon Kerouac. Michelle Robbins and her sister, Keri. Janette Reeve. Someone flicked my ear from behind, but all I heard was a giggle lost in the crowd.

Now, there were those who understandably felt a little threatened by my new status as a celebrity in our town. Perhaps they thought some of that Pee Wee Gaskins horror would rub off on them. Maybe they worried I had somehow brought it on myself. There might've even been a few who suspected I really *had* begged the man to take Alejandro's life. But no one confronted me directly—just a few side-eyes and quick look-aways throughout the day, especially in the lunchroom.

Somewhere in the midst of all these encounters, I actually ate lunch.

"David!"

Andrea called my name from the back of the line and I quickly joined her, my appetite budding to its full growth. It seems my own kids love to bitch and moan about how awful their school lunches are, but I'm telling you back in the day, in Lynchburg, South Carolina, at Mayewood High School, the food was mighty fine, made you wanna come back for more.

"Hey there," I said. "What're they serving?"

"Pizza."

Jackpot, I thought. Their pizza came in perfect rectangles, which somehow seemed unnatural, but it was one of my favorites. All I had for Andrea was the highly intelligent response, "Yum."

"Having an okay day so far?" she asked.

"Actually, yeah. If I was sitting at home I'd be completely insane by now."

She nodded as if she completely agreed.

We sat with a couple of kids whose families went way back with mine—Trevor Jacobs and Todd Eldridge. Todd had been at the Fox Pen but I'd never really gotten a good chance to talk to him—there always seemed to be a couple of drunk old men between us. Trevor, a stocky dude who was absolutely born for the life of a farmer and could probably wrestle a full-sized bull to the ground while sipping a cup of coffee, started the conversation.

"Sucks, man. What that guy said about you." Coming from Trevor, that was as sincere a statement ever made.

I was halfway through a gigantic bite of pizza, which hadn't disappointed. "Thanks. It's all kind of stupid, huh."

"It's not stupid," Andrea said. "It's scary as hell is what it is. You're handling it like a champ."

"Sure are," Todd interjected. He was a man of few words, but one of the smartest kids in school. He had about a 50/50 chance of being completely bald by the age of 20, however. Trevor and I had a side bet on exactly when it'd happen, that Todd didn't know about.

"What really *did* happen?" Trevor asked. "That night at the Fox Pen."

"Zip it, Trev," Andrea warned, growling with her eyes, if such a thing were possible.

"Nah, it's okay." I was in a good mood, a better one than I probably deserved. "Ask away, boys, I'm ready to talk about it."

Trevor raised his eyebrows. "Well? What happened?"

Andrea leaned closer to me. "David, don't ruin a perfectly good day. We don't need to talk about that psycho."

I sighed. "There's not much to tell, anyway. I mean, come on. I was scared shitless—I can barely remember a thing. I was in bed and something woke me up. Some creepy dude was standing in my room so I jumped off the bunk and ran for my life. I acted like a chicken, but I swear I didn't sit there and beg him to kill Alejandro."

"We know you didn't," Todd said. "And there ain't a person in this town that wouldn't have done the same thing."

I suddenly had a thought, then, and it wasn't a good one. The tone rang false in how Todd made his pronouncement, and I remembered the old axiom that if something seems too good to be true, then it probably is. Everyone was being *too* nice to me. In an instant the whole day shifted a little, and I could just envision Mrs. Moore announcing over the intercom the day before that I was to be treated with kid gloves upon my return. I'm sure she said it a little more principal-like, but I was now certain of it.

"David?" Andrea prodded my shoulder.

"Oh. Just spaced out there for a sec." What was I gonna do? I mean, it was better than the alternative. I could just see kids lining the hallways, throwing tomatoes at me, chanting *Candy-ass, candy-ass, begged for his life back...*

"Did you guys hear about his son?"

This little bombshell of a question came from Todd, and not only did it come out of nowhere, my mind had traveled too far away to know what in the world he could possibly be talking about.

"His son?" Andrea asked. "Whose son?"

"Pee Wee Gaskins. They talked about his son in the paper today."

I stared at Todd, feeling like the air had been sucked out of the room. He suddenly seemed pasty and pale and sweaty, and I wanted to up the bet that his hair would vanish before he graduated, well before 20. Hearing him say Gaskins' name, hearing him mention a son, dreading what was about to come out of his mouth made all the world sickly, ghastly, warping my vision.

"What're you talking about?" I managed to get out in a husk of a whisper.

Todd could sense my mood and answered tentatively. "Pee Wee has a son that lives up in Florence with his mama. Nothing to worry about. Just thought it was interesting."

I knew he was holding back. "It's okay, Todd. Tell me what the paper said about it. About him."

Poor Todd had shrunk in his chair. "Man, I shouldn't have brought it up. Sorry."

"Just tell us," Andrea said. Her curiosity had obviously overcome her concern for my mental and emotional well-being.

"He's our age, I guess," Todd replied after a few seconds of hesitation. "And that lady that wrote the crap about you went up and interviewed *him*. Said right there in the article that his mama gave permission, which seems sick as hell to me."

"The paper interviewed a 16 year-old kid?" Andrea asked, voicing the disbelief I felt in my heart. "How could she do that?" I didn't know if she meant the mom or the reporter, Wendy Toliver. Maybe both.

Todd gave a shrug as if to say, *How the hell do I know?*

"What did he say?" I asked.

"Maybe you should just read it."

"Tell us." I had to know. I didn't *want* to know, but I had to know.

Todd sighed. "Just a bunch of crap about how his daddy's misunderstood, that he's being blamed for all this because he's different, a hermit type. And because he works for the mortuary. Then he, uh, said that it was your fault everyone's blaming his daddy and that maybe they should blame *yours*. And... that you're the only one—well, you and Andrea, I guess—that saw him in the woods that first time. And then in the cabin at the Fox Pen."

"But the man disappeared," Andrea almost yelled. "If he's so innocent then why did he run off? Plus, the cops say they have all kinds of evidence that it's him. This is bullshit."

"I'm just telling you what it said!" Todd recanted. "Don't shoot the messenger, sheesh."

I didn't know how to feel. My good day had taken a nosedive.

"Whatever," I said, standing up. I looked forlornly down at my half-eaten pizza, thinking it a shame that such a beautiful piece of culinary art was going to waste. "I'm not going to let some bonehead kid of a serial killer ruin my day. Let's go to Chemistry, dammit."

We went to Chemistry.

. . .

4

"I read the article," Andrea said. "Found the paper in the library. Mrs. Ridley didn't want me to see it—hid it under a stack of comics that she asked me to re-shelve. For a librarian, she's not the brightest fish in the pond."

She and I were walking home, another school day in the books. Officer Mark Fuller slowly followed us in his patrol car as we made our way—my very own secret service detail. Every once in a while, I'd give him a wave and I'm sure he felt stupid waving back.

"You should've snagged it," I responded. We'd turned the corner to my street—without saying so, Andrea had obviously decided to go out of her way to see me home. Late afternoon heat melted all over us—so much for the brief cool spell that morning. "I guarantee my dad's already burned it in the fireplace."

"It didn't say much more than what Todd told us." I didn't believe that for a second. Andrea wasn't the type to hide things from me to protect my tender little soul, but we'd never dealt with something quite like this before.

"Well what *did* it say?" I asked.

"The guy's a moron. The reporter tried to avoid directly quoting him as much as possible, but when she did... Let's just say this kid learned everything he knows from the Sunday funny pages."

"That's the most non-answer answer I've ever heard."

She reached out and lightly touched my arm. "I swear, there's nothing that really stands out. He just talked about his dad all defensively, saying that half the stuff people have heard is a bunch of horse-patootey. And yes, he used those words. *Bunch of horse patootey.*"

"Well, if half of it *is* true, that's plenty."

"Exactly."

We walked in silence for a minute or two, my house just up ahead. She'd still avoided telling me anything about the article, and I didn't have the heart to pursue it too heavily.

"You won't believe what his name is," Andrea said when we stopped at the foot of our gravel driveway. My mom was sitting on the front porch and gave us a lazy, hot afternoon wave. "Hi, Mrs. Player!" Andrea gave her a double thumbs-up, which seemed outrageously absurd in the circumstances. Then she turned back to me and raised both eyebrows, a mischievous grin lighting up her face.

"What?"

"His name. The Gaskins kid. I said you won't believe his name."

"His dad goes by Pee Wee, so it's gotta be something like... Scooter. T-Bone, maybe?"

"Ha. No. His name is Dicky."

I stared at her and she stared back. Then we both burst out laughing.

Feeling better—definitely better—I gave her a hug and invited her inside for an after-school snack. As if she had ESP, Mom had baked cookies, and there was cold milk in the fridge.

5

An hour later, I walked outside with Andrea and asked Officer Fuller to give her a ride home. He said that he would, seeming relieved to break up the mind-numbing job of watching over my house, but only if I rode with them. That way he wouldn't get his balls busted for leaving me alone—his choice of words.

Andrea and I sat in the back seat of the patrol car like criminals, whispering to each other.

"You promised me this morning that you'd take your turn with *Where's Antony?*," she said, her breath hot on my ear.

"Yeah." I had goosebumps and wanted her to keep talking.

"And you didn't."

"Oh, yeah. Sorry."

"Well, then go for it, before we get to my house."

"Can't you just take another turn? You're way better at it."

She pinched the skin of my forearm, just enough to smart. "This whole game was your idea, remember? So come on. Amaze me with your brilliance."

"Fine. Okay, where's Antony, where's Antony, where's Antony..." I rattled my brain, hoping to come up with something that could come within a mile of her dark and twisted versions. "I think it should have something to do with a clown."

"Oh, yes. Definitely a clown. This should be good."

I took a dramatic breath of preparation. "Okay, Antony just enrolled at Clown University a couple of weeks ago, and so far he's been doing pretty well."

"Wait, is that a real place?"

"Of course it is." I tried to sell it as best I could. "It's in, um, Kansas. Kansas City, I think."

"That's in Missouri, Professor."

"Oh yeah. Anyway, that's where it is. Kansas City. And Antony is just killing it in his beginner classes. You know, things like... Juggling 101. Face Painting. How to sew clown costumes. Uh... how to make your feet unnaturally big. Things like that."

Andrea gave me a tiny laugh but it was enough to keep me going.

"So things are going peachy. Then one morning his professor of... you know, the guy who teaches them how to pack into those tiny cars? His name is Doctor Spitz."

"Wait, the same Doctor Spitz as your last story?"

"The same."

"What're the odds he'd be a proctologist *and* have a Ph.D. in Clown Car Packing?"

"I know. It's crazy."

"So what happened?"

I looked at Officer Fuller's eyes in the rear view mirror and saw the light of laughter there, though I didn't know if he could hear us. "This Doctor Spitz asks Antony to come to his office because there's a problem. And Antony has no choice but to say yes, even though he's getting a bad vibe from the clown doctor. A creepy vibe."

Andrea nodded, looking as genuinely interested as one could be playing such a stupid game. I reminded myself that Antony was all too real to her, no matter how ridiculous our stories got, and that dampened my enthusiasm. The last thing I wanted to do was to hurt her, and suddenly I couldn't think of where to go next in the tale.

"Okay, creepy vibe," she said, "he has to go to the guy's office. *And?* What happens?"

"Um, well," I struggled to end this, not enjoying it anymore. "It's bad."

"Good. I want it to be bad."

Maybe this did *help her*, I thought. Maybe it really did. So I finished what I'd started.

"Doctor Spitz tells Antony that he's not good enough, that he doesn't have what it takes to be a proper, scary clown. That clowns aren't meant to be cute and funny— their actual purpose is to scare the bejeezus out of small children. Antony tells him he's wrong, that he *does* have what it takes. Doctor Spitz says nope. Nope, you don't. Antony says yep. Yep, I do. They argue like that for awhile."

"Saying nope and yep?" Andrea asked. "Really?"

"Paraphrasing."

She nodded as if that made perfect sense. Behind the scenes, my mind was actually on a roll now, and I knew exactly where this ridiculous story was going.

"Finally, the professor relents, says that Antony can stay in the college if he proves himself with the small car clown trick. Antony promises to do whatever it takes. Doctor Spitz tells him he has to go to the cemetery, dig up 20 corpses from the freshest graves available. Then he has to stuff them in a small car that the professor keeps in his, uh, clown garage. Antony thinks this is the coolest idea in history and does it. I'll spare you the details. Let's just say 24 hours later, there's a tiny car in a clown garage stuffed with 20 dead bodies—most of them having rotted for at least a couple of weeks. It smells bad. I'm talkin' *ripe*."

"I bet."

"Antony wipes his hands with satisfaction, smearing guts and brains all over his coveralls."

"He was wearing coveralls."

"Yeah. What else?"

"Got it."

The car came to a stop and I realized we were in front of Andrea's house. Office Fuller turned toward us, his elbow jutting through the little window in the middle of the protective glass.

"Go ahead and finish," he said. "I have to know how it ends." He smiled, kind of a *Kids these days* smirk, but I couldn't really blame him.

"Yeah," Andrea added. "So far it sounds like Antony is just having fun with dead people. I bet he loved every minute of it."

I shook my head, patting her hair like she was a foolish child. "Okay, here's the best part. Doctor Spitz says to Antony, 'Alright, boy, your turn to get in. Time to prove yourself.' The color drains from Antony's face, and of course he doesn't want to do it. Begs the professor not to make him do it. But Doctor Spitz suddenly turns mean, turns into a raging clown. Yeah—he's been wearing clown makeup and a costume this whole time. I didn't tell you because I wanted it to be a... plot twist."

"This is so fantastic," Andrea deadpanned.

"Think of the scariest clown you can possibly imagine."

She and Officer Fuller looked at me with blank expressions.

"No, I mean literally. Close your eyes and... conjure it up in your minds. I don't have the skills to describe how horrifying this guy was. Is. Whatever."

Andrea shut her eyes for a moment, then opened them with a curt nod. "Got it."

I glanced at Office Fuller, who rolled his eyes. "Yeah, me, too. Looks like you."

"This horrible clown professor grabs Antony and drags him to the car, stuffed with corpses. He's super strong and lifts Antony off the ground and stuffs him through the door, the passenger side door. If you were there, you'd see that there isn't any room for this guy—the thing is filled top to bottom with bodies—but Doctor Spitz makes it happen anyway. He gets violent, using his strength and his fists to pound on Antony, hitting him, pushing him, forcing him into the squishiness of all that rotting flesh. Finally, only Antony's face is exposed, the rest of him... submerged, mixed in with bodies that have broken apart to make room for the poor son of a bitch. Doctor Spitz is smiling now, gray blood and sticky guts dripping from his face, and he doesn't say a word. He just reverently puts his hand on Antony's cheek and pushes, shoving it into the bloated butt cheek of a dead body, his nose and mouth slipping perfectly inside a wrinkle, cutting off all his air. The professor then shuts the car door—he really has to lean into it, you know, use that crazy-ass clown strength to make it click—and watches as Antony suffocates, drowns in a mass of decaying... flesh."

I paused, and felt a little giddy at Officer Fuller's wide eyes, Andrea's slightly open mouth.

"The end," I said.

No one spoke for at least 30 seconds. Then my personal security guard broke the silence.

"You're a sick little fella, aren't you?"

"He does it for *me*," Andrea replied, reaching out and taking my hand with a soft expression on her face, as if I'd just recited her a love poem.

"Well, that's sweet and all," the officer responded, "but I think your mama is about to have a conniption fit, wondering why you're inside a cop car."

Andrea and I looked at the house, saw her mom leap off the bottom step of the porch and sprint toward them, her face lit up in alarm. She was wearing a robe and nightgown, in the middle of the afternoon, her hair up in curlers.

"Crap," Andrea said as she opened the car door. "Don't worry, I'll calm her down and explain why we got arrested. You know, for telling bad clown stories to cops."

Her mom was yelling her name, now, standing on the sidewalk with arms folded and eyes aflame. Andrea leaned forward and kissed me on the cheek.

"Bye, David," she said as she got out of the car. "Thanks for the *Where's Antony?* story. It might've been the best one yet. See ya."

"Bye," I said, feeling content.

The door slammed shut and Officer Fuller quickly started the car and drove off. I twisted in my seat to watch through the back window as Andrea pulled her mom into a hug and whispered quiet mysteries into her ear.

6

Life poked along for a few days, nothing of note in the news. No one went missing, and no bodies were found, headless or not. I went to school, hung out with Andrea, did homework, did chores, always with the constant companionship of Officer Fuller, somewhere in the background, probably trying to avoid any further stories concerning one Antony Llerenas. Summer weather seemed here to stay, still early and a little bit fiercer. I made the noble decision on behalf of my friends and family to put on a couple extra layers of deodorant each morning.

On Saturday I went to the movies with Andrea, Trevor, and Todd—I felt bad for "shooting the messenger," to use his words —and we had a gay old time, just like they used to say in the *Flintstones*. We saw a scary flick (*Pet Sematary*, not as good as the book but still spooked me enough to clutch Andrea a couple of times like a frightened toddler) then ate burgers and shakes at a little dive called *Dairy Keen* (a downright ripoff of *Dairy Queen*, but no one ever complained). After that we all helped my dad dig a huge trench out behind the tobacco field, and to this day I have no idea what it was for. I have an inkling he made it up to keep us busy, and to keep my mind off darker things. He probably refilled the ditch with a backhoe at some point when I wasn't around.

All of this is to say that by the time the sun set, I had sweat out enough water to irrigate our crops for a week, and every last muscle in my body begged for respite. After some weary good-byes to my friends, after a nice supper of pork chops and baked potatoes, after an hour or so of watching the Braves game with my dad, after a weekend day of happiness and hard work, I toddled off to bed.

Sleep hit me before my head had time to properly indent the pillow.

7

For many years, my mind blocked what happened next in the middle of that sultry, heat-soaked night. Before it came back to me in recent days, I had sometimes dreamed about it. Believed that it *was* just a dream.

It certainly started that way. I was lying in a poppy field—just like the Technicolor one in *The Wizard of Oz*—with Andrea, and we were both eating ice cream cones. We almost floated we were so happy, and she kept licking at that icy white goodness like it might have the audacity to melt before she could get to the crunchy cone. Dreams don't usually make a whole lot of sense, and maybe since I was a teenage boy, she suddenly transformed, in an instant, from licking her ice cream to licking my face. I giggled and guffawed, but it felt good, and she kept right at it.

Then I woke up to darkness.

Several hard things poked my back, like little twigs.

All manner of insects sang their nightly mass all around me.

I felt a breeze skittering along the ground, rustling the leaves of trees and bushes.

And something was licking my face.

I yelled out in fright and swatted at whatever loomed above me, then scooted backwards, my hands scraped by the harsh undergrowth of the woods. It had been a deer taking nourishment with its tongue from my cheeks—I saw its white tail flashing in the darkness as it hip-hopped away, startled by my rudeness. Instinctively, I wiped my face and realized that something had been smeared across my skin. Something rough and grainy.

"I turned you into a human salt-lick."

The voice came from my left and startled me so much that my heart lodged in my throat, preventing me from even the slightest cry of fright. I backed away again, crab-walking straight into a prickly bush. Terrified, I froze, as if the branches of the bush had ensnared me like a spider's ropy gossamer.

"What?" I tried to say, but it came out more of a squeak.

"Be sure to stay where you are," the person responded. It was a man, his voice somehow gravelly and whispery at the same time, as if he wanted to disguise his identity. Maybe my eyes were still adjusting, but I couldn't see him at all. "Stay where you are, at least for now. I've got things to say."

Of course I knew who it was. It had to be Gaskins. But how had he gotten me out here? Why was he using that weird voice?

"What did you say?" I asked, my nerves calming just enough to allow me to speak.

"That I want you to stay where you are." The sound of his voice was demonic, almost comically so. But this didn't lessen the fear I felt, not at all.

"No, the first thing you said," I clarified. All four of my limbs trembled, as if I'd awakened inside a refrigerator instead of the warm woods, barely having cooled from the relentless heat that day.

"That I'd turned you into a human salt-lick." Leaves and undergrowth rustled nearby as he repositioned himself, and I now could make out the shadow of his head and torso—he appeared to be sitting, cross-legged and comfortable. I kept hearing a low crinkly sound, steady and regular, as if his lungs were full of candy pop rocks.

"What does that mean?" His words had horrified me even before I'd fully registered what he'd said. Plenty of movies had prepared me to think this guy would string my body up and salt my remains, eat me later for dinner.

"You live in South Carolina, boy. You know what a salt-lick is."

I rubbed my face again, felt the sandy residue that had been smeared on my forehead and cheeks. He'd wanted to attract a deer, lure a deer there to lick my face.

"Why?" I asked, so much disgust wrapped up in that one word.

"Because I was told to. To scare you."

I expected him to say more, but he didn't.

"Are you going to kill me, Pee Wee?"

I sensed a brief movement from him, then there was a click

and a light flashed in the darkness, blinding me completely. Covering my face with a forearm, I squinted, tried to see something amidst the brightness.

"I'll wait," the man said. "I'll wait until your eyes adjust."

It seemed a weird thing to say but I kept trying. Finally, images came into focus. He was sitting as I'd imagined, and he wore a sweatshirt and khakis, holding the flashlight in his lap, pointed at his chest. There was something unusual about his face and... and then I saw it all at once.

He had a bag over his head.

It was a plastic grocery bag, loose and shiny and crinkled, its handled-ends tied around his neck to keep it secure. Only because I was so familiar with the place myself, I could see the logo of Rexall Drugs printed amongst the bumps and valleys of the thin plastic. He'd cut a slit near his mouth, and the entire bag contracted and expanded with each of his breaths, causing the sparky pop-rock sound I'd noticed earlier.

He clicked off the flashlight and everything went black— except for the after-image of his bag-wrapped head, glowing in my vision, somehow scarier than the real thing. My entire body tingled with fear. His voice rasped from the darkness.

"Remember, now, I told you to stay where you are. For the time being, anyway."

"Okay," I said.

"I have a knife. I'm just letting you know. I have a knife. It's very sharp."

"Okay," I repeated.

He didn't speak for a while, leaving my mind to worsening thoughts. The woods had grown silent, the insects abandoning me to my own fate, not wanting to watch the terrible things that seemed destined to happen. I tried to build my courage, tell myself I could fight this man, especially if he *only* had a knife. Or at the very least I could run. Surely. I didn't have to let Gaskins hurt me.

Continuing his terrible Batman impression, he finally said, "You must be wondering why I've ensconced my head within this handy and convenient grocer's bag."

His words disturbed me, increasingly with every sentence that came out of his mouth. I had a hard time believing that Pee Wee Gaskins even knew some of these words. *Ensconced?* He'd always seemed so simple, so uneducated.

"Why the bag?" I asked, admitting my curiosity, which was genuine even in the middle of my terror.

"Because I don't want you to know who I am."

I hadn't expected that, hadn't even considered that he might not be Gaskins.

"I know who you are," I said, maybe being a little too bold.

"You think I'm Pee Wee Gaskins. And maybe I am. Maybe I'm not. Maybe I'm Donald Henry Gaskins, and maybe no one ever asked him if he liked being called Pee Wee. Maybe I'm someone completely different. Maybe I'm his son, or his father. Maybe I'm someone he's never met. Maybe I'm his victim, or maybe he's my victim. Maybe I'm someone who doesn't actually exist because within the sphere of your knowledge you don't know who I am. If you don't know who I am, do I exist at all?"

The words poured from him now, almost uninterrupted for breaths.

"What matters is that we are here, in the woods, in the dark, and we're sitting before each other, wondering who the other might be. Who the other might *really* be. We all have bags on our heads, David. All of us. Some of them have slits for air and some of them don't. Some of them are visible, some invisible. And when the bag doesn't suffice, then the head must come off. It's how we identify our worthiness to be in this world. Do you understand what I'm telling you?"

I didn't. I really didn't. And I was too scared to tell him that.

"You don't understand, I can tell. No need to speak. I know

all there is to know when it comes to our heads and the bags we wear. I know all there is to know about you."

As he spoke, I heard the telltale signs of him shifting, standing up, coming toward me. I let out a little whimper and backed further into the prickly bush. Suddenly hands were on my pajama shirt, yanking me out of the growth and tossing me onto my back. Then he straddled me, sitting atop my chest, pinning me to the ground by digging his bony knees into the flesh of my arms. It hurt, and I struggled helplessly to free myself—he'd always seemed a tiny man, but I couldn't overcome his strength.

"Stop moving," he said, still using that ridiculous scratchy voice. "Stop moving right now."

I obeyed, the terror filling every last nook and cranny of my body, bulging and pressing.

"It's finally time to see what kind of head is on your shoulders."

A grocery bag slipped over my head, his hands pulling its top edges tightly down to my shoulder then pushing them against the ground below my neck, so that a tight sheet of plastic now covered my face, pressing down, cutting off the air from my nose and mouth. Panic leaped through my nerves, a sheer panic I'd never felt before—not even in my earlier encounters with Pee Wee. Ignoring his orders from just seconds earlier, I kicked out with my legs, squirmed my arms, twisted my torso, fighting uselessly against his advantage and surprising strength.

I mumbled, tried to scream, but there was no breath to support it, no air to form the sounds.

"Stop!" he whispered violently, clamping his hand against my mouth. "Stop and prove that you can handle it! Stop resisting!"

Not knowing what else I could possibly do, I obeyed him once again. Fighting every instinct that screamed through my body, I stilled myself, stilled everything, my arms, my legs, my torso. I held my breath instead of trying to find it from somewhere it wasn't. I lay without moving at all, resembling the life-less corpse I was about to become. I felt as if I were melting into the ground, my entire existence at its end. Images of my parents and siblings flashed through my mind. I saw Andrea in the dark-ness of my closed eyes.

There was a ripping sound and suddenly air rushed onto my face, into my nose, into my mouth. I sucked in a breath, then another, then another, hearing the bag crinkle as I blew them back out.

"That's it, that's it," the man said, as soothing as if he spoke to a newborn baby. "That's the way. Way to prove your worthi-ness. Such control over your own body. That's the way."

Now that air once again filled my lungs and provided oxygen to my heart, the only thing that consumed me was a confusion so pure and bewildering that I questioned my own sanity.

"Why?" I mumbled. "What's going on?" I expected no answers but it was a relief to speak, to *hear* myself speak. It meant I was alive.

"I'm going to stand up, now," was the only answer I got, still in the raspy voice of something straight out of *The Exorcist*. "I'm going to stand up and you're not going to move. Do we have an agreement?"

I nodded, numb from the experience, the bag now lying loosely on my face. The man got to his feet. The release of pres-sure as his weight lifted off of me sent another wave of odd elation through my traumatized body. Although I desperately wanted to rip the grocery bag from my head, I didn't dare move.

"I'm going to walk away," my attacker said. "I want you to lie here, for at least 30 minutes, and think about the things I've said. 30 minutes. I'll know if you don't. Trust me on that one." He gave me a light kick. "Nod again, tell me that you understand."

I did as he said, hating the sound of the crinkling bag as my head bobbed three times. And then, just like before, nonsensical words flowed from him in a torrent of bafflement.

"Good. We all live in a crowded world, David. Only a few actually belong. Soon you'll be learning about the Reticence and the Waking, about things unseen, about why you're involved. It's a beautiful curse and a beautiful blessing, David, and only a few know of that beauty. Those who don't know how to use their heads will lose them. You be sure and hold onto yours, now. Never take all that flesh and bone that connects it to your body for granted. Oh no, never do that. Even the strongest can be... severed."

His insane rant apparently finished, I felt his presence leave my side, heard his rustling footsteps as he walked away. Something released inside of me, a dam that had been holding back emotions until they filled to bursting. Now released, they flooded my spirit and I curled into a ball, shaking with sobs.

How had my life turned into such a living hell?

How?

CHAPTER ELEVEN

I-20 Freeway
July 2017

I

Various forms of H2O made up my world, now. The sky abovewas nothing but a gray mass of cloud, so thick and heavy that you couldn't distinguish a single swirl or tail or wisp. Just flat grayness, like the end of time itself falling down to consume us. From that mass of cloud, rain fell in torrents. I'd seen heavier in my day, but this was consistent, relentless. Two days had passed since they'd found the body—bereft of its poor head—in the swampy backwoods of my parents' property, and unless it happened during my tenuous thefts of sleep, the rain had not stopped for a sparrow's breath. And below us—beneath our feet, along the roads and ditches, in the fields and parking lots and gravel driveways—water ran in tiny rivers and streams, gathered in a million miniature ponds. The news folks on TV had thrown the word "flood" around so much that you could tell they wished it had a few reasonable synonyms, something to break up the monotony.

In short, it was raining cats and dogs.

I drove through this world of water along I-20, heading west toward the city of Columbia. Now, when I was a kid, going to Columbia was like going to New York City for a country bumpkin from Lynchburg, and it still held a lot of charm for me. I liked its southern architecture and wide streets and mix of old and new. And it was one of the few big cities south of the Virginias that didn't feel *too* city-ish. Today was not a pleasure visit, however. Today had only one purpose, and then I planned to hightail it back to my family as soon as possible.

Today, I was going to see Andrea Llerenas.

I'd even called ahead and warned her.

I needed her. I needed her in a way that defied any sense of reason—it had been a year or two since we last got together, and we'd kind of lost touch. Not out of any kind of malice or ill will— nothing of the sort. Over the years we'd remained as good of friends as possible when one moves on in life, finds a career, a family, a new home. It's a rare thing for high school chums to stay as close as they once had, even high school chums from a small town. But I was extremely grateful that we'd done the best we could.

After an hour or so's drive, I exited into downtown Columbia, barely catching the sign before I passed it, my mile-a-minute wipers straining to do their job on the huge windshield of the minivan. It was like the high forehead of an obnoxious, balding neighbor. With my phone precariously balanced on the dashboard directly in front of the steering wheel, I visually followed the GPS map to her apartment complex, the sultry British voice of Siri politely giving me step-by-step directions in case I was too stupid to follow the clearly marked turns.

Andrea lived in a high rise—which for Columbia meant it had about 20 stories. As I pulled into its underground parking structure, the sudden lack of raindrops thudding on the roof and windows of the van almost popped my ears with the silence. I was impressed with the place. Clean cement, plants and flowers and trees planted in all kinds of surprising places. The walls of the parking decks even had decorative carvings of exotic animals that were part creepy and part beautiful.

On the third deck, I pulled into an empty spot and turned off the minivan. And then I sat there, staring at a ridiculous carving of seals skimming atop the ocean. Now that I had arrived, I was scared out of my mind. Last year I'd forgotten the annual Christmas card to her—which wouldn't be so bad if she hadn't *remembered* in such a spectacular way, writing separate notes for each child in my litter, with a small, sentimental gift attached to it. A yo-yo, a gift card, a bag of bite-sized Snickers, something else.

And so I sat there, parked within 100 feet or so from my childhood best friend, soothing my nerves with cheap hot chocolate from the gas station, prepping myself on the greeting, the requisite ice-breakers, the hugs, the kisses on cheeks, the order of questions and scoping and sharing of funny stories from the good old days. I wanted to go in with a master plan, able to change tactics on a dime, go in the direction I needed as soon as the chance presented itself. This had to be a success. Bad things were happening to my family, and I was here to ask Andrea for help, as she had once helped almost 30 years ago and many times since.

Someone tapped on the window, so hard and so unexpectedly that I shrieked, jumped, and banged my head on the glass.

It was her, of course.

For some reason, I didn't move. Just stared. Age had been neither kind nor cruel to this best friend of my youth—her hair dark and pulled back into a ponytail, her face without makeup, the tiniest of wrinkles at the corners of her eyes. She peered back at me with all the wisdom and kindness and smartassy-ness that I remembered from the good ole days. She cocked an eyebrow as if I'd gone soft in the head.

"Did you come to see me or my parking garage?" she asked, her voice muted by the window.

"Oh," I said in response, like a complete imbecile.

She took the situation under control and opened the door, swinging it wide and then reaching down to pull me into a hug. This released all of my nervous and awkward inhibitions and I hugged her back, fiercely feeling the years melt away and almost smelling the springy scents of the woods in which we walked so many countless times in our youth.

"Hey," I said. "It's really good to see you and I know I'vd sucked at keeping in touch, lately, and I'm sorry. But man, I really need you right now."

She made a joke of pulling away to escape, unclasping my hands from her neck, as if she'd had enough of my foolishness. But then concern creased her features and she didn't release my hands from her grip. She squeezed them.

"What's wrong?" she asked.

"A lot."

"Hooboy." She bent back over and kissed me on the cheek. "How about we go inside, make a cup of coffee. I just got back from the grocery store—wanna help me carry them up?"

"Nothing's ever sounded so good. Absolutely nothing."

2

We didn't say a whole lot at first. I was a little surprised by both the weight and volume of her considerable grocery take—at least five plastic bags dug divots into my fingers that almost burst from the pressure by the time I swung the items onto the kitchen counter in her apartment. She unloaded and mechanically told me where to put things like instant grits and cans of chili beans and Oreo cookies and something called quinoa that I silently swore to never try. I quite proudly put the milk away without needing any direction, however.

We spoke of this and that—what the kids were up to, how her job was going, how my job was going, why she ate quinoa, etc.—but nothing that stayed in my memory for more than 30 seconds. With each product put away into its carefully ordered spot, we seemed to take a leap backward in time, comfort and ease replacing discomfort and awkwardness. Without hearing her say it, I felt forgiven for my recent lack of Christmas card skills.

She put on a pot of coffee—for me, I guess—and then proceeded to make herself a cup of chamomile teaWith stunning morbidity this made me think of Betty Joyner at the Rexall Drug, and how—unless she'd figured out a way to travel through the universe approaching the speed of light to slow her relative age to ours—she was surely dead by now, buried in the ground. For a quick instant I pictured her body in the casket, decay already having taken her lips, exposing the teeth that might last forever, always grinning.

"Shall we sit?" Andrea asked, handing me a cup of steaming coffee. Relieved to escape dark thoughts of Mrs. Joyner's smiling corpse, I offered thanks and nodded. We sat down at the corner of her kitchen table, the 90-degree angle of the wooden edge the only thing between us.

"So," I began, taking a careful sip of my lava-temperature beverage. "I'm impressed you've yet to ask me what in the hell I'm doing here. Thanks for that."

She held her cup in both hands as if she relished the warmth of it. "You mean you didn't just come to say hi? To your best friend from high school?" She smiled to take the bite out of it. "I'm just kidding. You've got four little monsters. I'm surprised you have time to take a dump, so I certainly don't expect you to pop in for movie night with me every weekend."

This made me laugh, partly as a coping device. I had no idea where to start with all this mess.

"I'm assuming you heard what happened... what's *happening*... back in our sweet little hometown?" Even as I asked it, I suddenly knew that she *hadn't* heard. That would've been the first thing she'd talk about when I'd arrived—actually, she probably would've shown up on my parents' doorstep the same day if she'd known.

"Never mind," I quickly followed up. "It's a tiny place in the middle of nowhere, a world away from here. Of course you haven't heard."

"What're you talking about? Is everything okay? Did one of your parents..."

"No, no, they're fine. My kids are fine." That's all I could get out. A stark hesitation took over me, so strong that I felt muffled by some unseen force. Was it really fair for me to bring Andrea back into all of this—she'd probably been going to therapy for decades to get over the horrific things we'd seen as teenagers. Maybe she was good now. Healed now. How could I do this?

"David?" she asked softly. "If you don't tell me what's going on, I'll be forced to punch you in the brain. What happened?"

A heavy sigh was the best I could do for a response.

"David." This time it held the warning of a viper about to strike.

I decided to move forward. To suddenly lie to her and hide things seemed like the biggest betrayal of all.

"A whole bunch of crap has happened since we came to visit my parents. You could go online and read *The Item* and you'd know everything."

"You're killin' me, Smalls," she replied. "Just spit it out. Please."

"Well, the first weird thing was that Dicky Gaskins showed

up. Knocked on my dad's door like that was a perfectly expected thing of him."

"Dicky Gaskins?" She said his name with all the loathing it deserved. "What the hell did he come to your house for?"

"I still don't know. But it gets weirder. He started choking on his own tongue and then my son saved him, pulled it right out of his throat." Something about that whole affair still tickled my childhood memories, like a person standing just outside my peripheral vision, stalking me.

"O... Kay." Her brow pinched as she pondered reasons behind such absurdity. She'd also had several high-salaried therapists tell her that she'd blocked some of our high school memories. Neither one of us had sought to bring them back.

"It gets worse. So much worse." My chest shuddered with a halting breath, my emotions threatening to spill over. *Wesley. My son.* That bastard had taken my *son.*

"Man, David. What is it?" She reached out and held my hand tightly in hers.

"Dicky Gaskins kidnapped my oldest kid later that day. Wesley. In the middle of the night, actually. Had him for three whole days and we still don't know what in God's name he might've done to him."

Andrea said nothing, but tears of shock brimmed the bottom edges of her eyes.

"But we got him," I said, breathing a long, cool rush of air into my lungs. "Safe and sound, at least by the looks of it. At least on the outside. And they arrested Dicky. But then just yesterday we found a dead body back behind my mom and dad's place, mostly buried in the swamp. I haven't found out who it was yet. *And*—" Actually saying all of this out loud made me realize just how much had happened, how much shit had hit the fan. "—Dicky escaped, evidently."

"Oh my—"

I held up a hand. "One last thing and then we can fill in the details. The body out back... it's head had been cut off. Just like..." I didn't need to finish, didn't need to say the words. She'd lived it with me all those years ago. Not everything had been blacked out by our frightened and traumatized minds.

Andrea sat back, her hands on her cheeks, her eyes frozen in a death stare. "This can't be happening. You can't be sitting here, telling me all of this. It can't be..." She trailed off, looking as shaken as I'd ever seen her.

"I'm sorry, Andrea. It was stupid for me to come over here and drag you into all this."

"No, no..." She seemed so dazed, so... unbalanced. "It's okay. It's okay. I just need... I just need to process this." Without any further explanation, she turned and slowly walked out of the kitchen and down the short hall of her apartment. I watched as she entered the bedroom at the very end and closed the door behind her, softly, its thump like the last period of the last sentence in a depressing novel. My heart ached with regret, not helped by the uncertainty of her reaction. Had I triggered something? Was she going to have a breakdown? Indecision wracked me, needling the surface of my heart.

I stood up, took a step toward her room, then stopped. She'd made it clear she needed some time, and I had to give it to her. Grabbing my cup of coffee so I'd at least have something to sip while I waited, I sat on her couch and looked dully at the wall opposite. My eyes immediately went to a frame perched atop her television. It held an old photo, a young man and young woman standing arm in arm, dressed in jeans and T-shirts, smiling with all the bird-flipping confidence of youth.

It was a picture of me and her, 16 years old.

3

She came out of her room 30 minutes later. It had seemed like seven hours, maybe eight, maybe a thousand, but I knew it almost to the minute because a digital clock sat right next to the old photo of us. Those were basically the only two things my eyes had looked upon while I'd waited.

When I heard the bedroom door open, I stood up, almost spilling the cup of coffee. I'd barely touched the now-cold beverage. She wasn't in my view at first—you couldn't see down the hall as I had been able to from the kitchen—so I anxiously waited for her to make an appearance.

When she did, the first thing I noticed was that she held a suitcase in her hand. She let it thump to the floor.

"Can I stay at your parents' place?"

4

I wouldn't have believed it if the best psychic in the world had shown me a crystal ball revealing things exactly as they would play out, or even if God himself had come down and given me the same vision on my TV in full-color. But less than two hours after I'd arrived in her parking garage, Andrea and I were in my car, driving east, back toward home. Her suitcase was packed safely in the trunk, the Ozzy's Boneyard channel played on the radio, and fresh coffee and tea from the gas station nestled in the cup holders, steam escaping out of the little sip holes.

All of this put a permagrin on my face, despite the heavy circumstances, and Andrea noticed.

"It's good to see you smile," she said. We'd just left the city limits of Columbia, had about an hour to go. Rain continued to pour from the darkly gray sky and my windshield wipers worked at full speed, their sound as soothing as the patter of the rain itself and the incessant swish of the tires on wet road. "You looked three steps from death the whole time we were in my apartment."

"I *felt* three steps from death." I took a sip of my refreshingly hot coffee. "But the instant I saw you with that suitcase... my spirits lifted. It's kinda like the old days, you know? I never would've survived high school without you."

"High school? Or Pee Wee Gaskins?"

Her tone was light despite the dark turn of the question. "Both. Definitely both."

"Well, we'll just have to figure it out all over again, now won't we? If this Dickwad or whatever his name is likes running around cutting peoples' heads off like his daddy, then we'll deal with him, too. Boom." She took a victorious gulp of tea, which must've scalded her throat something fierce. "Ow. That's hot."

This made me think of something. "I guess the movies aren't so wrong after all."

"Huh?"

I glanced over and laughed when I saw her look of puzzlement.

"It's something my kid and I are always noticing. In movies. Like, cop movies, crime, whatever. Or anything that shows an office."

"David, what in the *hell* are you talking about?"

I laughed again. "In the movies, whenever some aide or what-ever brings coffee for everyone, in those ugly generic cups they always use, the main characters always grab them and gulp them like water, tipping way higher than a normal person would. They're so obviously empty, just props. I swear it's in every movie ever made. They never sip it like it's actually, scaldingly *hot*. And you just did that."

"That's because I felt empowered and invincible. And I forgot that it's hot."

I shrugged, then made a show of sipping my coffee very carefully and loudly, my lips jutting out like a chimpanzee. "Like I said, maybe I was wrong about that."

"So far we've had a very enlightening conversation."

"Haven't we?" I held out my cup and she graciously tapped it with hers. "Cheers."

"Cheers," she returned. "It's good to be back together." I wondered if she was mocking me, but I could tell from the corner of my eye that she was gazing out into the bleak rain, deep in thought. "Time is weird. Something that happened last week can seem a million years ago, but things that happened when you were a kid seem like yesterday. I don't think it's as linear as we think it is."

I nodded, wondering if we were about to launch into an existential, philosophical discussion. I didn't know if I wanted to or not—I was just happy to be with her again.

"I'm really sorry how things worked out, Andrea. Really."

She swatted at the air between us. "Oh, please, none of that guilt trip bullshit. It's not on you, not on me, not on anyone. You went to college, got married, had 70,000 children... I don't have any regrets and I hope you don't, either. I'm just saying that this is nice, that you're the best friend I've ever had and now I remember that. And I don't wanna forget it. So just promise me we'll keep in touch a little better than we did. Deal?"

"Deal. Absolutely. I want that as much as you do."

"And let's forget this cheesy conversation ever happened."

"Also a deal."

"But *without* forgetting that we're going to keep in touch."

"Also a deal as well."

"Okay, Mr. Redundant. I'm glad that's settled, then."

We drove on, into the storm.

5

We were about 20 minutes from Lynchburg when our conversation finally turned to what had been going on in Andrea's life the last year or so. It started with her mom, and Andrea's voice was as melancholy as the rain falling from the sky.

"She's in a home, over in Augusta. I tried to find a good place in Columbia but nothing quite fit, not even close to the one she ended up in. Lots of azaleas and oak trees and little ponds to sit by. She loved nature, that woman, so I found somewhere she could enjoy it."

"Man," I said. "Sorry to hear that. Does she have... dementia?"

"Oh yeah. It's pretty bad. Thankfully the one thing she always does seem to remember is me, though not a lot of our memories together. At least she's never called me by a different name. Once that happens, I'm gonna lose it, I swear."

I felt terrible that I hadn't even known about this. "How about we go and see her once we've figured everything out back home? We could go there on the way back to Atlanta in a couple weeks."

"Thanks, that'd be nice. I guarantee she remembers you. I told her about our little game, by the way."

I jerked my head so fast to look at her that the car swerved a foot or so. "What? No way. You told her?"

"Not until recently, at night, almost like bedtime stories. It made her laugh and cry but overall I think she liked it. We even tried a few rounds between each other. Hers sucked, though. Stuff like heart attacks or dying in a car accident. No creativity whatsoever."

I took all this in, feeling kinda weird.

"She loved you, ya know," Andrea said. "She really did. She must've said at least a thousand times over the years, 'Why didn't you marry David? Why, why, why didn't you marry David?' I tried to tell her things don't always work out like they do in the fairy tales."

"Don't they usually get eaten in the fairy tales?" I asked.

"Not in the Disney versions, which were the only ones I knew."

Andrea seemed lost in some kind of deep reverie. I wanted to forget about the past, not talk about it anymore, because it could only go downhill. But she kept going.

"All these years, and we've never gone back to what happened the night they captured Pee Wee. Worst night of both our lives and I barely remember a thing. And I know you saw things that I didn't."

Her tone was slightly accusatory. "You know I blocked out most of it, too. Every therapist I've ever gone to got less out of me than the one before. We were *16*, Andrea. Trained soldiers can't handle some of the trauma we went through. We're lucky that we lived through it, even more so that we survived psychologically."

"Speak for yourself," she half-muttered, and I couldn't tell if she was joking.

"Andrea, I swear on the life of my kids that I've never held anything back from you. Not one thing. What happened that night... I can only remember it as flashes of this and that, none of it good. Why do you think they took me to a treatment facility for six weeks? I couldn't sleep, couldn't eat, couldn't stop trembling. It's no wonder that my mind blocked out what it could—some kind of defense mechanism. I'm not sure I'd be here if I could recall everything perfectly."

I was rambling, no doubt about it. Speaking of things I hadn't talked about in years, not even with my therapist or my parents.

"What does it matter, anyway?" I asked. "They caught the guy and the murders stopped. Who cares exactly how we got there. I mean, have *you* held anything back?"

"No. I just feel like we went through all that shit together but then didn't get to *finish* it together. I've always felt like something is missing inside of me. That's all."

This was the first time we'd ever had this conversation. It left me dumbfounded and I went silent. The night in question was more like a series of colors in my mind instead of specific images and occurrences. Dark colors, colors in 3-D, spattered with blood.

"I'm sorry, David," she said after an uncomfortable couple of minutes. "It sounds like I'm sitting here blaming you or something crazy like that. I promise that's not it. I'm just trying to say I have genuine, real regret that I don't know how it all came to an end. It's obviously not your fault. I'm sorry I brought it up. Sincerely sorry, not pouty sorry."

"No, no, it's okay," I said, though probably not very convincingly. This whole idea to drive out to Andrea's place had been going along so well, and now it felt like we'd hit a huge patch of quicksand, sinking away from the world.

She reached over and squeezed my shoulder. "Honest to God. I'm sorry. It's like... not remembering makes me feel like I didn't do everything in my power to save you."

I gave her a quick look, tried to show her with my eyes that, of all things, she certainly didn't need to apologize.

"Andrea," I said, "I have absolutely nothing but good feelings for you, top to bottom, through and through. If you've felt guilty or regretful about anything—*any* of this shit—then that breaks my heart. We were *kids*, man. It's like Pee Wee's last victory over us that we still beat ourselves up about stuff. He really did a number on us."

"*That*, he did."

I wanted to ask about her dad, Antony, the subject of our cruel game in the past. *Maybe he's dead*, I thought, and I'm not ashamed to admit that would've made me glad, indeed. Maybe he'd even gone out spectacularly, doomed to one of the awful scenarios we'd imagined for him. But we'd spoken of enough dark things, and I made a mental note to ask her later in the night, hopefully over drinks. Plenty of drinks.

We rode on a for a few minutes in silence, and the tension in the air thankfully melted away. Especially when we saw the exit leading to our old hometown. Without saying a word, I knew she looked forward to those last miles driving through the country, the farms, the fields. Although today they'd be drenched in rain, that wouldn't take away from the magic of the land in which we'd been raised.

"Home, sweet, home," she whispered, echoing my feelings.

I turned onto a narrow two-lane road and headed toward Lynchburg.

6

"Guys, you remember Andrea, my best friend from high school."

We'd just walked into the house, and all four of my kids were there to greet us. My guess was that Hazel had been watching the rain through the window—she loved a good storm, a lot like her daddy in that regard—because she excitedly opened the door before we'd even reached the porch steps. Now we were inside, everyone standing there with that slightly awkward stance one takes while you wait for the ice to break. So far there was no sign of my parents.

"It's been a couple years but come on," I said when no one really responded, other than Hazel stepping up close and beaming a smile up at Andrea as if she hoped for candy or money. "Wesley, I know you remember."

He just gave a goofy smile in reply, and I was a little heartened that this was such a regular response from him. Maybe he'd started the path to recovery.

"Nice to see you guys again," Andrea said, her gaze sweeping all four of them, her voice filled with warmth. "Although you were teeny tiny." Logan stared at her with absolutely no expression whatsoever.

"You always send us something cool for Christmas," Hazel replied. "Last year daddy said a cuss word and said he forgot to send you a card."

"Aww, how sweet." Andrea tilted her gaze at me. "He's always been so thoughtful."

Hazel giggled, and I offered an apologetic *I give up* shrug to Andrea. "If I forget to send you something next year, I promise to cut off every finger on my right hand."

"Alright, you all heard him," Andrea said. "I'm gonna hold you to that."

Hazel giggled again. (Giggle is the only proper word for her.)

"Why don't you have a seat and I'll go find my parents. You four entertain Andrea for a few minutes, okay?"

"We'll be just fine," Andrea responded, taking Hazel by the hand and walking over to the couch. She sat down, Hazel sat in her lap, and Mason plopped down next to them. Wesley did so on her other side. Logan just continued staring as if he didn't quite know what to make of her.

"Logan," I said. "Mind your manners. Be right back."

7

I found my dad in the back shed—one of its three steel roll-up doors open to the wind and weather—as he hammered away at something on his workbench. I swear the man went out there just to break things apart and put them back together sometimes. He'd never been the most social of butterflies, and he always found an excuse to escape to his shed or work around the farm.

"What's up, Old Man?" I asked him just as he yanked a nail out of a piece of old wood.

Startled, he turned to me and watched as I shook some of the rain off of my shirt and hair. The shed of a farmer was a human institution, coming in all shapes, sizes, and materials, but always with that same musty, sawdusty, tainted smell. Simultaneously sweet and rank, a raw and primal scent that reached through your nose and down into your gut and stayed there. I liked it, and I'm not sure if that's because of my upbringing or because it's actually pleasant. My guess is the former.

"Well, hey, there, bub." Dad put down his medieval torture devices and wiped his hands on the work apron he wore. "Didn't expect you back so soon. What'd she do, spit in your face when you showed up?"

"No, she welcomed me with open arms, thank you very much. In fact, she came back with me. With a packed suitcase."

"Oh, hell." He gave me a knowing look.

"We're just friends, Dad. Always were just friends, still are. But it makes me feel better to have her around in a pinch."

"If you say so. We can put her up in Patsy's room, I reckon. Not that it matters to you yahoos, sleeping out in the living room no matter how many beds we've got."

I took in a deep breath, relishing the pungent smell of the sanctuary, as I looked around the old place—its endless rows of haphazardly stacked shelves, mounds of beat up, rusted machinery, hundreds of tools on iron hooks and nails, bags of feed and seed—some so old they'd probably expired in the last millennium. There were bikes and tricycles, balls of every sport, most of them flat, boxes stacked on boxes, their contents so mysterious they could make a reality show of opening them up. There was an ancient tractor—having long given up its sputtering ghost —parked on one end, a new one parked on the other. In the middle section there were about six generations of lawn mowers, their blades long dull. That old shed was full of just about everything known to man, and I often wished I could erase my memory and freshly explore every square foot, discovering its many treasures one by one.

I walked up to Dad and gave him a hug, wet clothes and all.

"Whatcha working on out here?" I asked. "And where's Mom?"

"Oh, she went to the grocery store, probably figuring out you planned to bring that lady-friend of yours back with ya. As for me..." He waved at the cluttered workbench as if his latest project should be self-explanatory. I looked around as if I could indeed figure his madness out, and my eyes noticed the steel cube of a safe tucked under his bench, the padlock still firmly fastened. I pointed at it.

"What's actually in that thing, Dad? Money? Please tell me it's money."

He shook his head. "Like I said, you'll find out when I'm dead. No offense, but I hope that's later than sooner. Patience, boy. Most things are better not rushed to be known. Some, never."

I crinkled my eyes at this mysterious statement. "So it's not money."

He grunted and swatted me on the back. "Why don't you go on back inside, now, let me finish up. Won't be long and your mom'll be home, we can start thinking about supper. Oh, she'll be wantin' to impress that girlfriend of yours, that's for sure. Maybe you'll get lucky tonight."

I didn't grace him with a response, only an eye-roll. Turning to leave, I couldn't help but glance at that damned safe and its taunting padlock one last time.

8

The rest of that day and evening was so nice, I could almost imagine that my son hadn't been kidnapped and no one had dumped a headless body on our farm. Andrea and my mom warmed to each other as if a single day hadn't passed since we were kids, and I learned about the last couple years of my old friend's life far more efficiently when Mom was in charge of the conversation. About her latest work in marketing, her running craze—she'd completed three marathons, which sounded like the worst torture imaginable—and I really felt dumb when she lamented the death of her dog, Spitz. My guilt slashed another notch in its belt.

Andrea and I helped with supper, a meal that in sheer scope rivaled most families' Thanksgiving dinner (let's just say that there was a turkey involved but it wasn't even the main course). I was glad for it, though, because it took a long time to prepare, and my kids hung around the kitchen, talking and laughing and trying to top each other at impressing my friend. I knew that on some level they probably hoped this might turn into something, finally, that maybe Andrea could be like a new mother to them.

Late into the evening, we found ourselves slouched around the living room like fat rock-hugging seals, lazing in the sun. Two or three hours had passed since our gargantuan meal, but I still felt as full as a grain silo in October. The Braves game was on, just like it was every night, and they were losing ten to three.

"Dadgum catcher has three passed balls tonight," my dad said from his mammoth chair. "The boy can't tell a curveball from his left nut."

Wesley, who'd more or less acted himself all night, though a little moody, looked at me as if he needed my permission to laugh.

"Dad, watch your language around the kids," I said automatically. I loved baseball as much as anybody on Earth, but this game had been decided in the bottom of the first, when the Mets scored six runs. "Why don't we play a game or something?"

Wesley grunted. Mason was asleep on the floor. Logan played with a wooden train set from the 60s. Andrea studied the ball-game on TV with exaggerated intensity, obviously trying to impress my dad. Mom was nowhere to be seen. Hazel perked up, though, ran over to me.

"I'll play a game," she said, literally bouncing on her toes. "If I watch one more quarter of this game I might have to go drown myself in the swamp."

"Inning, sweetie. They're called innings." Her lack of nomen-clature had nothing to do with being a girl, only her age. She knew sports better than any of my other kids.

"Oh yeah. And in hockey they're called periods. Like I'll have one day."

This made me sit up straight as a two-by-four, and even Andrea made a sound that was somewhere between a *Ha!* and a cry of shock. Wesley once again looked to me for approval to laugh.

"Honey, that's..." I was at a complete loss for words. I had no idea if she'd been making a joke or not, and I realized my future parenting a teenager of the female persuasion was going to be one hell of a ride. "I don't know. Yes, I guess you're right. It's the same word. Funny, huh."

My face was scarlet, and Andrea had a hand over her mouth, trying not to outright guffaw at my haplessness. Dad seemed completely oblivious to the entire situation.

"So, about that game," I said.

"Dad, can I talk to you for a second?" Wesley asked. "Alone?" It came out of nowhere, and seemed so adult, that I floundered for a bit, almost unsure that he'd actually said it.

Andrea came to my rescue. "Hazel, why don't we play check-ers? I see a board on that shelf over by your grandpa. Your dad and Wesley are gonna go talk in the kitchen."

"Yeah," I said, standing up. "Yeah, come on, Wesley. You guys have fun. Hazel, remember you have to jump if you're able to. None of that baby checkers stuff anymore."

"I *know*, Dad." She was already pulling the thing off the shelf, almost stumbling over Logan in the process.

Wesley avoided my eyes as he stepped past me on his way to the kitchen, and as I followed him, a litany of thoughts ran through my mind. My eldest son had been *kidnapped* for crying out loud, and we'd barely said two words about it since. My certainty that we should move on, act like normal, play and eat and laugh—it all crumbled during those few steps it took me to walk out of the living room. We should've gone back to Georgia the next day, should've gotten him right into a therapist, should've... My heart was sinking. The decision to stay with my parents had seemed so right—how was I supposed to know that Dicky Gaskins would escape from jail and dump a dead body in the swamp? What was Wesley about to tell me?

"Dad, can I go camping tomorrow night?"

He stood by the refrigerator and I faced him, three feet away. Both of us had our arms folded, serious looks on our faces, as comical as the question he'd just asked.

"Come again?"

"Jeffrey and Brett texted me. They're going camping by the river. They said it's fun when it rains like this because it's so high."

I stared at him, sure he was putting me on. Jeffrey and Brett were his cousins, my sister Evelyn's kids. But if this had been all he wanted, why had he needed to ask me in such dramatic fashion, alone? And who in the holy hell would want to camp in the rain?

"Uh, son, have you been watching this downpour? Camping in this weather is out of the question. Especially..." I hadn't told him about Dicky Gaskins and his Great Escape yet, hoped I never had to. I sighed, tried to cover up my mistake. "Especially after everything that's happened. You need to be with your family. I need you to be close to me. Why don't we ask them to spend the night over here?"

"Dad, come on." I studied him as he replied, looking for clues that this hadn't been what he really wanted to talk about. "They have a camper trailer, so it's not like we'd be sleeping in the mud." He sounded about as convincing as a rookie crop auctioneer.

"Wesley, what's this really about? Why'd you want to talk to me in here?"

He hesitated just long enough to know I'd hit the nail on the head, but he didn't give in.

"Nothing." He feigned a look of surprise. "I just didn't want the other kids to know or they'd beg to go, too."

"Uh-huh."

"Dad. Serious. I just wanna go camping. It's with my cousins."

I didn't have the heart, not yet, to tell him the real reason he couldn't go. "I don't feel good about it. I was driving in that storm today and it's bad, only supposed to get worse. Let's just go eat at the Compass tomorrow night and have a big sleepover like the good old days. Okay?"

"Well, can I at least sleep over at their house instead of here?"

He got me with that. Damn, kids are good at what they do.

"I, uh, I guess. Maybe. We'll see." My hemming and hawing was an embarrassment. After what he'd been through I hated the idea of disappointing him.

"Dad. Come on."

I stared at him, longing for the days when they were two years old and you just told them, *No, you can't have another cookie.* There were a lot worse things than a kid wanting to hang out with his own cousins. I could ask Sheriff Taylor to send a patrol car to watch at my sister's house while he was there.

"Okay, fine."

"Awesome, thanks." He turned to leave but I reached out and grabbed his arm.

"Wait." *Now's my chance*, I thought. He was in a good mood for the first time since the incident, and we'd yet to dig deeply into what had happened. "Let's talk for a sec."

His face melted a little, and I understood completely. Of course he wanted to forget about it, maybe even pretend it never happened. I didn't blame him. So I kept it simple.

"Are you doing okay? I've been bustin' my balls trying to think how I should act, what I should say... You went through something pretty traumatic."

He nodded, looking at the floor.

"Maybe it'll help to talk about it," I suggested. "You know me, bud. No judgment, no pretension, no bull... crap. You can tell me anything."

"I know." He took a breath as if he might say more, but then just let it out, full of silence.

Man, this was fragile. So fragile. I was so out of my element I might as well have been naked, standing on a rubber chicken, singing instead of speaking. I didn't want to lose him.

"Listen, we don't need to rush it. I'm ready, though, drop of a dime. Just say the word and we can talk through things. I really do think it'll help."

He nodded again, his face awash with relief that he'd escaped having to speak about what had happened just yet—other than what he'd told the police, which was a whole lot of nothing. What if he was holding back? What if that monster had done something to him, and he was too ashamed to tell anyone?

I put my hands on both of his shoulders, suddenly filled with emotion, my eyes glazed with tears. "Listen to me. Okay? Look at me."

He lifted his eyes, did as he was asked. Our gazes locked onto each other, perhaps more deeply than ever before. I tried to pour my soul into that look, putting as much feeling as I could into my expression.

"I love you, son. We kid, we joke around, we can be goofy as hell and cynical and sarcastic. And maybe I don't say it enough. But you need to..." I faltered, choking up as much as if I'd swallowed an entire egg in one gulp. My love for this skinny human standing before me was astronomical, geological, universal, eternal. It swelled within my chest so powerfully that I didn't know if I'd ever be able to speak again.

"Dad?" he asked weakly.

I swallowed, doing my best to recover, but when I finally spoke again there was a definite squeak to my voice. "You need to know how much I love you. It's beyond anything I can put into words. And I'm sorry you went through... what you went through. I'm sorry I wasn't there to protect you."

"I love you, too, Dad."

It was so simple but almost broke me. I pulled him into the fiercest hug imaginable, threatening the strength of his rib cage as I'd done Hazel while searching in that corn field, and let the tears wash down my face, knowing he couldn't see them. Even now, as I write these words, I shake with frustration that I can't properly convey the love I felt for him in that moment, and other moments in the near future. To his credit and to my great joy, he hugged me back as desperately as I held onto him. Finally, finally, I pulled away, no longer ashamed to let him see that I had cried. Maybe it would show him what I couldn't find the words to describe.

"You've looked more attractive in your life," he said.

A laugh exploded from my chest, intensified by the pure emotion sizzling through my veins. I probably sprayed him a little, but he had the kindness not to wipe it away. "Hilarious."

"Thanks for letting me spend the night at the cousins' tomorrow."

"Yeah, yeah, of course. It'll be good to hang with Jeffrey and Brett."

He smiled, looking like his old self, then turned and jaunted back toward the living room. I watched him go, feeling for all the world like I'd just been had, in a way. It didn't matter. Nothing could take away from the moment we'd shared. I did, however, make a mental note to call my sister first thing tomorrow and talk things through.

9

An hour later, everyone was in position to sleep for the night except for Andrea. She sat by me on the couch—my bed—with the three youngest kids sprawled on the floor at our feet. Wesley was already snoring on the recliner, his mouth hanging open like a whale about to suck in some brine. *That's a good sign*, I thought. Sleeping like he's got no care in the world. He'd left the lamp on, and a Joe Hill book lay sprawled on his chest.

The two floor fans were running at full blast, making the entire room a wind tunnel.

Andrea had to talk directly into my ear to be heard. "How do you people sleep like this? If you don't freeze to death, you'll go deaf from all that noise."

I patted her hand like she was a simpleton. "Ah, you have a lot to learn. This is what you call pure bliss. That soothing sound, the feel of a breeze on your face. It's better than sex."

"Then I'm guessing you've only done it four times." She pointed at each one of my kids in turn.

This made me snicker; I couldn't help it. "Good one."

She leaned into me, put her head on my shoulder. There's some old saying about slipping into an old pair of shoes, which has to be the worst possible analogy for anything associated with

Andrea, but it was something like that. This was how it had always been in high school. We flirted, we kissed, even did other things. But we were never... committed. Never in a true relationship. We were friends, powerful friends. And we'd gone right back to it.

"This is why I came begging for you," I said. "This. I needed this. I needed you."

She patted my chest. "I know. It's all like it's meant to be, like no time has passed. I'm glad I'm here."

I swung my arm up to put it around her, squeezed her into a hug. "You ever wonder—" I began, but she smashed a finger against my lips.

"Not now. I'm tired. Please let me fall asleep like this. That fan's kind of soothing."

Smiling with satisfaction at her enlightenment, I shifted to get a little more comfortable, and she shifted with me.

Then I fell asleep with the wind on my face.

10

The next morning, Andrea and I were at the Sumter library the second it opened. Rain fell in sheets outside, and the wind had made our umbrellas all but worthless. In a short sprint that couldn't have been more than 40 feet from parking lot to door, my clothes were half-drenched.

Shocking even my numbed senses, I saw that Grace Habersham still worked as a librarian. That woman must've been even older than Betty Joyner when I was a kid, and if your memory serves you, you'll recall I thought that lady was pushing 90 back *then*. Yet here was Mrs. Habersham, looking exactly as I remembered during my countless trips to the library as a child. I was pretty sure she wore the same outfit as well, a big-collared, frilly blousy thing with a skirt that kissed the floor as she walked. She was a vampire, the only explanation. A matronly one to be sure, but a vampire.

"May I help you kids?" She asked when we entered the front doors, frazzled by the beating we'd taken from the storm.

Andrea looked at me. *Kids?* her expression said. I was just relieved that the old lady didn't recognize me.

"Yes, ma'am," I replied. "We'd like to look at old records of Sumter and Lynchburg. Newspaper articles, census reports, land records, stuff like that."

"Why, certainly, dear. Follow me and I'll show you the Historical Records Room." She gave a cute little wave and walked toward the stairs in the back. One set went up, one set went down. "Now, it's in the basement, so I hope that doesn't spook you too much."

"I think we'll be okay," Andrea responded, as sweet as could be. "We kinda like dark, scary places."

The little old lady twittered the laugh-version of toodle-loo. "Just go right down these stairs and head to the very back. You won't miss it."

"Thanks, Mrs. Habersham," I said.

She gave me a long look. "I know you, don't I? You probably came here as a young boy."

For some reason that comment pricked my heart. But I wasn't in the mood to reminisce.

"Sorry, ma'am. Just visiting." It was the best non-lie I could come up with in a pinch.

"Well, hope ya'll find whatcher lookin' for. Just holler if ya need any help." She smiled, though I thought I saw a spark of suspicion somewhere in her eyes.

Andrea and I headed down the stairs, holding hands.

II

I didn't know exactly what we were looking for. Anything. Everything. Nothing. But I had been restless all morning and I wanted to do some research about the old days, read the original newspaper articles about Pee Wee Gaskins and all the crap that happened back then. Dicky, son of Pee Wee, had said some strange things, choked on his own tongue, kidnapped my son, threatened him, escaped from jail. A headless body had been found on my parents' property—just like the bodies in '89. I needed to know everything I possibly could about the Gaskins family, the original murders, and what had happened since. If nothing else, I needed to refresh my memory if possible—it seemed I only remembered about half of what I experienced at the time, and not the worst parts at that.

For Wesley, for my family—hell, for all of Sumter Country—I needed to do this.

Just in case.

For two hours, Andrea and I split up, perusing, digging, reading, with no real direction to our search. It's really hard to find something when you don't know what it is. But searched, we did. I started with the obvious—the articles written in *The Item* when it all went down—and I was surprised at what little detail had been provided. By the time Donald Henry Gaskins, aka Pee Wee, had been caught and captured, more than 10 bodies had been found, all of them submerged in various places within Pudding Swamp. But Pee Wee grew himself a Big Mouth while in the Big House, and some say he bragged he'd killed more than 100 souls. Like any rational person, I figured the truth lay somewhere in the middle.

Ironically, after all the nasty things he'd done, it was a murder he committed while in prison that finally put Gaskins on Death Row. He was executed nine years later, almost to the day. I knew none of this, as I purposefully blocked that man out of my life

once and for all after he'd been captured. But the details fasci-
nated me, now. Apparently, it's tough to find the time or necessi-
ties to cut a man's head off while locked up in maximum security,
but Pee Wee was able to construct a fake radio packed to the hilt
with C-4 explosive. That's what killed a man named Rudolph
Tyner.

This story didn't disgust me. I only found it... odd.

One of the articles stated that Pee Wee later claimed that
"the last thing Tyner heard was me laughing." Apparently, once a
mean son of a bitch, always a mean son of a bitch. In fact, for a
while there Pee Wee laid claim to a moniker which fit all too well
in my opinion: The Meanest Man in America. Although it's
strange. Before things happened, I hadn't thought of him as
mean, necessarily. Just creepy. Sad and creepy. Small and sad and
creepy.

I found another article about the sting operation the police
and FBI held in conjunction to capture Pee Wee, but I put it
aside. At least for now. My memories of that night in particular
were mostly hidden away in a very dark corner of my brain, and I
suddenly changed my mind. I *didn't* want to light a candle to it.
As I write my tale, I find myself wishing I could've kept it locked
away forever.

"Hey, David, come look at this."

I was happy to tear myself away from that trip down memory
lane, anyway.

"What ya got?" I asked, walking over to where she studied
something laid out on a table.

"Look at this land deed, from like 200 years ago."

I put my hands on the table and leaned in to take a gander,
but all I saw was a plot map and a bunch of stuff written in
extremely slanted, old-timey cursive that looked like chicken
scratch to me. My eyes hurt at even the thought of trying to
decipher any of it.

"What's it for?"

"As far as I can tell, it's for the property where your dad grew up, before he married your mom, sold this land, and took over the Fincher's farm. See those areas with the shaded ink? I think that's the Pudding Swamp sections that cross the property. It's kinda over by Mayewood."

"Huh. Interesting."

She put her hand on top of mine. "No, that's not what I wanted to show you."

"Then what is?"

She held my gaze for a second, then pointed at a black line near the bottom of the page, right above which some of that chicken scratch had been written. I thought I saw the name *Player* right away. And then...

"David," Andrea whispered. "The Players and a family named Gaskins jointly purchased this land way back in the late 1700s."

I sat down, said nothing, having no idea what it meant.

She looked at me. "What the hell?"

CHAPTER TWELVE

Lynchburg, South Carolina
June 1989

I

After I woke up in the woods, after a man wearing a plastic bag on his head taunted me, after he put a bag on my own head and gave me the next terror of my life, after he said all those weird things about something called a Reticence and a Waking and that I'd soon find out why I'm involved and after he threatened my life...

After all of that, I obeyed him and waited 30 minutes. To be safe, I let at least an hour go by, shivering in the darkness, watching the shadows for bag-headed men. I sat in a pool of trauma, aware of it, even at that age, aware that I couldn't possibly survive things like this without psychological damage. But there was nothing to be done. So I sat up, pulled my legs to my chest, hugged them tight, trembled, and waited.

I finally sneaked into the house, into my room, into my bed, relieved beyond description that my parents didn't wake up. As an adult, my decisions over those next 12 hours or so seem ludicrous, outrageous... Well, childish: I decided not to tell my parents or the police, at least not yet. I don't know why. I couldn't explain it then, even to myself, and I can't explain it now. But I know it was based in fear, maybe even Fear with a capital *F*. Because it had become a personal noun, a living entity, a beast, a presence, hovering above me, below me, within me.

I was scared to death to do anything. Fear stopped me. Pee Wee—or someone working with him—had become a magical creature, donning a mask, appearing in the night like a dream, waking me in the woods to haunt me. If I told, he might swoop in and punish the boy he'd chosen to torment. I didn't know why he'd chosen me, what he had meant when he said that I was involved somehow. It couldn't have been just that I'd seen him in the forest that night, sawing away...

A frightening thought came as I lay in my bed, thinking through these things. What if he'd been spying on me, watching me, guessing my movements? What if he murdered George Holloway that night *because* I was going to be there? The trail Andrea and I had walked was a popular one, and we'd gone there many times. Maybe he'd chosen me from the very beginning.

For what?

This is only a sampling of the things that raced through my mind as I lay curled in bed, waiting for morning. There were darker things that didn't stay with me, as would be the case with a lot that happened over the next few days. Memories that would end up dormant for decades before rising from the ashes. Although I didn't sleep, I did make one resolution that made me feel a little better: there was one person I could tell. One person I *had* to tell.

Andrea.

First thing tomorrow.

2

The next morning, I walked down Main Street in Sumter, pretending that Officer Fuller didn't slowly coast along the road behind me in his police cruiser after he'd dropped me off. He must've fallen asleep during the night, having missed quite the show. Or, for all I knew, Pee Wee had somehow put him to sleep. The way my mind was working, the way Fear paralyzed my actions, this only brought relief. I had convinced myself during the long night that Pee Wee would grow tired of games and kill me if the cops got involved again. He had become mythical in his powers.

I took in my small town as I walked along the sidewalk, taking comfort in what had always been there, steady and unchanging. The heat was already beginning to boil on the long street, despite the early hour, the sun just peeking over the eastern edge of the Main Street buildings. It reflected brightly off the windows on the west side, which in turn made the cars parked along the curb shine, as if they'd all just been scrubbed clean.

I passed by shops and businesses that had been there since I remembered, and probably decades before that. They were packed in on both sides like old toy blocks that had lost some of their shape, nothing quite clean or straight, some leaning this way, some leaning that way, not a one of them matching its neighbors in height or width. Windows were permanently fogged by age in most storefronts, topped by once-colorful canopies faded by the sun, the canvas worn and torn. The signs were my favorite, most of them vintage, making the entire street seem like something plucked out of the fifties.

Simon Says Sandwiches: Free Cokes on Sundays!

Billy Ray's Salon (The whole town sniggered at the fact he called his cheap hair-cutting place a *Salon*, as if he'd trained at a cosmetology school in Paris or something.)

Lemmon's Furniture: Everything Always 30% Off! (This made no sense to me then, makes no sense to me now. If it's always 30% off, then by definition it's *never* 30% off because that's the normal price.)

Parker Savings and Loan, the "S" in Savings a dollar sign. Of course. Of all the places in downtown Sumter, this business always held the least interest for me. It just might've been the only place on Main Street in which I'd never actually set foot.

Grandma Sycamore's Antiques, whose namesake had to have been dead for at least a century because her store looked much older than that.

The Chat and Chew, a little burger joint that my dad had been known to call, The *Rat* and Chew.

Bob's Books, where you could find used paperbacks, comic books, and magazines aplenty, but if you wanted to see the dirty stuff in Bob's back room you had to be 18 years old. It was in this place I first learned the wonders of caped men and women in tights (in the comics section, not in the naughty back room).

There were other places, all as familiar as the pecan trees in our yard. *The Sumter Public Library*, where the ageless lady named Mrs. Habersham ruled with iron hair instead of an iron fist. *Ed & Whitey's, The Compass, Whittacker Mortuary, Rusty's Auto Shop, Rexall Drugs*, of course. At least five or six clothing and department stores that hit all the demographics accordingly.

Seeing all of this, walking by these pieces of a life that had stayed constant, and had always been safe, a haven for weekends and holidays, warm summer nights... It made me feel better, gave me courage to talk to Andrea and figure things out.

I finally reached Delilah's Diner, a place that served breakfast all day and I couldn't fathom anyone ever ordering otherwise. You can mess up a salad. You can mess up a steak. But unless you take the bacon off the skillet too early, you can't mess up breakfast.

A bell jingled as I stepped inside, cool air making my sweat-skimmed skin tingle. Andrea was already there, sitting at a table in the back corner. She waved goofily, mocking the very idea of meeting at a diner like melodramatic grown-ups in a bad romance movie.

I headed toward her, noticing that some of the old fellas from the Fox Pen—the ones who'd kept us in stitches with their ridiculous stories and arguments—were lined up, like ducks in a row, along the bar that ran the length of the diner. Kentucky, the moss-bearded dairy farmer; Mr. Fullerton, the town lawyer who was taller than Paul Bunyan; old Gramps, crouching over the counter with both arms circling his plate as if someone might snatch his food before he could wolf it down; Sheriff Taylor and a couple of his deputies; Branson; a few others—they probably all loved this place because it was one of the few things left in the world that was older than them.

Most of them ignored me, but Sheriff Taylor gave me the head nod common to those parts, and Kentucky did a double take, as if Jack the Ripper had just strolled in. He covered it up with a hasty smile.

"Mornin,' Mr. Player," the old dairy man said. He had some egg in his beard, which probably improved its scent.

"Hey, there, Kentucky." His last name was Fryerson, but no one called him Mr. Fryerson.

He gently grabbed my arm just as I reached him. "Hey, if old Henry hadn't come along, there wouldn't be but *one* Dixon boy today!" He let out a low, rumbling chuckle that turned into a food-throated cough. "Remember that story?"

"Yeah. That was a good one." It really had been, the story of the Dixon boys throwing their poor dog off the side of the watchtower. A little dark, but no doubt entertaining. "Don't eat too much, you might get fat."

He downright guffawed at that one, rubbing his generous belly as he turned back to his food.

I walked up to Andrea and bent down to kiss her on the

cheek, then sat across from her at the table. It seemed very New York-ish, a fitting conclusion to what she'd started with the overzealous wave when I'd entered the diner.

"How goes it?" I said in greeting.

"It goes. I ordered you grits, eggs, and toast from Francis. Since I did all the work, I guess I'll let you pay for it."

"That's really sweet. Thank you."

She leaned forward, putting her elbows on the table. "So you were being pretty cryptic on the phone this morning. Speaking of, my mom says thanks a lot for waking her up. Our phone has the worst ring of all time. Sounds like a cat ripping its own heart out."

"Wow. You sure know how to go dark sometimes. Tell your mom I said sorry."

She waved it away. "Oh, please. That woman loves you to pieces. So... what's up?"

My spirits had been lifted by my walk through town, but now reality hit. Last night's insane, creepy encounter with Pee Wee had in fact happened, and it was time to tell her about it.

"Last night... This is gonna sound really weird, I have no idea how it happened, but I woke up in the middle of the woods. In the middle of the night. And Pee Wee was out there. I think it was Pee Wee. He had a... plastic bag over his head with a slit ripped near the mouth. So he could breathe. Told me a bunch of scary stuff, then he left."

Andrea stared at me, an odd look on her face. I realized she half-thought I was kidding.

"In a nutshell," I said dryly.

"What in the world are you talking about?"

I could tell she'd quickly recovered, realizing there's no way I'd joke about this stuff, but that didn't mean that my quick version of the story made a lick of sense. I was about to respond when Francis Daniels seemingly popped out of thin air to put our food on the table.

"Ya'll enjoy," she said, already five steps away by the second word.

Surprisingly, I actually felt hungry. I scooped up some grits, pushed a bit of egg on it, blew the heavenly mixture off, then shoved it in my mouth. The salty goodness filled my whole body with warmth.

"David," Andrea said, approaching annoyed. I'd scared her, I could tell.

"Sorry," I said, although I took another bite. "I'm just kind of going crazy. But it really did happen. Someone drugged me or... something. Then I woke up in the woods. And some Baghead was out there acting like a freak."

Andrea was slowly shaking her head. "This is insane. I... My mind can't even process this. What's this about a plastic bag on his head?"

I told her the story, beginning to end, filling in every detail I could remember. I kept my voice low, of course, but the diner was loud enough I didn't worry about being overheard. But even I had a hard time believing the words that spilled from my mouth. When I finished, I took an enormous bite of food, making some point I didn't even understand.

"I don't know what to say," Andrea said quietly. "You know I don't like the F-word all that much. Being Catholic and all."

I nodded, even though I'd known plenty of Catholics that must've missed that rule somewhere along the line.

"But this is effed up, David. Royally. We've gotta go to the police. *Today*. Is Officer Fuller out there?"

"Yeah, but something's holding me back. I don't know."

"Are you insane? We *have* to tell them."

My head felt so heavy I had to hold it up with my hands, elbows on the table. "I know. I know. But I'm scared to death. It seems like he's always right around the corner. If I go to the cops, I don't know, maybe instead of messin' with me he'll just chop my friggin' head off."

Andrea sighed, visually frustrated, almost shaking. "I'm scared, too."

"Hey, there David. Andrea."

I looked up—*way* up—and saw Mr. Fullerton standing next to our table. Kentucky was right next to him.

"Hey," I replied, rather weakly.

"How you holding up?" the lawyer asked.

"Okay, I guess."

"Your mama and daddy doing well?"

I nodded.

"How about you, Ms. Llerenas? You and your mama doing alright?"

She shrugged unconvincingly. "Yeah, pretty good, I guess."

"Life can be a real pain in the... bee-hind sometimes." He returned his attention to me. "I was real sorry to read that article in the paper about you. Such a shame." I couldn't quite tell if he meant because he thought it was bogus or because he was disappointed in me for throwing Alejandro under the bus. "I know I can't do much, but I took care of your bill. Least I can do."

"Oh. Oh, well thanks. That's really nice... You didn't have to do that."

"We're always here for you and yours, son. Always."

"That's right, boy," Kentucky added. He'd cleared his considerable beard of its egg ornamentation. "If I catch hide or hair of that peckerwood Gaskins, I'll string him up myself before the cops can say, 'Stop! In the name of the law!'" He chuckled at this, though I failed to see the humor. I did, however, appreciate the sentiment.

"Thanks, Kentucky."

Mr. Fullerton folded his arms, took on a contemplative air. "Hard to figure out old Pee Wee Gaskins, ain't it? He's been getting in trouble with the law his whole damned life, been in prison more times than you can count. But I didn't know he had it in him to do this."

I hadn't known that about Pee Wee. I'd always thought he was just a quiet man with no friends. But having seen him saw a man's head off, it didn't surprise me that he'd had run-ins with the police before.

Kentucky cleared his throat then spoke up. "Did ya'll know that Gaskins' kin goes back purtin near 200 years in these parts? Hell, maybe even longer. Just like my family and yours, David. Settlers of Puddin' Swamp itself."

This *did* surprise me. First I learned he had a kid, now I learn his family's been in the same county as mine for centuries. Maybe it wasn't a coincidence after all that he hated me so much. For all I knew, our families had once been like the Hatfields and McCoys, squabbling for so long they'd forgotten what the argument was about. The idea was ludicrous, but I felt it impossible to believe there wasn't something to our shared history.

"Damn, boy, you okay?" Kentucky asked.

I was doing that thing where you stare off into space, probably with slightly crossed eyes.

"Sorry. Just thinking."

"Looked like you'd done gone and had one of those anyaclisms. Eyes as blank as roadkill possum. You sure you're okay?"

"I believe the word you're lookin' for is *aneurism*," Mr. Fullerton interjected. "Not whatever the hell that was you said."

"Well laws, ain't you smart? Didn't know you'd up and come a brain surgeon all a sudden. Remind me to call someone else when I have my own anyaclism."

"Aneurism."

"I reckon we'll agree to disagree." Kentucky winked at me and leaned closer. "Just tryin' to cheer you up, boy. I'll have one of my fellas deliver ya'll some free milk and cream later. Sound good? Say hi to your folks for me."

"Thanks, Kentucky. Mr. Fullerton."

"Stay in school, kids," the lawyer said, giving a not-so-subtle head-tilt toward his friend.

They both gave us a warm smile then headed off to do whatever people like that did during the day. As soon as they were out of sight, I noticed our waitress, Francis Daniels, standing nearby, looking straight at us. Her face was as pale as the ghost she must've just seen.

"You okay, Francis?" Andrea asked. "They said they paid our bill."

The petite woman came closer, her hands trembling as she put them on the table, seemingly to steady herself. She'd wedged a folded-up piece of paper between two of her fingers.

"This... This is for you." She dropped the paper and hurried off, disappearing through the swinging double-doors that led to the kitchen.

Andrea and I looked at each other for a second, as if time had slid to a stop. Then we both reached for the hastily folded note Francis had left behind. Andrea got it first, opened it up, read what was written. Andrea's olive skin didn't look so olive anymore.

"*What?*" I asked.

Instead of answering, she just handed me the message. I took it with trembling fingers and let my eyes fall upon its words. The handwriting looked like that of a child's:

> *You will both go to the Honeyhole.*
> *You'll do it immediately.*
> *If you're not there within an hour,*
> *both of your mothers will be dead by sunset.*
> *Tell the police, they'll be dead by sunset.*
> *I'll have some fun before they die.*
> *I promise.*

Blood rushed to my ears, a roar that almost drowned out the buzz and hum of the diner. I could feel Andrea staring at me, but I couldn't look away from the sick, twisted message. The Honeyhole. Everyone in town knew what the Honeyhole was—a little pond-like depression where the runoff from one of the largest sections of Pudding Swamp drained, water almost constantly cascading from a culvert that jutted out from the levee. State Road 58 ran atop that levee, and anyone who'd ever walked along the boardwalk at Woods Bay State Park to watch for alligators had driven on SR58 to get there.

"David?" Andrea whispered.

I finally tore my eyes away and looked at her. My entire chest bulged with a suffocating fear.

"What do we do?" I asked.

Andrea snatched the note from my hands in reply and stood up from the table, her entire body shaking from anger. Before I could stop her, she marched over to the double doors and stepped through them just as Francis had. Belatedly, I hurried to follow her, reaching the doors just as they stopped swinging. I pushed the greasy things out of my way and entered the kitchen.

The place was noisy: clanking pots and pans, the scrape of spatulas on griddles, the hiss of steam, the roar of fire on the grill, people talking over each other to call out orders and confirm them, yell out "Order up!" when they were done. I spotted Andrea in a back corner, apart from most of the action, where Francis was cowering in a plastic chair as Andrea shook the threatening note over her head.

"Who gave this to you?" I heard her yell.

Francis shook her head, staring at the floor, her hands clasped between knees that knocked rhythmically. I'd known this woman for years—at least on a peripheral level—and I'd never seen her like this. A grown woman as frightened as a child.

"Francis," I said, as soothingly as possible, putting a hand on Andrea's arm so she'd stop dangling the note like a guillotine over the poor lady's head. "Did somebody threaten you? The person who gave you this note?"

"I can't say anything," she murmured, barely legible over the chorus of kitchen sounds. "He said he'd kill me, my whole family. Please just *leave*."

On most levels, you're aware of your age, your youth, your maturity, even though you come out of your mama thinking you're as smart as any adult in the room. And in that moment, it appalled me that this woman, well over 30, maybe 40, was allowing such a burden to fall upon people less than half her age. I simultaneously felt pity and loathing.

"Come on," I said to Andrea, gently grabbing her upper arm. "Let's go."

She yanked it out of my grip and berated Francis. "So it's okay for us to go there and die? To protect your family? Was it Pee Wee Gaskins? Huh?" She asked the questions too quickly for anyone to answer, much less a frightened mouse of a woman.

"Just come on," I insisted. I'd quickly abandoned my accusations of cowardice on this person, perhaps feeling some premonition of a distant future, when I would do anything—*anything*—to protect my own children. "We know very well who it is and we have no choice. Come *on*."

Andrea seemed to shrink in defeat. "I'm sorry, Ms. Daniels. I'm sorry." She looked at me, her eyes and expression so full of stress and terror I almost gave up. Almost decided to take our chances with the police. But I knew, fundamentally knew, that we couldn't do that. We had to play Pee Wee's games until we could figure out a way to end everything at once.

"Let's go," I said to Andrea. From somewhere, a modicum of courage had found its way into my heart. "We have to go, and if we don't leave now, we won't make it in time." I braced myself for her to argue, but she didn't. Only nodded. We were on the same wavelength.

"Sorry, Ms. Daniels," she said one last time, then handed me the note as if she couldn't bear its weight anymore. When we stepped through the kitchen doors, I wadded the paper up and shoved it in my pocket.

3

We ditched Officer Fuller. I felt bad about it, knew I'd get in trouble, but we both agreed that getting dropped off at the sight in question probably constituted "Tell the police," as Gaskins had warned us not to do. After consulting a moment at the front door of the diner, peeking through the window at Fuller, sitting in his car as he read the newspaper, we decided to go back into the kitchen and exit via their back door. We didn't ask permission; we just did it.

From there it had been easy to sneak down the backstreets to the closest bus stop, hop on, and head out of Sumter. Luckily there was a drop off at Fryer's junction (where the Pit Stop gas station could sell you everything from crickets to condoms, amongst more ordinary SKUs like bread and milk) and that left us only a half-mile hike or so to the Honeyhole. After all was said and done, we reached the little trail that snaked off of SR58 with just under ten minutes to spare.

"We made it," I said quietly. We'd barely spoken during the trip, the fear we both felt acting as a shield to any speech. What could we say? Other than discuss our complete idiocy at walking into a mousetrap.

"When's the last time you were here?" Andrea asked. We stood side by side, staring at the narrow path—nothing more than a trail of dirt too foot-trodden to grow weeds. It slipped down a small incline from the road and vanished between two pine trees. I could already hear the splash of the draining water as it fell into the small pond. Behind us, on the other side of the road, was a broad stretch of Pudding Swamp, black, without ripples, full of mysterious creatures, Cypress trees jutting from its surface like tendon-trailing fingers.

"I don't know. Last summer, maybe. I guess we out-grew it." The place was a haven for adventurous swimmers and dads teaching kids to fish. Some rich dude from Florence was rumored to stock the thing every once in a while.

"What do we do, David?" The unease in her voice only made mine stronger.

"No idea. But like I said on the bus, there's no way he's going to kill us. He could've done that a dozen times by now. He just wants to torment us for some reason. Play with us."

"I'd hardly say, 'there's no way,' but maybe we're his key to showing off to the media. They always say serial killers like the attention."

Or maybe this was our last day on Earth. "Plus he said he'd kill our moms if we don't do this."

"Let's just go down there," Andrea said. She took a deep breath then walked forward. I wanted to yell at her to wait, to give me another minute to think about it. But I stayed silent and went with her.

We slipped through the pine trees and followed the dusty trail as it skirted a semi-circular ridge, slowly descending until it reached the back edge of the pond known as the Honeyhole, about 40 feet below SR58. Looking up, I saw the round cement culvert, maybe two feet in diameter, jutting out from the mound of earth and rock built up beneath the road. The pipe extended about 10 feet, like someone had planted a giant paper towel roll into the side of the levee. From the dark, open face at the end of the cement cylinder, a heavy, steady stream of water poured out, falling a couple-dozen feet until it splashed into the pond. Perpetual ripples radiated out from the white-water point of impact, bouncing off of waves that had rebounded from the shore, making the entire pond look like the surface of a busy swimming pool. The pond itself was probably 50 feet across, almost perfectly circular, completely surrounded by trees.

It felt like another world, a surreal oasis hidden from the rest of civilization. Ironically, that's what made it so popular, and I was shocked to see no trace of another person—I'd never, not once, had the place all to myself. What was Pee Wee up to?

"There's no one here," I said, stating the obvious.

She twisted her neck looking this way and that. "He's hiding somewhere. Watching us."

This gave me a wave of chills that travelled and ricocheted across my skin as surely as the ripples on the pond. My eyes immediately darted from tree to tree, sweeping across the shoreline from where we stood to the other side, where the ground sloped back up toward SR58. Sunlight filtered through the forest canopy, creating a million discrepancies of shadow and bright reflections, especially as the light winked and flashed off the wavy pond. I didn't see a single sign of Gaskins or anyone else. This didn't make me feel better. Not at all. I imagined him up in a deer stand, far off, aiming a rifle, its scope pinpointed to my head.

"Maybe it was a test," I said. "He just wanted to see if we'd do what he told us to do."

Andrea finally broke off her searching gaze and focused on me. "I can't believe we came here. Something's wrong. It feels... haunted."

The constant roar of the waterfall provided the only real soundtrack to our surroundings—just loud enough to mask the crickets and birds. There was definitely something eerie about the Honeyhole today, as if a fourth dimensional shadow had been cast, a darkness we couldn't see with our physical eyes. With every passing second, almost counter-intuitively, my shackles rose higher and higher as no one made an appearance to terrorize us. The hair on my arms stood straight up, every single one of them.

Andrea and I waited for another minute or two, slowly turning in circles as we tried to see the woods in 360 degrees. Still no sign of anyone.

"Can we leave now you think?" I asked, my own voice startling me. It seemed to echo off the chamber created by the carved-out pond against the levee.

"Could it have been a prank?"

"By *who*?"

She just shrugged.

"Let's give it five more minutes," I suggested. *Maybe he won't show up*, I thought. *Maybe he's been caught by the police. Or maybe he's killing our moms.* I whimpered a little at this horrible direction my mind had gone. "No, let's go. Let's just go. We did what he said."

"Amen, hallelujah. Come on." She'd barely finished those words when she suddenly screamed, pointing at something behind me. I spun around.

On the other side of the pond, someone's head had poked out from behind a wide oak tree. A plastic bag had been pulled over the head, its handles tied tightly around the person's neck, just like the man who tormented me the night before when I'd awakened in the woods. Because of the bag, I couldn't see any facial features, but whoever it was obviously stared back at us. The bag contracted and expanded with each breath, and I could see the slit that had been cut open near the mouth. Shuddering with horror, I could only stand there, my eyes locked on our visitor.

Andrea's hand slipped into mine and squeezed.

The bag-headed person lifted an arm from behind the tree, slowly, slowly, the index finger extending into the age-old position of pointing. Once the arm got to about a 45-degree angle above the horizontal, it stopped, the finger overly rigid, directing us up and back toward the road. Scared at what I might see, my eyes followed the line of indication, my head slowly turning to the right. I sensed Andrea go rigid the instant I sucked in a gasp.

There was a man standing on top of the culvert.

He stood right at the end of it, where the water gushed out, keeping his balance with both arms extended. This person also had a bag on his head, tied the same way, breathing through a similar slit, the thin plastic bulging and retracting like a diseased heart. He wore a T-shirt and raggedy jeans, skinnier than I was, his feet adorned by old Adidas high-tops.

It wasn't a man.

It was a kid.

I barely had time to register this when the kid took his own turn pointing. In dramatic fashion, he slowly brought his right arm forward until his extended finger pointed directly at us, and then just above us. He jabbed it a couple of times and I realized what he meant. He was pointing at a spot *behind* where we stood. Almost crying out in fear I spun around to see what he'd motioned toward.

A third baghead, just 10 feet from where we stood.

Andrea clutched me and I clutched her. A soft moan escaped the back of my throat, just as a shiver of fright rattled my spine. Our third visitor was short but looked to be a grown man judging from his weathered hands and demeanor. He had his back to us and, just like the other two, a plastic grocery bag concealed his head, its handles tied in a tight little bow. He was close enough that I heard the crinkling sound as the bag collapsed and billowed out rhythmically. Despite the hot weather, he wore a black and blue flannel shirt and faded jeans— from years of wear and tear, not some 80s fashion statement holding on at the end of the decade. He remained still, facing the other direction, his two feet planted in the pine straw and leaves as if he'd grown there.

Behind us, the water rushed out of the culvert, splashed eternally in the Honeyhole. There was no other sound. I risked a glance over my shoulder and saw that the kid still stood on top of the cement shaft; the other man still hid behind his tree, poking his head out to watch the festivities. They'd both lowered their arms.

"What're we supposed to do?" I yelled, my voice directed at the first man we saw. "Why'd you tell us to come here?"

And then they went through the same ridiculous charades as before, as if they were automated dummies in a Disneyland ride. The man behind the tree pointed at the kid standing on top of the culvert. Then the kid pointed at the man behind us. When I returned my attention to him, he slowly turned his head to look back at us, the bag twisting, bunching up around his neck. Andrea and I were still arm in arm; we instinctively took a step away from the third man. Even though we couldn't see his eyes, I felt them upon us, staring through the plastic. He seemed to stay like that forever, unmoving, craning his neck almost unnaturally over his shoulder.

"Please don't hurt us," I said, embarrassed at my weakness.

"Let's just run," Andrea whispered to me.

I shook my head, knowing that wasn't the answer.

The man now turned the rest of the way around, slowly, his invisible gaze staying focused on us, until the front of his entire body faced us fully. I wanted to say something, anything, reason with these people. My fear had turned numb, like I was getting used to this insanity.

"Who are you?" Andrea asked. "Are you Pee Wee?"

The man tilted his head to the right, as if he hadn't understood her.

"Is that your kid back there?" She jabbed a thumb over her shoulder. "Is that what serial killers do nowadays? Train up their children to take over the family business when they're sick of murdering people?"

The man tilted his head the other way, and it reminded me of nothing so much as the scarecrow in *The Wizard of Oz*, though this guy seemed even dumber, a lot scarier.

A twig snapped behind me. I spun to see the first man

approaching us along the shore of the Honeyhole, walking as if he strolled along in a park. This guy also wore a flannel shirt, red and gray, but matched with khaki pants instead of jeans. If they attacked, we'd have no choice but to run—and I thought we could pull it off. But not yet. Not quite yet. Motion up by the culvert made me look that way. The boy had tight-roped himself back to the steep slope of the bank beneath the road, and began to climb down it on his hands and knees. Not knowing what else to do, I kept my eyes on him. After slipping and stumbling a couple of times, he made it to even ground and walked toward us, calmly. Soon we had all three of these bag-headed weirdos within 20 feet.

"I swear if you guys try to hurt us—" I started to say but Andrea interrupted me.

"We'll go for the kid, first," she said flatly. "You might kill us, but we'll hurt that kid somethin' fierce before it's all said and done."

We were both naturally addressing the first man we'd seen— he was roughly Pee Wee sized, from what I could remember—as the third one seemed dumber than rocks. In my mind, we'd seen Pee Wee first, then his son, the one supposedly named Dicky of all things, and then someone I couldn't begin to guess at. I could only think of him as Baghead.

Pee Wee raised his right arm, just as he had done earlier with his left arm, nice and slow, and pointed at Baghead. Andrea and I shifted, looked over at him. He hadn't moved an inch, his feet still planted like roots. The situation had become so awkwardly bizarre that I wasn't even sure that what I felt was fear anymore. I had that strange sense of a nightmare—scary, but deep down feeling like a dream.

Baghead moved.

He took a step toward us.

It startled me enough that I flinched, then Andrea and I backed up several feet. Still holding onto each other's arms, we now stood on the very edge of the small pond. Pee Wee was to our right, his son to our left.

Baghead took another step. Then another. His movements matched the earlier idiocy of his tilting head. Another step, almost lurching. It was like someone was trying to possess his body, or control it with a remote of some sort. Another step. Another.

He wasn't heading directly at us. His line, if he kept at it, would lead him to a spot between us and Pee Wee. Baghead took another step forward. Another. Each one seemed a labor for him, often taking a second to catch his balance, as if he were walking the gymnastics beam. Another step. Three or four more and he'd be at the edge of the Honeyhole.

I had absolutely no idea what the hell was going on.

Andrea leaned in and whispered, "We need to get out of here. Now."

"Just a second." A morbid curiosity had taken over me, an urge that felt unclean but irresistible. I was being unfair to Andrea but I couldn't help it, despite a building guilt. Making it worse, I knew she'd never leave without me.

Baghead had continued to move, and now stood on the very edge of the shoreline.

He stepped into the water.

His foot made the same splash and plunking sound of a large rock. He brought his other leg forward, swished it into the pond at least two feet beyond his first step. Not hesitating like before, he now kept going, sloshing his legs one after the other as he waded deeper and deeper. Soon the dark, wavy surface had reached his upper thighs, and the outer most drops of the waterfall cascading from the culvert smacked onto his bagged head, each one sounding like a slap.

Completely mesmerized, I couldn't take my eyes off of this man who'd just marched into a small pond. I barely sensed the other two in my peripheral vision, and they also were looking toward the middle of the Honeyhole. Andrea's hand squeezed my forearm, almost slipping from the sweat that soaked both of us.

Baghead adjusted his stance, looking down into the water as if he searched for something, moving his body this way and that as he lifted and dropped his feet. Eventually he'd turned all the way around, now facing us again, though he didn't look our way.

"David," Andrea whispered fiercely. "You're starting to piss me off."

"Okay, just..."

Baghead bent his knees until the water reached his neck, leaning forward slightly while he reached down with both arms. There was obviously something on the bottom of the pond, and his efforts made it look like he was grabbing it, getting a solid grip, now lifting...

He straightened his legs, his torso rising from the water, streams of it cascading off his shoulders. Then something else came up, something bulky, wrapped in drenched material that Baghead held onto with both hands, their tendons standing out with the effort. As the water washed off the object emerging from below, I saw more details but still couldn't tell what it was. It looked like a big slab of meat wrapped in cloth, a stubby, bony, gristle-lined...

I let out a scream, as shrill a sound as I'd ever made in my life, before or since. If Andrea made any noise I'd never know, because mine drowned out all others. But she did collapse backwards, recoiling from the horrific sight of a beheaded human in the not-so-loving arms of Baghead. I fell with her—our butts thumping into the soft ground of the woods. All the while, my eyes never left the fright show currently playing out in the Honeyhole.

Baghead stood perfectly still, his hands firmly clenched within the soaked folds of the decapitated corpse's clothes—a black shirt from the looks of it. The water having drained off, now reduced to gray-colored tears dripping from the ghastly sight, I could clearly see the gaping, open wound where a head had once been attached. It had long since bled out, leaving a meaty mass of discolored tissue, polka dots of severed bones and tendons scattered throughout—some bigger than others.

Who, I thought, panicking. *Who is that?*

I pulled Andrea into me, squeezing her like a security blanket. My heart sputtered as countless potential names ran through my head, despite most of them not even matching the size and weight of the body in Baghead's hands.

"I wanted you to see this," a strangled voice spoke.

It was Andrea's turn to scream this time, a startled yelp even as I flinched for what seemed like the tenth time in the last ten minutes. Pee Wee had walked up to within three feet of us, his bagged head looking down at where we sat, huddled together. He'd used that same disguised, rough voice, and continued to do so as we looked up at him.

"I wanted you to see this." He gestured toward Baghead and his victim in the middle of the pond. "The Reticence grows stronger. I can't never be cured because of the pact our families made. But I will keep, keep, keep haunting you and taunting you and making your life a living hell so that you suffer the sins of our ancestors! Do you understand me, boy? It'll end with my son!"

He was screaming by the end, all but losing the guttural disguise, his voice now laced with lunatic shrieks. Taking two steps closer, he leaned forward, his scarecrow-looking head coming closer and closer to mine. As the bag retracted into the contours of his face when he breathed in, I saw his bluish lips, his crooked, yellow teeth through the jagged slit. I thought I saw shadows of his eyes behind the thin veil of plastic.

"I don't know what you're talking about," I said weakly, trembling at this man's instability. Why had we trusted him? In all my life, it had to have been the stupidest thing I'd ever done.

"Just let us go!" Andrea screamed, rising from the ground a few inches, spit flying from her mouth. "You freaky asshole!"

Pee Wee lurched forward and slapped her, then slapped me before I could react. We both fell to our backs, more from shock than pain or force. The sting on my cheek was nothing compared to the horror rebounding through my nerves.

"Don't talk to me like that you..." He stopped, breathing hard, the crinkle of the bag inflating and deflating on his head like constant sparks of static electricity. "I don't even need you," he then said, almost in wonder, as if he'd just had a revelation. "I don't need you, girl. The only one I need is David."

He reached to his back pocket and pulled out a hunting knife, the blade at least eight inches long. Then he held it out in front of him, twisting it this way and that as if trying to get the sun to glint from its surface, the tip pointed at Andrea.

"All I need is David," he whispered. Then louder, "What do you think, boys? Should we stick this thing like a pig?" He turned his head toward Baghead, still clutching the dead body in the middle of the Honeyhole. Baghead shook his head back and forth with exaggerated but slow movement, making sure he was understood.

"Aww, now. So soft, ain't ya. What about you, boy?" Pee Wee looked at the younger one, standing a few feet down the shoreline. "Think we oughtta make our friend David a widow? A widow at the age of 16. Sad."

It hit me that he'd stopped using the gravelly voice, maybe having forgotten in the rapidly changing events. From what I could remember, which wasn't much, he sounded like the Pee Wee that had shown me a shovel as a child and confronted me in a cabin before murdering my friend, Alejandro.

The boy, who had to be his son, nodded firmly.

Pee Wee leaned close to me, holding the knife in the air to his right, its point only inches from Andrea's neck. "What about you, David? What's your vote? Want me to slit her throat so you can be done with all her naggin' and bitchin'? Maybe we can find you a nice gal in Columbia. Big improvement, you gotta believe me."

I could barely find my voice to answer. "No. Please. Please don't hurt her. Please." I couldn't bear it. I couldn't bear the thought of him killing yet another of my friends, and especially not her. My body shook with silent rage at the thought.

Pee Wee straightened up, the blade falling to his side, where it hung loosely from his fingers. "The boy votes no so it's a tie! Two to two. What about you, girl? What's your vote?"

Andrea stared back at him with all the hatred one human can have for another. But she shook her head.

"No's the vote," Pee Wee pronounced, speaking through his bag like a complete lunatic. "Let's tally them up, then. That's, uh... According to my old math teacher, that'd be three to two in favor of *not* cuttin' your throat and making the world a better place. Sadly, my vote's the only one that counts so that's one to nothin'."

I decided, then and there, in the very instant he said that only his vote counted, that there was no way on hell or Earth that I would permit him to harm my best friend in the world.

He stepped closer to Andrea, looming directly over her, his shins practically touching her knees. Then he knelt down, one forearm draped across his thigh, the other hand holding up his knife, studying it with overly curious eyes as he twisted it, pointy end toward the sky. The torment-your-victim shtick had run its course. I felt Andrea tense beside me, as rigid as I'd ever felt her, her right fingers squeezing my bicep for support.

Pee Wee went back to his gravelly voice. "I think we'll start with the thro—"

Andrea's body twisted, releasing like a spring that had been coiled against its strength. At some point, to neither my notice nor Pee Wee's, she'd loosened a rock from its moors in the sandy soil, gripped it with her left hand. She swung it up from the ground, leaning into me for leverage, and smashed the heavy chunk of granite directly into Pee Wee's face. He screamed a most un-serial-killer-like scream, something that sounded more like a toddler being ripped from the arms of his mother for preschool. The plastic bag ripped, his head twisted back, and I saw two things fly in a straight trajectory from his injured mouth —a short squirt of blood and a single tooth, its broken edge white against yellow.

There was no time to consider this, no time to exult in the payback. Andrea was already scrambling to her feet, pulling me up with her. I slipped once but then got my own feet underneath me, even as Pee Wee screamed at the top of his lungs, howling outlandish curses. I quickly scanned our surroundings, looking for the best options of what to do now, but Andrea took control. She grabbed my hand and started running, straight toward the boy who stood on the shore of the Honeyhole. As we closed the gap between us—he hadn't moved a muscle, and I could only imagine the look of shock hidden beneath his bag—I heard a splash to my left. Baghead had dropped his headless burden. He now swung his arms and swayed violently side to side as he moved as quickly as possible through the water, heading in our direction. Once again he struck me as clumsy, not of sound mind, his movements somehow those of a child, stressing urgency over practicality. I knew we could outrun him.

"Stop!" The boy in front of us yelled, actually holding out a hand, palm toward us. What the hell did he think he was, a traffic cop? "Stop or my daddy—"

Andrea didn't slow a bit, pushing him to the side as we ran into him. He fell, his body splashing down into the shallow edges of the Honeyhole. She moved past but the kid kicked out a leg as I ran by, and it was just enough to trip me. I fell shockingly fast, my face slamming into the soft mud of the shoreline. And then he was on top of me, trying to slide his arm around my neck from behind.

Something in me exploded. Some lit fuse touched the packed incendiaries of everything that had happened to me, that had destroyed my childhood, that had taken the last vestiges of any semblance of innocence from my life, forever.

I roared out a battle scream and flailed my arms and legs, twisted my torso, expending every ounce of energy I could mine from my depleted supply. I connected with his face with an open-handed slap, stunned him. He shifted to his left and I took advantage, throwing my weight toward him to keep his momentum moving until he had flipped to the ground. I climbed on top of him, then unleashed a fury of punches, pummeling him with both of my clenched fists. As my knuckles ripped into his plastic-lined face, I felt the connection, a jarring that traveled through my bones, all the way up my arms until the force shuddered in my chest.

I kept at it, feeling a primal joy I didn't know existed, wanting nothing more than to beat the living shit out of this vile pustule who'd contribute to our misery that day. His bag had ripped open, come halfway off, exposing the boy's face, but I had never seen him before. He had no features that stood out to me, half-blind from the mad adrenaline that rushed through my veins and pulsed in my ears.

"David, come *on*," Andrea insisted, tugging hard at my shirt. Her strength surprised me as she pulled me from my perch atop the kid, though my swings never stopped. I had punched that bagged face at least a dozen times, and I'm sure the one that missed, hitting open air with my right fist, as she finally yanked me off of him, would've finished the job. I would've been an ender of life. I continued to reach for him as she got me to my feet, enraged, filled with an euphoric lust to kill this symbol of the troubles that had haunted me. But he was left on the ground, groaning and whimpering like a coward.

"He's half dead!" Andrea shouted. "Run!"

I then saw that Baghead had almost reached the edge of the

Honeyhole, unleashing some roar of his own, a sound that was straight from a haunted house of dead orphans, shrill and demented. His arms flailed like mine had, though his purpose was balance. He was only six feet away.

"Come on," Andrea said again, pulling me behind her as she ran.

We reached the vine-and-bush-tangled slope, started climbing toward SR58, pulling on weeds, stepping on roots. Behind us, I heard water sloshing off wet clothes as Baghead finally accomplished his slog through the Honeyhole and emerged on shore. We'd scrambled halfway up the incline when I looked back. The man, drenched and dripping, stood just past the kid—who had sat up, attending to a bloody nose—with his hands on his hips, staring at us through that wilted bag of his.

Instead of pursuing us, he spoke, using that same disguised, rough, graveled voice I'd heard Pee Wee use; the bag puffed out with his words.

"Better run, boy," he said, sounding more intelligent than I'd given him credit for. "Won't be no appeasing him this time. Ya'll gone too far."

I'd stopped my ascent, unable to look away. Baghead stood there, still as the trunks of trees that surrounded the Honeyhole, hands perched on those hips, staring back. Breathing heavily. His plasticky hood still pumping like a heart. It struck me that the faux-deep voices of the two men were close enough that I couldn't say for sure which one had been the man to taunt me outside my home the night before. Pee Wee was smaller in stature, but maybe not enough to tell at night, in the dark of the woods.

"David!"

My head snapped around and I looked up the slope to see Andrea at the top.

"What the hell are you doing? Come on!" She made as if to climb back toward me.

"No, stop!" I shouted. "I'm coming."

Yanking on every branch and vine I could see, I pulled myself the rest of the way up, cranking my legs into the loose dirt to help. I reached her, we stood, we hugged, we looked down the slope together. Now partially hidden by the trees, I could see that Baghead had gone to help the boy I'd beaten to within an inch of his life. Pee Wee had crawled over to them both. Water gushed out of the culvert, down, down, down, its splash the only sound in the forest. They seemed to have no intention of making chase.

Battered, more inside than out, I grabbed Andrea's hand and we ran down the narrow road, along the levee, back toward town.

"That was so stupid," I said as we picked up speed. "We're going straight to the police."

4

The next hour was a whirlwind. We'd gone about a mile and a half when Officer Fuller's car screeched up to us, doing a 180 before he was able to stop in the dust off of Parker's Lane. He jumped out of the car, yelling and screaming at us, even though I could see the immense relief on his face the entire time. We told him what happened, his eyes getting bigger with each word. He called it in on his radio, explained what had happened as we had, told them it was at the Honeyhole, got us in his cruiser. He booked it for the police station, his siren and lights working on overload. He'd told dispatch to make sure someone called our parents.

As Andrea and I huddled in the back seat like criminals, like Bonnie and Clyde, I knew there'd be no more messing around. There'd be no living like normal, having a cop parked outside to watch over us. There'd be no going back to school.

Until and unless Pee Wee was captured, my life could never be the same.

5

Later, I sat in a tiny room, a room that was used to interrogate criminals. They'd placed Andrea in another room. My mom had come, hugged me, cried, hugged me again, cried. Repeat and rinse. She was pretty distraught, and now—more than back then —I understand why. I understand on a level most people don't and can't. Of all the things I've wished for throughout my life, one of the biggest was this: that I could go back in time and comfort my sweet mama on a deeper level, love her just a little harder. Oh, the things that woman went through.

My dad hadn't shown up right away, and the deputies in charge—Sheriff Taylor was out and about doing his thing—decided to go ahead and take statements. My mom, and Andrea's mom as well, had insisted on being in the respective rooms with us, and they had every right to do so. It took an hour or so, but I finally told them every little detail I could think of, then told them again. And then a third time. There'd been no need for Andrea and me to get any story straight, so I felt no stress over our tales straying from each other. But I have to admit the atmosphere gave me pause now and then, made me wonder if somehow I could say the wrong thing, end up in the slammer for the murder of that poor headless sap being exhumed from the Honeyhole as we spoke.

I wondered and wondered who it was. Living in a small town, odds were pretty good you knew someone when they had their head sawed off and dumped in a pond. With my dad being late, of course I had jumped to the worst case—that it was him. This thought haunted me until he finally showed up—haunted me even though my mom had assured us that he'd called from a pay phone and that he promised to hurry back from his errands down in Lake City.

It was him, I told myself. *My dad is dead. My dad's heartbeat is as gone to this world as his head is gone from his body. Pee Wee set someone up to fake his voice on the phone. He's dead, he's dead, he's dead...*

And then he walked into that little tiny room, my mom on one arm, Sheriff Taylor on his other side. Relief filled me like air after a long dive to the bottom of a pool.

There were more hugs. More tears. A lot of "What the hell is going on?" and "How the hell did this happen?" I felt bad for Officer Fuller, because my mom had pretty much decided that everything in the world was that poor sucker's fault. Andrea and I had told the truth about sneaking out on him, but I think it helped Mom to have a scapegoat. Dad didn't show much emotion, just a stunned pallor that made him look twenty years older.

I soon found out why.

"Honey," he said gently to my mom, "would you mind giving me a few minutes with David? You know, man to man stuff."

Even then, even as a kid, I knew that was about as low a thing as you could say to a distraught mother. Or a perfectly happy mother, for that matter. She looked my dad dead in the eyes, as fierce as I ever saw her, and said, "Unless you plan on tellin' the Sheriff here to get his deputies and drag me out kickin' and screamin', there's no way in Satan's hell I'm leaving this room."

Dad showed neither anger nor surprise. Nothing, really. He just replied with something along the lines of, "ayup, okay."

Dad sat down. Mom sat down. Sheriff Taylor sat down. The three of them faced me across the rectangular table. The door to that broom closet of a room had been closed without my noticing. The air was stuffy, warm. Something was up and I knew it.

"Son," my dad began. "The Sheriff and I had a long talk. This... thing that Gaskins is doing with you... Well, it defies explanation. Our families have a history, I'll admit"—this is the first I'd ever heard of such a thing—"but this goes beyond the pale. The man seems hell-bent on tormenting you instead of..." He didn't need to finish.

I nodded. "He didn't even have his friend chase us after Andrea knocked him with that rock."

"Exactly. Which is why..." He lowered his head, unable to find the words.

"Edgar, what is going *on*?" my mom asked.

He sighed and leaned close to her, whispered something indecipherable in her ear. I strained to catch a word or two but had no luck. She started shaking her head back and forth so hard I thought it might topple off. My dad grabbed her arm; I could tell from the way his tendons poked out and his muscles flexed that he was squeezing hard enough to hurt. She winced, tried to pull away. Failed. He said more words, the harshness of his whisper filling the room, yet still impossible to work out. My mom wilted. Forgetting everything else, I felt an anger toward my dad like never before, maybe for the first time in my short existence.

But he turned away from my mom, kind of throwing her arm away from him as he did so. She looked in her lap, defeated. I sat and stared, utterly bewildered at this behavior from both of them.

Sheriff Taylor cleared his throat. "Look, David. This is a touchy subject but we've put a lot of thought into it, even before... whatever the hell that was today."

"I take it you didn't capture anybody?" I asked.

The Sheriff shook his head, looking more embarrassed than regretful. "No. All we found was the body, some blood, and torn remnants of the plastic bags you told us about. Seems they left them behind."

"Let's cut to the chase," my dad said, placing his elbows on the table and leaning halfway across the table. "David, this has to end. It *has* to end." He paused, letting that rather obvious state-ment float through the air for a few seconds. "And there's only one damned way to do it. We promise you'll be safe. You'll be protected by more men than it takes to run a state dairy farm, I swear to God Almighty above."

I held my breath, waiting for the ball to drop. Sheriff Taylor finally had the guts to come out and say it.

"Dammit, David. We're going to use you as bait."

CHAPTER THIRTEEN

Lynchburg, South Carolina
July 2017

I

The rain fell from the sky. Relentless, unstoppable.

I personally supervised my son Wesley being dropped off at his cousins' house to spend the night. An officer named Scott Wright had been put in charge of surveillance, and I was actually tired of hearing his voice after at least a dozen promises to stay vigilant, not sleep, watch the house every second, walk around the premises every hour on the hour, die before anyone brought harm to my son...

That didn't make me feel any better. None of it did. Frankly, if something happened to Wesley, I'd feel zero percent better knowing that this brave policeman had died in the effort to stop it.

My sister, Evelyn, made similar promises, though she never went so far as to offer her life in exchange for Wesley's. But she did guarantee one hell of a country breakfast come morning. I asked if I could come over with the other kids to join in, and she said something to the effect of, "You bet you're ass, little brother." In terms of protection, at least her husband had more guns than a cobbler has shoes. And maybe he kinda relished the thought of hunting something besides deer for a change. Life in the South.

Now I stood with Wesley, just him and me under the protection of the porch. Rain pattered on the sloped roof, sloshing off in sleets, and thunder rumbled in the distance. Evelyn had gone back inside with her sons Jeffrey and Brett, and officer Wright said he wanted to do a walkabout before he took up his post for the night, military-grade umbrella bloomed and held rigidly above him. He used that word, *walkabout*. It had an ominous feel to it, like something a soldier would've said in Vietnam. I almost changed my mind, based on that one word alone, but in the end I relented. The honest truth was I didn't see how he'd be any safer at my parents' house than this one.

"Well," I said, rather pathetically. "Guess I'll head back to the farm."

"Dad, there's nothing to worry about." He pointed up at the house. "Uncle Jeff kills enough deer to feed my high school wrestling team for a year. One idiot named Dicky won't be a match for him. *If* he gets past that cop, which he won't. We'll be safe."

"I don't want you alone," I said. "None of that nonsense from the movies where you think, oh, I'll go out for a walk or oh, I'll go get some snacks out of the basement. You stay with your cousins and your aunt and uncle. Play Monopoly or something."

"Monopoly? No one's played that since 1996."

"You weren't born in 1996."

"Exactly."

I pulled him into a hug, and he more or less returned it, as much as one can ask from a 16-year-old boy. I didn't let him go when he naturally tried to pull away. I whispered into his ear.

"There's a lot of stuff about my childhood you don't... Stuff I've never told you."

"You mean about Pee Wee Gaskins?" They knew the basics. Only the basics.

"Yeah. Having his son around... It just makes me nervous. How ridiculous is it that he escaped from the frickin' jail? That Sheriff Taylor's nowhere near as good as his daddy. I'd boil his balls over a campfire if I could get away with it."

This made him snicker, and that made me feel better.

I finally released him and took a step back. "We'll come back in the morning, eat some of that breakfast grub Evelyn's so famous for."

"Mmm," he said, rubbing his tummy. "I can feel the cholesterol clogging my arteries already."

I scoffed. "Yeah, like you need to worry about that. We should have you eat lard straight out of a bucket, put some meat on those bones."

"Don't worry, Dad. Someday I'll get fat like you."

With that, everything seemed as normal as it could get. I gently swatted him on the shoulder, told him I loved him, thanked the good Lord he kinda grumbled it back, and sprinted for my car, soaked by the time I finally let the wind slam the door shut.

2

That night, I slept where Wesley had slept—in my dad's van-sized chair, its cushions enveloping me like foam-spray insulation. Reclined all the way back, it was as good as any bed I'd ever had the fortune to lie upon. Hazel had complained, wanting me on the couch within her reach, so I sat with her and talked awhile, until she was too tired to complain when I moved for the chair. Mason and Logan were practically on top of each other, both of their mouths wide open enough to catch any rat that might scuttle by and take a peek at their tongues. Andrea had told me she was too tired to think, much less talk, and had tonight taken my sister Patsy's room. I'd gone in to check on her, as if she'd signed up to be one of my kids, and she'd been sound asleep. For about three seconds I considered climbing into bed next to her for a snuggle, then thought better of it. She might wake up in the middle of the night, think me an intruder, and kick my ass.

And so I lay on the famous chair, fans blowing all around me, no other sound or movement in the world. I reached over and turned off the lamp perched atop my dad's trusty side-table, its surface scattered with the day's newspaper. He always said he'd switch to an iPad the day they cranked his coffin into the ground at Parson's Cemetery. Right before the light vanquished, I saw the headline about the body I'd stumbled upon in the swamp behind the house, but I had no interest in reading another word about it. Turned out we didn't know the victim, who'd done it, or why somebody would want his head. But I had to assume that everyone in town suspected the same thing I did—that Dicky Gaskins had taken up his papa's trade.

My eyes adjusted to the darkness. Shadows came into focus, the room took on depth. I saw the sweet silhouettes of my children, unmoving, sleeping, hopefully dreaming of better things than my gruesome discovery. I thought of Wesley and his cousins, probably playing video games or watching an R-rated movie I'd forbidden him to watch without me. Surprisingly, I felt he was safe, that all of my kids were safe, that I was safe. I don't know what brought me that peace. Maybe the plain fact was that Dicky Gaskins scared me about as much as a crawdad.

After discovering the old land record, Andrea and I hadn't found much else to write home about in our library research. Yes, the Player and Gaskins families went back a ways, apparently. But our only real evidence of that was the joint purchase of the land on which my dad had been raised. It seemed impossible to me that I hadn't known this, and my mom and dad seemed just as oblivious when we asked them about it. A weird expression crossed my dad's face when he pleaded ignorance, however, but I couldn't imagine why he'd lie about such a thing. I grilled him until he made it clear that I was annoying the hell out of him, but he still offered no answers. My plan was to ask around town until someone did.

Sighing, I looked up at the ceiling, thought of the many times I'd heard the creaks and groans of footsteps up there, completely inexplicable. A chill sprinkled goosebumps across my skin, though it wasn't necessarily scary or creepy. Grandpa Fincher didn't frighten me all that much, not really. As my gaze traveled along the old, yellowed tiles above, I thought maybe I could hear him walking up there, even now. Probably impossible over the roar of the fans, but my mind told me I heard it, and I believed my mind.

Don't worry, old man, I thought, trying to project the words to the otherworldly dimension where ghosts liked to hang out. *Your boy David's got everything under control.*

A warm glow traveled along my body, filled me with certain joy. I have no idea how to explain it, but I happily accepted the feeling and soon fell fast asleep.

3

We were running late the next morning. I blamed the youngest, Logan, as I usually did because he can't put up much of an argument. But this time it was legit. He'd had one of those rare starts to the day where he performed the Double Whammy before the sun broke above the pecan trees—he'd puked *and* pooped his pants. The former happened upon waking up, the latter when he'd gone outside to play with Grandma because he felt better.

But then, of course, he had too much fun to tell her about the pending emergency in his bowels. I only had to clean up the first mess, and I care not to remember the details. Mom took care of the other.

Finally, about a quarter after 10, we were on our way to Evelyn's. I'd been texting Wesley since I left him, for my own peace of mind and to practice my text-joking skills. Some things are only funny when delivered via cell phones, you know. I'd tried a gem on Wesley, involving a toilet, Logan's mishap, and the word *chocolate*, but all I got in return was one of those damn laughing emojis with tears streaming from its eyes. Kids these days.

At least I knew he was safe.

"Daddy?" Hazel asked when we were a couple miles out from my sister's place. Andrea sat next to me in the passenger seat, kids in the back; my parents had driven separate.

"Yes, my beautiful princess?" I replied.

"Is it ever gonna stop raining?"

"Oh, probably. You never know. Maybe we'll have ourselves an ocean in Sumter County soon. Wouldn't that be fun?"

"Daddy, was that your idea of a humorous joke?"

This was Hazel's far-beyond-her-years way of verbalizing an eye-roll.

"Yeah. Wasn't it hilarious?"

"Totally failed to land, Old Man."

Sometimes I honestly couldn't believe the things that came out of her mouth.

"Dad?" This time it came from Mason. I think Logan had done his usual and fallen asleep way in the back.

"Yes, my handsome prince?"

"Do you think Uncle Jeff'll let me play with his guns?"

I cringed again. "*Play* with them? You mean, like, load them up and let you go around town shooting things? Probably not, son."

He then repeated Hazel's exact line. "Dad, was that your idea of a humorous joke?"

I loved these little people so much. Letting out a courtesy laugh, I pulled the car into the gravel drive that led to Evelyn's house. Cornfields hemmed in on both sides, and driving slowly down it had always been one of my favorite things on earth. The eerie stance of the green stalks, packed in and blocking your view, making you feel as if the world had been cut off. I loved that creepy feeling, the goosebumps, born from such childhood pop culture as *Children of the Corn* and a cheesy but terrifying made-for-TV movie I'd seen way too young. It was about a murdered man stuffed in a scarecrow suit to hide the body, but who decided to come back from the dead and kill the bastards who'd done it. I'd been home alone, and had turned on every light in the house until my parents returned.

I also loved the crunch of the gravel under my tires, and the pouring rain just added to the otherworldly effects, as rain always does. Some people may disagree rather strongly, but to me, a good storm improves everything but outdoor barbecues and baseball games. All in all, I was feeling much better about life.

We exited the cornfields and entered a wide expanse of yard, my sister's house plopped right in the middle. It wasn't your typical farmhouse because they'd torn down their old one and rebuilt recently—more like your typical ranch-style home that was always magically bigger on the inside than it looked from the outside. A million tiny splashes sparkled on the roof as the rain fell and fell and fell.

A police cruiser squatted stony and silent underneath a carport on the left side of the yard. It was too dark to tell for sure, but I saw no sign of Officer Wright in the driver's seat—I wouldn't have been surprised if Evelyn had invited him in for breakfast, though. Or he could be reclined, snoozing away, forgetting his duty to protect my son. This didn't scare me, however. If anything had gone wrong, Evelyn would've lit up the cell towers until they exploded from overuse.

I pulled the car up as close as possible to the sidewalk leading to the front door, put the thing into park, cut off the engine. The heavy taps of raindrops on the roof and windshield now became a roar, and I suddenly felt as drowsy as if I'd been drugged.

"You guys care if I take a nap?" I asked. "Papa's an old man, tired."

"Forget, it, Daddy," Hazel answered. "You can bet your pants there's bacon frying in that house."

Mason made a long *yummmm* sound. "Oh yeah. I swear on my left pinkie toe I'm gonna eat at least 20 pieces of bacon. I'm gonna eat until I puke all over Aunt Evelyn's floor."

He said this with such a happy voice I half thought he meant it.

"Alright, fine, I won't take a nap. Mason, wake up Logan. Then let's make a run for it."

It was only 30 feet, max, but we were drenched by the time we reached the porch.

4

Evelyn did her best to crack my spine with the hug she gave me, and I did my best to return its ferocity. I knew that my siblings had always felt a little guilt over the misadventures of my 1989 summer, since they had all been out and about, all over the world at the time. Some in college, some starting careers in exotic places like Deer Park, Washington, others running off to get married. No one had been around, and I know they felt bad about it to this day. No matter how many times I assured them that was nonsense, I still sensed it in the little things, like the hug my big sis had just given me.

"What a week you've had," she said when we finally let go of each other. "I'm so sorry, little brother." She'd been the only one out of all of us to return to the homeland, live out her life much like our parents had. Although I was always a little jealous, I never had the guts to take the leap, myself.

"I know," I said solemnly. But the last thing I wanted was to dwell on the bad stuff. The house smelled of bacon, my kids were bouncing around the room—except Mason, who'd already asked Uncle Jeff three times about the gun safe—and I wanted to see Wesley, make sure he was alright. So far there'd been no sign of him or his cousins. "It's been hard on all of us. Thanks again for helping lead the search parties."

She pshawed me to high heaven then gestured us to sit, sit. Jeff gave me a smile and a knowing nod toward Mason.

"If he's annoying you," I said, "you have permission to lock him in the turkey coop."

"Nah, he's good. Come on, boy. Help me with a couple of things and I'll let you shoot the hell out of some old coke bottles."

Mason's grin just about reached his ears and they set off out the back door. Hazel and Logan had found a box of toys and other wondrous mysteries that Evelyn had pulled out before we arrived—I noticed one of those old Fisher Price record-player things with the plastic grooved-discs and felt a surge of nostalgia. It was gonna be a good day, dammit.

Evelyn and I plopped down on the couch where we could have a perfect view of Hazel and Logan exploring the wonders of that big wooden box.

"Breakfast'll be ready in about 10 minutes," my sister said.

"Don't tell me the boys are still asleep?" I asked.

"Wesley sure is—haven't seen a peep of him this morning. Lazy like his daddy, I reckon. Brett and Jeffrey went out early to dig some trenches by the creek, fill sand bags. Jeff's worried about it flooding up near our pump house. All this rain, ya know.

It's like the angels hadn't taken a piss for months and decided to all dump at once."

My sister liked to say such things. My brothers were worse. I had the slightest alarm build in my chest, however. No real tangible reason, but my good mood evaporated. I had to check on things. Immediately.

"What'd the cop do?" I asked. "He's been out there all night?"

"Yep. Never even came in to use the bathroom. But he hasn't budged from under the carport."

I stood up, so quickly my head swam for a moment.

"You okay?" Evelyn asked.

"Yeah," I replied absently. I needed two minutes to put my mind at ease. "I'll be right back."

"Well, alright, then. Why don't you go wake up that sleepy head while I finish breakfast. I went all out." She got up from her comfortable perch. "Let's just say that we have three options of grits." With a smile she walked off for the kitchen.

Something deeply unsettling had birthed inside me. A little worm that wiggled its way through my innards. I walked over to the front door, saw a few umbrellas standing inside a tall, antique ceramic vase that looked like it had been made for just such a thing. I grabbed the biggest one and opened the door, then popped the thing open with a click of a latch. It bloomed wide and I put it over my head as I stepped into the torrential rain.

Drops of heavy water pattered on the thin sheet of plastic above my head, even as the wind picked up, tried to rip the umbrella out of my hands. I steadied it, leaned forward, and marched straight for the police car. My feet splashed through puddles, and cold water soaked all the way up to my arms as it blew under the protection of my pathetic canopy. The car sat dark and wet, covered in droplets despite being parked under the open-sided carport. I think Jeff had built the structure for a tractor way back in the day—they had a full garage for their own vehicles.

I stepped under the roof and let the umbrella fall to the side —I balanced it on the gravel-covered ground without closing it. Then I stepped up to the passenger side window and leaned in, shielding my eyes with both eyes so I could get a decent glimpse into the gloomy interior.

At first I didn't know what I was seeing. Officer Wright was definitely inside the car, slumped against the window on his side, eyes closed. I'd wanted to take a nap myself just a few minutes earlier, so I couldn't completely judge the man. But then the shadows softened, things became clearer, my eyes adjusting to the lack of light. His neck bent at a weird angle, and his hands seemed oddly placed on his lap, unnatural, mainly because his palms both faced up.

In this matter of scant seconds that I observed him through the window, the dreadful realization of what happened dawned upon me, all at once. I sprinted to the other side of the car, looked through the driver's side window. A little more light reached the car from the gray sky on that side of the port, and the first thing I noticed was the color red.

Red smeared along the inside of the glass, as if someone had unsuccessfully taken one swipe with a rag to clean it off. Red, flat and wet, squeezed between the surface where the policeman's head rested against the window. Red, all over his face, spattered in droplets. Red, rimming his lifeless eyes, which stared at the rain though I knew he couldn't actually see anymore.

Officer Wright was dead.

I didn't take another second to investigate, because my sister's words now took on an all new meaning, almost hanging in the air like they'd been formed there by an old man's pipe smoke. What had seemed harmless now meant the end of my world. Jeffrey and Brett had left early that morning; hadn't seen a peep of Wesley. *Lazy like his daddy, I reckon.*

I ran.

Sprinted from the carport and into the rain, the umbrella as forgotten as a stranger's face on a train. Splashed through puddles. Bounded up the steps in one leap. Tore open the door, shouted Wesley's name, my voice so laced with panic that Evelyn's face appeared around the corner from the kitchen, too stunned to speak. I bolted for the long hallway that ran most of the house's length, the various bedroom and bathroom doors facing each other like the cells of an old prison. I knew which one my son would've slept in—knew it from years of him doing that very thing on summer visits.

Third door on the left.

Door closed.

I yanked it open, my grip almost breaking the knob from its frame. In the short time it'd taken me to get there, I had imagined the worse. Someone—my mind pictured Dicky Gaskins without the slightest effort—had come to this house, murdered Officer Scott Wright, sneaked into my sweet sister's house, found my son, killed him where he slept. Or, perhaps like before, he'd taken him again. Taken him away from me a second time, after we'd already saved him, a thing for which I couldn't have forgiven myself if I lived to be a thousand years old.

In the far corner of the dark room, blinds still closed, a sleeping bag lay in a long puddle, bunched and rippled. I leaped forward in two steps, slid to the floor, slammed both of my hands onto the cloth. They met resistance, the hard shoulders of a young boy.

"Wesley!" I yelled, a booming rip of a sound.

He turned toward me, the topmost edge of the sleeping bag toppling off to reveal his sleepy face. He squinted, grunted, moaned.

"Wesley," I repeated, though this time it was only a whisper.

"Hey, Dad," my son said.

5

I made a decision that I probably should've made a day earlier. Come hell or high water—and with Dicky Gaskins on the loose and rain falling like God's very own tears, either one was a viable possibility—my family wouldn't separate again. No sleepovers, no babysitting, no hide and seek, no trips to the grocery store with Grandma. Except for maybe—*maybe*—the brief moments it took a person to shower, I planned to keep all four of my kids within my sight until we went back home to Georgia.

The day that followed my grim discovery in the cop car was a strange mixture of fear, relief, and rock-bottom boredom. We all felt afraid—how could you not when someone had murdered an officer of the law right under your noses? Daylight helped, as scant as it was under the thickly clouded skies, and being together helped. But the fear in my children's eyes—even Logan, to whom we hadn't explained one iota of what had happened—made my heart ache. Despite that, the rescue-relief of thinking the worst about Wesley and then finding him sound asleep on the floor still inflated my chest with enough happy air to offset the deflation of everything else. And the boredom...

Sheriff Taylor wouldn't let us leave, saying he had federal agents up his ass about procedure and protocol, scene of the crime, witnesses, all that *Law and Order* shit. So we sat around, together, in the living room, not doing a damn thing. The weather had knocked out the cable and every station on the radio sounded like static and fuzz, broken up every once in awhile with a drumbeat or shriek of guitar. The Wi-Fi sucked, making Netflix or Hulu a pipe dream. So we played Monopoly— mostly because Wesley had made a joke about it and I wanted to prove it could be fun. Checkers and chess as well, and Evelyn kept us fed. We each took our turns with a grumpy old lady from the FBI, asking us the same questions over and over again, but not a one of us knew a single thing about how or why that poor

Officer had been killed or who had done it (though if it had been put to a vote, Dicky would've won in a landslide). I didn't even know the method of his untimely demise—all I'd seen was blood and a whole lot of it.

It was a day to forget. Even Hazel had a hard time being bubbly.

Sequestered.

Bored.

Scared.

Rain falling like a son of a bitch, its incessant patter loud but silent, a thing none of us would ever notice again until it stopped. Andrea stayed by my side, never saying a word about the dark happenings that had descended on our old town, just being my friend, taking over with the kids when she could tell my will had fainted within me.

That night, long after the sun had set, its passing marked only by gray turning to black, they finally let us return to my parents' house. We slept in the living room, as always, Andrea snuggled with Hazel on the couch, me on the floor with Mason and Logan, Wesley reclined in the World's Largest Chair.

It was a day not that long ago, and yet I can't remember a single phrase uttered, or who played whom in the games, much less who won. I don't remember the food we ate or the face of the grumpy old FBI woman. I can't recall a thing but the fear, the relief, the boredom. Those three things swirl into the rest of that long day like colors, mixing together until all I see is a blob of tie-dye. We slept, and the next day began.

My eyes fluttered open, early that morning. Gray light glowed behind the blinds.

Dad stood above me like an obelisk, his face hidden in shadow. He dropped something onto the carpet, right in front of my face. A newspaper. I blinked a few times, then lifted myself onto an elbow. The paper had unfolded to reveal the front page, above the fold, where they always told you the very worst things. I stared at the biggest headline for a very long time:

FIVE MORE BODIES FOUND IN SUMTER COUNTY

I read the article, each word taking me back in time—it was like my dad had taken out an old paper saved from my 17th summer, the details strikingly similar to what Pee Wee Gaskins had done back in the day. Bodies found in swamps, brutally murdered, some of them missing heads. How could Dicky be so much like his demented father? How? The possibility that someone else was doing it didn't even bother crossing my mind. It had to be him. One Gaskins carrying on the family legacy.

I sloughed back to the floor and stared at the ceiling. The horrors of my childhood had returned, fully. Returned to spite me, to make sure I knew that my escape all those summers ago was a sham, that I didn't *deserve* to escape the fate destined for one David Player. Karma wasn't about to let me get away with the mistakes I'd made the first time around. Mistakes I was starting to remember all too well.

Hours passed before everyone else woke up. During those lonely hours, I wished that the ghost of Grandpa Fincher would float down through the ceiling and scare the life out of me. I needed the distraction.

CHAPTER FOURTEEN

Lynchburg, South Carolina
June 1989

I

I hadn't seen Andrea in two days.

Now, with the wisdom and cynicism of time passed, I look back and doubt myself when I remember how hard that was on me. I can only imagine what others may think, those who didn't live out those terrifying weeks as I had. But I tell you, Andrea and I were already best friends *before* Pee Wee Gaskins swooped in and made life a living hell. Those dark days then solidified our bond into something like granite—hard, unbreakable. A thing on which others might shatter their teeth if they didn't handle with care.

It wasn't fair. I needed her. She needed me. It wasn't fair.

Bait.

I sat on a cheap bed in a cheap motel—one of those old-school jobs with a long line of attached rooms, all the doors facing directly onto the parking lot—my feet propped up, pointing at the tiny TV that had been showing episodes of an ancient series called *The Andy Griffith Show* all day long. Such was my boredom that I had been trying desperately to figure out a great mystery about this old, black-and-white show. The main character was a sheriff, and his name was Andy Taylor. *Sheriff Taylor*, just like the man in charge of protecting the great city and county of Sumter. Then why in the hell was it called *The Andy Griffith Show*? Imagine if they'd called *TJ Hooker*—the finest cop series of my generation—*The Bill Shatner Show* instead? The idea was preposterous.

These are the types of mundane conversations I had with myself while doing absolutely nothing in my little prison of a motel room.

They'd put me in there the very day we'd escaped the freak show at the Honeyhole. The FBI agent put directly in charge of my safety—a little wisp of a man named Agent Jackson who didn't seem capable of protecting himself, much less me—explained that the motel and its surroundings were far easier to monitor than our farmhouse. Cops were supposedly planted in several spots, their whole purpose supposedly to keep David Player and Andrea Llerenas alive.

She was there, same motel, somewhere. That's what was making me so angry. It seemed beyond unreasonable that we couldn't have some time together, at least a few hours. I was heavily traumatized, and she was the only one who truly understood. I needed her, but my pleas and explanations fell on deaf ears. If I'd heard one more person tell me to "trust us, we know what we're doing" or "your safety is our only concern right now" I would've punched said person in their nether regions, up top or down below, whichever caused the most damage.

I didn't know much about the plan to capture Pee Wee Gaskins and his minions, those other creeps at the Honeyhole, all of them hiding their faces behind plastic grocery bags. I'd never been a huge fan of the word "bait"—something about it implied cheating to me, which was why I'd always been more of a hunting fan over fishing—but having it applied to me brought things to a whole new level. I was going to serve as bait. Andrea, too, for all I knew. And although the exact details of the plan hadn't been revealed yet, I'd been assured by no less than 10 people that the risk to my life was zero.

Zero? *They must really think I'm stupid*, I thought to myself many times during those couple of days holed up in the motel. The odds of dying by lightning bolt while taking a dump in a porta-potty were extremely small, but certainly not zero. Laying a trap for a serial killer, using teenagers as bait... I was pretty damn sure I'd rather take my chances in the porta-potty.

Barney Fife said something smarmy while adjusting his gun belt on *The Andy Griffith Show*. Sheriff Andy Taylor took it in stride, then offered some wizened advice that could apply to any situation, be you a socially awkward deputy of the law or a kid about to lay in wait for a murderer. Soft music accompanied the sheriff's age-old wisdom, and for some reason another black-and-white video popped in my mind—*Psycho*, by Alfred Hitchcock. My eyes wandered over to the motel bathroom, where I could see the shower curtain in the mirror.

Maybe that was the plan. I'd take a shower and wait for Pee Wee Gaskins to sneak in with a knife, ready to slash me to death just like Anthony Perkins did to Janet Leigh. We could even play that iconic music—the reen-reen-reen scream of the violins—to make it feel authentic. The cops could hide in the toilet...

Someone knocked on the door, startling me out of my ridiculous line of thoughts.

My feet swung off the bed and onto the floor, my hands pressed to the mattress, leaning forward as I looked in the direction of the knock. Fear was like an icicle in my throat. But I had no reason to be scared—guards were stationed both in front of and behind my room, and several more in the general area. My parents were in the room next door to me, where at the moment they were hosting Sheriff Taylor and Agent Jackson, probably discussing just how they planned to dangle their youngest son on a string for Pee Wee, like a carrot in front of a mule.

But none of that mattered when I heard the tapping of knuckles on wood. There was only fear.

"Who is it?" I shouted, trying to sound steady.

"Open the door."

I leaped to my feet and did as I was commanded because it had come from a very familiar and friendly voice. Andrea stood there with her arms folded, looking back at me with a sideways smile. A man in a suit stood right behind her, a white dude who looked like he slept during the day like a vampire, and he didn't seem too happy.

"You talked them into letting us hang out?" I asked hopefully.

"Something like that," she replied. "Let's just say I can pitch a fit with the best of 'em when I need to."

"You guys have a half-hour," the ghostly agent said. "And if I get in trouble, I'm gonna tell them you bit me." He turned away from us and stared out at the parking lot, but I was pretty sure I'd seen a trace of a smile before he did.

I took a step back, swinging the door wider. "Well, come on in, Aunt Bea!"

"Huh?" Her puzzled look made me feel a little giddy—I was just excited to have her there.

"Aunt Bea!" I replied in my very best southern drawl. "Ain't you come to make me dinner? Mmm-mmm, Aunt Bea, you have outdone yourself this time!"

She came inside, giving me an overly exaggerated look of worry. "This is how you've been dealing with things? Watching old TV shows? Learning sexist lessons about the women-folk doing all the cooking?"

I only laughed, and it was as genuine as they come.

We sat on the bed, legs folded up beneath us, facing each other.

"So what's going on with you?" she asked. "Have you heard much?"

"Not really. Even my mom and dad won't tell me what the plan is. I've basically been sitting here for two days, eating McDonald's and watching TV, listening to my mom tell me over and over again that everything will work out."

Andrea nodded with her lips pursed. "Sounds a lot like what I've been doing."

"More people were killed, though," I said. My dad had left me the paper that morning, saying I deserved to know what we were up against. "Some woman named Kenzie Dunford—they found her at the dump, right where the swamp borders it. I guess she was pretty... rotten, decomposed, whatever. But they think Pee Wee did it because... you know."

"Her head?"

"Her head. There was another guy, too. Can't remember his name—I'd never heard of either one of them. He was more recent, I guess, maybe even last night."

Andrea sighed, slowly shaking her head. "How in the world can he keep getting away with it? I mean, this guy's tromping around, leaving bodies all over the place, storing their heads somewhere... It's not like we're in New York City for crap's sake. There are only so many trees and barns he can hide behind."

I shrugged, feeling a little hopeless. My excitement over her visit had been spoiled.

"What do you think they're gonna do?" she asked. "They can't *actually* be serious about using us as bait, right?"

"I think so, but I think it's something more like a trick."

"What do you mean?"

"Like... I don't know. It's not like they're going to put is in a box, propped up with a stick that's got a string tied around it.

Right? Pull the string when Pee Wee runs in to snatch us? There's no way it's something like that."

Andrea adjusted to get more comfortable, lying down, resting her head on an elbow-propped hand. "So maybe they're going to use a decoy? Or just try to make him think we're somewhere, been moved somewhere..." She groaned and rubbed her eyes. "I don't know. It hurts to use my brain."

"That's the gist of it," I agreed, these thoughts really just coming to me as we spoke. "I bet they're planting fake evidence or making fake phones calls or whatever. We just gotta hold tight and get through this."

"I miss the good ole days when we thought there was just one of him."

That realization had been weighing me down, too. Having one maniac haunt your town was bad enough, scary enough. Seeing those two others with bags on their heads, obviously in cahoots with Pee Wee, made things unbearable. It was like a sign at a haunted carnival: *Three killers for the price of one, come one, come all!* I could almost envision the creepy carny hawker standing beneath it, yelling those words to the crowds as they passed him by, heading for the bearded lady or the four-legged man.

"Yeah," I finally said, not sure what else to say. "When they catch 'em, we're gonna party like it's 1999."

"They will," she said. "And no, we're gonna party *until* it's 1999."

"Deal." I held up an invisible glass of champagne, and she pretended to click it with one of her own, then made a show of sipping it like a lady, pinkie raised.

"Why you, anyway?" she asked.

I looked at her, not liking the heavy weight of that simple question.

She sat back up, only a few inches away from me. "Seriously, David. There has to be a reason, right?"

I nodded, remembering what Pee Wee had said to me at the

Honeyhole. "You heard him. My grandpa supposedly *took* something from him."

"Yeah, but *what?*" It was an obvious rhetorical question—neither one of us could possibly know—but it still frustrated me.

"How am I supp—" I caught myself. Sighed. "It can't be money or anything like that. The Gaskins don't quite strike me as the *Beverly Hillbillies* if you know what I mean." Rumor had it that Pee Wee lived in a shack in the middle of nowhere, without any electricity or running water. Or used to anyway. He'd been on the run since we saw him in the woods that first night when it all began.

Andrea was slowly nodding her head, deep in thought. "You're right. What could it be? What could your grandpa *possibly* have taken from him that would make him... *do* this? Some kind of family heirloom, maybe? Or it could be, like, a metaphor. Your family picking on his family."

"Do I dare ask my dad?"

"You told the police, right? I did."

"Yeah, I told them. But not around my dad. I mean, I know they asked him about it, but he hasn't said a word to me. For some reason I don't wanna bring it up, like he'll think I'm accusing him or something. Hard to explain." I grabbed a pillow and shook it, squeezing it with both hands as if I wanted to strangle the fluffy thing. "I hate this!" I shouted. "I just want it to be over!"

Andrea was moving toward me, reaching out with her arms for a hug, when there was a rapid knock at the door. It scared the hell out of both of us, and I'm not sure which one jumped the highest.

"Who is it?" I yelled out.

The door opened and my dad's head poked through the gap. I could see my mom trying to get a peek, right behind him.

"Hey, son," Dad said. "Our meeting's over. Just thought we'd come visit with ya for a bit."

I glanced guiltily at Andrea, not even sure why. Pee Wee Gaskins had me all messed up.

"Come on in," I said rather absurdly.

"Great!" Mom said cheerily as they entered the room. "We've got chicken!"

2

There aren't a lot of axioms in life that are always true, 100% of the time. But here's one of them: If you live in the south, and you're having a bad day, fried chicken will *always* make you feel better.

A half-hour after my parents barged into the room carrying two buckets of greasy, smelly, gloriously cooked bird, I sat back against the wall at the head of the bed, licking my fingers to no avail. At that point, only a full shower with scalding hot water could cleanse my oily, glistening skin. Rogue smudges of grease had gone all the way to my elbows.

Andrea had left, summoned by the same pasty gentleman from earlier, appearing a little more comfortable now that the sun had started to go down. Andrea's mom had ordered in some Chinese food and was patiently awaiting her, he'd said rather briskly, and off they went. I could see the bulge of a weapon under his sport coat, and that gave me some relief.

"Did ya get enough?" my mom asked, perched on the far corner of the bed. "There's still almost a full bucket over here." She gestured toward the cardboard tub sitting on the dresser, its bottom third dark with seeping grease.

"Mom, did you want me stuffed like a turkey so I'd make better bait?" I rubbed my tummy and tried to laugh, even though I knew it had been a terrible, absolutely awful joke.

"Not. Funny." She gave my dad a look mean enough to singe his eyebrows.

"Sorry," I said. "But can't you guys tell me what's going on? What the plan is?"

"David, listen..." My mom faded off what she was going to say when my dad stood up from his chair and walked over to where she sat, looming over her, his face pinched and angry. She cowered, just a tiny flinch, but in my eyes it was as if he'd slapped her. What was *with* this? First with the cops, now in my motel room—Dad pulling this alpha male shit on my mom. I'd never seen him act like this.

"What's..." I couldn't quite find the words to pose a question.

My mom had been staring at the floor, avoiding Dad's eyes. But now she looked over at me. "Everything's going to be okay, son. You'll see. This bait nonsense isn't as bad as it sounds."

"I think David and I better have a chat," Dad said, his tone laced with warning and completely directed at Mom. "Why don't you go next door—I'll be there in a jiffy."

She stood up, brushing her clothes, straightening her blouse. And to her credit, she looked my dad square in the eyes, their noses practically touching.

"Any harm comes to my boy," she said, making her husband's earlier tone sound like it came from a cartoon bunny, "I swear to Heaven above that this world will never have *seen* such wrath before."

With that, she came over and gave me a kiss on the cheek, then marched out of the room without another glance at my dad. She slammed the door behind her, its thump like a shout in the silence of her wake. It took a moment for Dad to recover, his eyes lingering on the closed door long after she'd left.

"Dad," I said, "what's going on? I've never seen you and mom like this."

He responded by slumping to the bed, sitting on the edge, his head falling to rest in his hands.

"Oh, son, there are some things in this world that you could never..."

He didn't finish, but I was annoyed, anyway. There's nothing so condescending as a parent telling you that some things you just can't understand until you're older. Even if it's true, let us figure that out on our own, I always thought growing up. Using it as an answer to genuine questions or concerns was nothing but a cop-out in my book. Although I've changed over the decades to believe what I so hated, at the least I've never uttered the words aloud to my own kids.

"*What*, Dad?" I pushed when he went quiet.

He lifted his head and turned toward me. "I tell you what. I give you my word that someday I'll tell you everything. There's a... history between our family and the Gaskins. A dark history. I don't have it in me to explain quite yet, but first things first."

Startled by his words, I sat in silence.

My dad was visibly frustrated, sweating, his hands trembling. "Listen to me, son. All I can say is... We have to catch Pee Wee. We *have* to. Do you understand me? We have to catch him tonight. Tomorrow. The next day at the latest. We have to catch him and be done with this. I know it's not fair to you, not fair at all. But I swear upon the lives of my ancestors, upon my own father, my own mother... I swear on the life of your siblings and my sweet wife... I will *not* let any harm come to you or to Andrea. You hear me? You'll be safe."

The tremor in his hands had traveled up his arms, to his entire body. In a weird juxtaposition, it reminded me of that slight shivering on Christmas morning that I could never quite get to stop as a little kid.

"Why's it so important to catch him?" I asked. "I mean, besides the obvious. What *history* do we have between our families? I didn't even know he had a son."

That last comment made him ball up his hands into fists and shake them above his lap. "He wasn't supposed to..." He didn't finish, choosing to let out his frustrations with a big groan.

I felt... strange. Like a thin veil that had always hidden my dad's true face was about to be lifted to reveal a completely different person than I'd always envisioned.

Dad abruptly stood up, his eyes on the floor. "Like I said, someday I'll explain all of this. Okay? I promise. But right now you just need to sit tight and do what you're told. We're gonna catch that son of a bitch and end this once and for all. If I have to do it all by myself, by God I'll do it." He walked toward the door, still not giving me so much as a glance.

I couldn't believe the immensity of things unsaid. Scrambling for one question among so many, I blurted out what first popped in my head.

"Well what's the plan? When are you going to string me out for bait?"

He had his hand on the doorknob, had already twisted it, but froze at my words. For several seconds he stood that way, unmoving. Then he slowly turned his head to look at me.

"Son, that's already happened. What do you think this is, a vacation? You're strung up on the fishhook already." He paused, maybe regretting the assholery of his response. "I'm sorry, David. I love you more than I could possibly express. But... we just gotta get through this." He opened the door and took a step over the threshold.

"Dad, wait!" I shouted. "What do you mean I'm on the fishhook?"

He stopped, turned toward me again. "Just like I said, son. We've got no choice but to use you as bait, finish this thing. Sorry for the piss-poor imagery, but we've got you strung up on the fishhook." He took a breath. "And now we're going to cast the line out, into the most rotten part of the swamp, just like any good fisherman. DNow do what you're told."

He shut the door before I could respond.

CHAPTER FIFTEEN

Lynchburg, South Carolina
July 2017

I

I didn't know what to do.

People were being murdered all over my old hometown. A cop had his throat cut right in the driveway of my sister's house, while my own son slept inside. And now we had two officers of the law keeping watch, one in the front yard, one in the back, while we sat in the home in which I grew up, doing absolutely nothing. My four kids were bored out of their minds, with all the time in the world to think about the scary things going on out there in the swamps and woods surrounding us. My mom did her best, playing games, making food, finding things on TV to watch. Dad had gone out to run some errands, answering his wife's protests by saying that if Dicky Gaskins wanted to mess with him, then bring it on.

Sometime in the afternoon I decided I was five minutes from insanity. I didn't know what to do—no. Even worse, I knew there was nothing I *could* do. Or should do. This wasn't like being a kid again, when the adults had lost their minds and decided to let a teenager act as bait for a serial killer. This time around we'd leave it to the police and wait it out. There were many, *many* things worse than boredom. But still, I was three steps from going bananas, as Hazel had once said when it rained for a week in Atlanta.

I cornered Andrea in the kitchen when I found her in there pretending to search for something in the fridge. The real reason she'd left the living room, I knew, was because Mason had asked her to play Monopoly again.

"Oh, there's the... mayonnaise," she said when she finally noticed me, arms folded knowingly, staring at her. She pulled out the half-empty jar and studied its contents. "Oh, good, looks like there's plenty."

"Yeah?" I questioned. "What're you lookin' to make? Mayonnaise on crackers?"

She rolled her eyes and put the jar back into the fridge. "I needed a break."

"Me, too. Kids are great, especially when they're at school or asleep."

"Very funny. You better not take those precious things for granted, you heartless bastard." She pulled out a chair from the table and sat down, then put an elbow on the table and plopped her chin into her open palm, blew air through her lips. "They *can* be exhausting, I'll admit. Who invented Monopoly, anyway? I hope that sadistic son of a bitch is rotting in a pile of fake money."

I took a seat next to her. "Pretty sure he made lots of *real* money."

"Yeah, whatever. Capitalist pig."

Wesley walked into the kitchen, gave us a cursory glance, then opened the fridge, started perusing its contents.

"What's up, big fella?" I asked.

"I'm about to drop-kick Logan through a window is what's up." He pulled out a stick of butter, leaving me flabbergasted as to what he planned to do with it. "If that kid whines about one more thing, it's gonna happen. I'll pay for the broken glass." He shut the fridge door and put the butter on the counter.

"Uh, Wesley?" I asked. "Please tell me you're not going to eat that stick of butter with a knife and fork?"

"At least spread some mayonnaise on it first," Andrea said, then snickered at her own joke even though Wesley didn't get it.

He breathed in and let out a heavy sigh. "I was gonna make some toast." He said it the same way he might've pronounced that he had three weeks to live, then stood there and stared at the counter.

Guilt washed through me—once again, I knew that he needed a therapist, a counselor, someone to talk to about what he'd been through. I fully planned to make this a reality as soon as possible—after the storm, after the trip, after the capture of Dicky Gaskins. After, after, after. My son needed something *now*. But like everything else on that long, endless day, I didn't know what to do.

I stood up and walked over to him, put my hand on his shoulder. "You okay, bud? I mean, I know nothing's really okay right now, but... I'm sorry. I wish I could make you feel better."

"Dad, it's fine." He turned his eyes on me and all I saw was sadness. "I just decided I didn't want toast after all. I'm fine." But he didn't look away.

I pulled the kid into a hug, patted his back like he was two years old and needed a burp. "This trip really sucks, doesn't it? Really, really sucks."

"I've had worse." He stepped back from me and attempted a smile. "When can we go home, though?"

The question hurt my heart. "They say the storm'll be over tomorrow." I sighed. "Look, I was thinking they'd catch Dicky and everything would be fine. But now I feel like an idiot. I tell you what—I'll try to talk Grandma and Grandpa into coming back to Atlanta with us. Maybe Evelyn and them, too. This place is kinda spoiled for a while, huh."

"Yeah, you could say that."

Andrea came up and squeezed him a good hug. "Maybe I could come, too?"

"Really?" Wesley responded immediately. The word was packed with so much enthusiasm and genuineness that my spirits lifted back up.

"Absolutely! But only if your cheap-skate dad promises to take us to a couple of Braves games."

They both looked at me. I was a little stunned at how quickly the shades of darkness had been lifted from the room. Peace filled me, and I couldn't wait to get on the road the next day.

"You know," I said, "I think the Nats are coming into town. I hereby swear in the name of the law that we'll go to all three games in the series. Lower level, even." That phrase almost choked itself out before escaping through my throat and past my mouth. "I mean, seriously. What dad in the history of the world has ever made a promise like that?"

"Group hug," Andrea said.

We did it, the arms wrapped around me feeling like those of angels.

"I do have one teensy-weensy condition," I said when we were finished, holding my thumb and index finger a millimeter apart.

"What?" the two of them asked simultaneously.

"Monopoly. Right now. Full rules, no short cuts, the three of us and Mason."

By the looks on their faces, you would've thought I'd requested a severed finger and toe from each of them. But I stood my ground and waited for their response.

"Dibs on the wheelbarrow," Wesley said.

"Fine."

"Who the hell wants to be the wheelbarrow?" Andrea asked as we moved toward the front room.

"I need something to hold all the money I'm gonna take from you," was Wesley's perfect reply.

I swore right then and there to help Mason win.

The world was back on its proper axis.

2

Mason didn't win. Neither did Wesley. I sure as hell didn't.

Andrea took it in an absolute rout. And she didn't mind gloating much, either, even going so far as to make a "raise-the-roof" gesture, pumping both hands toward the ceiling like a deranged gorilla. It was so quaint and endearing that I didn't even bother ridiculing her dorkiness.

Dad had been gone all afternoon, returning home with enough buckets of fried chicken to feed half of Sumter County. It brought back memories of a day long ago that I'd spent every year since trying to forget, but my mouth and stomach didn't complain at all as I downed two drumsticks, a wing, two thighs, and every scrap of the biggest breast ever to be sliced off a chicken.

The rain appeared to be tapering off, the light tap-tap-tapping on the roof almost a shock to each of us—we'd gotten so used to the steady roar of the downpour that our ears didn't quite know what to do with this new sound. I stood at the window, watching the scattered raindrops splash into the thousand little lakes of the front yard—it was like Minnesota out there. One more day of this and there would've been some serious flooding.

Andrea came up to me and rubbed my back for a second. "Looks like there's a light at the end of the tunnel. You sure about leaving tomorrow?"

"Oh, yeah," I replied. "I don't know why I didn't think of just dragging my parents along earlier. This place is kind of ruined for awhile anyway." *Maybe forever*, I didn't say aloud. Grandpa Fincher might've been listening with his ghost ears right above our heads.

"And..." She hesitated. "You sure about me coming along?"

It touched me that she asked that, that she hesitated, that her voice betrayed just how much she longed to go. I turned to her.

"Are you kidding? I will go out into those puddles and get down on my knees and *beg* you to come with us if I have to."

She hugged me and I squeezed back. Maybe, after all these years...

"Everyone's in a good mood," she whispered. "If you're gonna tell your parents, now's the time. They need plenty of hours to pack their old-people stuff."

I laughed at that, probably a little harder than it deserved. "You're right. I'm nervous, though. My dad likes traveling about as much as he likes Richard Nixon. And yes, he still talks about Richard Nixon. Don't you dare ask him about it."

"Well, put on your man-panties and get her done."

I kissed her, right there in front of the whole family. By the time I was done, every man, woman, and child in the room was staring at us, eyes wide open. It had worked out perfectly. I cleared my throat and posed the question.

"How would everyone feel about packing up Grandma and Grandpa and kidnapping them back to Atlanta?" There was a cheer from all four of my kids—even Logan, who just imitated Mason. "We'll even ask Jeff and Evelyn to come."

Another cheer. My mom beamed with pleasure, as if she'd been waiting for me to get off my ass and suggest we get the hell out of Dodge. Dad looked contemplative, but he was doing that slow nod with his lips pinched, as if he'd just heard an idea so wise he couldn't believe he hadn't come up with it himself. *Looks like we have an arrangement*, I thought.

"Great," I said. "We'll leave first thing in the morning. Now, five bucks to anyone who can stuff another piece of chicken down their throat..."

3

I decided to put each kid to bed in a very individual way that night. It was our last one at Grandma's for a while—*forever, maybe*, I tried very hard not to think—and this house and home was sacred ground to me. I wanted it to feel the same to the four precious things that made up my brood, and I hated that the damn Gaskins family had done their best to ruin that dream. We'd have one last, wonderful, peaceful, beautiful, memorable night. We'd try to forget that there were cops outside and a lunatic on the loose.

Logan was first up. Mom and Dad had been packing for at least an hour, acting like they were about to head out on the Titanic. I would not have been the least bit surprised if my mom had dragged out Grandma Fincher's old trunk, but thankfully she settled for a suitcase roughly the size of an airplane bathroom. Wesley was in the shower, Hazel reading a book, Mason studying the rules to Monopoly—the kid surely thought he could find a loophole to nullify Andrea's grand victory earlier. She sat on the couch, eyeing him suspiciously.

I had Logan all tucked away into several blankets on the floor, right beside the fireplace.

"How's my Wolverine?" I asked him. No one had turned on the fans yet, so I didn't have to yell at the top of my lungs.

He yawned—the little guy resembled a lion more than a wolverine (whatever the hell that is)—and stretched, then curled back into a ball and closed his eyes, pulling his favorite blanket up to his chin. The thing was two layers of flannel, stuffed and quilted and covered with *Star Wars* characters—it would've been my favorite, too. I tickled his back.

"Uh, Logan? Did you lose your tongue somewhere?"

He made a sound that somewhat conjured a "Huh?"

"I asked how you're doing there, partner."

"Good, daddy. Thanks."

This made me laugh, not even sure why. "You excited for our big road trip tomorrow?"

His eyes popped open. "Yeah. Can we have Mountain Dew?"

"All you can drink. We can save the bottle for you to pee in."

He giggled like any tiny kid would at the mention of bodily fluid. "What about poop?"

"We'll probably have to pull over for something like that. It'd be hard to get that in the bottle without making a mess. But you can fart all you want."

"Eww," Andrea said from the couch with a scrunched up face. "Seriously? Who's the four year old? Logan, your dad is disgusting."

Logan liked that response and giggled harder. I showed my displeasure by reaching for the closest fan and twisting the dial to full blast. That wondrous breeze and soothing sound made me want to lie my head down next to Logan's and welcome the sweet bliss of sleep. But I had three kids to go.

"Hey, Wolverine," I whispered directly into his ear.

He twisted to look up at me, made that "Huh?" grunting sound again.

"I love you."

"Love you, too."

"How much?"

"All the way to the ceiling in the room with the green couches *and...* all the way around the world." This is a sacred phrase in our family, and I can't bring myself to describe its origins. Some things I will keep in my heart.

"Good," I said. "That's how much I love you, too."

I hugged the little man, squeezed him tight, praying this precious child never had to experience some of the horrors his brother and I had seen.

"Nighty night, Wolverine."

"Night, daddy."

Next up, Hazel.

4

She was as sweet as always, that girl. After reading some of her latest conquest—*Matilda*—out loud to me, she finally put the book down and snuggled into my arms.

"I can barely hear myself think with that fan on," she said. "I know you couldn't hear me reading." Little did she know she sounded like a 50-year-old woman.

"You want me to turn it off?" I asked.

"Are you crazy? I'd rather turn off my brain."

"That's my girl." I hugged her a little tighter. My kids really knew how to bring me joy.

"Daddy?"

"Yeah, sweetie?"

"Sometimes I feel bad cuz I forget things about Mommy."

I kissed the back of her head, surprised at just how much her comment had hurt. "It's okay, Hazel. I promise. We'll always have the pictures and videos to remind us. She's out there some-where, remembering you, and that's enough... goodness to fill the whole universe. I wish you could understand just how much that lady loved you. Someday you might have kids of your own and understand how you can love someone so much it actually feels a little like pain."

"I already do understand."

She didn't elaborate, and tears moistened my eyes enough that one dropped out, splatting right into her hair.

"You're wise beyond your years," I said.

"You always say that."

"That's because it's true. You're smart enough to be President."

"Am I smart enough to be you?"

"Okay, now you're just trying to get something. You need to borrow money?"

She giggled, and if my goal before bed was to get each of my kids to do so, then I was already halfway there.

"What're we gonna eat on our trip?" she asked.

Kids could change the subject on a dime, a magical gift, especially when food was involved.

"Hmm, I don't know. I'm kind of in the mood for *Combos*. The pizza flavored ones."

"Those are gross. I was thinking more like *Cool Ranch Doritos*."

"Oh, you wanna kill us all with your breath? Okay, cool."

"At least I don't get the toots like you and Mason."

If I had an additional goal to include flatulence in each kid's conversation before bed, then I was two-for-two.

"At least mine aren't as stinky as Mason's," I said as solemnly as possible.

She laughed again, and I figured I was about done, here. But I didn't want to let go.

"You tired, sweetie?"

"Yeah." She shifted out of my embrace and pulled her pillow close like a teddy bear. "I better get a proper sleep for our trip tomorrow."

Smiling from ear to ear, I gave her last one kiss on top of the head. "Oh yes, you should. I don't want a mopey dopey all the way home."

She smiled, already half-dozed. I left her to it.

5

"It says it right here, Dad."

Mason pointed at a rule deeply imbedded within the minutiae of the Monopoly instructions. We were on the carpet, somewhere between Hazel and Logan, both of whom were breathing the deep sighs of sleep already. At least that's what it looked like —I couldn't hear much over the blowing fan.

Mason eyed Andrea—reading an old and dusty National Geographic on the couch—then shifted to have his back to her. I looked over his shoulder to read the line he'd indicated.

"Huh," I grunted.

"There's nothing about putting 500 bucks in the middle. Or the taxes and fees. Landing on Free Parking has nothing to do with that money!"

I was impressed with my son's determination and research capabilities. Andrea had insisted on utilizing the old made-up rule despite Mason insisting it wasn't actually in the official instructions. Looked like he was right.

"Break it to her gently," I said, throwing an amused glance back at Andrea. She knew all too well what was up. "Maybe wait for the drive back. That way she can't escape when you rub it in her face."

"Good plan."

"Let's get you to sleep, okay? Long day tomorrow."

"All riiiight." He said it with that drawn out, whiney voice as he folded up the Monopoly instructions and tossed them aside. "I guess she can have one night thinking she won. But I can't wait to bust her on it in the car. And we have to do a rematch!"

I thought I might need medication when this rematch took place, but we'd cross that bridge when we came to it. "I'll be rooting for ya. Now let's get some sleep."

He mumbled something unintelligible, and I left him to his

sweet dreams, filled with piles of money and monocled men in top hats.

6

Wesley had already dozed off when I sat on the armrest of Dad's chair. I looked down at him, studying his features—his foppish hair, his teen-oily skin, his hardening jawline. You never noticed your kids' changes from day to day, but every once in a while, in a moment like this, it hit you hard and heavy just how much they'd leaped forward in age. How had the little baby I'd once held in my arms and for whom I'd changed poopy diapers turn into this man-child lying before me? It now took considerable movement of my head for my eyes to travel from his head to the tips of his toes, when I used to see his whole body in one glance.

My little boy was all grown up.

I grabbed the blanket that was draped across the back of the chair and fluffed it over Wesley, then tucked it under his chin like the good ole days when he slept in the car-shaped toddler bed. He rolled over to his side, pulling the blanket along with him, turned away from me.

"Goodnight, bud," I said. The other fan stood next to his chair; I turned it on.

Andrea walked up, grabbed my hand, then pulled me along behind her as she went to the kitchen. Mom was in there, emptying the dishwasher. When Andrea saw her, she seemed disappointed. Maybe the plan had been for us to make out while we munched on snacks—seemed as good a time as any to break the ice and return to our teenage glory years.

"Hey kids," Mom said, as if she'd read my thoughts and wanted to play along. "I think your father and I are finally packed up and ready to go. He just went out to check some of the irrigation lines, make sure the flooding hasn't broken anything."

"What?" I asked. "Right now? It's pitch black outside."

Mom waved it off as if to say, *Whatcha gonna do?*

"Should I go help him?"

"Nah. I think he wanted some time to think before we head out to your place."

"Are the cops out there with him? I better make sure they keep an eye out."

"David," Mom said firmly. "Nothing's going to happen to your dear old dad. He took his handgun with him." She laughed at that, making me wonder if she'd slipped herself a gin and tonic or two after he'd left.

"Well, why don't you at least get some sleep. Come on. We'll finish putting those away for you."

She thanked us and left, leaving us to it.

"I can't blame him," Andrea said as she put away a casserole dish, seeming to choose a spot randomly. "This house is so small I can't get you alone to save my life, and with all the rain I think everybody's got a case of cabin fever."

I stacked some plates then put them in the proper cupboard. "You wanted to get me alone, huh? Ooh la la."

She shook her head endearingly. "You're so adorable. Actually, I wanted to show you something I found on the Internet. Somebody must've fixed the connection now that the storm's ending."

I stopped, everything else on my mind vanishing with a snap. "Really? What'd you find?"

"This really old site that talks about... weird stuff. Really weird stuff. Most of it's about things in the south, especially in South Carolina. Let's just say the Lizard Man... ya know, what old Gramps used to go on about at the fall festival? There's a whole page on him. It. Whatever."

My hopes for groundbreaking information collapsed like a sinkhole. "Oh," was all I could get out.

"But there's something else." She grabbed the utensil bucket —which filled me with joy; I hated putting away forks, spoons, and knives—and walked over to the correct drawer, opened it. I realized then that she was remembering all of this from our childhood, from the many times she'd been over here. My parents hadn't changed a thing in all these years.

"What is it?" I asked, leaning back against the counter. We were done with our chore.

"Let's go back to my room and I'll show you." She closed the utensil drawer with a soft thunk and put the bucket back into the dishwasher. "My iPad's in there."

"Uh-huh," I said. "I can see what's going on here."

"Oh please." Another head shake—one which I fully deserved—but then she kissed me on the cheek as she walked past. I quickly followed her.

7

About 10 minutes after our dishwasher escapades in the kitchen, Andrea and I found ourselves lounging back on Patsy's bed— poor Patsy, never there to defend her former domicile—snuggling, all four eyes in the room focused on the glowing face of Andrea's iPad. She dexterously moved her fingers across the bright surface, as skilled as the techiest, nerdiest teenager around.

"This is it," she said.

I stared at the screen. The website looked like something programmed back in the 90s, with almost no aesthetic upgrades since. Called *Legends and Myths of the Deep South*, the landing page had hundreds of lines of text, each one of them underlined to show it provided a link to what was described. The entire page was a jumbled mess, the font tiny, the kind of website where your eyes start hurting before you've clicked on a single thing.

"There's so much weird stuff on here," Andrea said. "Sometime you just need to dive in and enjoy the ride. Your ancestors are basically insane."

"That's what makes us special," I murmured. "So what're we looking for on here?"

She scrolled the page a few inches, more and more underlined hot links appearing from the bottom like credits in a movie. "This one right... That one." She pointed at a line squished amongst many.

I had to lean closer and squint my eyes to see the stupid thing. It said:

PURITAN HEXES RIVAL THEIR MOST DEMONIC COUNTERPARTS

I gave her the most baffling expression I could conjure. "Uhhhh..."

"Will you just read the article?" she asked, obviously annoyed. "Give me a little credit?"

"Sorry." I began reading, and paragraph by paragraph, two things became most prominent in my mind: First, that whoever wrote the article had either quit school or stopped trying to learn grammar around the second grade, and second, Andrea must've smoked something funny to think this crazy stuff had anything at all to do with our situation. I mean, this garbage was talking about Puritans and Quakers and curses and bloody sacrifices.

"Just keep reading," she said when I couldn't stop myself from eying her questioningly again. "All the way to the end."

The background of the story went all the way back to precolonial times, when Native Americans still ruled the continent and the only people exploring this far north of what is now Mexico were mostly Europeans fleeing religious persecution. Schoolhouse tales of ships like the *Mayflower* and places like

Jamestown, starvation and disease, brutal battles with those native to this land, futile attempts to plant crops and establish settlements. As glamorous as that one *Peanuts* cartoon might've made it seem, life back then was an absolute hell.

But apparently, things weren't bad enough for them, so they invented new problems, and this was what the article focused on —a completely bonkers rivalry between the Puritans and the Quakers. The hypocrisy, even in the poorly worded article, astounded me. Puritans came over here because they were being persecuted back home, and what was one of the first things they did once they had some resemblance of a new home in a new world? They started persecuting the living shit out of those claiming to be Quakers. I'm talking nasty, awful, horrible shit. Things like quartering bodies and sending the bloody parts back to their families, or old classics like burning people alive at the stake.

And there were darker things, tales of curses and hexes placed on the Quakers, stuff that conjured images of Satanism or witchcraft more than it did of pilgrim Christians running around with their tiny wooden crosses. The one that struck me first was a curse placed by Puritan holy men on pregnant Quaker women—according to the madness I was reading, their babies were born with the skin inside out, no eyes, no tongue, no fingers, no toes. *Egads*, I thought. Another one was described as a hex put upon fathers, making them full of insatiable bloodlust, no matter how many of his own family members and townsfolk he murdered. It all intrigued me enough that I committed to research this craziness later for curiosity's sake.

Still, I had no idea what any of this had to do with my family or the serial killer running around Sumter County. As fascinating as it was, all I wanted to do was snuggle up with Andrea and go to sleep. Tomorrow, we'd escape all the nonsense of my home-town, anyway. My mind wandered and I started to skim a little, wondering just how many sadistic things these people could come up with.

My eyes stopped on a single word. They stopped as suddenly as if some kind of magical, visual wall had erected itself in their path.

That word was *Gaskins*.

"What the..." I whispered.

"Told you," she replied.

I had to backtrack, having spaced it so much that I had no idea in what context that plague of a name had just appeared. Jumping back to the last part for which I knew I'd been well focused—something about putting a hex on cow's milk so that anyone who drank it got such an extreme case of diarrhea that eventually they'd die of dehydration—I began reading again, paying close attention to each and every word on the digital page.

Several families from those harsh, cruel days decided that enough was enough and broke off from the main settlements of both the Puritans and the Quakers. Families from *both* sides, making a pact of peace, despite knowing that the secret pact would be viewed as heresy from their respective peoples. They broke off and fled south, as far as they could reasonably go, eventually settling in the swampy central lands of the Carolinas. The article then listed a few names of these families, and Gaskins was one of them. Player was *not* included—I read the short list twice to make sure.

Andrea was obviously bursting at the seams to get my take on what I'd read—even though I couldn't quite get past seeing the surname of Pee Wee and Dicky.

"*Well?*" she asked. "Could any of those names be relatives of yours? On your dad's mom's side, somewhere up the line on any maternal side?"

I had no answer—genealogy wasn't my forte. Fincher and Player were about the only names I knew for sure. All I could get out to her was, "How on Planet Earth did you find this article?"

"Google is your friend," she replied. "I sifted through a bunch of junk but eventually landed on this gem."

I let out a weary sigh. "Not that it means a whole lot. I mean, what? Do you think the Gaskins family is cursed or something? Cursed to hunt down people and chop their heads off?"

"Don't be a smart ass," she replied, yanking the iPad out of my hands as if I didn't deserve it. "The key is that the Gaskins family goes *way* back, and we know that yours does, too. And yes, running around chopping people's heads off is weird and creepy and unusual by anyone's standards. So the fact that we have this weird-ass article about Puritans and Quakers putting hexes on each other and fleeing to where we now live... *and* that it involved the family of the guy doing it now and his dad who did it before him... *and* that both of these crackpots seem to have a thing for *your* family... I mean, come on. Maybe it means something."

"Yeah, I guess." An enormous yawn bloomed from my chest and I was powerless to hold it back, mouth stretched wide. "Sorry. I'm just so freaking tired. And I don't think any of this can help us tonight. Rain check?"

She looked so disappointed. "It's your family, not mine."

I pulled her into a hug. "Sorry, really. It means a lot that you're doing all this research. Means even more just that you're here. My kids worship you."

"They might like me even more than they like you," she said.

"I think that's a good bet, actually."

She took a deep breath, let it out. Feeling her against my chest brought an amazing sense of peace. As much as sleep beckoned, I couldn't wait to get on our way in the morning, especially with Andrea along for the ride.

"Let's go to bed, then," she whispered.

"Together?"

"No way. That'll confuse the hell out of your kids."

I doubted that. It seemed like something they said on TV or in the movies, but I didn't wanna push it. Plus, we still had a very dark past to overcome before we took too many steps forward.

"I'll head for the couch," I said, giving her one last squeeze. "You don't have a fan in here, anyway, so it never would've worked."

She responded with a genuine laugh, and I was reminded of an old *Seinfeld* episode when George learned to leave immediately when a joke landed properly. I stood up, held my hands toward the ceiling.

"That's it! I'm out of here! Goodnight!"

She looked at me like I'd sprouted a couple of horns.

"*Seinfeld?*" I asked hopefully.

"Ugh. I hated that show."

Exaggerating a heavy sigh, I said, "First *Led Zeppelin*, now *Seinfeld?* That's okay. I forgive you."

"Goodnight, sweet David." She smiled.

"Nighty night."

Feeling like a kid again, I left her room and closed the door.

8

Darkness ruled the house.

I lay on the couch, awash in its comfort and the soothing hum of the double fan action which blew air in conflicting currents throughout the room. I didn't know if my dad had come back into the house yet or not, and I was too tired to check. I figured he was okay or my mom would've pitched a fit by now. We had two policemen outside our home. Others patrolling the streets of Lynchburg and all of Sumter. Dicky Gaskins couldn't possibly be brave or stupid enough to come anywhere near my parents' home.

Tomorrow we'd awaken, bright of spirit. Mom and Dad together would make us a spectacular breakfast, the works, emptying out all the goodies from the fridge and cupboards for one last feast before our journey. Things would be packed into cars, seating arrangements made, movies downloaded onto a plethora of electronic devices, headphones tangled everywhere. Smiles and relief and dreams of new beginnings. The darkness of the past that had made Andrea and I go our separate ways... that darkness could end. We could be what I always wished us to be. Friends. Best friends. Family. And if the world spun on a perfect axis, tilting within all known laws of physics and love, then maybe something magical could happen. Perhaps the eternal pain of losing my wife could soften into something humble and sweet and full of good intentions. Maybe, just maybe, Andrea could be mine and I could be hers, despite our awful parting two decades ago.

I'm not sure I actually believed these things I was telling myself. If my life had proven anything to me, it was that the Gaskins could overcome any obstacle in the world to traumatize my family. But I can honestly tell you that I felt safe. Content. Hopeful. I had no right to—I feel adamant now that something deep inside of me must've been screaming for attention, raking its nails against the hardest walls of my heart, begging me to listen. I did not, and I'm not sure it mattered at all, except in this: I can't say with certainty that I did my best to prevent the events that were about to unfold in lightning-quick fashion. And that's a true dagger.

If any of these prescient thoughts were present in that moment, lying there, in the dark, content and tired, comfortable, enjoying the breeze and lullaby of the fans, the presence of my children, the cocoon of my childhood home, then they were on a level so subconscious that I only guess at them now. At the time, in that moment, my mind drifted in happiness.

I fell asleep.

CHAPTER SIXTEEN

**Lynchburg, South Carolina
June 1989**

I

A noise, from the bathroom in the back of my motel room.
I was still sitting up in bed, unable to sleep after the
things my dad had said before leaving me all alone. Things about
bait and fishhook and doing what I'm told. I had nodded off a
couple of times, but I'd snapped awake instantly. I didn't want to
sleep until I knew something about the plan. Anything. More
than once I'd almost gotten up, ready to march out of there and
demand to see Andrea, knock on every door if I had to. But the
courage to do this heroic act never came, and I sat still in the
silence. Even the low hum of the air conditioner, mounted under
the window, had shut off.

And now, a noise.

Scraping. Like a leafless branch rubbing against the screen of
a window.

The lamp on my nightstand still shone with a dull yellow

brightness, and I was glad for it. That sound in the darkness would've conjured up everything from Freddy Krueger, blade-claws outstretched, to the Grim Reaper, his finger of bone pointing at me from a black robe. But in the light, I figured a rat had gotten loose, or maybe one of the guards was out back, patrolling the alley behind the motel.

It stopped, and I thought nothing more of it.

2

At some point I had truly drifted off, my body slouching over onto its side, my back to the bathroom. The scraping sound returned, this time louder. At first it entered my dream, lumber-jacks suddenly appearing at the fall festival, sawing away at a gigantic log with one of those broad two-person jobs. Back and forth, back and forth, their faces all smiles...

I snapped awake, spinning myself around to look at the rear of the room, at the mirror, at the open door of the bathroom. I saw nothing. But the sounds of something hard and rough scraping against metal or wood—I couldn't tell what exactly—filled the air, a regular rhythm, just like the men sawing away at the log in my dream. The noise bounced off the walls and ceiling, making it impossible to tell from exactly where it came. But it was *loud*, and I whimpered a little in fear.

"Hello?" I asked, feeling silly when I heard my own voice.

The sound stopped almost immediately. This didn't make me feel better.

Keeping my eyes on the bathroom—wasn't that always where the killer waited, hiding behind the shower curtain, waiting for you to sling it open?—I scooted to the far side of the bed and reached for the telephone on the nightstand. It came out of its cradle and into my hand. I gripped it firmly. Not wanting to look away, I did so anyway, quickly scanning the buttons on the phone. The whole dial pad suddenly seemed like gibberish, another language, not making sense. Then I saw a button labeled, FRONT OFFICE.

I pressed it, heard a few rings, then a click. Nothing moved in my small room, not even a shadow.

"Hello?" a quiet voiced asked on the other side of my call.

"Yes, can you please connect me to my parent's room? It's right next to mine. Room one-nineteen."

"That's your room or the one next to yours?"

"The one next to mine. The one I want you to call for me."

"Okay, no problem. Can you verify the name that room's listed under?"

"Um, yeah. Uh, Edgar Player."

I jumped when I heard it again—this time, just one long, slow scrape before it stopped, like a small piece of metal dragged across rough cement. It had definitely come from somewhere in the back of the motel, behind my room. Outside, somebody messing with the wall. The motel clerk still hadn't responded to me.

"Listen," I said, barely able to speak over my rising fear, "I'm here under police protection. Can you tell them that something weird's going on right outside my room? In the back."

Scraaaaaaaaaaaaaape. Clink. Clink. Clink.

I let out a yelp. "Seriously! Someone's trying to break into my room I think!"

The guy on the other end didn't say a word.

"Hello? Hello?"

Nothing.

I slammed the phone down and jumped out of bed, ran for the door to my room. Feeling an icy chill, as if someone was right behind me, about to touch my shoulder, I ripped open the door and almost screamed when I saw a policeman standing right in front of me.

"Ho there, boy," the man said, holding his hands out as if I were a lunatic with a hostage. I didn't know the guy—he was chubby, brown uniform, eyes bloodshot as if he'd been sipping from a flask on the sly all evening. "It's okay. I heard you shouting. What's going on in there?"

I couldn't believe how hard I was breathing, and the words were a struggle. "Someone's... trying to... break into my room. From the back."

"Break in?" He looked past me, brow pinched, leaning one way then the other. "You sure?"

The question struck me as totally absurd. "Yes!" I shouted. "Can't you hear it?"

But of course the sound had stopped. To the cop's credit, he didn't start laughing at me or pat me on the head. He just nodded and said, "I'll check it out. May I?" He raised his eyebrows, flicked his eyes past me. I stepped to my left and he strolled in with not a care in the world, as if we were going to watch TV together.

"Sonny's patrolling the alley back there," he said when he reached the bathroom. Without stopping he walked into it, flicked on the light, then swept aside the shower curtain, flinching ever so slightly before we both saw that it was empty. "Just heard from him on the radio... Couldn't have been more than, oh, five or six minutes ago, I reckon."

I didn't appreciate the implication in his voice—that I was dreaming, prone to fantasy—but what could I say? "Well... I swear I heard something. A really loud scraping sound, like... more like sawing, like someone trying to cut through the window screen, or maybe even the wall."

"Uh-huh," the cop said, standing on his tippy-toes to peek out the small window. "Don't see hide nor hair of nobody out there. Not sure a man could squeeze through this winduh to be honest. Maybe a toddler could." He had a good chuckle at that, and suddenly I was offended. My fear washed away in my anger.

"I'm not making it up! Somebody's out there! Call your...

friend on the radio!" I don't know what had come over me, shouting at an officer of the law like this.

He turned around, and I expected him to smack me with the back of his hand for such disrespect, but he just had a little smile on his face. I fumed but forced myself to stay silent.

"Now, now, no need to get uppity there, young man." He finished surveying the bathroom then came out, took a look at the small vanity then poked his head into the closet. There wasn't a whole lot he could investigate. "Look, there ain't a chance in Kingdom Come someone's gonna break through that winduh and come after ya. Now stay put right here and I'll holler at Sonny on the radio. That make ya feel better?"

To this day I can still feel the man's condescension, as if it pulsed out of him like microwaves. "What if he doesn't answer?"

"Then I reckon I'll go back there myself and check things..." He'd been walking toward the door but stopped, staring at it. "Son, did you close that when we came in?"

It was shut, all right, but I couldn't remember for the life of me if I had done it or not. "I guess so?" I said as a question, almost feeling like I'd done something wrong.

"Huh," was all he said in return.

My fear came swooshing back, replacing the anger. It was as if I were only capable of feeling one or the other. The room had almost no hiding places, but my eyes wandered to the bed, and I wondered...

"Could he be under there?" I asked.

The cop went over to it, kneeled down, lifted the crumpled blankets and had a peek.

"Nah," he said. I liked him again for at least checking. "Let me give old Sonny a holler, now. He's probably back there bored out of his mind. Maybe he was doin' somethin' funny to pass the time and gave you a fright."

Like what? I wondered as he pulled the walkie-talkie off of his belt. *Sawing wood for a campfire?* It was 90 degrees outside.

He turned a knob to a certain channel then held the device up to his mouth, pushed the side-button. "Sonny, Sonny, this is Jessie up front. How's it hangin', good buddy? Over." The radio squawked, but no reply came. The 10 seconds we waited felt like three minutes. "Sonny, get off your dairy-air and pick up. This is Jessie up front. Everything fine and dandy back there? Over."

Another squawk. Another 10 seconds of silence.

"Sonny? Sonnnnny? Man, come on. Pick up."

Squawk. Silence.

"Sonny, I'm gonna open up a can of whoopin' sauce if you don't pick up in three, two, one..."

Squawk. Silence.

The officer let his radio-holding hand fall to the side. "I'm fittied to beat that man to a pulp," he whispered under his breath. But he had genuine worry etched on his face. "Listen," he said to me, "I'm gonna call someone over to keep an eye on your room, then check out what the heck's going on with Sonny. Leave that door, locked, ya hear? Don't worry, I won't head back there until we get you another fella to stand watch."

"Okay." I didn't want him to leave me, and had the absurd notion to grab his arm and lean all my weight on it, tell him he'd have to drag me along with him.

He must've seen the fear in my eyes. "Don't worry, son. We've got—"

Scraaaaaaaape.

The drawn out noise filled the air, a soundtrack to any haunted house. The officer stopped mid sentence and grabbed his gun on instinct, pulled it out and started waving it around the room like he expected an ambush. I felt a cool rush of terror and jumped onto the bed, completely out of instinct, as if our biggest threat was the carpet turning into lava, a game I'd play with my kids far in the future.

"What the heck was that?" the cop asked.

Scraaaaaaaaaape.

It was an awful, awful sound, mostly because I didn't know what it was. Feeling a brief and irrational burst of glee that I'd been proven right, I yelled out, "I told you!"

Scraaaaaaaaaaaaaaaaaaaaape.

Suddenly it was obvious where the noise was coming from. Above us. With quick hindsight, my mind readjusted how it had heard the sounds. The first instance had been over by the bathroom, the second somewhere between there and the middle of the room. The third one...

With almost comical slow motion, the officer raised his eyes toward the ceiling directly above where he stood. I followed his gaze, saw an expanse of white tiles up there, most of them yellowed, many with dark stains from a hundred past storms that had been too much for the roof to hold back.

Scrape.

It was short and quick, definitely coming from exactly above the cop.

The officer stole a glance at me, put his finger to his lip in the international sign for *Shut up, let me take care of this.* I nodded, scared out of my wits at this point, shivering as if the temperature had plummeted. Waiting to see what happened next.

Slowly raising his arm, the officer finally pointed his gun at the spot right above his head.

"Who's up there?" he yelled. I jumped as surely as if he'd fired a bullet.

The ceiling creaked a little, then again. My mind immediately leaped to the most ridiculous explanation—that Grandpa Fincher's ghost had finally decided to move out of the farmhouse and haunt this motel instead. As silly as it sounded, for at least three or four seconds I genuinely considered the possibility, hoped for it—much better than the alternative.

"I said who's up—"

The ceiling tiles above him collapsed, a downward explosion of plaster and metal and insulation that rained upon the officer like rocks dumped from an excavator. In the middle of all that cascading debris, I saw two feet, two legs, a body. It all happened so fast, a blur of motion and color, my thoughts unable to keep up with what my eyes were seeing. Impossibly, I saw the person who'd jumped through the ceiling land on the policeman's shoulders, his thighs wrapped around the cop's neck from behind, legs dangling down his chest as if they were readying for a chicken fight in a swimming pool.

A mere shadow in all that swirling dust, the intruder raised an arm and I saw a flash of metal near his hand, a knife. He plunged it downward, the blade sinking into the soft flesh of the officer's neck, right below his chin, right in the nape between the collarbones. The cop screamed, a gurgling sound that was somehow worse than the three distinct ribbons of blood squirting from his wound. He collapsed to his knees, the killer still perched atop his shoulders, the cop holding both hands against his neck, trying to stop the life from spilling out. I was so horrified that I scooted back on the bed until my shoulders hit the wall, unable to tear my eyes from the murderous scene before me.

The cop gurgled again, made a coughing sound that sprayed blood from his mouth. Then he fell forward, his killer stepping from his body as if he'd intended to descend that way all along, and the suffering, dying policeman's face slapped the hard carpet floor. Finally, finally, I was able to look away, look up, see what spawn of evil had fallen from the plaster sky.

The man had a plastic grocery bag on his head.

Tied at the neck, collapsing tightly to his skin with every inhale, ballooning out with every exhale, that crinkling sound all too familiar from our encounter at the Honeyhole. The small slit at his mouth revealed just enough for me to see the grimace beneath. I knew it was Pee Wee, could tell from his stature, his stance, his lips. He stared at me through the bag, towering over his victim, catching his breath. Blood dripped from the point of the knife which he held by his side, still gripping its handle in a tight fist, as if he wanted one more kill. He spoke to me, using that same gravely voice like before.

"Tonight's the night. You wanted to be bait, well I've come to snatch it and gobble it up." He turned to face me fully, pointed the wet, crimson blade at my head. "There's no hook, though. You ain't got no idea how many connections I have in this county, boy. Crazy runs in the family."

Something in me snapped, yanked me from my petrified state as surely as if someone had dumped a bucket of ice water on my head. With a burst of searing adrenaline, I pushed myself off the bed and ran for the front door, but he'd anticipated that move and jumped in front of me, swiping the knife in an arc that made me fall to the floor to avoid it. Before I'd even fully landed I was scrambling with my arms and legs, like a dog dropped into a puddle of mud, finally getting enough traction to catapult myself in the opposite direction, this time toward the bathroom. Barely gaining enough balance to stay on my feet, I sprinted for the opening, sensing him right on my tail.

I made it inside, grabbed the edge of the door, threw all my weight into shutting the thing. It slammed closed, my eyes catching one brief glance of him charging toward me. Just as it clicked his body rammed into the cheap wood, seeming to shake the entire building. I screamed, fumbled for the knob, quickly twisted the button to lock it—just in time; it rattled from Pee Wee trying to open it from the other side. Then he banged on the door with both fists, relentless, thunderous, not stopping.

"Leave me alone!" I screamed. "Help! Somebody help me!" I screamed that phrase over and over and over, pounded on the back wall of the shower, hoping to wake my parents up. It seemed impossible that they could've slept through all of this commotion and an icy dread filled me that maybe they were dead, stabbed in the neck just like the chubby cop. "Help me!" I yelled again, feeling as if my throat would rip itself to shreds from the effort.

The door bounced in its frame, screamed against the hinges. Then again. Then again. He was ramming it with his shoulder. I immediately looked to the only other way out, jumped on top of the toilet's closed lid, twisted the bar that locked the window above it. Then I heaved upward, sliding the glass open. It was small, narrow enough that most people wouldn't have a chance to get through. But I could do it, skinny runt that I was. I'd *have* to do it. But then came an abrupt awareness of complete silence, not sure how many seconds ago it had started.

I stilled myself, listened, looked toward the door, hoping against hope that other cops had found us, or that Pee Wee had given up and run away. Both seemed foolish, preposterous. My heart wrapped with despair, I turned my attention back to the window. Placing my hands on the bottom sill, I bent my knees, ready to jump up for leverage so that I could squirm my way through. Just as I leaped, throwing all strength into my arms to catch my weight, a face appeared in the opening, looking back at me from the dark.

A face hidden by a thin layer of gray plastic.

I screamed and twisted my body, completely losing control, my right shoulder banging into the sharp edge of the window frame. Then I fell to the ground, my ass hitting the toilet then smacking into the linoleum floor. Shuddering from horror, I scooted sideways until I ran up against the far wall, the closed door now to my left, looming above me. The apparitional face had disappeared from outside, but I knew it hadn't been a figment of my imagination. Pee Wee's friends were with him. Son. Cousin. Father. I had no idea who these monsters were.

A sharp bang against the door made me jump. Not a thump this time, a bang, something smaller and more focused hitting the wood. Another bang. Another. I curled up into a ball, at a loss for any option. Pee Wee hit the door again and it cracked.

Then again and again. Once more and the crack became a hole, splintering inward. I caught a flash of his fist. He hit it once more, then gripped some plywood shards and ripped them back toward him, widening the gap. Bloody fingers reached through and gripped more shards, yanking them off. The jagged hole was now several inches wide, about a foot tall, right in the middle of the door. Abandoning myself to doom, I crawled over the side of the tub and collapsed inside, tearing the shower curtain off of its rings and down on top of me. Receding back to my youngest self, I pulled the edge of the plastic sheet up against my chin, seeking its protection like the blankets of childhood warded off those fanged monsters waiting in the closet or under the bed.

I stared at the broken gap in the door, waiting for my fate. At the moment I could only see the closet on the other side, the long mirror on its sliding door at such an angle that only revealed the yellowed ceiling above.

Pee Wee's head appeared, crumpled plastic masking his face. He spoke again, his voice the growl of a crocodile.

"I have something to show you."

Baffled, I wanted to shut my eyes but a primal, morbid curiosity kept them open. Pee Wee disappeared again but an object of blood and horror quickly replaced him. I whimpered, knowing immediately what it was. The head of the policeman, his nose mangled, his mouth open in a silent scream of terror, his face splashed in red paint, looking back at me with a death stare, his own eyes open but empty of life.

He pulled the head away and reappeared with his own—I could just see the features of his face behind the thin sheet of crinkled plastic. Even though I finally squeezed my eyes closed, wishing him away like a nightmare, I heard his next words perfectly.

"I'm gonna do somethin' a lot worse to you, boy."

CHAPTER SEVENTEEN

Lynchburg, South Carolina
July 2017

While sleeping on the couch, surrounded by my family, only hours from our scheduled trip back to Atlanta, I dreamed of that night from almost 30 years ago. So much of it had been blocked from my memory, but in the dream it was all there, every detail. Although separated enough from my younger self to *know* it was merely a dream, observing more like a bystander than truly reliving it, I felt the fear and terror of that poor kid. My heart ached for him, as if he were someone else, not me.

Then I woke up.

It was dark, the only sound that of the twin blowing fans.

Someone was standing there, observing me.

It was still the middle of the night, pitch black, but the silhouette of a man leaned over my body, a dark, featureless head looking down, only a couple of feet from my face. I flinched and scrambled to get up, fend him off, fight tooth and nail, but then I heard my dad's voice.

"It's okay, son. It's me."

Weirded out, I reached my arm down to the carpet, feeling around until my fingers found the cell phone I'd dropped there before falling asleep. I picked it up and turned on the flashlight function, not wanting to be in the dark another second. It was just after midnight.

"What's going on?" I asked, shining the light toward my dad but not directly in his eyes. Dressed in his old-man pajamas, he'd straightened up, and oddly he had a hand hidden behind his back, as if he'd brought me a surprise. I directed the light toward his side as I leaned over to see what he was holding, but he shifted to make sure it stayed hidden. "Dad?"

He didn't respond, just stared down at me with a weird expression, kind of vacant, like maybe he was sleepwalking. I swung my legs around to the floor, then pushed off the couch with both hands and stood up. As I did so, he took a couple of steps away and shifted again to keep his front toward me. He held his arm behind him more than he needed to, almost comically.

"Dad. What's going on? Is everything okay? What've you got back there?"

"It'll all be over," he mumbled, barely audible over the roar of the fans. I mostly read his lips. "No more rituals. No more pacts. No more murders. I swear on my own life I'll end it. Once and for all." He trembled as he spoke, still with those vacant eyes. It seemed as if he were in a trance.

"Dad, you're really freaking me out. What in the *world?*"

Instead of replying, he turned and bolted for the hallway that lead to the kitchen and his bedroom. I reached out for him on instinct but it was too late. He ran from me, instinctively leaping over Mason's sleeping body, forgetting to remove his hand from his back, now fully in my view. I shone the light directly at the closed fist pressed against his body and saw what was gripped there.

A syringe.

A syringe with a silver needle that glinted in the light.

What the hell?

I quickly swept the light around the room to make sure all of my kids were safe and sound. Wesley in his chair. Mason, Hazel, Logan, on the floor, all of them snuggled up in their blankets. When I shone the light back on Wesley, preparing to follow my dad, his eyes were open; he shut them as soon as I looked, trying to pretend he was still asleep.

I walked up to the chair and leaned close. "Wesley?" I whispered. "You okay? I think Grandpa is sleepwalking." *Hiding a needle and syringe behind his back*, I didn't say.

Wesley just moaned and rolled over to face the wall.

I straightened up and looked down at him for a moment. Something was weird. Off. The air in the room had a cloying solidity to it, despite the two fans blowing at full blast. I felt so unsettled I almost had to sit down.

But my dad. Dad had gone bonkers.

Hoping the kids could somehow sleep through it, I reached across Wesley's body and turned on the side-table lamp. A glance down showed him wince, but other than that he didn't stir. I had to do it, couldn't stand one more second of that room being dark. After another quick sweeping gaze of the room, where all seemed well and the kids slept soundly, I went after my dad, toward the kitchen, flipping on lights with every step. As the house came to life, glowing and bright, I felt much better.

Dad wasn't in the kitchen.

I marched to his bedroom, gently opened the door. I'd never turned off the phone's flashlight, so I shone it inside, where I could see my mom sound asleep on her side of the bed. No sign of dad. Unless he'd hidden in the closet, he wasn't in there.

I shut the door then turned around and leaned back against it. Took a breath. Turned off the phone's light and slipped it into the pocket of my shorts. Then I did a quick search of the rest of the house—bathrooms, bedrooms, closets. I even looked in Patsy's room, where Andrea snored in bed, but he wasn't there. He'd left the house, even though I'd never heard any door open or close. For the life of me I couldn't think of what had overcome my dad.

The cops keeping guard, I thought. Maybe he'd gone out there to talk to them.

I walked back through the house to the kitchen, where a door lead to the back porch. It was closed but not locked, making me think he'd quietly slipped out, trying to trick me. I opened it up and stepped through, flicking on the porch light at the same time. My right foot had barely landed on the smooth cement when I saw it. A sight that instantly changed the night.

A policeman lay sprawled across the steps on his stomach, arms bent awkwardly beneath his body. His eyes were closed, mouth open, a string of drool connecting his lower lip to the top step. I couldn't tell if he was dead or alive, but the thing jabbed into his neck made my heart stutter.

It was the syringe, jutting out like a stuck harpoon from the body of a whale.

My dad. My dad had gone completely insane.

This thought was only half formed when every synapse in my brain fired at once upon the same thing, the only thing that mattered. My kids. Something evil was in the air this night, and I had to protect my children at all costs.

I turned away from the incapacitated cop and ran back inside, through the kitchen, down the hallway, burst into the living room where I could already see my three kids who'd been sleeping on the floor, still in the same positions. But just as my heart slipped into the safety zone of relief, I looked down at my father's oldest chair, the relic that had been around since the dawn of human civilization.

Wesley was gone.

No, no, no, no, no, no, no, no...

The word became a chant in my head, a drum beat of panic, a taunt that it was all happening again. I turned in a complete circle, my eyes searching every corner of the room. There was no sign of my eldest son anywhere. I looked past the front door then immediately jerked back to it—the front edge was just slightly ajar, by a centimeter at most. Leaping over my children, I sprinted to the front, ripped open the door, ejected myself onto the front porch and down the steps, where the halogen light in the front yard revealed an ephemeral world of moonish glow and angles of shadow, crystalline reflections on the countless puddles created by the storm. Most of them were connected, the yard more of a lake than anything else.

Scanning left and right, spinning, looking everywhere my feeble sight allowed, I saw no sign of Wesley. Nothing.

Then I stopped, realizing something else. I saw no sign of *anyone*.

Where were the other cops? Where was our protection? What was going on?

Bathroom, I thought. *Maybe Wesley's in the bathroom.*

I went back toward the house, jumped the steps in one leap, went through the still-open front door. Remembering that horrible night just last week, feeling an awful since of déjà vu, I once again jumped over my sleeping kids and bulleted for the closest bathroom. Almost stumbled across the threshold. Turned on the light. No one. I went to the only other one in the house. Turned on the light. No one.

Déjà vu, déjà vu, déjà vu.

Maybe I was still dreaming. How could two events be so similar? How could my son disappear right under my nose twice in the same week? What was my dad doing?

Too many questions. Too much craziness. The stress of it threatened to stop my heart altogether, my blood churning through my veins, breaths impossible to catch, my chest tightening up...

Andrea. I needed Andrea. She was the only thing I could hold onto, keep myself sane. Panic and fear threatened to snap my last tether to reason.

Running, now. Through the hall, into the living room, leaping for the third time over Hazel's body, then Mason's. I reached Patsy's room, didn't bother knocking, opened the door.

"Andrea!" I shouted.

The name had barely escaped my lips when all the lights in the house went out.

"David?"

Andrea's voice in the abrupt darkness, the silence. The winding down of the two fans in the living room reminded me of something dying, adding a note of melancholy to everything else, my breaking point closer and closer.

"Right here," I whispered, fumbling to get the phone out of my pocket, then to turn the flashlight function back on. It beamed into life and I shone it at Andrea's bed. She recoiled, shielding her eyes, as she stood up. "Sorry." I pointed the light at the floor.

"What's going on?" she asked.

I almost lost it. Barely able to breathe, barely able to think, every muscle in my body coiled up into knots, I almost collapsed onto the floor, so overcome with terror at what might be happening, the uncertainty of it all. Of what to do.

She must've sensed it because she came to me, grabbed me by the shoulders.

"David, what happened, sweetie?" The kindness, the steadiness in her voice brought me back from the brink.

My breaths came in short, tight, painful bursts. "The power just went out! My dad's gone nuts, poisoned one of the cops, then took off. I can't find Wesley. Oh man, Andrea, he's not in the house. I don't know what to do. I went outside and didn't see any other cops."

To her credit, she bypassed the usual "What are you talking

about?" or "Are you crazy?" questions and took me by the hand, marched the both of us back into the living room where the kids hadn't yet been awakened by my frantic search of the house. Not knowing what else to do, I shone the light on the empty chair in which Wesley had slept.

"Okay, call 9-1-1," she said. "We have to at least get that ball rolling and then we can keep searching for him and your dad."

"Okay," I replied, already bringing up the dial pad on the phone. I tapped the three ominous numbers, held the device up to my ear.

"What about your mom?" Andrea asked.

It was hard to speak but I forced out the words I needed. "Still in bed. Maybe go get her and bring her in here. I can't leave my kids, not for one second. Not again. If we're gonna search for Wesley then we're gonna do it as a group."

A woman answered my phone call as Andrea sprinted out of the room. "Hello, what's your emergency?"

I told them my son was missing, then sputtered out the details as quickly as I could, explaining that we already had officers at the house looking over us but one had been attacked and I couldn't find the other. I begged her to hurry, to get us some help, then hung up. As we'd spoken, I knew I had to call Sheriff Taylor, probably should've done it first.

Andrea came back into the room, my poor mom walking with her, dazed and scared, eyes still full of sleep. I gave them a quick nod and called the sheriff. It rang seven times then went to voice mail. Frustrated, I hung up but then called him right back, waited through the interminable rings, and left a message.

"Sheriff, this is David Player. Something really weird's going on over here, please call me back ASAP. My dad and Wesley are missing." I tapped the red "End Call" button then hurried over to my mom, pulled her into a hug. My words had scared her to death.

"It's okay, Mom," I said, hating the words even as they came out. Nothing was okay. "We just have to figure this out."

"Figure what out?" she half-yelled. With the fans shut off along with everything else in the house, her voice shattered the air. "What happened to them?"

Finally, all the craziness had broken through the barrier of my kids' slumber. All three of them were stirring in their blankets on the floor. Anxiety filled me to the breaking point—my concern for Wesley, for my dad, mixed with the stark need to protect the younger ones right at my feet. In all of my life, I don't know if I've ever felt the crushing weight of uncertainty like I did in that moment.

"I don't know," I whispered, the phrase filled with varying levels of meaning.

Andrea took action, picking Logan right off the floor, along with his blankets, then plopping to the ground next to Mason. With Logan nestled in her lap, she gently gave Mason a shake and completed his wake up. He looked at her with squinting, wondering eyes. I snapped out of my frozen state, took my mom's hand, then walked to Hazel, pulling on my mom so that she sat on the floor with me, very close to where Andrea sat with Mason and Logan. I placed the phone on the ground so its light beamed toward the ceiling, casting the entire room in an eerie, faint glow.

"Sweetie," I whispered, tapping Hazel's shoulder. "Hazel."

She turned over and looked at me, not quite as bleary-eyed as Mason had been. She smiled, in that instant ignorant to whatever was happening all around us, happy to be stirred, probably excited to begin our journey to Atlanta.

"Come here."

I wrapped my arms around her and picked her up, pulled her close. Without saying a word, the six of us instinctively moved toward each other, shifted when needed, scooted here and there, until finally we were huddled as closely as possible, our backs pressed against the frontside of the couch. I sat in the middle and spread my arms wide, pulling them all into me, like a hen with her chickens. I wished for wings of steel to protect them.

There was no way I could leave those kids. Wesley was 16 years old, just months away from the world calling him a grownup, able to fend for himself to some degree. And my dad had dropped to the lowest of my priorities for the night. But these young ones... No way. I'd stay put, wait desperately to hear the wail of a siren or the buzz of my phone. Making a decision, any decision, brought me some peace. I closed my eyes and took the deepest, fullest breath I had all night.

The house was as still and silent as an empty cathedral, the lone candle of my phone burning its bluish flame into the ancient white tiles of the ceiling.

"Son," my mom said. "I don't understand what's happening."

"The police'll be here soon," I replied, in no mood to talk. "Maybe Dad and Wesley had to take care of an emergency, I don't know." I had no explanations, and I didn't want to make up any.

"Okay," she said quietly, and I leaned over to kiss her forehead, thankful for the intuition she acted upon, to let things play out, avoid all the unnecessary talking and speculating.

Andrea found the hollow between my neck and shoulder, pressed her head into it. I could actually feel my artery bouncing off her skull as it thumped to my heart's rapid beat. She sat to my right, Logan in her arms, Hazel in mine, Mason pressed between us on the floor, half smashed to death. My mom was on the left, grasping me tightly, a life preserver keeping her afloat in this sweeping tide of terror that threatened to destroy our house, our home, our life.

Genuinely shocking me, my kids said almost nothing. I'd expected a bombardment of questions and complaints, whimpers and tears. They weren't stupid—not even close—and no matter what they'd heard or hadn't heard, they knew the shit had hit the fan on this night. They knew we were in a heap of trouble.

And that was the maddening part for me. I knew we were in trouble, too, but had no clue as to what that meant. I wanted to scream in the agony of my ignorance.

My van.

The thought struck me so specifically, like someone had lit up fireworks in my brain to spell it out in sparkling, bursting flames. *My van.* Right outside that front door. I could grab Dad's shotgun, keep my precious babies in a tight huddle, make a scrum of sorts, all of us on top of each other for protection, out the door, down the steps, to the van. If anyone jumped out at us, I'd blow them to bits with the shotgun. Get in the car, lock the doors, give Andrea the shotgun, rev the engine, and drive like shit out of a goose, flying hot and heavy until we were away, far away, to safety. This is what we had to do.

Time to act.

"Kids, everybody, get up." I lifted my arms away from Andrea and my mom, feeling badly that we'd *just* settled down. "Come on. Get up. I'm gonna get dressed really fast."

It sounded absurd, but I planned to throw some jeans on, slip into shoes. Quickly. I couldn't imagine driving off in my jammie shorts. No one complained as they shifted and moved into position to push themselves up from the floor, the strange night entrancing them to silence, to turn off their minds and do what they're told.

"Just stay right here," I said. "Huddle up."

Everyone had stood by now, and they joined each other in a group hug. Andrea eyed me, her expression full of questions, but I could tell she worried that any discussion would only frighten the kids. She trusted me, and it meant the world.

My bag was at the end of the couch, mostly in shadow. I'd tossed my jeans on top of it earlier and now grabbed them, hopping on each leg in turn as I pulled them up. I zipped and buttoned, then felt the reassuring bulge of the keys in my front pocket.

"You guys okay?" I whispered, rummaging for socks. In my entire life, I'd never heard the house so completely silent. "We're gonna jump in the van and drive out of here, okay?"

I found socks. Put them on. Put my shoes on. Tied them. All the while, my mom tried to convince me that we couldn't leave without Dad and Wesley. Andrea did her best to shush her without the kids seeing. I eyed her as well, trying to telepathically tell her to shut the hell up. She finally got the message and closed her mouth. I felt so awful for her but I just didn't know what else to do.

I picked up my phone, shone the light toward the carpet. "Okay, now it's your turn."

We wasted another couple of minutes, walking around in a group, allowing each of them to at least put on pants and shoes —I knew they'd feel more comfortable like that, and I was desperate for anything that might help alleviate the fish-out-of-water awkwardness of the night.

No more than five minutes after we'd stood up from our cuddle-station by the couch, we all stood together by the front door. I had my dad's shotgun gripped in both hands, trying to ignore the looks of terror each one of my kids kept throwing at it. Tears poured from my mom's eyes, but she did her best to keep in the accompanying sobs. Andrea had a hand on my elbow, her fingers squeezing to show her support. My gaze swept across my children. Hazel. Mason. Logan, wrapped in his grandma's arms.

Bravery beamed from their scared faces, and the trust they put into me—complete, total, unquestioning—was enough to shatter my heart.

"I promise we're going to be okay," I said. "I love you guys."

"Love you, Daddy," Hazel said back. Logan leaned his head on my mom's shoulder; Mason did his best to smile.

"Okay, then." I held the shotgun with one arm, a finger resting on the trigger, the barrel pointed toward the floor, and opened the front door with my other, just enough to peek outside.

A man stood on our porch.

He had a bag draped over his head.

CHAPTER EIGHTEEN

Lynchburg, South Carolina
June 1989

P ee Wee Gaskins knelt right before me, his bag ripped off, looking at me with his devil-kissed eyes.

"Time to go for a ride, David." Abandoning his gravel-voice, he said it in a quiet, eerie tone that was far scarier.

After he'd shown me the head of the police officer through the busted door of the motel bathroom, then his own head appeared in the hole to announce that he was going to do something worse to me, I had no concept of options. None. I sat there, on the floor, arms wrapped around my knees, and I trembled. The terror had consumed me to a degree that I almost didn't feel it, numb, the same way that scalding water in a hot tub feels lukewarm after 10 minutes, barely noticeable. I shook, and awaited my fate.

Pee Wee had reached through the hole and unlocked the door, then opened it. He stepped inside, stared down at me through the thin veil of his plastic bag, breathing in and out. After an excruciating wait, where eventually I stopped looking up at him and focused on the floor, he'd grabbed the side of the bag on his head and ripped it off. My eyes shot back to him.

And then he'd knelt down and told me we were going for a ride.

"Where to?" I somehow managed to ask.

He didn't answer for a second. His hair was greasy and matted from the bag, thin on top. He had pockmarks on his cheeks, made worse by sporadic stubble that looked more like fungus. Noxious breath leaked from his crooked nose and his crooked mouth, which was slightly open, revealing yellowed teeth with bits of white in every gap. The man was as short as I remembered him, but for the first time I noticed how tightly ripped with muscle were his arms, neck, and shoulders.

Sawing off heads is good exercise, I thought.

"You'll find out," he finally said. "It's time my family gets a little payback for what *your* family has done to us."

"What do you—"

His hand whipped out and cracked me across the cheek. I cried out, held my hand up to my face. Four-fingered shocks of pain pulsed beneath my soft skin.

"Don't speak again, boy. You hear me? Don't speak again unless I ask you to."

I didn't so much as nod, not knowing what might set him off. Although I'd hated him plenty well before that moment, the sting of his slap turned it into something visceral, monstrous, world-shaking. I hated him so much—many sleepless nights lay in my future, when I'd stay awake for hours, imagining my hands at his throat, squeezing until his face turned purple and the life went out of his eyes.

Pee Wee grabbed me by the shirt and made me stand up as he did.

"Follow me," he said. "I hear one peep out of you, I'll cut your mama's throat. You try to run, I'll cut your mama's throat.

You try to hurt me, I'll beat your mama *then* cut her throat. You got it?"

I nodded this time, not daring to leave his question unanswered. What *had* happened to my mom and dad? I knew they weren't next door, sleeping the night away with all this commotion going on. I felt a flutter of panic that took my breath.

"Come on, then."

He walked out of the bathroom. I followed. He went to the door of the motel, stepped outside—he didn't hesitate, didn't take a moment to peek around the corner to make sure no SWAT member had a rifle aimed at his head. He just strolled out of there like he owned the place, and something told me that he did. Or his relations did, anyway, and the way he talked, that distinction didn't matter much. I followed.

We made our way across the parking lot, all the way to the other side, where two cars were running, someone at the driver's seat in each one—all I saw were heads and shoulders of shadow. Pee Wee stopped at the rear of the first one, a white Mercury Tracer—the thing hadn't been washed since my twelfth birthday by the looks of it—with a hatchback. The large window was caked in dust, but several people had left clever phrases carved into the residue.

PLEASE WASH ME
MY DRIVER'S A DICK
CLEMSON SUCKS

Just below the window, a couple of bumper stickers represented the high IQ of the vehicle's owner.

CALL 555-5555 IF YOU WANNA F*** YOURSELF
I HATE LIBS

The scrawled messages and sticker phrases made me sick inside, a glimpse into darknesses from which I'd been relatively sheltered. Even more strongly than I'd felt it in the motel, I just wanted to be home, safe and sound, the terrible, hateful world a million miles away.

Pee Wee leaned over and pushed a button to make the hatch-back pop open; hydraulics hissed as he swung the large door toward the sky. My gaze had fallen to the ground, where I watched two tears drop out of my eyes and fall, seemingly in slow motion, finally splatting on the asphalt at my feet. But after the hatch opened, in the corner of my vision I saw arms and legs inside the trunk and I quickly looked up.

Bodies.

I took a step backward, embarrassed at the Texas-sized gasp I inhaled. My hands flew up to my mouth like an old lady sighting lovebirds behind the bushes.

Bodies. At least four of them, tangled up like tag-team wrestlers, dressed in blood and matted hair and torn clothing. Two were police officers, two weren't. Before the horrible thought could even enter my mind, I could tell that none of them were my parents or Andrea or anyone else I knew.

"Oopsie daisy," Pee Wee said. "Wrong car."

He reached up and gripped the edge of the hatchback door, then slammed it shut. The thunk jolted me like a gunshot. Shaken, I followed Pee Wee as he stepped over to the rear of the other idling car, this one a little cleaner but a lot older. The thing was like a boat on tires, a silvery Cadillac from the 70s that had a trunk bigger than my closet at home. He took a key out of his pocket and stuck it in the keyhole, turned till it clicked. As the lid popped and opened up by its own momentum, I braced myself to see more dead people.

The trunk was empty.

"Get your skinny ass in there," Pee Wee said, gesturing with annoyance at the vast cavern before us. "I won't ask twice."

Too smart to hesitate or ask dumb questions, I did as I was commanded, clambering over the bumper and lip of the trunk into the voluminous space. I had the most irrational thought that at least it was carpeted instead of exposed metal, might even make for a comfortable car ride.

I turned over and looked back at Pee Wee but he didn't return my glance. He just slammed the lid closed, another jolting thunk that made my heart skip a beat, and I was in utter, complete darkness.

The tears came hard and fast, so much so that it hurt. I sobbed, curled up into a ball, fighting the urge to kick and scream and beat my fists against the metal above my head. I cried for several minutes, wondering what horrible fate awaited me, waiting for the car to drive off. But nothing happened; we didn't move. The vibration of the running engine stayed smooth and steady, something I felt all the way to my bones. I had no concept of time, but it seemed as if at least a half hour passed before I heard the jangle of a key being inserted into the trunk's keyhole again.

It popped open, lifted toward the sky.

Andrea was standing there, her face hidden in shadow.

"Get your ass in there," I heard Pee Wee say. "Don't make me ask twice."

Just like I had done, she climbed aboard without complaint or hesitation. Pee Wee slammed the lid shut, and she and I immediately wrapped ourselves around each other for comfort, sobbing without words. A nearby door opened and closed.

This time, the car drove off.

CHAPTER NINETEEN

Lynchburg, South Carolina
July 2017

The man stood on the porch, wearing a grocery bag wrapped around his head—just like the old days, with a slit in the mouth—his eyes hidden behind thin plastic. I'd made a shuddering, almost chortling sound when I saw him, something that even in that moment of terror embarrassed me. Hazel and Mason and Grandma screamed, in unison, as if they'd practiced by a piano earlier. Logan didn't see it because his face was buried in my mom's neck.

Andrea reacted in no way I saw or heard, but she quickly ushered everyone back into the living room, pulling and pushing when needed, until they were huddled by the couch. I hadn't moved a muscle, paralyzed by the fear of my childhood. Staring at the intruder as he stared back at me, the bag inflating, deflating, inflating, deflating, his nose prominent when the plastic compressed against his face.

I held no pretensions of bravery, but I had a gun and this man didn't.

Pulling it up to aim the barrel at our visitor, I leaned the shaft against my body as I reached out and opened the screen door with my free hand, then kicked it open. I stepped through, now holding the shotgun with both hands, bringing it up higher so the thing pointed right at the man's face.

"Who are you? Dicky? Huh? What's going on? Where's my son?" Every word louder than the one before it. I got no answer but one—the man tilted his head to the side, something I'd seen 30 years earlier from Baghead, standing in the Honeyhole over a headless body.

I couldn't stop the tremble in my arms; the gun shook so much I finally brought it back against my chest to steady the thing. But it still pointed at the intruder's hidden eyes.

"Who are you?" I screamed. "I will blow your brains out!"

Without saying a word, the man bowed his head, then slowly turned in a circle until his back was to me. I shoved the barrel forward and smacked him between the shoulder blades, causing him to stumble a step or two, but he didn't react. After a pause, he walked forward, slowly and deliberately, showing no rush or fear of my gun. He went down the steps, started walking across the yard. I followed him, bracing the wide butt of the weapon against my upper shoulder, looking down its shaft toward the departing menace, not that I needed to aim much with a buck-shot-spraying cannon like the one in my arms. I willed myself to shoot.

But I couldn't do it.

I couldn't shoot a man in the back.

"Hey!" I shouted. "*Hey!* Where's my son?" He kept walking, didn't turn around, in no hurry. I almost blasted the gun toward the sky but I didn't want to terrify my children any more than they already were. With no porch light, and no streetlights within miles of our home, the creeper soon disappeared into the darkness. I saw no trace of him.

My breath came in short, painful bursts. I turned around,

went back inside, saw Andrea and the others on the couch, so tightly packed together they looked like a giant with multiple arms and legs.

"Come on," I said. "Let's make a break for the van. Hurry."

Andrea scrambled up, holding Hazel in her arms, shooing Mason along before her. My mom was right by her side, clutching little Logan; his whimpers were a dagger to my heart. I held tightly to the shotgun, swearing to myself I wouldn't hesitate next time—if someone, anyone, got in our way again I'd blow a hole into their chest.

We went out the door, a little group of terrified souls, me in front, everyone else right behind. I held the gun out before me, scanning the porch, the steps, the yard. Andrea had my phone, pointing the flashlight in front of us, although its glow quickly dissipated in the wide open yard and air of the night. Sweeping the barrel of my weapon left and right, left and right, we stepped to the edge of the porch, went down the steps. Besides the crickets and cicadas singing their musical haunt of the dark, the only sounds I heard came from my children, sniffles and moans and whimpers.

The van was only 20 feet away, pulled up on the gravel drive that semi-circled through the front yard. We walked toward it as I desperately wished for eyes in the back of my head so I could see everything around us.

"Take the keys out of my pocket," I whispered to Andrea.

She shifted Hazel to one arm—no small feat, I tell you; that girl was growing an inch a day—and slipped a hand into my right pocket. The keys jangled as she pulled them out, then a chirp boomed in the night as she unlocked the doors. The lights flashed, too, almost blinding; I had to squint and look down for a second.

When I returned my attention to the van, something moved on the other side of it, popping up over the edge, like a jack-in-the-box. I yelped, saw the shiny, crinkled plastic of another

Baghead, the man throwing his arms into the air and yelling, "Boo!"

My kids screamed, every single one of them. Andrea yelled my name; Mom shrieked, a sound that was as inhuman a thing as I'd ever heard. My last reservation, my last tether to rational, humane action snapped. Letting out a yell of frustration, I gripped the gun as fiercely as I could and ran around the side of the car, just as the second intruder started sprinting away, making a beeline for the cornfield on the north side of the house. I raised the barrel, aimed it forward.

"*Where's my son!*" I roared.

No response. Only running, away, his back to me, almost gone.

I fired.

The boom and flash of it rocked the night, as if thunder and lightning had struck all at once, splintering the air around us.

It also tore dozens of bloody holes into the man who'd been fleeing. He stumbled forward and fell flat on his face with an oomph and a splat. Then the world went back to darkness, crickets, cicadas. The cries and soft moans of my family. All of it barely heard over my own breaths, like the panting of a winded dog, as I stood there, staring at what I'd just done. Though I couldn't see much, the guy wasn't moving or making a sound. Nothing.

For the second time in my life, I'd killed another human being.

CHAPTER TWENTY

Lynchburg, South Carolina
June 1989

The ride was a bumpy one.

I'd never had any reason in my life to be in the trunk of a car, much less with the lid closed, vehicle moving at high speeds, my body jolted by every rock and pothole we ran over. At least I had Andrea there, her arms wrapped around mine, my arms wrapped around hers. I wished I could see her face, but having her to latch onto was enough to keep me sane. We slid along the worn-out carpet of the trunk with every swerve and sudden turn, hitting our heads, banging our knees, rolling, banging our heads again. With every jostle and bump, we held onto each other tighter, until I thought I might squeeze her to death, saving our captors the trouble.

When we hit a stretch of straight road, our bodies stable, I felt Andrea's hot breath in my ear as she whispered to me.

"What're we gonna do?"

I'd seen a lot of movies where this exact thing happened to the hero, I'm sure—though nothing specific came to mind.

Therefore, with Hollywood being my only possible resource, I came up empty.

"I got nothin'," I said, reaching deep to pull the slightest trace of humor from my stressed, coiled, knotted core. "But I'm scared, I can tell you that."

"Me, too."

I wanted desperately for her to keep talking. If nothing else, I needed her voice. But she went silent, her mouth and nose digging into my neck, wetting my skin with her breath. What was there to say? Tens of thousands of words must've been stored somewhere in my subconscious, but I couldn't put together the slightest phrase to give either one of us comfort.

We rode on, the hum of the engine and thrum of the road beneath the wheels seeming to taunt us, as at any other time such sounds would've soothed me to sleep.

"David!" Andrea whisper-shouted some few minutes later. "David!"

"What?" I replied quickly. "What, what, what?"

She moved out of my arms and leaned up on one elbow—the silhouette of her shadow leered over me a bit in the tight space. "This is a trunk. Which means it probably has a spare tire right under us, under the carpet. Where there's a spare tire, there's a crowbar."

A crowbar. The thought was both exhilarating and terrifying. I seemed a long way from having the guts to swing a crowbar at anyone, much less a bunch of lunatic murderers. Maybe Andrea could go berserk like she had at the Honeyhole.

"Okay," I said rather dumbly.

"Then move."

The next minute and a half was an exercise in body contortion and flexibility. First we had to pick a corner from which to pry up the carpet, pull it back as we scooted as far away as possible, slip the material under our knees, then search the cool metal surfaces beneath us with our hands. All while

crawling over top of each other, blind to the other's movements, with a good bump on the road now and then to keep us
honest. I felt wetness in my hair after one particularly bad
knock, touched it with a finger, winced at the sting and slick of
blood.

"Feel the tire?" she asked.

My fingers had just brushed across the hard rubber. "Yeah.
What if they can hear us?"

"They can't." She said it with such conviction that I decided
to believe her.

Our skulls smacked together at least three times as we felt
around the tire, slipping fingers into any crevice possible, trying
to find a damn crowbar. The only thing I got for my trouble was
a scrape across my thumb that made *it* bleed, too. This stupid
trunk was proving to be a worst enemy than the man who'd
locked us inside, although I knew that'd change very soon.

"Holy shit. I found it!" Andrea yelled way too loudly. Her
sentence had barely ended when the driver slammed on the
brakes, hard. Both of us catapulted forward, slamming into each
other and the front side of the trunk at the same time, aches and
pains erupting in places I'd forgotten existed. I heard the clank
of the weapon she'd found as it flew from her hands and banged
against the roof then back down on the metal we'd exposed.

Andrea groaned. I groaned. The driver of the car turned off
the ignition, the resulting silence so deep that I heard a tinny
ringing in my ears. Mostly on top of Andrea, I rolled off of her
and onto my back, my whole body cramped and achy.

"We need to put the carpet back where it was," I said as
quietly as I possibly could. She grunted agreement and we once
again went through the body contortions necessary to get it laid
out flat, covering the spare tire, like it had been before. I
relaxed, my back on the carpet, face-up again.

"Switch with me," she whispered. At the moment I was
closest to the rear of the car, where the trunk would open.

I tried my best to see her, but the darkness was complete. "Why?"

"Whoever opens that door, I'm going to bash their head in."

"That's a terrible idea."

"Why?"

"They might kill us!"

We whispered so lightly I couldn't imagine anyone inside or outside the car could hear us. But then one of the car doors opened, followed by the ding-ding-ding of the vehicle's warning system—either the lights were on or the keys were still in the ignition—and the door didn't close. Footsteps on gravel told us someone was walking to the back of the car; the direction seemed to indicate it had been the driver. Whoever it was, he or she stopped just on the other side of the metal from where I lay prone and vulnerable.

"Hand me the crowbar," I said in a panic.

"Switch with me!" she repeated.

"No time! Just hand it to me."

"Pop it," a voice right above us said, muffled by the metal. Something clunked and the lid of the trunk rose a few inches, faint light pouring in. It was just enough that I saw a long, thin object hovering right in foot of my eyes.

The crowbar.

I grabbed it from her and slipped it under my leg.

Just in time. A man lifted the trunk door as high as it would go, then stared down at us. His features were hidden in shadow but I could at least tell that he wore no bag on his head.

"This is our stop," he said. I didn't recognize the voice. Not Pee Wee. "Get out, we've got a short little walk."

"Okay," I said stupidly. With a groan I swung my legs over the lip of the trunk, then pushed off the carpet to get my butt on the lip. I kept one hand hidden behind me, firmly gripping one end of the crowbar. I knew I had less than three seconds to decide whether or not I had the balls to use it as a weapon, and thoughts flashed through my mind like frames of a film. My life was in danger. Andrea's life was in danger. My parents, too—they could even be dead already for all I knew. And there might not be another chance that night to have a hard rod of metal at my disposal, unbeknownst to a stranger who stood two feet from me.

"Hop down, you little shit," the man said. "You're just as stupid as your mama by the looks of it."

He took the decision out of my hands. Bracing my legs against the bumper for leverage, flexing my body in all the right places, I swung the crowbar from the trunk and arced it through the air; its clawed end whacked into the man's shoulder. He gave a yelp of pain, stepping back a couple steps as he rubbed the spot where I'd hit him. I leaped onto the ground and came after him, raising my weapon again, but he sucker-punched me right in the stomach; I collapsed to the ground in a fit of coughing, trying to suck in air as quickly as it heaved out of me. Nausea swept through my guts. The crowbar lay on the gravel, right in front of my eyes.

The man lightly kicked me in the ribs. "Like I said. As stupid as your mama. Time to pay the consequences."

I braced myself for another kick or something worse. Instead he turned on his heels, the tiny rocks crunching under his shoes, and stepped back over to the car. I looked up from where I was curled into a ball, clutching my stomach, just as he reached inside the open trunk and yanked fiercely on something with both arms.

Andrea.

Pulling her by the hair, he heaved her out of the vast, dark space, then threw her on the ground, about 10 feet from me. She landed in a heap as she let out a scream, then somehow maneuvered herself to catch my eyes with hers. They were stone-cold, full of bravery, and I guessed that mine looked the exact opposite. I knew she wanted me to do something, but I had no idea what, and even if I did, I doubted I'd find the courage to do it.

She broke eye contact, then tried to get to her feet; the man kicked her in the small of her back, making her collapse again, her cheek smacking into the gravel. He kept the heel of his shoe where he'd kicked her, put his weight on it. Andrea moaned, then screamed, even as she squirmed unsuccessfully to get free.

The man turned his head toward me—I could see just enough of his features now to be sure I'd never met him before. He had a squashed face, a flat nose, scraggly hair.

"Boy," he said, "I reckon we need you tonight, but this little brat ain't nothin' but some insurance. Ya hear me?"

He knelt down, placed his knees on her thighs, one each, then put his hands on the back of her neck. I glanced at the crowbar, so close to me—he obviously had no fear of me whatsoever, knew that I was too chicken or too weak to fight back, to hurt him. I slowly slid my hand out from beneath my stomach, inched it closer and closer to the handle-end of the bar.

Andrea's attacker had both hands wrapped around her neck, now, and I could tell he was squeezing because she made choking sounds and wiggled her middle section, thrashed with her arms, kicked with the bottom half of her legs. All of it to no avail. He weighed enough to keep her down, was strong enough to kill her. I had my doubts that he'd go that far, at least so soon in the night, but I didn't have the luxury of making assumptions.

Andrea gagged, coughed into the dust and rocks, kicked her feet. But her efforts had weakened.

"Boy," the man hollered at me. "Your stupid mama ever teach you the birds and the bees? Better yet, she ever show ya how it works?"

My spirit broke. My mind broke. The world collapsed into a single collage of horrifying images, floating in my mind. My parents, dead, their heads chopped off. Andrea, raped, killed, her head chopped off. Leaving me alive and alone to watch it, live with it. I snapped.

Gripping the crowbar as if it tethered me to my own heart, I jumped to my feet and ran as fast as my legs could cover the ground between me and Andrea's attacker. I didn't yell, didn't scream, instead using all that energy, channeling it—along with the rage that threatened to erupt inside my chest—all of the power known to me and some not. All of it into my skinny little arm.

The man saw me coming. Completely unimpressed, he casu- ally let go of Andrea's neck and rocked back on his knees, ready to spring to his feet and swat me away like a fly. But he was too late. Something had happened to me, had made me monstrous and strong for one brief moment. Bursting with hate and anger, I raised the crowbar above my head, then swung it 100 times harder than I had before. He raised his hand to ward it off, but he was too late for that, too.

The claw end of the crowbar crashed into the top of his head with a solid thunk, sinking in all the way to the shaft of the bar itself. He screamed. I screamed as I yanked it back out, ripping brains, skull, skin, hair. Then I hit him again, this time right in the temple. His screams cut off and he fell off Andrea, collapsed in an unnatural position to the side of her. He went still, didn't move in the slightest. I hit him one last time to be sure, then stood there, heaving breaths in and out.

Andrea had scrambled away from the scene, facing the other direction, on her hands and knees, choking and spitting. I dropped the crowbar, so full of adrenaline I didn't know how I could ever come back down to Earth from the realms of violent ecstasy in which I floated.

I sensed a presence behind me. I turned to look, the world spinning far more than it should have. Three people stood over by the car. No, just one, their forms jittering, then melding together; my vision could hardly keep up with the speed of my churning metabolism.

Pee Wee watched, his arms folded, showing no emotion whatsoever. He'd observed the whole thing, I knew it. Watched without trying to stop me.

"It's in your blood, son," he said. "You know that, right? The violence. It's in your blood. That's the real reason you were able to kill him. Old Cousin T-Bone wasn't much good for nothin' anyhow. May he rot in peace."

My heart had started to slow, just a little, but not enough to speak.

Pee Wee pulled a gun from behind him, pointed its barrel at me.

"Time to go, now. Just a short walk. Bring her along if ya want." He nodded at Andrea, who seemed to be recovering, sitting still in the grass just off the gravel road.

"Where?" I managed to say.

He answered, though it made no sense.

"To the House of Tongues."

CHAPTER TWENTY-ONE

Lynchburg, South Carolina
July 2017

After shooting the Baghead who hoofed it for the cornfield —filling his back with buckshot—I ran to Andrea, my mom, my kids. Sweeping the shotgun along with my vision as I turned in a circle, I scanned every direction, trying to spot signs of anyone or anything suspicious. Nothing.

"Get in the van," I said. "Quick."

We all acted. I took Logan from my mom's arms as she opened the automatic side-door closest to us, then Andrea ushered Mason and Hazel inside as soon the door had slid far enough. Their grandma went next; I handed Logan to her when she took a seat, then pushed the lever to close the door. Andrea sprinted around the van to the passenger side and a few seconds later we both slammed our doors shut at the exact same moment. Before anything else, I engaged the locks throughout the vehicle, feeling the smallest hint of relief at the simultaneous series of thunks. With the key in my pocket, all I had to do next was push the ignition button—the van's engine came to life with a surging roar, followed by a steady hum.

"Seat belts!" I shouted, feeling a little ridiculous.

I shifted the gear into drive and hit the gas, anxious to leave the house of my childhood for the first time I could ever remember. The tires spit a few pebbles and tufts of sand then caught traction, propelling us forward. We shot toward the spot where the man had fallen on his face—our headlights illuminating the shiny polka dots of blood that littered his body—before the curve of the gravel driveway turned us away from him back to the road in front of our house. I was just about to hit-the-pedal-to-the-metal and gun it out of there when I saw something move out of the left corner of my eye. A figure, a person.

I slammed on the brakes, purely on instinct, curiosity winning over sanity.

"What're you *doing?*" Andrea snapped at me.

Ignoring her, I stared out the window. A Baghead had come out of the cornfield, stepping from between the stalks like Malachai in *Children of the Corn*, every bit as creepy. He had no weapon I could see, his body still mostly lit up by the peripherals of the headlights. Taking slow, steady steps, almost ritualistic, he walked up to his friend, cousin, brother, whomever I'd killed. Then he bent his head to look down, stared for a few seconds, peering at bloody death through the thin veil of a cheap grocery bag, which pulsed with every breath.

"David, get us the hell out of here!" Andrea yelled, whacking me on the arm.

She was right. Of course she was right. I slipped my right foot from the brake and pressed it to the gas pedal. We spun out a little, then surged ahead once again, leaving a cloud of dust and spitting rocks to the new stranger who'd emerged from the fields. In my last glimpse of him, he'd raised both arms to cup his hands around his mouth, his body language suggesting that he was shouting as loudly as possible at us, leaning forward with the effort.

But I couldn't hear him, not a single word. And if I dared stop again, Andrea would probably kick me out and drive off herself, leaving me behind. I almost did it anyway, telling myself it might've been about Wesley or my dad. A clue. A direction.

Or a trap. A diversion. This was no time for me to turn into a complete idiot.

We hit the road, spun just a little in my over-exuberance to turn left, then the tires found their home against the asphalt. We zoomed ahead, the lights creating a consistent, eerie halo of misty white in the near distance while we drove, as if the night were so dark my lights could only penetrate its outer surface. My hands trembled so I gripped the steering wheel as tightly as I could, squeezing my fingers into stillness.

"Where are we going?" Andrea asked.

I thought of my son. I thought of my dad. Of my mom, right behind me.

I thought of my three kids back there with her.

"I don't know."

Remnants of rain slicked the road, filled the divots and potholes. Puddles and practical lakes hemmed in from the sides, the swamp that veined our small town having swelled in size more than I'd seen since Hurricane Hugo. Another couple of stormy days and we would've turned into Venice. The tires swooshed through the wetness, the darkness over us like a veil on the world, a world that had shrunk in size to only include us, enclosed within a moony light that traveled as we traveled.

Wesley, I thought. *My son.*

Pain and guilt wracked me in equal measure. What was I doing? What in the hell was I doing? I slammed on the brakes, skidding to a stop after a one-quarter turn that terrified my children. Whimpers and moans turned to wailing and screams.

"I'm sorry," I whispered.

"What is it?" Andrea asked, her voice shockingly calm.

"What's going on?" Mom said at the same time, *pretending* to be calm.

I leaned forward until my forehead settled against the steering wheel. When I spoke, my voice cracked with emotion. "I don't know what to do. The police aren't responding, Sheriff Taylor isn't, Dad isn't, Wesley isn't. What am I supposed to do?" I jerked back in my seat with that last question, slammed my fists against the dashboard. "We have to go back, find them. How can we leave?"

"You're scaring the kids," my mom whispered, spooking me from right behind my ear.

"They should be scared!" I shouted. Closing my eyes, I wished I could take it back. "I'm sorry, guys. I'm sorry."

Andrea reached over and took my hand. Squeezed. "Is there a safe place we could leave your mom and the kids? We could do that, then go back and look for them. Or find out where the cops are in this tiny town."

"Evelyn's, I guess." But even as I said it, the image flashed in my mind of that dead cop slumped against the window in his car. Nowhere was safe. Nowhere.

"David."

I'd never heard my name said so ominously. It came from Andrea, and I knew something was wrong. I looked up, into the rear view mirror. Headlights, coming on fast.

"Oh, shit," I whispered, though I had no way of knowing it was trouble. The odds were even against it—how many people could be driving down this road, for any number of reasons? Possibly, maybe, hopefully, it might even be a policeman or FBI agent.

Unsure of my actions, I put the car back into drive and pulled off to the soaked side of the road—only a few feet lest I sink into the surrounding swamp. I thought for a second, then shifted the car into park. I just couldn't make a decision to drive forward or backward. I couldn't.

The approaching headlights got bigger and brighter, making me think it was a truck. My heart leaped into overdrive as it came right up behind us, veered a little to make room, came up alongside, started to pass us...

The truck's tires screeched with pressed brakes as it swerved, its back end fish-tailing away from us, its front end stopping directly in our path. I immediately shifted into reverse, my foot moving toward the gas pedal, my head turned toward the back to scout our escape route, when Andrea shouted at me.

"Wait! Don't go!"

I paused, panic searing through me, looked at her. "What?" I shouted. "What?"

"They're holding up a sign!"

I faced forward again, focused on the passenger-side window that sat right in the beam of my headlights. Like she'd said, someone held a sign against the glass, a large piece of white paper that seemed to shine of its own accord. A message had been scrawled across it, hastily but neatly, with a black magic marker:

House of Tongues
NOW
Or Wesley dies
Get in, alone

I stared at the words, completely unable to look away or act. I felt nothing inside, as if someone had shocked my system with a human malware that erased my hard drive. At least the part that had feelings, emotions. Everyone in the car was silent, even my kids. The numbness that consumed me at seeing the message was unlike anything I'd ever experienced before.

Memories were coming back. Like hearing a song or smelling a scent that takes you to another time and place, I was being swept away, swept to that night long ago when I'd been taken to the House of Tongues.

"David?" Andrea whispered, seeming to sense that I'd fallen into a semi-trance.

"Yeah?" I replied weakly.

"You can't go back there."

I couldn't answer, couldn't say anything. If I had a soul, it had fallen into an abyss.

"Protect my kids," I said. "Protect my mom. Take this van and drive. Drive until you hit the Georgia state line. You have a shotgun. Use it if you need it."

"David," she said sternly. My mom said my name in the same way at the same time.

I opened the door.

"David!" Andrea reached out and grabbed my arm but I gently shook it off.

Then I looked at her, all the fierceness of the evil world in my gaze. "Protect my family."

"David, no! No!"

My mom screamed at me from the back. "Close that door and drive away, David. Right now!"

The truck waited in front of us, idling, a stream of exhaust rising in the eerie light.

"Daddy?" Hazel said in a trembling voice.

"Dad?" Mason.

"Daddy?" Logan.

With the open-door alarm dinging, I turned around and faced my children. Hazel, her sweet face wet with tears, her eyes full of questions. Mason, pale and afraid, wilted. Logan in the far back, as confused a kid as ever was. I loved them to bursting, but we weren't complete. Not without Wesley. Not without their eldest brother.

"Do you guys trust me? Have you always trusted me?"

I waited for their nods and got them, one by one.

"Do you know I love you, more than any dad has ever loved his kids?"

More nods, a few more tears.

"I swear to you, I'll be okay. I'm going to save Wesley and Grandpa, then we'll all be back together. I swear it. Okay? I need you to be brave and go with Grandma and Andrea. You can pray for me if you'd like. And for your brother."

More nods, more tears. Their bravery humbled me to a level I didn't know possible, and solidified the oath I'd just made to them. One way or another; somehow, someway; if I had to reach down the gullet of hell itself and pull Satan's heart out with my bare hands, I'd do it. When dawn came, my family would be alive and safe. *All of them.*

I looked at Andrea and she looked back at me.

"There's no choice," I said.

She waited. Nodded. Blinked, squeezing out a couple of tears.

"David, you can't do this," my mom pleaded. "You can't do this."

"Mom, I love you. I love you more than life itself."

I jumped out of the car, slammed the door closed before anyone could say another word. I expected a door to open, someone to chase me, but no one did. Andrea knew what had to be done, and she'd taken charge of the loved ones I was leaving behind. I walked toward the truck. The sign in the passenger window had been taken down, but a hand appeared in the dim light of the interior. It made a hitchhiking fist, thumb extended, pointing to the back of the truck, its meaning clear.

I grabbed the lip of the truck bed with both hands, placed a foot on the bumper, then vaulted myself into the back. I sat down, legs crossed, my back against the side. The truck peeled out, spraying mud onto the front of my van, then sped away. I watched the van recede, but the lights were too bright for me to see inside. To see the faces of my family.

I raised my right hand against the rushing wind resistance.
I waved.

It's my turn this time, Andrea, I thought as I lowered my arm.
This time it's my turn.

CHAPTER TWENTY-TWO

Lynchburg, South Carolina
June 1989

We walked through the woods, Pee Wee right in front of us. He had a flashlight, illuminating a narrow path through the brush and weeds and undergrowth. Another man was behind us, a bag on his head, a thing that now seemed almost normal to me. He, too, had a flashlight, directed at us in case we made any sudden moves. Andrea and I held hands, our fingers slick with sweat. We'd probably been hiking for 20 minutes since we left the gigantic Cadillac, where a dead man lay next to it, his skull bashed in by a crowbar.

I'd killed a man, and so far I felt no remorse.

I did feel sick inside, queasy, unclean. But not remorseful. These people had put me through hell, and they all deserved a similar death. Worse. And if they thought Andrea and I were just gonna be nice little lambs going to the slaughter, they had another thing coming. Not that some monumental, heroic bravery had taken over me—the honest truth is that I was scared shitless. But I'd also had enough of their antics, feeling as if we'd reached a point where we had nothing to lose anymore, a point with only two options: beg for mercy or go down fighting. I hoped in my heart I'd choose the latter when all things came to a head.

On and on we walked, through the gloomily lit tunnel of the trees.

"Where're you taking us?" Andrea asked. No one had spoken for a few minutes and her voice just about wiped out the courage I'd been building up—I almost jumped out of my pants.

Pee Wee stopped. We stopped, too, or we would've run right into him. Without turning around, he answered in a tone full of annoyance.

"I already told you where we're going. The House of Tongues."

"Well what the hell is the *House of Tongues?*"

I almost cheered at the defiance in her words.

This time, Pee Wee *did* turn around, shining his flashlight up under his chin to create the classic ghoul face. When he spoke, his face twisted with creepy shadows. "It's exactly what it sounds like. I ain't no poet."

He spun around and started walking again. The Baghead behind us gave a nudge in our backs with his flashlight, and we stumbled forward, trying to keep up. A few minutes later, we exited the trees and entered a small clearing, maybe 30 feet wide, where not only the trees but even weeds, bushes, scrub—everything—had been cleared. Pee Wee and the Baghead both were shining their lights around, either looking for something or trying to impress us with our location. I wasn't, in the least.

Only one thing broke up the bare ground of the clearing, and I had no idea what it was. Some kind of shaft, almost like a chimney, made of old stones and mortar, rising 20 feet from the ground. It was cylindrical, about as wide as one of the huge pecan trees in our front yard, and tapered off a little toward the top, ending in a jagged circle of broken rock, reminding me of a beer bottle that some brawler broke against the bar to ward off a drunken foe. The surface of the shaft looked ancient, covered in mildew and moss, a sickly greenish hue mixed with gray.

"That there's been around since the Revolution, kids," Pee Wee said, sounding more than a little fanatical, like a deranged docent in a museum. "The House of Tongues is right under it. Come on, now."

He walked forward, his light making the tall structure's shadow sway back and forth against the trees like a drunkard. We followed him around to the other side, where there was a square hole built into the bottom of the shaft, no more than three feet high, sealed by an iron-banded wooden door. The whole thing seemed like a tower in a castle—maybe Rapunzel had been imprisoned up top, though I saw no sign of her hair.

Pee Wee took out an old-school key and slid it into a keyhole, turned it; a click sounded and the door opened slightly. The noise reminded me of the Cadillac's trunk, and that made an ominous situation even more ominous. Pee Wee crouched down and placed his palm against the wood, pushed it all the way in with a creak. Darkness waited on the inside, complete.

"Follow me," he said, then he leaned forward onto his hands and crawled through the opening.

I looked at Andrea but she was too busy staring at the square of blackness where Pee Wee's feet had just disappeared. The Baghead nudged me with the point of his finger.

"Get in there," the man said with that gravelly voice I hadn't heard since the Honeyhole. I was massively confused as to who'd been who whenever I met these psychos.

Andrea went ahead of me, dropping to her hands and knees and crawling forward. I did the same, right behind her, and as soon as she crossed the threshold, faint light appeared on the inside. I entered next, into a tiny rounded chamber that looked much like it did on the outside, rough stone blocks mortared together in haphazard fashion, the circumference of the chimney narrowing the higher it went. A few tubular fluorescent bulbs hung like Christmas ornaments from rusty nails, their wires zigzagging up the curved face of the flat rocks. The glow was unnatural and uneasy on the eyes.

A metallic staircase spiraled its way downward from a small landing at the door, and Pee Wee had already descended a few steps, so that his eyes were almost even with mine while I still knelt. Andrea stood on a step to the right and above him, looking up the shaft of the chimney. I joined her, glad to stand back up to my full height. The place smelled dank and rotten, the air surprisingly cool. The lights buzzed over our heads, an unpleasant sound that matched everything else about the place. Baghead was the last to enter, shutting the door behind him. I felt as if I'd been sealed in a tomb, and hoped it wasn't true.

Without saying anything, Pee Wee started clomping his way down. We followed.

The steps clanged and the entire metal structure of the spiral staircase trembled, rattled as we descended into the depths below. There were also metallic groans and squeals that echoed off the walls, the sounds ricocheting up the stone shaft until they hit the top and bounced back toward us. Soon it was an eerie cacophony of reverberations and perpetual squeaks that made my head hurt. The slight swaying of the steps made me dizzy.

The stench seemed to worsen every time I put a foot down. Rot. Decay. Moldy wetness. We'd gone 20 steps. Then 40. I couldn't fathom what the purpose of this place had been in those long-ago years when it had been built, dug into the earth. But I feared finding out the source of those foul smells. The fluorescent bulbs above us had lost their effectiveness, the air darkening, but I could sense a reddish glow coming from below. *Magma*, was the word that came to mind, a river of lava, just like Mount Doom in *Lord of the Rings*. But the temperature was plummeting, not the other way around.

We reached the bottom.

I heard the scruff of Pee Wee's shoes when they left the metal mesh of the steps and scraped across a dusty stone floor. Andrea and I exited the staircase right after him, entering a long, narrow tunnel constructed from the same blocks of stone as the shaft we'd just descended. A red lightbulb hung from the ceiling, the only source of light, creepy as hell, as if someone's blood had evaporated into the air. At the end of the corridor, another iron-banded door stood closed.

No one said anything. I was holding Andrea's hand and couldn't remember how long we'd been doing so. Pee Wee walked ahead, all the way to the door. We followed him, the gun-toting Baghead right on our heels. This routine was getting old, but that didn't mean I was anxious for it to end. A visceral fear, something deeper and more sickening than I'd felt before, crept into my nerves and bones. The stark realization that my death awaited me on the other side of the door... I didn't know how to bear it, shaking from the panic.

Andrea squeezed my hand harder, brought it to her lips, kissed my knuckles.

"It'll be okay," she whispered. Her words bungeed me back to sanity, at least for the moment. We all stood in front of the menacing door, its cracked wood and rusted iron bands looking as old as England.

"This is the House of Tongues," Pee Wee said in a scratchy whisper, something demonic about it. "I expect reverence when we enter. Do you understand?"

I felt so helpless, knowing we should fight, attack these two monsters before we were opened up to even more on the other side of the door. But I couldn't. I had no capacity to act.

So I nodded instead.

"Are you gonna kill us?" Andrea asked, holding onto her dignity. "You really think you'll get away with all of this?"

"No." He answered with absolutely no doubt in his voice, as if he'd accepted the consequences of his many murders, felt that it would all be worth it. "Now, are you going to be reverent?"

Andrea was fuming, but she seemed to sense that the time to fight back had not yet presented itself. She nodded as meekly as she could.

"Good." Pee Wee unlocked the door and pushed it open.

A rancid breeze blew outwards, as if the chamber within had exhaled after holding its breath for millennia. I gagged, held my nose, coughed at the same smells we'd already been accosted with, but magnified tenfold. Pee Wee reached around the frame of the door and flicked a switch; lights flickered to life beyond the opening—lights with the same buzzy glow of the fluorescents in the stairwell. He paused at the threshold to look back at us, then made a gesture with his head for us to follow him in. Then he stepped inside, and so did we, entering a room with a low ceiling, bordered with wooden shelves on all sides, about 20 feet square. Several lightbulbs hung from the ceiling.

The shelves were mostly spare, but one wall of them had been filled with sealed mason jars, lined up end to end, the glass of each touching its neighbors on both sides. An amber-colored liquid filled each one, a large, pale chunk of something floating within every single jar. The bottles were labeled with white stickers yellowed from age, messy handwriting scrawled across the faded surfaces.

In my life, I've felt the presence of true darkness, of evil, of things that have haunted and will continue to haunt me until I take my very last breath. But at the top of the list, far ahead of whatever may come in second place, was the feeling I got in that room, in that moment, looking at those shelves, stocked with sealed, dusty mason jars.

Pee Wee swept an arm slowly through the air, in the direction of the jars, as if revealing a brand new car to a winner on a game show.

"Behold," he said in a reverential voice. "The tongues of our ancestors."

CHAPTER TWENTY-THREE

Lynchburg, South Carolina
July 2017

The warm air rushed against my skin, blew my hair into a tangled mess, as the truck drove through the night. I sensed the turns before they came, shifted my body in anticipation, though I'd only been to this place once in my entire life. The memories were coming back hard and fast, some of it masked as intuition, and not in any type of order that made sense.

But I remembered the castle-like tower, with its broken-tooth crown. I remembered the iron-bound doors. I remembered the spiral staircase of metal and rust. Worst of all, I remembered the wall of mason jars, each one filled with an amber liquid, keeping its precious cargo safe, floating, and preserved.

Tongues.

I shuddered at the thought, at the memory. The purpose of the tongues still eluded me, however. Why did Pee Wee have them all? What had he said on that horrific night so long ago? I couldn't quite recall. Not yet. But the memory waited, patiently, eager, on the other side of some veil that I didn't understand.

The truck slowed and turned onto a barely-there dirt track that vanished quickly into a heavily wooded area. The canopy of branches and leaves looked like a cave rimmed by the headlights of the vehicle, its destination dark and foreboding. Although impossible, it all seemed familiar to me—that tree, that bush, the rocks along the trail, the way the path curved slowly to the right. In my countless visits back home since I'd graduated from high school, I hadn't been back to this spot or this general area, even. The growth of the forest would be completely different from when I was a teenager. But still. I was coming back to the place where my horrors culminated, climaxed, marinated into the meat of my being.

I was scared, like the child I had been.

The truck stopped.

A cloud of dust washed over us, shining in the headlights like fog, then dissipated. The truck doors opened, and two men got out, both of them wearing the uniform of old, the most ridiculous uniform I could possibly imagine for people of such evil. Grocery bags on their heads, the handles tied around their necks, cut slits through which they could breathe.

Having been through all this before, I found a seed of bravery mushed within me.

"Seriously?" I asked, throwing all the scorn I possibly could into the word. "Still with the stupid bags on your heads? What are we, in kindergarten? Show your faces, cowards."

The one who'd been driving looked at me through his thin veil of plastic. Tilted his head. How often had I seen that gesture?

"Where's my son?" I asked. Something was slowly trickling into my veins and muscles and heart. Desperation. These bastards didn't know it, but once I saw my son, once I saw even the slightest sign that he was alive and well, I would go on a rampage, killing like a demon released from Hell until Wesley was freed. I, nor he, had anything to lose now. They would kill us eventually, soon. And I knew it.

The Bagheads didn't respond. The driver rounded the truck and came to stand by his companion. Then he pointed into the woods, in a direction I already knew. The way to the House of Tongues.

"Is he there?" I asked. "You took him there, did to him what you tried to do to me?" I knew the answer to this even as I asked it, but I needed confirmation, a stamp of approval for my pending rampage.

The Baghead who'd been in the passenger seat finally spoke. He used the voice of old, the disguised voice, the voice of crushing rocks.

"We won't fight you. Follow us or the boy dies."

Neither one of them waited for a response. They turned and started walking away, down a tiny deer trail that I hadn't noticed until they slipped through the bushes that framed its entrance. The two men were soon replaced by swaying branches and darkness.

I jumped out of the truck and ran after them, slipping into the thick growth of vegetation. I couldn't think anymore. Only act. Unlike the night all those years ago, fear for my own safety didn't exist. It should have, because I had three other kids dependent on me, but the numbness was complete. Forward. Forward. Forward.

I caught up to the Bagheads, slowed to a brisk pace right on their heels. Their flashlights cast a sporadic spray of brightness on the low canopy above us, eerie and dizzying. They didn't speak, and I didn't speak. The nocturnal insects serenaded us with their night song; the soggy leaves and pine straw squished beneath our feet. I studied the build of the two men, wondered if there was any way I could take both of them. As soon as I had

Wesley in my sights, I planned to do whatever it took to put them down.

We entered a clearing, the clearing from my childhood. The stone-brick tower still stood in the middle, though it seemed half as tall as I remembered. Both Bagheads shone their lights upon the tightly curved shaft—its crown still jagged, its sides still filthy, strewn with moss; the whole thing looked like a smokestack from an industrial revolution-era factory. Seeing it made my heart icy cold.

"Is my son down there?" I asked. Images of the House of Tongues were flashing through my mind, the memories of it coming together like pieces of a jigsaw puzzle.

The two men turned to look back at me, the bags on their heads crinkling with the movement. They said nothing, just stared through the plastic. I was so fed up. Fed up with how I'd been treated as a teenager, fed up with how I was being treated now.

"Why are you doing this?" I asked, trying to keep my calm. "What do you have against my family? Against me? What did I ever do to the damned Gaskins?" My breaths were quick and shallow, my lungs difficult to properly fill with air.

One of the men took a step toward me, then another. He leaned closer, his bagged, shadowed face only a few inches from mine.

"Your family is accursed," he said, with no attempt to disguise his voice. It was Dicky. I knew it was Dicky. He said the last word with exaggerated emphasis on the syllables. *A-curse-ed.* "And for 200 years, you've made us accursed too."

His words didn't baffle, didn't confuse. They only angered. I shook from it as I spoke.

"I'm glad that you backwoods, inbred, dumbass Gaskinses can feel better when you blame all the things you've done on everything and everyone but yourselves, but it ends tonight. I swear to God that it ends tonight." I breathed in and out as heavily as if I'd just run a half-mile without stopping.

The Bagheads stood there, saying nothing in reply. Several seconds passed.

"Where is he?" I shouted. "Tell me where he is!"

Still nothing.

Fuming, I barreled forward, stepping right between the two men; I bumped their shoulders with mine, throwing both of them off balance. But I didn't stop—I headed toward the small square door that I knew waited for me on the other side of the stone tower.

"Ya might not like what ya find down there," Dicky said from behind me.

I stopped, couldn't help it. Turned to face him and his partner.

"Take off that stupid bag," I said. "Stop acting like a damned child and take it off!"

I don't know how to describe the amount of anger that flowed through me in those moments without repeating myself incessantly. But it was a living thing, a consuming thing.

"Take it off!" I screamed, then I was running forward. I reached the man I thought was Dicky, grabbed at his head. He didn't resist. My fingers found the bag where it had been tied around his neck, dug into the thin plastic, gripped it. He still didn't resist, even as the momentum of my efforts pushed him several feet. I stayed with him, using both hands now to rip at the material. The plastic resisted at first, but once I snipped it the whole thing burst apart, flimsy shreds falling across his shoulders.

It was...

It was my dad.

I didn't understand. I didn't understand at all.

Stumbling backward, two steps, three, four. Staring at my own father, his hair disheveled and sweaty, his face haggard, his eyes full of glowing pain. He said nothing, looked back at me with as blank an expression as I'd ever seen on his face, so empty that I doubted my initial recognition of him for a moment. But it was him. A confusion as big and complex as the universe filled my soul. And still he said nothing.

Stunned, I looked over at the other Baghead—the one who *had* to be Dicky—as if he'd explain and make everything okay. It was all an innocent mistake, a joke, a prank. There was no way in hell, no circumstance under the sun and moon, no possible explanation for why my dad was here with Dicky Gaskins, disguised in the childish hood of my lifetime enemies.

"What's going on?" I said in a low voice, asking the grass and trees as much as anyone else. Nothing, absolutely nothing made sense in my life right then.

But Dicky responded anyway; he left his ridiculous bag atop his head but made no effort to mask his voice.

"Our families are stuck, David," he said, as if I'd asked for directions and he was obliged to answer. "Doesn't matter how many decades you spend tryin' to forget, tryin' to deny it. We're as tied up as chicken wire, man. Ain't nothin' gonna change that."

I stared at him, either dumb or dumbfounded, I didn't know which. "What are you talkin' about, Dicky? I swear if you did anything to my son..."

"Ha!" He barked the word, not an ounce of humor buried within it. "If I've done anything to your son. The nerve you've got, David. For 200 years *your* family has been doing things to *my* family, but all you can go on about is one little person. One person out of hundreds. You ain't nothin' but a damned son of a bitch."

I couldn't take this for one more second. I leaped forward, grabbed his shirt with both of my hands. I yanked him close to me, his bag-hidden face only inches from mine.

"Stop talking in riddles!" I yelled, sprays of spit sounding like raindrops on the thin plastic. "Where is he! What'd you do to him! Did you kill him? Huh?" I screamed every word.

Dicky made no effort to fight back, hanging almost limp in my grip.

Surely just to rattle me, he answered in that gravelly, Batman voice.

"Course we didn't kill him, you dumbass. There's a lot worse things than *that* you can do to a man. Man or kid alike."

I let go of his shirt and pushed him to the ground; he fell flat on his back, let out a painful-sounding grunt.

"One more time," I said, hearing the danger in my own voice. "Where. Is. He."

Dicky leaned himself up onto an elbow. "He's right below us, David." He pointed a thumb toward the dirt and weeds beneath his body, as if pointing at Hell. "He's down there doin' what it is we been doin' for two centuries."

"What, Dicky. What's my son doing? Why don't you enlighten me."

He didn't respond for a few seconds, and I almost gave up—I was just starting to turn back toward the broken tower, the door, the spiral staircase, my son—when Dicky spoke four words that made the hairs of my entire body stand on end.

"He's using a saw."

CHAPTER TWENTY-FOUR

Lynchburg, South Carolina
June 1989

After Pee Wee had lead us into the long, dank, stone-bricked room with its shelves of preserved human tongues, the Baghead who'd come down with us grabbed Andrea and me by the arms and guided us past it all, made us sit in two wooden chairs with their backs against the far wall. The revelation that the mason jars contained tongues had really shaken me, made me sick to my stomach. Stunned, I sat down without fight or complaint, grabbing Andrea's hand for support. A tether to sanity, reason, some kind of hope.

Pee Wee untied the plastic bag handles around his neck and pulled the bag off, then scratched his fingers over his crew-cut hair. I stared at him, the pock-marked face, the weasel-like eyes, the lean, taut figure. A huge scab and bruise marked the spot where Andrea had hit him with a rock. He wore scruffy jeans, an old work-shirt with a name atop the pocket so faded I couldn't read it, and dusty work boots. Standing before us, he folded his arms, looked down at the floor. A half-minute or so passed in silence; the other Baghead didn't remove his disguise as he stood by the door through which we'd come. The world's strangest watchdog.

"Why'd you bring us here?" Andrea asked. She hadn't given up with these types of questions, though everyone in the room knew they weren't going to get us anywhere. I thought that by demanding information, it was her way of showing bravery, showing she didn't plan to cower in fear.

Pee Wee focused his gaze on her. "You didn't have to be a part of this, ya know. This is between the Player family and mine, not yours. You and your mama could head back to Mexico for all I cared, but you're here now, ain't ya? Tough shit I say. It's what you get for jacking me at the Honeyhole."

"I'm just as American as you," she replied defiantly.

That inflamed Pee Wee. He stepped up to her, slapped her across the face for the second time in a week. She didn't so much as whimper, just straightened her head and glared back at him. I hated myself for being too chicken to do anything about it.

"That don't seem to work on you none," Pee Wee said. Then he slapped me just as hard. My face snapped to the right, the blooming pain of it like a whoosh of lit gas. My eyes stung with tears.

"Stop it!" Andrea screamed.

I braced myself for another whack, but it didn't come. Pee Wee took a step back and folded his arms again, his skin flushed and sweaty now.

"If you kids think this is all gonna end with somethin' as easy and quick and clean as death, you can toss that right out your heads. Oh no. That ain't how this whole things works, ya see. No, sir. No, ma'am. Uh-uh. This here's about torment. About payback. This here's about makin' things balanced betwixt our families. Got it?"

His eyes were trained on mine as if he expected an answer.

"I don't get it," I said meekly.

"That's 'cause your daddy's too weak to tell you the truth. To tell you your history. Your Grandpa Player was yellow-bellied, too. Your whole damn family line's been too craven to follow our pact, keep things... manageable. They keep trying to pawn it all on us, one-sided. It's enough to make a man... Angry."

I wanted to ask. Ask the obvious and simplest of questions, but I literally could not speak. Pee Wee obliged us by answering the unspoken.

"It's a curse, boy. A curse upon our ancestors, yours and mine both. From those pricks, the Puritans. You study them in school, I reckon? You know what the hell a Puritan is?"

I nodded, squeezing Andrea's hand at the same time. We had to do something. Had to. The tension in the air was thick, something awful and dark ready to shatter it. This man was totally unstable.

"Did you know you're a Quaker?" Pee Wee asked.

The question took me so much by surprise that I found my voice.

"A *Quaker*?"

Pee Wee turned his attention to Andrea. "Girl, you know what Puritans and Quakers are, don't ya?"

I watched her as she nodded, nothing else. But I could tell her mind was spinning, trying to come up with a way out of this shit show.

"They hated us," Pee Wee said. "We hated them, too, but they had all the power. *All* the power." He paused. "I wanna read you a scripture. Ya'll probably too busy committin' whoredoms in the woods to read much of the Good Book, I'm sure. But you're gonna listen to this one. Understood?"

He waited. I nodded. Andrea nodded.

"Proverbs," he said, having calmed down, back to the reverential voice he'd used when we first entered. "Proverbs, chapter 10, verse 31. Either one of you know it?"

He waited. I shook my head. Andrea shook her head.

Then he recited the scripture as if each word were as sacred as the tomb of Jesus. "'*The mouth of the just bringeth forth wisdom; but the perverted tongue shall be cut out.*'"

He went quiet, perhaps hoping we'd ponder the meaning. My eyes naturally went to the bottles lining the shelves on the other side of the room, full of tongues, according to Pee Wee. I wondered what kind of evil was going on, here.

"We were cursed to kill," Pee Wee said. "Cursed to shed the blood of our fellow man, commit the ultimate sin. Passed down from generation to generation by the perverted tongue when pulled from our throats, then cured by its cutting out. It's our curse and our blessing. It's also why we remove the heads of the sinners, because it's the dwelling place of their perverted tongues. We become *their* curse and their blessing."

He's more than crazy, I thought. *He's... gleefully insane.*

"You're gonna see the ritual, now," Pee Wee said, barely above a whisper. "The Reticence and the Waking. The passing and the cure, all in one night. Then it'll be *your* turn to carry the torch for a while. Don't that sound fun?" He looked behind him, toward the Baghead standing guard. "Bring him in."

The man nodded and opened the door, letting a boy about our age into the room. He was short, skinny, brown hair mussed and greasy, long enough to hang down around his eyes. His face was bruised and battered, as if he'd recently had his ass kicked— the Baghead I'd pummeled at the Honeyhole. At first I thought his eyes were wild with fear, but after a moment I realized it was something more like fanaticism. His gaze darted here and there and his hands fidgeted at his sides, his whole body tense with some kind of excitement.

"This is my boy, Dicky," Pee Wee announced. "Pretty close to your ages, I reckon, though I ain't got a clue what year he was born. Don't matter none. He's here to help out with somethin' just a little bit wonderful. Things been goin' along the same for long enough. Tonight we're gonna put the hand on the other foot, or whatever the hell that damn phrase is."

I stole a glance at Andrea, my eyebrows raised to the roof. I had no idea what was going on, and based on her own baffled expression, neither did she. But something about her demeanor gave me pause. I couldn't quite place why I thought it, but she seemed poised to strike, like a snake coiled up before a mouse. I'd seen her this way once before.

"Come here, Dicky," Pee Wee said. "Come on over here. I want these kids to get a good look while we turn the page on the old Player book. Time for the Gaskins' chapter, ain't it."

Dicky, still trembling with anticipation, came over to stand by his dad, both of them only three or four feet in front of us. Pee Wee put his hand on the boy's head and patted, like he was the family dog.

"Remember what we went over?" Pee Wee asked.

Dicky nodded. "Yes, sir."

"Good." He stepped over to a cloth bag that had been set against the wall and knelt next to it, rummaged inside. Then he pulled out a mason jar—full of the same amber liquid as the others lining the shelves, though nothing floated inside—and a hunting knife, the gleaming blade over half-a-foot long with a serrated edge for cutting skin and meat. He held these items up for everyone to see, then placed them on the floor, next to the bag. Then he stood up and took his place next to Dicky again. "Let's get started. You ready?"

"I'm ready," the boy responded.

I stared with sick fascination, almost forgetting the circumstances. Andrea and I still held hands, our fingers as wet as if we'd dipped them in a swimming pool. Dicky had a quick façade of fear flash across his face, but then it was gone.

"Here goes nothing," Pee Wee said, stabilizing his stance as if he expected the room to start shaking from an earthquake, hands held out before him. He concentrated on those hands, and

I half-wondered if he was about to do a magic trick. Then he reached up to his mouth, which he opened wide, and stuck several fingers inside, pushing on his own tongue. He kept at it, grunting, shoving his hands deeper and deeper, forcing his tongue to the back of his throat. He gagged, choked, coughed, but didn't stop whatever he was doing. Dicky looked up at him with wide-eyed wonder.

Then something must have happened, because suddenly Pee Wee went completely silent and took his hands from his mouth, arms dropping to the side. His mouth gaped open, his cheeks a little puffed out, something obviously wrong. His face showed discomfort, and he tapped his son on the shoulder then pointed desperately at himself, pointed at his throat.

"He just choked himself," Andrea whispered, her voice creepily steady.

I knew she was right, as little as I understood why.

Pee Wee Gaskins had just shoved his own tongue down his throat.

CHAPTER TWENTY-FIVE

Lynchburg, South Carolina
July 2017

Dicky's words had frozen me for a second, telling me that my son was down in the House of Tongues using a saw. I gaped at him, standing next to my dad, who looked so completely out of his element that it begged for a laugh. Pieces of the puzzle of my memories had been snapping into place left and right, but there were still some things that remained fuzzy. Not that it mattered. Whatever Dicky had just meant with what he said, there could be nothing good about it.

I finally got ahold of myself and turned away, sprinted for the stone tower and its door on the other side, like I'd meant to do a minute earlier. Dicky had a gun and I knew it, but he had orchestrated this entire evening, and if he'd wanted me dead, I'd be dead. I didn't know what his ultimate objective was and didn't care, my mind only allowing one path forward before anything else could happen: reuniting with Wesley.

I reached the broken column of stone bricks and rounded it, stopped by the wooden door with its iron bands. The waist-high door hung slightly ajar, dim light shining from within, leaving a long line of yellow across the weeds of the clearing. I dropped to my knees, pushed the door open, crawled inside. Everything about this place came back in a rush right before I experienced them again, its smells of rot and mold, its damp, dirty interior, the hanging, buzzing fluorescent tubes, the sounds of the rattling stairs. I jumped to my feet as soon as I cleared the threshold, flew down the spiraling stairs as quickly as my feet would move.

I jumped over the last three steps and landed on the cement floor, ran down the hallway to the next door, also made of cracked boards, rusty metal bands keeping them together. It was closed. Not slowing, I rammed my left shoulder into its warped surface, throwing every ounce of my weight forward, the soles of my shoes actually leaving the ground.

Crack.

Two of the boards splintered even as the door itself collapsed inward, swinging all the way open and crashing into the wall on the other side. I fell to the floor, trying to scramble back up even before I'd fallen all the way down. I remembered this room, the shelves, the sparse furniture, the mason jars filled with amber liquid and tongues—though there were far less than last time I'd been here. I was able to get to my feet, obtain my balance, observe what was in the room of my haunted childhood.

Blood.

Bodies.

Death.

Stench.

My son.

When I saw the scene of nightmarish horror that lay before me, for a split second I thought it unreal, a figment of my imagination or the setting of a ghoulish film. Stumbling to the side, then backwards, I crashed into the shelves of bottles that had been there for decades, several of them tipping over to the hard floor, cracking as they spilled their reeking contents all over the place. I hardly noticed as my hands sought for purchase, trying to steady myself while my reeling mind did the same on the inside. I stared at the display of gore, filling my vision, time slowing as I took in the grisly details.

Three bodies. No, four.

Three of them were dead, without any doubt, the reason clear—their heads had been sawed from their torsos, lying next to them with strings of meat and bone and gore trailing between the space through which they once connected. The amount of blood was astounding, so thick that on first glance it seemed a pool of crimson, deep enough to wade into, dive into, leap into, legs clenched in a cannonball.

And then there was the fourth body. The one cradled in Wesley's lap. I looked at him, and the person cradled there, with such despair that my life almost ended along with those who'd expired, scattered across the room like abandoned trash.

Wesley sat on the floor, legs crossed beneath him, a woman's back draped across his thighs, her head dangling off one knee. Her hair spread across the cement in a fan, her legs splayed out on the other side. She twitched a little, a slight spasm that might've been my imagination, but her eyes seemed glazed with death. There was movement near her neck, a gruesome thing that tried to block itself from my reasoning mind at first sight. I had no choice but to focus, now, no choice but to see what was going on, see the truth, see the horror.

Wesley had a handsaw in his hand, gripping the handle so tightly that his fingers shone white through crimson wetness. He sawed back and forth, back and forth, in a rhythm so steady that my heart told me he was possessed, hypnotized, under some kind of demonic spell, though I believed in none of those things. But I saw no possible reason within my sphere of understanding that could explain what my seventeen-year-old boy was doing. None.

"Wesley," I said, my throat cracking on the word. I cleared it.

"Wesley." Louder, with more strength. "What... I don't know what they've done to you, but you need to stop. Right now. Stop... doing that to her. You've hurt her enough." What I really wanted to scream was, *How could you! How could you do this, Wesley!* But I knew he was in some kind of trance, his entire psyche teetering on fragile, thin ice.

His eyes slowly rose to meet mine. His arm moving the saw slowed.

"Dad?" he asked in an innocently baffled voice. It seemed he couldn't reconcile the awful things of this place with his other life, his real life, the one where I was his father. How had Dicky done this to him in just a matter of days? How?

"Yes, Wesley. It's me. Your dad." I moved closer to him, literally taking this one step at a time. I took another one, having to lift my foot over the leg of a dead woman who lay sprawled in the middle of the room, on her stomach, headless. I was about ten feet from my son. "Please listen to me, okay? The Gaskins did something to you. This is not you, your real mind. I don't know what the hell they did but I'm here, now. Okay? Dad's here."

He stopped sawing at the woman in his lap. She was obviously past saving—the twitch I'd seen was her body moving from the inertia of the handsaw cutting away at her gristle and bone.

"Just put the saw down, okay?" I asked, taking another step. "We'll figure this out, we'll get you out of here. I'm not gonna let anything else bad happen to you. I swear on my life."

His gaze on me seemed empty of acknowledgement, but he nodded anyway, threw the saw to the side. It clanked and slid to a stop in a smear of blood. Then I rushed forward, grabbed the woman by her shirt and lifted her off of him—not caring at this point about any kind of delicacy or respect—then collapsed to the floor next to Wesley, pulled him into my arms. He didn't resist, but also didn't hug me back. The stench of human flesh and gore made me gag, but I held it in check. Sticky blood covered my hands, my face where it leaned against Wesley's; blood seeped into my pants from the ground beneath me.

"We're gonna get you out of here," I said, trying to stay sane. "Come on. We'll figure everything out one way or another." *Prison. They're going to send my son to prison.* It took every bit of my collapsing will to move forward, moment to moment. I put my arm beneath his, readied myself to lift him to his feet. "Come on, help me out."

Then I heard the echoing bangs of the stairs—someone clomping down the metal spiral at the other end of the hallway outside that room. Dicky. Armed. Coming to fulfill whatever sick destiny he'd set up for us tonight. I had no choice but to pull my arm back from Wesley and leave him there, sitting in a pool of his own crime. I jumped to my feet.

I remembered, now. I remembered the last few details from so long ago, as clearly as if someone had projected a movie of my past onto the stone wall.

I knew exactly what I had to do.

CHAPTER TWENTY-SIX

Lynchburg, South Carolina
June 1989

I'd never been properly trained how to react when a man shoves his own tongue down his throat until the air is cut off, depriving him of the sustenance of life. Which Pee Wee had just done, right in front of us. I could only stare and gape, hope that he died quickly. Andrea reacted by shaking, almost uncontrollably, but I couldn't rip my gaze from the ghastly scene before me. Pee Wee had collapsed to his knees, both hands wrapped around his bulging neck, his face purpling as his eyes—big, wet, white—threatened to pop from their sockets.

Dicky sprang into action, the sudden movement spurring a feeling of great disappointment inside of me before I really understood why. But quickly, I knew. He was going to save him. He was going to save his dad, the last thing on Earth I wanted to happen. But did I act? No, I didn't. Cowardice glued my ass to the chair. Andrea let go of my hand and stood up, her entire body tensed, but she didn't make a move.

The scene before us played out like a tragic comedy. Dicky, as young as us, had obviously been tutored beforehand on how to deal with choking. He almost calmly stepped behind his dad and wrapped his arms around the man's chest. Then he squeezed hard, twice. Pee Wee made the slightest of sounds, a tiny crackle of sorts, as he then let himself fall to the floor. Dicky straddled his chest, leaned forward, and worked at his dad's face—pinching his jaw forcibly, shoving a hand inside his mouth, digging as if for gold. Pee Wee violently coughed then, an explosion of phlegm and noise, as Dicky scooted off of his body. Pee Wee rolled onto his side, heaving and gasping and coughing, normal color slowly returning to his skin. The tongue had been dislodged, and my worst enemy hadn't died. I had the strangest urge to laugh.

The room grew quiet, still, as Pee Wee regained his composure. I stared at him, perplexed by what I'd just seen. He got to his feet, looking down at his son, still on the cement floor and breathing heavily. Then he looked at Andrea, standing only a few feet away.

"Did ya like that, girl?" he asked, his voice strained from the bonkers choking incident. "Were you scared that Papa Gaskins might not make it?"

Andrea had grown still, herself. She seemed relaxed, now, towering over me as I continued to sit like a craven. No visible tension in her, certainly no shaking. And she didn't respond to his taunts.

Pee Wee appeared to be taken a little aback. "Well ain't you a brave one?" He stared her down for a few seconds more then returned his attention to his son. "Boy, stand up."

Dicky did as he was commanded. I tried to read his expression but came up empty.

"Now listen to me, and listen real good," Pee Wee said. "Once we're done with the next part, I ain't gonna do a whole lotta talkin' if ya get me. See that bottle there?" He pointed at the one he'd taken from the bag, over by the wall, the hunting knife right next to it.

Dicky nodded. "Yes, sir."

"I'm gonna cut my tongue out, son, and I don't want you to stop me, ya hear? No matter what, no matter how much I scream, no matter how much I cry. I'm gonna cut it out and then I'm gonna put it in that bottle of formaldehyde to keep it preserved. Plain and simple. And when you're ready, when you're all well and done with what needs to be done, you're gonna take a bite out of that son of a bitch. Got it?"

I felt a blackness open up in me, a terrible gulf into which I wanted to fall. What madness was this? What lunatic's dream had we just stumbled upon?

I almost shrieked when Pee Wee suddenly whipped around to look at me, his eyes blazing as he stared into mine.

"The Reticence, boy. The Reticence and the Waking, that's what this is. The curse and the cure, right before your eyes. Then it's gonna be your family's turn for a while. It *will* be, or under God in Heaven I'll slaughter every man, woman, and child alive with a drop of Player blood in 'em. Mark my words and doubt not, boy. Tell your daddy what I just swore to you. Just to prove it, I'm gonna kill your little friend before we wrap things up. Better her than your mama, right?"

"You're crazy," Andrea said, the type of statement my future kids would deem worthy of Captain Obvious. "You're insane and you'll never get away with this."

Instead of responding, Pee Wee walked over to the wall, bent over, and picked up the knife with its gleaming steel and serrated edge. He twisted it in front of his face, closely examining its deadly potential—it was like a flashback to the Honeyhole incident. Then he sauntered over to stand just inches away from Andrea. Every natural alarm system known to the human race clanged inside my skull, trying to wake me up to the horror blossoming before my very eyes but I only sat there, scared and weak.

Pee Wee brought his blade forward, its pointy end aimed at my best friend's face.

"You have no idea," he whispered. "You have no idea the pain my family's been through. All because of my ancestors, things I ain't got nothin' to do with."

"Oh, please," Andrea replied. "If you really think that then you haven't met my dad. I think he's got your ancestors beat in the asshole competition."

I absolutely couldn't believe her bravery. It changed me, forever.

"It's not my..." Pee Wee, visibly frustrated, dropped his head and sighed. "*My* ancestors were cursed by the Puritans. Don't you get it? I can't kill David—his family's as mixed up in this bullshit as much as mine. But I can *hurt* him. Oh, I can hurt him in all kinds of ways, ways worse than death." His gaze found me when he said the next line. "All the Players have done for 200 years is try to get out of the pact, make it all about the Gaskins."

"I don't know what you're talking about," I said weakly. Andrea shifted slightly, planted her feet, moved an arm, all of it very subtle but noticeable from my lower vantage point. "I didn't even know that our families knew each other."

Pee Wee stared hard at me. "The sins of the father shall be passed down, the Good Book says. I don't care what you know or don't know. But this all ends with my son, and that's a fact." He looked back at Andrea, then changed his grip on the knife, holding its handle in a fist as if he planned to rear back and drive the blade into her eye. "Be sure and watch, Davey boy. I ain't allowed to kill your sorry ass, but I sure as hell can—"

Before he could finish his sentence, Andrea did exactly what she'd done at the Honeyhole. Her entire body twisted like a coiled spring that had been released, her arm swinging in an arc from behind her. She held a chunk of brick in her left hand, gripped tightly in her fingers, jagged, chunky red clay like a growth on her palm. Pee Wee had no chance, no chance at all.

He'd just started to duck, just started to pull his arm up as a defense, but both actions were too late. Andrea's violent swing connected, hitting the same mark as at the Honeyhole; the brick slammed into the side of his head with a horrible clunking sound. Pee Wee collapsed to the floor without making a sound.

Andrea screamed, stepped forward, held the brick up again over her head, looking down on Gaskins. She fell to her knees, right next to where he lay, even as she brought the brick down with all of her strength. Right before it hit Pee Wee's face—a thing that I'm certain to this day would've killed him—Dicky tackled her from the left, knocking her to the ground; he landed on top of her. The brick had dropped from her grip and thudded against the cement floor, about five inches from Pee Wee's face. He was groaning, holding both hands to the gash on his temple, rocking side to side.

I stood up. Ran over to where Andrea was fighting at Dicky, shoved him off of her. She leapt to her feet, gave me a look filled with bloody rage, then she sprinted to the wall of glass bottles, started swinging her arms wildly. She swept several jars off the shelf and they crashed to the floor, breaking in a loud, shattered chorus. More fell, more broke apart, the sound unbearable, mixed with the splashing of liquid, as if some crystal beast were being slaughtered. Dicky had stood back up, and he went at Andrea, his face a demonic scowl. I rushed forward and stuck my foot out, tripping him. He hadn't seen me, sprawled forward with no chance to break his fall, cracked his face against the cement.

But it did nothing to deter him; he scrambled to his feet, even as the broken glass all over the floor cut up his hands. He moved toward Andrea again; I moved toward him. Andrea swept another dozen or so bottles off the shelves—jars shattered everywhere; that disgusting liquid splashed onto the walls; preserved, gray, meaty tongues flopped and bounced. Dicky was almost to her; I was almost to him.

"Stop!"

The word was like a crack of thunder, a boom of such power that all three of us obeyed. We froze, our last steps crunching on broken glass, standing right next to the wall of bottles that now lay half-empty, its contents strewn across the room.

A Baghead stood in the doorway. He held a shotgun, pointed it at us. He cocked it while we watched, a heavy clunk of a sound that echoed off the low ceiling.

Using the disguised voice I'd now heard far too often, the man said, "Get away from that wall. Get away from the jars." He jabbed the end of the shotgun toward the opposite wall. "Now."

Dicky, Andrea, and I scooted ourselves to the other side, each step precarious over the sea of glass at our feet. Crunches filled the air.

"If any one of you makes a move toward me, or toward Mr. Gaskins, I'll shoot you in the head with buckshot. You won't like it. Trust me for a second."

All three of us breathed heavily, backed against the cool stone of the wall. The Baghead also breathed, his plastic bag puffing, retracting. He walked forward, twisting his body as he passed us so that the barrel of the shotgun still pointed in our direction. Glass cracked and crunched beneath his boots. He reached the spot where Pee Wee had fallen—the man still lay prone, moaning in pain, hands covering his face.

Baghead knelt beside him, shifted the shotgun to one hand while reaching down with the other. He picked up the knife that had dropped out of Pee Wee's grasp when Andrea bonked him in the head with that brick. He looked at the blade for a moment through the thin plastic, then back up at us.

"Go on, now," he said with his guttural voice. "Go get the police and bring them back here. Old Pee Wee ain't goin' nowhere."

I wasn't sure I'd understood his words they surprised me so much. Not a one of us moved a muscle.

"Go get the police!" Baghead shouted. "Now!"

That kicked us into gear, especially Dicky. The poor kid seemed even more traumatized than us, as if maybe he'd broken out of the trance enforced on him by his dad. We hurried for the door, for the hallway, for the spiral staircase leading to freedom above. I was the last one to reach the base of the stairs, which rattled under the weight of the other two as they ascended, and I took one last look down the hallway, still able to see through the open door through which we'd just escaped. What I saw then was an image my mind immediately rejected, refused to believe was real. Even worse was the sound that came with it, rushing at me like a living beast. I think the whole affair had been mentally blocked by my abused psyche by the time I reached the outside air just a few seconds later. But, after the passing of decades, when I returned to this place, I'd finally remember.

Baghead had taken the knife in one hand and opened Pee Wee's mouth wide with the other. Then he started cutting at Pee Wee's tongue, even as the injured man screamed like a thrashing, choking demon. Baghead ignored him. Kept at it.

We fled that place of horror; we fled until we were safe.

I never saw Pee Wee Gaskins again.

CHAPTER TWENTY-SEVEN

Lynchburg, South Carolina
July 2017

I

Dicky.
He was making his way down the spiral staircase, every one of his steps loud and clanging. I could almost feel the rattle of the metal reverberating through the air. He came with such confidence, the same confidence that had doomed his dad. I grabbed a bottle from the shelf and moved into position, waiting on the inside of the door that led to the hallway, hiding myself just out of view from the stairs, hoping Wesley didn't give me away.

I heard Dicky reach the bottom, step off the twisted metal structure, heard the scrape of his shoes against the cement as he came toward me. Closer. I heard his breaths. Wesley still sat where I'd left him, looking as dazed and sad as anyone I've ever seen. Covered in blood. I brought the liquid-and-tongue-filled

Mason jar up to my chest, firmed my grip on it, holding the thing like a football with my right hand. Waited.

Dicky Gaskins, almost 30 years after I'd last seen him in this room, stepped through the doorway and into the House of Tongues.

I swung my arm, just as I would've thrown the ball, but instead of letting go, I held tight to the rounded jar, held tight until it smashed against the side of Dicky's head. The instant it hit, the instant I heard the sickening thunk, felt the shudder of the impact travel up my arm, saw his mouth opening in a scream, a vision flashed in my mind, of Andrea doing this very same thing to Pee Wee so long ago. The horrible wheel had spun once around.

Dicky cried out and stumbled, crashed into the wall of mason jars. Several of them toppled off of the shelves and crashed against the hard ground. I went after him, raised my arm, brought it down, aiming to crush his skull. He partly deflected my swing with his shoulder so that the jar only grazed him. Then he punched me in the stomach with a solid fist, heaving it up from his lower position. I grunted as the air whooshed from my body, leaving behind what felt like a vacuum. Sucking for a breath, dry-heaving, I rolled over onto my back, clutching my abdomen. Dicky sprang atop me, put a hand on my throat. His eyes showed no trace of perception or lucidity, his face a mask of pure, animal rage, snapped from sanity. He growled like a rabid dog, wrapped his hands around my neck, and squeezed.

I batted at his arms with mine, tried to grab his hand, tried to gain purchase. His strength was shocking, pinching the life from me, pinning me down, throttling me. I couldn't breathe, couldn't scream, couldn't so much as cough. My chest ached, begging for air; white spots danced above me, like little wisps inviting me to the underworld. The world itself began to fade.

Air rushed in.

I didn't know what had happened. Dicky was no longer on top of me. My body's instincts had triggered, pulling in breaths one after the other. Pain wracked my entire torso but the relief of air in my lungs overpowered all else. My vision cleared.

Dicky had backed up to the frame of the door leading to the hallway. His face contorted in agony, he was staring angrily down at the handle of a knife, which jutted from the meaty part of his upper arm. Wesley stood over both of us, but somehow seemed smaller, looking more like a child than I'd seen him in years; tears carved white paths down his bloody cheeks. His expression contained all the terror and all the fear that he must've felt since all of this had begun.

"Not my dad," he said, a whimper of words he barely got out. "You promised."

"I don't care anymore!" Dicky shouted at him. "I'll kill every last member of the Player family! The pact is over!"

It was that word that did it. *Pact.* It was that word that sent me over the edge.

I became rage and rage became me.

Hearing screams, hearing roars, knowing they were mine even though they seemed to come from another soul, another dimension, I pushed against the floor with both hands, throwing my body toward Dicky. My shoulder hit his chest—I drove him into the wall as hard as I could. He tried to recover, tried to retaliate, but the surge of adrenaline that had exploded inside my system made me invincible. A lion couldn't have stopped me. I grabbed him by the hair and slammed his head against the wall, once, twice, three times. Stunned to oblivion, he ceased resisting.

"Wesley, sit down over there!" I yelled the words, though I hoped my son understood the object of my searing anger. I pointed at a spot next to the woman I'd seen Wesley carving at upon entering the room earlier. The bloody saw was still there, on the ground. "Sit down! Right there!" I pointed again.

I grabbed Dicky by the shirt, gripping the material in both of my hands, and dragged him across the floor, thumping his body over other bodies with a strength that felt endless, infinite. I breathed pure air, my lungs full like never before. Clarity pierced my mind and I felt no pain, anywhere. I had become a god of energy.

"Sit down!" I yelled again. Wesley plopped next to the poor woman's head. I dropped Dicky next to him—the man moaned but didn't move. I knelt, then reached for his head, placed it between my thighs. Although I didn't and never would believe a single word that had come out of Pee Wee's, Dicky's, or my own dad's mouths about curses and cures, the only thing that mattered was that my son believed it. That was the only explanation.

"Don't worry, Wesley," I said as I picked up the handsaw. "This ends right now. He put a curse on you and this'll make it go away. Simple as that. You just have to do what I say, no matter how weird it gets."

Wesley nodded, though he didn't meet my eyes.

I had no doubts, no hesitation, no fear.

With my left hand, I squeezed Dicky's cheeks until his mouth popped open. The handsaw was in my right. The task seemed logistically impossible with the tool at my disposal, but technicalities didn't matter. A piece. We only needed a piece. I grabbed his slimy tongue and yanked it out, ignoring the grunt of pain that escaped his throat. With the tip exposed—purple, skimmed with milky white—just enough for my gruesome purposes, I went at it with the saw. There was blood. There were screams. I had to grab Dicky's head and slam it into the cement to stop his violent reaction to the pain. I sawed at his tongue, cringed at the rubbery resistance.

Soon I held a tiny chunk of meat in my fingers.

Repulsed, it took every ounce of my newfound but quickly fading strength to prevent myself from emptying the contents of my stomach. Wesley stared at the piece of tongue with wide eyes, glowing with revelation. He knew that whatever they had done to him—that if it were real, then so was the solution, the cure, right in front of him. For 200 years it had been so, and it was so tonight.

After everything—after all the death and horror, the blood and terror—he did something so simple, so absurd, so final. My son had the bravery to do this thing that made no sense.

He reached out and took the chunk of meat.

Popped it in his mouth.

Chewed.

Swallowed.

"Okay, that's my boy," I said. Then I stood up and held my hand out to him. "Come on. Your job is done. Mine's not."

He took my hand and stood up. I made him leave, told him to wait on the spiral staircase, out of sight. Once he did as he was told, I quickly took care of two tasks in that blood-spattered room.

Then we left that place of hell and I've never been back.

2

The rain had returned with an exclamation point.

It poured from the dark sky, the sound of falling water overpowering everything else; the ground outside the House of Tongues was a marsh, sucking at our feet as we ran toward the truck left behind by Dicky. My dad sat in the passenger seat, his form nothing but a silhouette I could barely make out. I had a reckoning to come with him, but I couldn't bear to do it in front of Wesley. But the fate of my traitorous father—a man I'd always loved while fearing him as well—had been determined with the drop of one last straw upon the camel's back.

He'd left us to Dicky. He'd sat in that damn truck and let

Dicky come down to finish us off, not to mention the countless and unknown things he'd done before that. My head still didn't quite grasp it all. I now knew with almost certainly that he was usually, if not always, the Baghead that had accompanied Pee Wee Gaskins, and I didn't understand it at all.

But that reckoning would come soon enough.

For the next little while, it was all about saving Wesley.

"I hate to do this, but I want you to ride in the back!" I told my eldest son, yelling over the relentless rain. "I have to be able to clean off that blood easily and it'd be way worse inside the truck. Maybe the rain'll wash it off for me."

"What about you?" he shouted in return. His eyes shone in the dark—I swear that they did—and I saw his old self returning in them. Those three words had not come from the same entranced zombie from down below.

"It doesn't matter about me," I said, already knowing my immediate future, accepting it with the heaviest of hearts. "Just trust me on this. Jump on in."

He did as I said; I watched his shadow leap into the bed of the truck.

I opened the door on the driver's side, got into the cabin— my clothes soaked as if I'd jumped in the swamp—and started the engine without looking at or saying a word to my dad. He sat still and silent, a sulk of a man. Getting the keys from Dicky had been one of the two tasks I'd accomplished in the House of Tongues before exiting. The other had been to stab him in the heart with a stray knife until he stopped breathing, the easiest thing I'd ever done.

I put the truck into drive and began skidding our way along the muddy clearing.

3

I drove through the wet night.

My mind was on Andrea. My mind was on Mason. And Hazel. And Logan.

Most of all, my mind was on Wesley.

An infinite array of terrible choices seemed to surround me, pierce me, penetrate me. None of them were good. And only one made sense. Thinking through these things one last time, I wanted to call Andrea, tell her what had happened, explain it all, hear the voices of my other three kids... but I couldn't. Not yet. I only needed another half-hour, a full one at most.

We arrived at my parents' house.

4

Dad stayed in the truck while I cleaned Wesley up.

He stripped naked outside of the house, where I hosed him down even as the rain did most of the work anyway. Then we went inside; he showered while I burned his clothes in the tiny fireplace of our living room. I added so much wood to make sure the job got done that I thought odds were even the house itself would burn down. The odds were also even whether or not I would care.

Wesley came out, dressed in fresh clothes, his hair combed. For all the hell he'd been through, he looked pretty damn good. I sat him down—my dad's chair beckoned like the throne of Zeus, and I couldn't even look at it, so we chose the couch, where in recent nights I'd held Hazel in my arms and shared stories of Grandpa Fincher's ghost in the attic.

I shuddered at the thought of what trauma my son must feel, and I didn't even know one tenth of what he'd been through. I knew the post-traumatic stress was coming, and coming hard. But all I could do was live in the moment and try to save him.

"Wesley," I said.

His eyes met mine, questioning.

"There'll be plenty of time for answers later," I continued. "You to me and me to you. But right now..." I sighed. "Right now I need to make sure of one thing. The most important thing."

"What, Dad? What're we gonna do? I... killed those people." He shook as he spoke.

"Don't say another word about it. Not now, not never. Not one word."

This confused him, maybe even offended his senses, so I hurried to explain, my heart in so much pain that it hurt to speak, as if the words pricked it on their way out.

"I can't even pretend to understand what this curse is within the Player family. And the Gaskins family. But if you believe it, then it doesn't matter if it's real. I know you, and I know that something was done to you to make you do those things."

He started to respond but I shushed him with a raised hand.

"No. Don't say anything. Just listen." I breathed in and out, the pain in my chest mounting with every passing second. "I'll keep it simple. If anyone goes down for this, it's going to be me. It's not gonna be you. Eventually I think I'll be able to weasel my own way out, too, but for now we have to save you. You were here, all night. You know nothing, absolutely nothing about any of the murders, nothing. Just... nothing. Understood?"

"Dad, you're crazy. How can I—"

I took his hands, trembling with emotion. "Listen to me, son. I couldn't bear... I could *not* bear it if you went to prison. Juvenile. Mental institution. Anything. I would die of a shattered heart, do you understand me? I already lost your mom, and I can't lose you. It..." I faltered, here, despite my every effort to stay strong. Tears poured from my eyes, my chest filled with something as large as the universe. "If you've ever held an ounce of love for your dad... Please... just do as I say, okay? If anything I'm being selfish because I'm doing what's best for *me*. Okay? This is what's best for me. I want you to do this for *me*."

Even as I spoke, I had no idea if what I proposed was even possible. Who knew what evidence waited in the swamps and in the woods and in that damned House of Tongues. But all I could do was try. If I had to fully confess to everything, just to deflect them from my son, I would do it. There was, simply, no other option. None.

"I need you to trust me," I said, wiping the tears from my cheeks. "Trust me like never before. No matter how hard it gets. You did nothing. Say nothing. We'll protect you with lawyers and you'll never say a word. Not a human on earth could possibly think..."

We stared at each other. I was out of adequate things to say. I had nothing else.

Pulling him into a hug, holding him tight, I whispered into his ear.

"Swear to me you'll not say anything. Ever. This is your gift to me."

"I'm so sorry, Dad. I'm so sorry." He broke down, then, wept into my shoulder. Sobbed. I squeezed him even tighter.

"I love you, Wesley. There's not a dictionary in the galaxy with enough words to describe how much. I love you." How inadequate the phrases that spewed from my mouth, like a leaky faucet trying to fill the oceans. I could only hope that he felt the power behind them.

"Lie down here on the couch," I said, finally pulling away. "I know you won't be able to sleep, but just stay here until someone comes for you. Okay? It's gonna be an incredibly hard day or two until things get figured out. But your job is easy. You know nothing, you say nothing. That's it. Deal?"

He nodded, still weeping. He pulled his legs up onto the couch and laid his head down.

"Somehow this will all work out. I love you."

"I love you, too, Dad."

My heart felt like a wretched chunk of dying tissue, but I left him there. Turned my back on him. Walked through the house to the kitchen. Picked up the landline phone. Called 9-1-1. Waited for an answer. Gave the man who answered our address.

"There's something terrible in our shed," I told him.

Then I hung up and went out the back door.

5

Buckets of water fell from the sky.

Wet darkness ruled the earth.

I opened the passenger-side door of the truck, saw my dad sitting there, the remnants of his grocery bag still ragged around his neck. I grabbed him by the shirt, hauled him outside. He didn't resist. Not letting go, I forced him to walk alongside me, through the rain, across the shallow lake of our yard, toward the looming shadow of our shed in the back. I'd exhausted my supply of emotions and heartache. This was my father, the man who raised me. He'd always loved me, taken care of our family through hard work and sacrifice.

But I felt nothing for him in those moments. Only for Wesley. For Andrea. For my other kids, for my mom, for the unending suffering that had now been brought down upon us. Pee Wee had used words like the Reticence and the Waking. Well, now it was time for the Reckoning.

We reached the triple rolling-doors of the rickety old building that contained at least 1,000 items of a century-old farm, from tractor parts to basketball rims. I chose the right door, heaved it up and open, my other hand still gripped in the soaked cotton of my dad's shirt. I pushed him inside, not unkindly, just with enough force to let him know the child was now in charge of the parent.

He stumbled a bit then grew still, looking at the wooden-plank floor with all the shame of his decades. I couldn't believe how different he appeared to me. I didn't have the capacity to understand how he could be the same man who'd raised me.

"I know what's in the safe," I said. A sledgehammer was attached to the wall, its heavy metal head nestled between two nails, the wooden handle hanging toward the ground. I grabbed it, hefted it in both of my hands. I didn't want my dad to have the satisfaction of hearing me ask for the combination to the padlock.

I walked over to the safe, lifted the sledgehammer high over my head, then threw it down, crashing its solid chunk of iron onto the lock. The vibration hurt my arms; the effort barely made a dent or spark to the lock. I lifted the hammer again, swung it hard. Again. Once more.

The padlock burst into pieces.

I dropped the hammer and knelt in front of the safe door, which had popped halfway open. I swung it all the way to my left and peered inside. There was only one item. A mason jar. Full of amber liquid. A meaty, elongated mass of flesh floating within. I reached in and pulled it out. A worn, yellowed, dusty label affixed to the glass had a name written in long-faded ink, the letters barely legible.

Pee Wee Gaskins.

Although I was several light years from understanding *why*, I had no doubt as to *what* anymore. My dad had been the Baghead who so often accompanied Pee Wee all those years ago. He'd been the one to drug me, drag me out to the woods, allowing Pee Wee to torment and taunt his youngest son. Or he'd done it himself, I don't know. He might've been the one who appeared slow-witted at the Honeyhole when I was a kid, maybe acting that way to ensure I didn't guess his identity. He'd also been at the House of Tongues back then, I had no doubt of it. Who knew what else—the details didn't matter. He'd been an accomplice in the very thing that defined the horrors of my life.

I walked up to him. Held the Mason jar and its disgusting contents in front of his face, shook it at him. Then I said the only word that could convey the storm of thoughts pounding inside my mind and heart.

"Why?"

For the first time in hours, my dad looked directly at me.

"To protect you."

It took a monumental effort not to rear back and smash the jar into his face. Instead I let it fall to my side, and I waited. Waited for him to explain.

When he did, genuine pain filled his eyes. "The Waking goes back 200 years, son. It's not like it's under my control. We had a pact with the Gaskins, something that worked for generations until that night you and Andrea attacked Pee Wee. I cut out his tongue that night, brought it here, hoping that somehow I could figure out a way to break the chain. But all it did was make Dicky angrier, hungrier for vengeance."

My breaths came short and fast, my chest rising and falling. He kept talking, all of it spilling out in a torrent of confession.

"We were cursed, David, cursed so long ago that no one remembers when it started. Our two families helped each other carry that burden until my dad messed everything up, broke the chain. They left me no choice but to right his wrongs, pay penance. I had to do those things to you or they would've killed our whole family, and years later I had to let Dicky pass the curse back to our family, to set things back to normal, back in balance. I had no choice, son! All I've ever wanted was to do what's best for my children in the long run."

Trembling, I replied, "What about Wesley? What about *him*?

Why would you let them do those things to him? How could you possibly sit back and watch them brainwash Wesley into... slaughtering innocent people? How?" I screamed it. The rage almost incapacitated me; it was all I could do to remain standing.

My dad's face hardened. "Because *you're* my son. Not him."

And that was it. I turned away from him and collapsed to the ground, my head in my hands. All night my heart had been hardening into a brittle shard of fragile pain, and now it shattered, the pieces jagged and sharp and cutting. My dad was crazy. My dad had lost his mind, utterly, if it had ever functioned at all. His words simply made no sense, and thus everything that had happened—the horrors of my childhood, the horrors of recent days—were all for naught. It was simply a trail of madness and blood.

I wept for him, for me, for Wesley, for my family.

Behind me, glass broke. It didn't really register. I couldn't get up, couldn't look. But then I heard choked gurgling sounds.

Spinning around, I knew what I was going to see.

My dad had slit his throat with a slice of glass from the jar.

He now lay on his back, blood spurting as he gagged and coughed. I crawled over to him, knew there was nothing I could do. But I put my hand on the wound, anyway, tried to staunch the flow.

His eyes found mine and he choked out a few last words. "Now... it's broken... forever."

My hand on his neck had shifted without my realizing it. I was squeezing his throat, trying to crush everything that lay within that frail passage of flesh. He would've died anyway, but I'm almost certain that I hastened the process.

His eyes faded shut; the life fled from him in one last breath. I fell back, rolled onto my side, staring at his dead body. The weight of everything I'd ever known and all that I didn't and never could understand threatened to crush me forever, as if the air of the shed had solidified into an igneous matter of infinite mass. I closed my eyes, able to live on for only one purpose. Andrea. My kids. Saving Wesley.

In the distance, I heard sirens.

CHAPTER TWENTY-EIGHT

Sumter, South Carolina
June 1990

One year had passed since Pee Wee Gaskins went to prison, relieved of the weight of his own tongue. Besides a private deposition, I did nothing to follow the stories or trial or anything relating to the worst man I'd ever known. My mom never mentioned his name again, and my dad changed in ways that I can only perceive looking back through the lens of decades passed. He was never the same, but I also have no solid memory of how he was. That makes little sense, which explains him perfectly.

Andrea and her mom were moving to Columbia, only an hour away by car, though my heart told me it was a drive neither she nor I would make very often. And it hurt. We sat at the counter in the Rexall Drug, saying our goodbyes, drinking one last coffee together. They planned to leave the next morning.

"Are you going to miss me?" I asked.

She took a careful sip. "Of course I am. At least once a week."

"I'm gonna miss you once a day. Easily."

"Aww. That's sweet."

"Yeah. It really is. I'm just that kind of guy."

She rolled her eyes. "I give it six months. In six months, you'll be sittin' on the john, reading the *TV Guide*, and you'll think... 'What the hell was that one girl's name? Angie? Angela? Antelope? Something like that. Oh, look, there's a rerun of *Dukes of Hazard* tonight!' Yep, that's what'll happen."

"Probably right, what can I say?"

She put her cup down and leaned close to me, turning serious so abruptly that I didn't quite know what to do.

"I'll always love you and I'll always remember you, David. Always."

"Same," I said, kind of choking on the word. "Always."

She hugged me, and I hugged her back.

After pulling away, she picked up her coffee and took a sip. "If it weren't for Pee Wee, I bet we would've gotten married someday."

"Really?" After all these years, she never ceased to surprise me with these conversations.

"Yeah. I think because of him, we could only always be best friends. Like, it made this bond between us that's not really right for lovey dovey shit. Just friends. Besties. We'll always have the darkness of Pee Wee buried inside of us, and that's not really the kinda thing eternal love is built on."

"Huh." I realized I completely agreed with her, though the thought had never quite articulated itself in my own mind. "Well, then that's just one more reason I hate the sumbitch, as Gramps would say."

She liked that, smiled me a nice big one, genuine. "Who knows. Maybe someday when we're old farts we'll end up in the same nursing home. I'll marry you, then."

"You'll still be hot. So will I. We'll be the hottest 80-year-olds to ever make out in a wheelchair."

"Maybe we'll have little old person babies."

"I don't really understand what you mean by that."

"Neither do I." She laughed, which made me laugh.

"We definitely had some good times," I said. "Hopefully we can forget the shitty parts. Like Pee Wee and dudes with bags on their heads."

"Not likely. But it'll get better. It will." She took my hand in hers. Time passed.

"I've been dreading this for weeks," I said. "Seriously. How am I supposed to say goodbye to you? It hurts really bad."

She nodded. "Yeah, it does."

We sat in silence for a while, taking sips of coffee to pass the time. It was a weird feeling. I didn't want it to end, but I couldn't wait for it to be over.

"Here's what we'll do," she finally said. "When the clock strikes the hour, I'm just going to get up and leave. Let's literally *not* say goodbye."

"Um... okay. That's actually the perfect idea."

"Awesome."

We had 20 more minutes, then. We talked nonstop, reminiscing about anything and everything except those dark times haunted by Pee Wee Gaskins and the Bagheads, which sounds to me now like a bad 60s band. I'm glad we avoided the topic, though of course we couldn't have possibly known that one day the terror of it all would come back.

At five minutes to the top of the hour, Andrea said, "Where's Antony, David?"

Our old game, something we hadn't done in a while. I put my fingers up to both temples and closed my eyes, hummed for a few seconds. "I'm gettin' nothing. Maybe he finally kicked the bucket. What about you?"

"I know exactly where he is."

"Oh yeah? Where's Antony?"

"He's sitting in a chair, watching TV, drinking beer. Hating himself because he blew his one shot with the most beautiful, kind woman in the world. That's enough for me, that he lives with all that regret."

"Well, he lost the best daughter in history, too," I said. "Don't forget that part. If I was your daddy I would've never left."

She laughed. "That's impossible creepy and sweet at the same time."

"It's what I do."

Somewhere from outside a clock chimed, the faintest, saddest of sounds.

"See ya around?" Andrea asked, slipping off of her stool.

"See ya around."

She kissed me on the cheek and left, the bell on the door clanging as she disappeared from my life.

EPILOGUE

I

There was a lot of evidence against me. The papers and local TV stations had already declared my guilt, declared me a monster, based on the weakest, scantiest leaks from the police department. I, for one, refused to speak, biding my time to see where the chips might fall. Until I heard a whisper against my son, I felt safe doing this. And so far there hadn't been a peep.

Time would tell. They'd found me covered in blood, after all, with my dad lying dead next to me, his throat slit a good six inches. They'd discovered the House of Tongues the same night, and there was no way to hide the fact that I'd been there. Forensics is the damnedest of things. Not to mention that Dicky's truck had been parked in my parents' front yard.

Time would tell.

My best defense at the moment was to keep my huge mouth

shut. I missed my kids beyond anything describable by the languages of humankind. It hurt, each and every day, each and every hour. But I had saved my eldest son, and that kept me solid.

Did I believe the crazy things claimed by my dad and the Gaskins? Rants about curses and cures, pacts and persecution? No. Not for a second. But the Waking had worked, and my son appeared as back to normal as one could be under the circumstances, seeing a therapist twice a week. The kids had transferred to schools in Columbia, only a 45-minute drive from my current abode of incarceration, and close to their grieving Grandma as well. Although I'd never asked for it, Andrea was taking care of all four of my children as if they were her own.

I'd loved her in my youth.

And I love her now.

2

Visitor's Day at the prison.

I sat in a hard plastic chair, the worst kind, the kind that makes your ass feel like it's folding in on itself, pinched with pain. A small desk fronted by a glass wall lay before me, a little old-school telephone handset hanging next to it. Andrea sat on the other side, my four children standing right behind her. The sight brought tears to my eyes every time they came, and I never tried to hide it.

I picked up the phone, trying not to think of the army of germs that lay encrusted on its surface. Andrea did the same.

"Hey guys!" I shouted, knowing they could kind of hear me through the window. "You have most definitely made my day! Man, you guys look great."

"We all miss you like crazy," Andrea said, the best part being that I could see she meant it.

"Oh, trust me," I replied. "I miss you more. All of you."

"So what's new?" she asked, with a twinkle in her eye that would've given Santa Clause a run for his money.

"Oh, ya know. Lots of sitting around. Stimulating conversation with the bank robbers. I read a book this week! *Harry Potter and the Something or Other*. That shit's insane."

"Daddy, shame on you!" Hazel yelled from the other side. I laughed with glee.

Wesley was smiling. Mason was smiling. Logan was smiling as he sat in Andrea's lap. Hazel even smiled through her scowl of rebuke over my potty mouth. They couldn't completely hide that look in their eyes, the one that hated our circumstances, the one that wondered just how guilty I was, the one that despised the prison as much as they despised my being inside of it. But they *tried* to hide it, and their love for me seemed to make it a doable task.

I had no way of knowing the current mental and emotional state of my eldest son, but he looked well enough. I had sworn before they arrived that I'd try my best not to think about it while they were there, so I stopped.

We chatted for an hour, each of the kids taking turns, fighting over the handset, half the time talking to me without it, yelling loud enough to wake the dead inmates rumored to be buried in the prison yard where we exercised. We spoke of video games and breakfast cereals, basketball and dance, movies and music, celebrity scandals and what everyone planned to be for Halloween. In a sign that he really had begun the journey back to the kid I'd always known, Wesley joked that he was going to dress up like a convict in my honor. I have to say, there was a part of me that was beginning to think he'd blocked the things that had happened from his mind, much as I had done three decades earlier. I hoped so. There were no Gaskins to come around in the future and jog his memory.

Alas, our allotted time of talking and yelling and laughing came to an end.

"We'll come back next week," Andrea said, kissing her fingers and touching the glass between us. I did the same, and then each of my kids did as well. It was the closest we could come to a group hug.

"Great. I love you guys. I really do." I choked up like usual, feeling no shame.

They turned to go and were just about gone, an officer opening the exit door for them, when Hazel suddenly sprinted back to my window, grabbing the phone before anyone could stop her. I'd hung mine up but quickly retrieved it, pressed it to my ear.

"Daddy?" Hazel asked.

"Yeah, sweetie?"

"I forgot to tell you. We visited Grandma's house and I know you didn't do any of those things they said you did! I mean, I already knew it, duh, but now I *really* know it! And everything's going to work out fine and dandy. He promised!"

"Well, that makes me happy, sweet girl. Wait, who promised?"

"Great-Grandpa Fincher! And he'd never tell a lie, now would he?"

She didn't wait for a response, just hung up the phone and ran back to Andrea and the other kids. I watched her go, watched them all go, waving until the door closed behind them.

Grandpa Fincher.

Huh.

I knew that sneaky ghost would help me out some day.

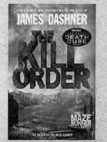
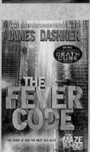

73 Years Later...
**Their ancestors survived the apocalypse,
but will Sadina, Isaac, and Jackie be as lucky?
A new spinoff trilogy from the author of
The Maze Runner**

JAMES DASHNER

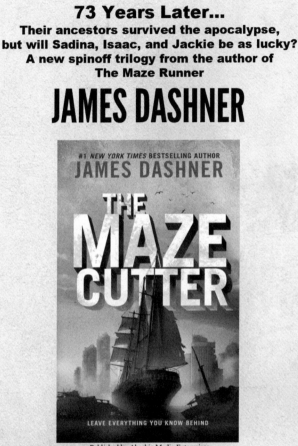

🐦 **@JamesDashner**

📷 **@DashnerJames**

JamesDashner.com

ABOUT THE AUTHOR

James Dashner is the author of the #1 New York Times Bestselling Maze Runner series (movies by Fox/Disney) including *The Maze Runner*, *The Scorch Trials*, *The Death Cure*, *The Kill Order*, and *The Fever Code*, and the bestselling *Mortality Doctrine* series (*The Eye of Minds*, *The Rule of Thoughts*, and *The Game of Lives*). Dashner was born and raised in Georgia, but now lives and writes in the Rocky Mountains with his wife and their four children.

Join the #DashnerArmy for exclusive content and giveaways at <u>JamesDashner.com</u>